Also by Jessica Blair

The Red Shawl
A Distant Harbour
Storm Bay
The Restless Spirit
The Other Side of the River
The Seaweed Gatherers
Portrait of Charlotte
The Locket
The Long Way Home
The Restless Heart
Time & Tide
Echoes of the Past
Yesterday's Dreams
Reach for Tomorrow
Dangerous Shores
Wings of Sorrow

For more information about Jessica Blair
visit www.jessicablair.co.uk

SECRETS OF THE SEA

Jessica Blair

PIATKUS

PIATKUS

First published in Great Britain in 2004 by Piatkus Books
This paperback edition published in 2005 by Piatkus Books
Reprinted 2009

A CIP catalogue record for this book
is available from the British Library

ISBN 978-0-7499-3607-5

Printed and bound in Great Britain by
CPI Mackays, Chatham, ME5 8TD

Papers used by Piatkus Books are natural, renewable and recyclable
products sourced from well-managed forests and certified in
accordance with the rules of the Forest Stewardship Council.

Mixed Sources
Product group from well-managed
forests and other controlled sources
www.fsc.org Cert no. SGS-COC-004081
© 1996 Forest Stewardship Council

FSC

Piatkus Books
An imprint of
Little, Brown Book Group
100 Victoria Embankment
London EC4Y 0DY

An Hachette Livre UK Company
www.hachettelivre.co.uk

www.piatkus.co.uk

ACKNOWLEDGEMENTS

I am grateful for the support of my family who are always ready with advice and constructive criticism. I thank my editor, ever ready with her expert advice to shape the book to its final presentation. I thank also all the staff at my publisher who do so much to see the book to its final destination – the reader. I must acknowledge all the authors on whose works I have drawn for background material. I should mention one in particular: *Yorkshire Fisherfolk* by Peter Frank (Phillimore & Co. Ltd, 2002), a valuable and erudite book on its subject.

For Ken, who called 'out of the blue' and changed my life.
Thank you for your friendship.
Also remembering Heather who played her part too.

Chapter One

'Maybe when you get back?' Georgina Holmes put the question with a quizzical smile on her lips.

The corners of her husband Gideon's kindly eyes crinkled as he placed his broad hands on the waist of his wife of twenty-three years. Their gentle touch told of the love he had experienced the first time he saw her on the quay of Whitby's east side in 1773, the year he had returned from his third whaling expedition.

The weather had been good for the last two days of the voyage that had taken him away from his home-port for six months. A calm sea and a favourable wind had meant good progress. The sight of Whitby's ruined abbey on the cliff top, catching the sun's rays, a welcome landmark for sailors nearing home, always set Gideon's heart racing. It had put him in a good mood. The voyage had been successful and, judging by the praise he had received from the Captain of the *North Star* for his enthusiasm and ability, promotion in the future looked certain.

As the ship had been warped to its berth beneath the streets of red-roofed houses that spilled down the cliffside to the river, his eyes were drawn to a girl among the crowds of relatives and well-wishers jostling on the quay as they strove to get a better view of those on board. Gideon had fallen instantly under her spell, and there and then had resolved to marry her if she was free. He swore that at some time in the future he would make her proud of him when he took out his first ship as captain from this thriving port on Yorkshire's rugged coast.

Someone had come to the rail beside him and for a moment his attention deviated from the girl, but it proved to be a decisive moment.

'Hello, Jack,' he greeted the young man with whom he had become friendly on this voyage. 'Tell me, do you know who yon lass is? That one with the pale blue bonnet and the grey shawl round her shoulders?' Gideon's gaze was on her again, drawn by the laughter in her eyes, joyous in the knowledge that a whale-ship was safely home from the rigours of the Arctic.

At that moment her gaze swept along the men crowding the rail, and stopped. She sensed she was being closely scrutinised. Puzzled as to why this should be and who might be studying her, she sought out her observer. Their eyes met. Across the gap between ship and quay a moment of time was stilled. The past meant nothing. The future beckoned with its gift of a life to be shared. Theirs was an immediate and binding love that promised to last through eternity.

'Aye, Gideon. She's Georgina Attley. Her father has a jet workshop near the bottom of the Church Stairs.' As he spoke Jack glanced at his friend, grinning when he saw the look in Gideon's eyes. 'Smitten, is thee? Ah, well, best of luck. Thee'll need it.' He did not enlarge on the meaning behind these last words nor add that he had been rebuffed by the same girl who had obviously transported Gideon into a dream world. All that his friend had taken in were the words 'Georgina Attley'.

They became the gateway to a world of happiness, an enduring marriage, three sons and two daughters.

'Maybe when you get back?' Georgina repeated her question when she did not receive an immediate reply.

Gideon gave her a loving smile. 'Aye, all right, lass.' Maybe she was right. At fifty, it was time to fulfil her desire and move to the west side of the river, where new buildings were being built as the town expanded, offering more salubrious dwellings to those who could afford them. It had been Georgina's dream for some time to live there.

'So I can look for somewhere while you're away?' Excitement shone in her eyes.

'Aye, lass,' he replied, then added a note of warning. 'But don't go completing any deals until I get back.'

'I won't, I promise.' She kissed him on the cheek.

He still held her round the waist and looked with teasing seriousness into the depths of her eyes. 'Now, lass, thee can do better than that.'

Love welled from the depths of her heart as she met his gaze, and then allowed a kiss on his lips to express it as eloquently.

When their lips parted he said with glowing affection, 'Your kiss will be my warmth in the cold of the Arctic, and your lips will be on mine through all the coming days when we are apart.'

'And my thoughts will never leave you,' she replied tenderly.

The door opened but Gideon and Georgina did not move apart. Their five children were used to seeing the constant expressions of love that passed between their parents and in them saw the foundations of the security that permeated their own lives.

'You boys ready?' Gideon asked.

'Yes, Pa,' Daniel and Edmund answered together.

'Good.' He cast a proud eye over them.

Daniel at twenty-two reminded Gideon very much of himself at that age. He was strong and broad-shouldered, his face tanned by the sun, wind and salt air. His six-foot-two frame, with its commanding presence, could not fail to be noticed, and appreciated, by many a girl.

His nineteen-year-old brother Edmund was shorter by three inches but, though he was thinner, there was still power in his frame. When the two eldest boys came into the room they were accompanied by Abel who, aged eighteen, was making his first voyage to the Arctic. There were boys who went at a much earlier age but Abel's parents had insisted, as they had with all their children, that he receive good education first. Now he was excited by the prospect of being gilded with the same aura that attached itself to his father, brothers, and all the whale-men of

Whitby. Theirs was regarded as a special calling, braving the icy seas and dangers of the Arctic, where they pitted themselves against whales sometimes twice as long as the open boats from which they hunted with hand-held harpoons. These men were hunters and often explorers too, sailing uncharted seas in search of their prey. Special in the eyes of Whitby folk, whalemen were always given an enthusiastic send off on sailing day; and on their return, when the cry of 'Whale-ship!' rang through the town, the cliffs, staithes and quays were crowded.

Gideon was a strict captain. He would not allow his sons to sail with him for he feared that family relationships might get in the way of his running the ship efficiently. A fierce disciplinarian, he was sometimes criticised for being too unbending. Once on board he was a different character from the mild-mannered man who doted on his family at home. Nor would he allow his sons to sail together on the same ship. Should tragedy strike, the loss of more than one of them would be impossible to bear. So today Daniel would be on the *Hunter* under Captain Fitzgerald; Edmund on the *Sunset* with Captain Webster; and Abel would be aboard Captain Horner's *Wanderer*, while their father would take his usual ship, the *Water Nymph*, owned by Sam Coulson, one of the leading merchants and businessmen in Whitby.

'All right, boys, say goodbye to your ma. We'd best be getting on board.' Gideon kissed his wife again and turned an admiring eye to his daughter Ruth who at twenty rejoiced in the same fresh beauty as her mother at that age. She reminded Gideon so much of his first sight of Georgina. 'It's good to have you back, Ruth. Look after your mother. You too, Rachel.' They nodded reassuringly at him and accepted his kisses.

Daniel, Edmund and Abel said their goodbyes, and Daniel voiced their concern for their sisters. 'Take care. This will be the first summer when there's none of us lads here to look after you.' The brothers had been solicitous for their sisters' welfare ever since they were youngsters. This had been a cause of chagrin to Ruth on more than one occasion but they took no notice of her protests that they were smothering her and she could look after herself. At twenty, three years older than Rachel, she had a likeable personality that was complemented by her attractive looks and capacity for friendliness. Though sometimes reserved, like her mother, it was a trait that could deceive, for Ruth had a strong character. For most of this last year she had been in France with her spinster aunt who had invited her to accompany her to the Continent, judging it would be good for Ruth to widen her experience.

Rachel had an independent streak, too, and though she sometimes revelled in her brothers' protective attitude she always managed to give them the slip when there was a special beau she wanted to see. She had no one to whom she gave particular attention but was never at a loss for an escort to a party or special function; her lively personality ensured that. Her round, bright face was usually wreathed in a sunshine smile and her startlingly blue eyes expressed her love of life.

Now, with their brothers sailing to the Arctic, the sisters experienced a new and welcome feeling of freedom. Though their mother would be at home to caution them occasionally, they relied on her inherent tolerance and trust, knowing they could twist her round their little fingers.

But across Whitby at that minute something was taking place that would alter the course of the future they had envisaged.

Sam Coulson pushed a bottle of whisky and a glass across his desk to his twenty-four-year old son. 'Get a good one, it'll be the last for five or six months if you keep out of the whisky houses in Shetland.'

'I'll do that all right.' Martin grinned at the thought of his first whaling voyage when some of the crew had introduced a youngster of seventeen to the whisky houses. In the gloomy atmosphere of a room filled with peat smoke trying to escape through a hole in the roof, the skirl of the pipes could not drown out the cries of the old crones who'd egged him on to try both whisky and girls – at a price.

5

Sam eyed his son closely. Sam's strength of character had been tested in the darkness of poverty and shaped on the anvil of his determination to rise above his beginnings and make a success of his life. Wealth had come to him through his shrewd brain and good eye for an investment, but he was a man who also knew what it was to serve in the Arctic seas – all traits that had been passed on to his eldest son who was the shining light in his father's eye.

Sam admired Martin's physical strength, though he himself did not lack power in a slim frame which had been honed by the rigours of a harsh early existence and the punishing life of the whale-ships. His thin pointed face had been leathered by the elements of sun, wind and sea. His dark eyes hardly ever smiled and there was always a slightly sardonic look about his mouth. He held most men in contempt and gauged them purely by their financial status. Ambition beyond measure had cultivated a ruthless streak in him that he was not averse to using to further his desires.

Now Sam leaned back in the chair behind his desk, sipped his whisky and eyed his son. 'You've thought about what I said?'

'I have. I'll make this my last whaling voyage.'

'Good.' Sam's knowing half-smile was full of satisfaction. 'You'll not regret it, Martin, I'll see to that. You can fulfil many of my dreams – expand on my ideas. We'll not let this business stagnate. A lot will depend on you. I have no faith in Ben who seems to seek only the pleasures of this life, and Eric will never make anything other than a whale-man. He's sailing with you again this year.'

'You shouldn't have indulged Ben with the same money as you did me.'

'I made a promise that when you reached the age of twenty-one each of you would receive two hundred pounds, and I'm a man who keeps his promises, Martin. You used your money wisely. In the last two years Benjamin seems to have used it just to have a good time. He must be coming to the end of it.'

'Unless his luck at cards holds.' Martin knew he was not revealing Ben's passion for gambling.

Sam snorted. 'It can't! And he needn't come running to me when he hasn't a penny. He'll get no more off me, and he needn't think he can sponge off Eric when he gets his. I'll see to that.' Sam fished a watch from his waistcoat pocket. 'Ah, plenty of time. Well, now that you have decided to give up whaling as far as voyages to the Arctic are concerned, I'll give you something to think about while you are away.'

Martin eyed him with curiosity, knowing there would be some intrigue behind these veiled words. His father had not become the town's leading merchant, with investments in a number of Whitby's thriving industries, without a capacity for seizing on some very slender chances. Sam Coulson had a reputation as a shrewd businessman, but one who would bend the rules and sail very close to the wind if it was for his own benefit. His dealings had brought him friends and also enemies, but Sam Coulson was always the one to come out on top and many a man had left Whitby rather than cross him a second time.

His ruthless attitude stemmed from his rough childhood, at the mercy of a father who drank, and a mother who did not care where he was. But Sam always had a streak of ambition in him he must have inherited from somewhere. It had roused in him a desire to escape from the squalor of his childhood and move in the upper echelons of Whitby society. He had done so first by toughening himself serving on the whale-ships. There he had seen the possibilities of making money in a trade that contributed much to the economic prosperity of the town. He took the view that if it did that for Whitby it could do the same for Sam Coulson. He saved and speculated, moving in and out of investments quickly until he had built up sufficient capital to take a share in a whale-ship. That share became two and then four until he achieved his ambition of owning a ship of his own and engaging a captain with a reputation for sniffing out whales – Gideon Holmes. Sam then wisely diversified and also acquired interests in shipbuilding, and the making of ropes and sails. He was ever on the look out to use his wits and further expand his investments. He loved the power that money brought him, and that had led him to the suggestion he was about to make to his eldest son.

'There is something I have never disclosed to anyone before but now is the time.'

His curiosity aroused, Martin raised one eyebrow in query.

'Over the years I have watched Seaton Campion create a successful business. It would be a great asset to Coulson's, and I mean to acquire it.'

The force and conviction in his father's voice startled Martin. 'What! But you and he are friends . . . the families are close.'

Martin was familiar with the story of how his father and Seaton had first met as boys in the Market Place. His father was being chased by an irate girl from whose basket he had just plucked a bag of cakes. He fell and would have been caught had not a stranger, Seaton Campion, grabbed him and yanked him to his feet. Seaton took Sam to his home which was very different from the hovel where he lived. He thought he'd be thrown out and told to keep away but instead was treated with kindness by Seaton's parents, who seemed to take the attitude that if their son liked someone then that person was all right. They were so easygoing Sam could easily have deceived them but it had never entered his head. Their acceptance of him changed his view of life. This was another world from the one Sam knew and he was determined to make something of himself and enter it. When they grew up the two friends both prospered in Whitby's commercial world, but in different ways. Sam, because of his tough childhood, had a ruthless streak that carried him along through many a shaky deal. Seaton achieved his position slowly and steadily, without taking chances.

'Seaton is content to be where he is, enjoying a comfortable living from his various interests,' Sam went on. 'I don't decry him for that or for what he is. In fact, I respect his perseverance and good sense. But that way is not me, I don't think I could ever curb my restless nature – be content with my lot as he is. I need to be always achieving.'

He paused to take a sip of whisky and Martin took the opportunity to ask, 'Where is this leading, Pa? What do you want me to think about while I am in the Arctic?'

'I want to create the biggest commercial enterprise in Whitby, a business that could wield influence beyond this town as Britain's mercantile strength increases.' The fervour of a visionary was in Sam's voice as he envisaged the future power within his grasp. 'And it will all be for you eventually, if you play your part.'

'Pa, I love the life of a whaler, the responsibility that I have as a harpooner. Something gets into your blood when you are locked in contest with a gigantic creature that could shatter you and your crew with its enormous flukes. And if that isn't enough of a driving force, there is always the magic of the Arctic calling me back. But . . .' Martin paused to emphasise the word and those that followed '. . . I'll forego all that to help strengthen this firm in any way I can.'

Sam eyed his eldest child with satisfaction. All his planning for the son on whom he had doted since birth appeared to be coming to fruition. He gave a slight nod as he said, 'I'm pleased to hear that. I wouldn't have got the same response from Ben. And Eric will only be happy at sea. He may be useful in that respect, of course.'

'The firm will be safe in my hands,' replied Martin in a tone that showed he would tolerate no interference from Ben whom he regarded as an unambitious wastrel. 'You and I will carry this business forward.'

'Aye, lad, we will that – and you'll produce the heir to secure its future. I reckon when you get back from this voyage, you'd better think of marrying.' Martin merely raised his eyebrows at this suggestion. His father chuckled before he went on, 'Oh, I know you play the field but I reckon it's time you settled down for the good of our enterprise.'

Martin's lips twitched with amusement. 'It sounds to me as though you have someone in mind?'

'Aye, lad, I have. Someone who could substantially expand our interests the moment you marry her.'

'Don't I get any say in the matter?' Martin asked warily.

'You do, but think on my suggestion carefully.'

'Well, who is it then?'

'Alicia Campion.'

Sam could not tell immediately how his suggestion had been taken. Was Martin horrified by the idea or did he approve, if only mildly? Sam pressed on.

'I have approached Seaton a number of times with the suggestion that we should amalgamate, but he's always refused. I think it can be achieved through Alicia. She's not bad-looking and has an attractive personality. And, think on, Seaton has no sons and as the eldest daughter she has to be in line for some or all of the business. Even if he shares it out between his three lasses they'll no doubt see the advantage of staking their shares through you.'

Martin started to chuckle. 'You're a wily old bird!'

Sam grinned. 'Aye, maybe I am. I haven't got where I am today without keeping one step ahead and weighing up all the possibilities. Well, how does it sound to you? You've known Alicia her whole life.'

'I agree she's likeable enough, and has something about her.'

'And, I imagine, a useful lass in bed.'

Martin was not taken aback by his father's straight talking. 'But maybe she won't have me?'

'Leave that to me. A few words in Seaton's ear, pointing out the advantages to be gained from such a marriage, should do the trick. As you indicate, Alicia can be a bit rebellious at times but she isn't one to go against her parents' wishes. You think about it while you're away.'

'No need, Pa. It's obvious we'd benefit the business if we could pull this off. I'll not scuttle that. Besides, I can still sow my wild oats elsewhere.'

'Aye, you can that, lad. I'll plant the idea in Seaton's mind then.' Sam raised his glass. 'Here's to the future.'

'The future!' Martin drained his glass and stood up. 'I'd best be going. Don't want to get on the wrong side of Captain Holmes before we sail.'

Ten minutes later he and Eric were making the traditional goodbye in the hall.

'Take care, you two,' said Sam, clamping his hands on each son's shoulders in turn, 'though I know you are in good company with Captain Holmes.'

The young men gave their sisters Sarah and Dina a kiss, and shook hands with their brother Benjamin. Martin gripped his father's hand and read his approval when their eyes met.

'Aren't you going to break your own rule for once and see your sons sail?' asked Benjamin, impatience at his father's stubbornness evident in his tone.

Sam's eyes were cold when they locked on him. 'You know my views about that. Watching ships sail is time mismanaged, and my time is money. You'd be better thinking more about those words and applying yourself to something useful.'

'There's more to life than making money.' Ben didn't wait for what he knew would be a sharp retort; he had heard it often enough. He turned to his brothers. 'I'll be on the pier.'

'And we will too,' chorused Sarah and Dina.

Martin and Eric picked up their bags and strode quickly from the house.

Sam watched them go. He always had to steel himself for this moment, not that he minded them leaving so much but their leaving for the sea always reminded him of his wife who had died four years ago. She had pleaded with him the moment Martin had reached his teens not to send their sons to the Arctic, but Sam had been adamant, saying that whaling was a part of the family business they should know about, apart from the fact that it would toughen them up for life. There was constant disagreement between his wife and him after that, and Sam's ruthless nature would not allow him to yield to her pleas. This had led to the disintegration of their marriage and to both of

11

them seeking solace in other arms, with their confrontations growing more and more bitter until her death.

An hour later Ben called up to the stairs to his sisters, 'Are you two coming?'

He heard a door bang and an answer of, 'Yes.' There was a scurrying sound and Sarah and Dina appeared. They ran quickly down the stairs, fastening the ribbons of their bonnets around their chins. They wore similar ankle-length pelisses. Sarah's was in navy blue with the thinnest of fur trim around the small collar. Dina's was scarlet, devoid of any adornment.

The sisters were very close, having found solace in each other's company during the sad years of their parents' feud. Though they dare not voice their opinions openly they blamed their father for much that had happened. They had witnessed his intransigence over the whaling issue during their impressionable years and it had left its mark. Nor did they see eye to eye with him over the gifts of money he had made to Martin and Ben, and would do to their youngest brother when Eric reached twenty-one, for he had refused them the same gift saying only that 'girls marry and are looked after by their husbands'.

Sarah, at twenty-two, had been engaged to the son of the owner of the alum works at Ravenscar south of Whitby, but two years ago tragedy had robbed her of the happiness she'd envisaged when her fiancé fell from some high cliffs while going to supervise the unloading of the cargo from a collier berthed below. She was only just beginning to get over the loss and was grateful for the support of her sister Dina who was currently courting Rowan North, newly promoted to boat-steerer for this voyage aboard Sam's ship the *Water Nymph*. Though he had respect for any man who signed on for a whaling voyage, Sam did not really approve of his daughter's relationship with Rowan who had been raised an orphan. He'd prefer her attention to be directed towards someone more influential and useful to the business. But a defiant Dina had always

12

opposed her father's hints and suggestions about this matter.

It was she who, as they left the house, voiced her pleasure at Ben's stance. 'You'll really rile Father one day with your constant criticism. Not that he doesn't richly deserve it, mind.'

'He should go to see his own sons off. I had more than enough of that harsh existence after just one whaling voyage, but I care nothing for his opinion of me. There are things about me he does not know and which I will only reveal when the time is right.'

From the garden of their house on the West Cliff they had a view across the river to the east side where the late-morning sun brightened the red roofs of the buildings climbing the cliff to the old parish church and the ruined abbey standing like a sentinel on top of the cliff, a welcome sight to many a home-coming sailor.

'Do you know how many ships are sailing today?' Dina asked as they hurried through the streets towards the riverside.

'I heard yesterday that four will be ready: *Water Nymph*, *Wanderer*, *Hunter*, and *Sunset*.'

'Good,' said Sarah, excitement in her voice. 'It will be a grand sight.'

Streams of people of all ages and levels of social standing were making their way to vantage points to see the whalers sail. The whale-men who would not see this Yorkshire coast nor their homes for nearly six months were widely respected by the townspeople.

'Where do you want to go?' asked Ben as they neared the bridge.

'The West Pier,' replied Dina quickly, wanting to get her opinion in first.

'Not the cliffs?' he asked, a little surprised at her choice. 'You get a better view from there.'

'But you are closer on the pier, and that means you see the crew.'

'All right. The West Pier it is,' Ben agreed. He exchanged a glance with his elder sister Sarah who raised her eyebrows in return, knowing that Ben was well aware of their younger sister's continued liaison with Rowan North, in spite of their father's disapproval.

They turned away from the bridge and joined the crowd of people already on their way to the West Pier. On the other side of the river folk were thronging narrow Church Street as they headed for the piers and staithes, while others were prepared to make the steep climb up the one hundred and ninety-nine steps to the cliff top. Though there would be sadness for some at seeing a loved one, be it husband, son, brother or sweetheart, sail to the Arctic, they thrust the dangers from their mind and assumed jocular expressions. This was sailing day for the whalers, a special day when these brave men deserved the best of send offs.

On reaching the West Pier, Ben quickened their pace and forged a way through the crowd to seek a good vantage point for his sisters near the end of the pier.

'All right here?' he queried, shepherding them to the edge of it.

'Yes,' they agreed wholeheartedly.

From their position they would see the vessels approaching downstream, towed by oared boats until they cast off and allowed the ships, with the wind in their topsails, to take to the open sea.

Around them people were jockeying for good viewing positions in a light-hearted way. Joking complaints and criticisms were made and good-humoured banter flowed in return. Pleasantries were exchanged, news imparted and opinions offered, but all the while a keen lookout was kept for any sign of movement from upriver.

'They're coming!' The first cry was eagerly taken up and swept through the crowd like a consuming fire that would not be controlled. Excitement charged everyone.

Ben turned automatically as he took up the cry, passing it on. The words faded on his lips when his eyes met those of a young woman a short distance away. He felt a singing in his

14

heart that would not stop. It told him that all the other girls with whom he had sought favour or had enjoyed Whitby's social life did not matter and would never be part of his life again. Her gaze, with clear interest and curiosity in it, met his before she demurely turned away to her companion.

He felt someone dig him in the side. 'Don't stare!' hissed Dina indignantly.

'Moonstruck,' commented Sarah, amused to see her carefree brother look so bewitched.

'Who is she?' he asked, for he knew his sisters had observed the direction of his gaze.

'Ruth Holmes,' replied Sarah. 'And that's her sister Rachel.'

'Gideon Holmes's daughters? Captain of Father's ship?' he asked in surprise.

'None other.'

'Why haven't I met her before?' asked Ben as if his whole life so far had been a desert.

'She's been away this last year, travelling the Continent with her spinster aunt who lives in King's Lynn normally but wanted to take advantage of the peace to see something of France. She thought it would broaden her niece's education if Ruth accompanied her. She is rather reserved, you see.'

'Then I think maybe her education should be broadened even further.'

'I don't think you'll get a chance to do that.'

'Oh, I will.'

Ben's remark was made with such confidence that Sarah and Dina read a challenge in it.

'We'll each bet you a florin that you don't get her to accompany you to the ball at the Angel next month,' they said, certain they would win.

'Done,' Ben agreed.

The excitement of the crowd intensified as the first ship was drawn downriver. Already they could see the people on the opposite cliff top waving and hear their cheers. The *Sunset* came abreast with the pier, its topsails catching the breeze. Her

15

crew lined the rail, climbed the rigging to be more conspicuous else, under orders, were already aloft, ready to loosen the main topsail. The ship passed close to the pier. The farewells became more animated. Calls were exchanged between those on shore and those bound for the Arctic. Smiles hid tears from loved ones, though there were also those who regarded this parting as a blessing: men who would be away from nagging wives, or women who would now be free from demanding husbands and able to find comfort in the arms of more considerate lovers.

The pilot boats slipped their ropes and moved out of the way of the *Sunset's* progress.

Ben saw Ruth's wave become more vigorous. Who was it for? A beau? His heart sank a little. He followed her gaze anxiously. Could he pick out the sailor for whom her farewell was meant among all those on the deck? His heart lifted with the relief he felt when his eyes settled on one particular young man who was waving with equal enthusiasm, his face broad with a beaming smile. Edmund Holmes. Ben had never met him but knew Ruth's brother by sight.

The *Sunset* passed between the piers, and met the first swell of the sea.

Ben turned his attention back to Ruth. At that moment she diverted her gaze from the *Sunset* to see if the next ship was underway. Her eyes met his for the briefest of moments but he saw interest and curiosity nevertheless. Then she leaned sideways and said something to her sister. They both turned their attention upriver.

The second ship was coming. A buzz ran through the crowd once more. When the *Hunter* drew near the pier Ben saw both girls wave with equal enthusiasm. This time he saw that Ruth's attention was riveted on Daniel Holmes whom he also knew by sight.

The *Hunter* took to the sea and headed north.

The *Wanderer* was close behind. Ben saw Ruth wave to her youngest brother, Abel.

One more ship to go. Even those who had already seen their

loved ones leave the safety of the river lingered. This was a Whitby whale-ship that was leaving and they would give her an equally warm send off.

Ben, seeing his sisters' attention concentrated on Martin and Eric's ship moving slowly downriver, slipped away from them. He threaded his way carefully and unobtrusively between the watchers on the pier until he was close to Ruth and her sister.

The *Water Nymph* came into view and he could sense excitement intensify in the sisters. By the time it approached them the boats had been cast-off and the wind was catching the ship's sails, driving the whaler towards the sea. Laughter was on their lips but there was concern in their eyes and a clear hope that all would go well with the voyage and that their father would return home safely to them. Their animated waving was returned by the man standing close to the helmsman. Then he raised his hand to his peaked cap and saluted them before turning his full attention to seeing his vessel safely from the river.

Ben saw Martin was aloft while Eric was busy coiling ropes near the bow. His younger brother straightened after finishing his task. They exchanged cursory acknowledgements. Next Ben turned his gaze aloft. He waved to Martin and received one in reply. He saw Martin give extra attention to Sarah and Dina but wondered if this was for their sake or for Alicia Campion's who had joined them. His speculation was short-lived because, with the *Water Nymph* taking to the sea, the crowds began to disperse.

Ruth and Rachel turned to leave the pier and almost bumped into Ben. Apologies sprang to their lips but died there when he smiled, doffed his hat, and said, 'Good day, ladies. Here to see your father sail?' His eyes, focused only on Ruth, twinkled with pleasure to have surprised them.

'Yes,' replied Rachel quickly. 'And our brothers.' She had noted that Ben's attention was really on her sister.

'They do not sail with him, I believe?' He made it appear as if he was addressing only Ruth.

She could do nothing but reply. 'If there was a tragedy and

a ship was lost then only one member of our family would perish.'

'A wise provision,' Ben conceded. 'But let us not dwell on such sombre matters. May I escort you good ladies home?'

'I don't . . .' started Ruth, but was immediately interrupted by her sister.

'There's Rowan's sister. I want a word with her. Excuse me.' Rachel gave her sister no chance to stop her, she was away as soon as she had spoken.

Ben smiled. 'It seems a decision has been made for you, Miss Holmes. So if you will allow me the honour, it will be my pleasure to see you safely home.'

Ruth was experiencing a mixture of annoyance and gratitude towards her sister. Though she was embarrassed at the way she had been left with Ben Coulson, she was pleased also to be able to make the closer acquaintance with this young man who had caught her attention in the crowd.

'Miss Holmes, it is very remiss of me. I have imposed myself on you without a formal introduction. I hope you will forgive me?' he said.

'There is nothing to forgive, Mr Coulson.'

'Ah, so you know my name?'

'And the reputation that goes before you.'

'Alas, I fear that reputations are frequently exaggerated. I understand you have been away from Whitby for a year? Stories can get out of hand in that time. Please allow me to show you that many of the ones concerning me are unfounded.'

Before Ruth had time to reply Alicia Campion, catching sight of them walking together, hastily left Ben's sisters and came over.

'Hello, Ben,' she said, pleasure evident in her voice and expression. 'I was hoping I would see you. I thought you might be here to see your father's ship sail.' She turned to Ruth. 'And you are back from your sojourn in France, I see, Miss Holmes. I hope you had a pleasant time and that you do not find Whitby too parochial?'

18

'Thank you for your concern, Miss Campion. I had a most enjoyable time in France, but I assure you I shall not be bored in Whitby.'

Ben caught the flicker of an eye in his direction and smiled to himself at this rebuff to Alicia, and the challenge to him that he thought he read there. Maybe Ruth Holmes was not such a withdrawn person as his sisters had made out. Maybe there was spirit behind the reserve she had cultivated. It would be tempting to find out.

Alicia made no reply but turned to him and said, in an attempt to freeze Ruth out, 'Are you going my way?'

'I'm afraid not, Alicia. I have promised to see Miss Holmes home. I saw you with my sisters. I am sure they would be pleased of your company.'

Anger surged through Alicia. How dare this interloper capture Ben's attention? Seething as she was, she controlled her feelings. She must not create a scene and appear no better than a common fishwife. She turned on her heel and strode away without another word.

'Oh, dear,' said Ruth, a note of amusement in her voice. 'I think you upset that young lady. I believe she may nurse certain sentiments towards you.'

Ben fell into step beside her and shrugged his shoulders casually. 'Just good friends. The Coulsons and the Campions are close. We saw a lot of each other as children, and still do.'

'But not in the same way you did as children.'

'No. People grow up.'

'And assume different relationships in their adult years.'

'Miss Holmes, let me assure you that there is nothing between Miss Campion and me – only friendship.'

'Do you say that about all the young ladies whose hearts I hear you have broken?'

'Have I broken yours, Miss Holmes?'

'Indeed you have not,' replied Ruth indignantly. 'That assumes a relationship between us that does not exist.'

19

'Did not the look in your eyes when we first saw each other a short while ago establish one?'

Ruth, annoyed that he had been aware of her interest in him, coloured. 'Of course not.'

'Well, we shall see.' Ben deemed this was the moment to change the course of their conversation, at least for the time being. 'Are you pleased to be back in Whitby, Miss Holmes?'

Almost taken aback by the change of subject, Ruth felt the hostility that had threatened to take her over disappear. In the short time she had talked to him she could not deny she had been attracted to this confident young man. He had an air of assurance that would have females of all ages vying for his company, like moths to a candle flame. He was handsome with a certain confidence that was entirely natural, not purposefully projected. His laughing eyes sparkled beneath the brim of his black top hat. A thigh-length coat was left unfastened to reveal a sand-coloured waistcoat that matched the trousers that came to the top of his highly polished black shoes. His waistcoat was worn partially open and beneath it he wore a white, high-collared shirt with a light blue cravat tied at the neck in a casual manner that nevertheless drew the attention.

'Indeed, I am pleased to be back with my family in the town of my birth.'

'You have missed it while you have been away?'

'I have.'

'And what did you think to France?'

'Like all places, it is beautiful in parts and not in others. If you are interested in architecture and fashion it is worth a visit but I did not find the French very welcoming. Have you visited that country, Mr Coulson?'

'I have not been so fortunate.'

'You have not travelled at all?'

'If you can call one whaling voyage travelling, then yes, I have.'

'Ah, I wondered why you did not sail with your brothers?'

'One voyage was enough for me. I did not relish the prospect but Father insisted that if his sons were to inherit any interest in his business, they must know something of it. Though he has diversified considerably, Father built his wealth on a foundation of whaling. Martin is different. He relishes the whale-hunt and says the Arctic is magical. He speaks highly of your father, as does Eric, and I know mine rates him highly as both captain and hunter.'

'I am glad of that. I know Father considers Mr Coulson a just and fair man where he and the crew of the *Water Nymph* are concerned, and I have heard him speak highly of your brothers.'

'I think he will lose Martin after this voyage. Father has been hinting that he wants him back here in Whitby to teach him more of the business which he will take over as the eldest son.'

'And what about you?'

Ben's eyes twinkled as he met her look. 'Ah, you *are* interested, Miss Holmes.'

'Purely as a topic of conversation,' replied Ruth a little testily, annoyed at herself for being caught out again.

'*That's* a matter of opinion. But –' he gave a dismissive gesture '– to answer your question, I have interests in the business but play no active part in it. On our reaching the age of twenty-one, Father gave both Martin and me a sum of money and allowed us to make of it what we would. Martin financed some fishermen in Robin Hood's Bay and has done well.'

'And your other brother, Eric?'

'Is not yet twenty-one, but I'm sure he will use his money to invest in something more directly connected with whaling. Maybe buy shares in a ship.'

'And what did you do?'

'Your interest does not wane, I see, Miss Holmes.' Ben laughed at the petulant look she gave him but went on quickly, 'I put mine to good use and have lived well off it.'

'A little riskily at times, from what I heard before I went away a year ago.'

21

He raised his eyebrows. 'I am flattered, Miss Holmes, that you were interested in me even then.'

Ruth looked hard at him and spoke firmly. 'One could not help but hear the rumours.'

'But you were sufficiently interested to remember them, and therefore me. Now I would like to learn more about you, and if you want to get to know me better too, I would be grateful if you would do me the honour of accompanying me to the ball at the Angel next month? That is, unless you are already spoken for?' He added the last remark out of courtesy though he had seen the interest flare momentarily in her eyes. He realised she had brought it quickly under control so as not to appear too eager.

'Mr Coulson, that is kind of you but . . .'

'There *is* someone else?' His face clouded with anxiety. He hung on her reply.

Ruth smiled to herself at his obvious distress. Ben Coulson was more than just a little interested in her and the feeling was mutual. 'No, there is no one. I do thank you for your invitation but . . .'

Relief overwhelmed Ben at the news that Ruth was not spoken for. He followed her 'but' by finishing her sentence for her. 'But with your father heading for the Arctic, you will need to ask your mother's permission? Have no fear, Miss Holmes, I will come in person to seek her consent.'

'You seem to have this all thought out.'

'It is no use dithering over such an important matter. The ball is only twelve days away. I will visit your mother tomorrow.'

Ruth gave a little smile. 'You appear certain you will succeed?'

'Indeed I shall, Miss Holmes. Your mother will succumb to my charms when I make this request.'

'We shall see. But aren't you forgetting something else?'

Ben looked puzzled and then shook his head. 'I don't think so.'

'I'm sure Miss Campion will be expecting you to escort her.'

'I can assure you that I have made no other approaches. Do you think eleven o'clock tomorrow morning a suitable time?'

'I believe so. I will mention that you will be calling. If it is not convenient I will send a message to your home.'

'Thank you for your thoughtfulness,' he said, and inclined his head.

As they strolled through Whitby, Ben noticed a number of glances thrown in their direction. No doubt several people would be curious about Ben Coulson's latest companion but he noted that others cast admiring eyes in Ruth's direction, the men no doubt wishing they were in his shoes and the ladies sizing up her elegant attire. Her red dress was cut on a simple straight line from a high waist. Two interweaving panels of blue embroidery ran up the front of it and branched around the neckline which was cut low to a point just above the waist, revealing the pale blue blouse worn beneath. The sleeves, each with a similar embroidered pattern, came tight to the wrists. A blue waist-length cape with a small turned-up collar was fastened with a clasp at her neck, while a small bonnet allowed her dark brown hair to peep out at front and sides and form a frame to her round, well-proportioned face.

The demure expression had returned as she faced him at the front door of her home in Grape Lane, but he read behind it the challenge of a spirited girl who was curious about him.

He doffed his hat and bowed slightly without taking his eyes off her. 'Until tomorrow, Miss Holmes.'

'My mother will expect you.'

Chapter Two

The March wind blew from the sea carrying a chill to every nook and cranny of Whitby, but in his heavy-duty coat with collar turned up Ben was protected from its icy grasp. Not that he would have noticed it anyway for his mind was preoccupied as it had been for much of the night with thoughts of Ruth Holmes.

His jaunty step carried him through the flow of people going about their daily business as he made his way to the bridge. He exchanged greetings with acquaintances and friends but resisted the temptation to stop and talk, for he was bent on a mission. He crossed to the east side and turned into Grape Lane.

Here he rapped on a dark green-painted door with a brass knocker shaped like a whale, to denote the house owner's trade.

The door was opened by a young servant dressed in black with a white apron tied neatly at her waist. Her hair was hidden by a white mob-cap.

'Mr Coulson to see Mrs Holmes,' Ben announced brightly.

'You are expected, sir. Please step inside,' she returned without hesitation.

He moved past her and waited until she'd closed the door. He found himself in a hall of simple proportions with a narrow staircase, edged by an oak banister, running from its left side.

'This way, sir.' The maid moved near a door to the right, paused, and turning to Ben, said, 'May I take your hat and coat, sir?'

He handed her his hat and shrugged himself out of his coat. The girl took them, knocked on the door and announced, 'Mr Coulson, ma'am.' She glanced at him and nodded.

He walked into the room to see a lady seated in an armchair which had been positioned to one side of the fireplace but turned slightly so that she had a view of the door without losing the heat from the fire that burned brightly in the grate.

'Good day, Mr Coulson.' Her voice held a note of cautious friendliness.

Ben was struck by the undeniable presence of the lady who greeted him. He sensed authority yet a natural kindliness in her attitude. Here was a lady of two parts, authoritative yet under-standing, firm yet pliable, able to switch between the two as circumstances dictated. This no doubt came from being the wife of a man who spent nearly six months of the year plying the lonely Arctic seas, and in the rest of his working life might be called upon at any time to carry cargoes to and from the Continent. During his absences she was both mother and father to her children.

'Good day, Mrs Holmes. It is kind of you to see me and it is a pleasure for me to meet you.' Ben gave her the warmest smile he could without appearing ingratiating. He bowed, and as he straightened his eyes met hers and there passed between them a mutual desire for plain speaking. There would be no shilly-shallying. Kindred spirits had met and they both knew it.

He felt a surge of relief but realised that, in spite of their unspoken understanding, he could not assume that the permission he sought would come easily.

Georgina Holmes had taken to this young man the moment he walked into the room. There was an air of cautious confidence about him. He would not be browbeaten and would stand up for what he thought was right. His reputation had preceded him but she was sensible enough not to prejudge, for she knew that rumours had a habit of containing untruths. She would make her own judgements and hopefully make them wisely, for she had no husband to help her. She eyed Ben as he walked towards her. She liked his smile, there was warmth there and fun too, both of which were reflected in his deep brown eyes. And he was so handsome! At Ruth's age she too would have fallen for this young man who held himself so well.

'Do sit down, Mr Coulson.' Georgina indicated a chair opposite her.

'Thank you, ma'am.'

'My daughter told me of your request to call on me.'

'I am more than delighted that she did so,' he replied. 'Did she tell you of the reason for my request?'

'She did indeed.' Georgina gave a little pause that set Ben to hovering between expectancy and despair. He searched her face but her expression gave nothing away. 'Well, Mr Coulson, let me hear it from you?'

'Mrs Holmes, I would like to ask if I may have your permission to take your daughter Ruth to the ball that is to be held at the Angel next month?'

Georgina pursed her lips thoughtfully. 'Before I give you an answer, I think you should tell me a little more about yourself.'

'So that you may judge if the rumours circulating about me are true?' He dared to put his interpretation of her request bluntly, but went on quickly, 'Yes, rumours there are and always will be attached to someone who likes life and enjoys himself. And rumours are frequently embellished, particularly by those who are jealous. I will not try to hide behind untruth, Mrs Holmes. I do like life and I do enjoy myself, but in whatever I do I set myself limits. Contrary to what some people would have you believe, I do not go beyond these. I respect the opposite sex. I play hard, and work hard too.'

'And what do you do for a living?'

'It may appear to some that I do nothing but spend my time between tavern and card table. I do admit that I'm not averse to either but, as I say, I have my limits. Some would say I sponge off my father, but that is not so, ma'am. My father is a harsh taskmaster, but that is not the reason I do not work for him. When I was given a small sum of money by him at the age of twenty-one, I was determined to make my own way in the world. I believe I am not doing too badly nowadays with

26

interests in a ropery and a ship-chandlery business. These interests occupy much of my time and mind, though they are not generally known and I would ask, ma'am, if that information could be kept between you and me?'

Georgina raised her eyebrows in curiosity and surprise. 'And the reason for this request, Mr Coulson?'

'My father thinks I am wasting the money he gave me. When the time is right, I want to surprise him.'

'Would it not be better for him to know what is going on?'

'No, ma'am. He and I don't see eye to eye over many things. I incurred his wrath when I refused further whaling voyages after my first. He has always thought that it is the only way to measure a man.' Ben cast her an enquiring look as he added, 'Maybe with a husband and sons in the whaling trade, you think the same?'

'No, Mr Coulson, I do not. It is every man to his own liking, I believe. Whaling is the way my husband and sons see to make a living for themselves. You are entitled to your own choice and I respect your decision to do what you believe suits you best.'

'You are a very understanding lady, Mrs Holmes.'

Georgina smiled. 'Ah, Mr Coulson, flattery will not influence my decision.'

'I did not think it would,' he replied with a twinkle in his eye.

'Mr Coulson, you have been honest and forthright with me and I admire that in people. I am sure you will show every respect to my daughter. Heaven help you if you don't!' Her lips twitched with amusement as she added, 'Ruth's brothers are very protective of their sisters.' She had risen as she was speaking and went to the bell-pull beside the fireplace.

A few moments later the maid who had admitted Ben to the house came into the room.

'Elizabeth, tell Miss Ruth I would like to see her.'

Ruth, who had been waiting in her room unable to settle to anything, was quick to respond to the call. She checked her rush in the hall, straightened her dress and ran her hands through her hair before entering the room.

'You sent for me, Mama?' She blushed as she cast Ben a quick glance.

He smiled to himself. He was seeing the demure Ruth today, rather different from the girl he had met on the West Pier and had judged could be high-spirited. He liked the mixture.

'I did, Ruth, do sit down.'

She did so and sat straight-backed with her hands placed carefully together on her lap.

'You already know the reason why this young man is here,' Georgina went on with her eyes fixed intently on her daughter, seeking any wavering from the request she had made. She saw none. 'Knowing as I do that there is a firm resolve behind that demure expression you are adopting, I have no doubt that if I refused permission you would find some way round it. If I locked you in your room, you would surely climb out of the window.' Georgina laughed when she saw the look of astonishment cross Ruth's face. 'A mother knows more than you think, having indulged in such escapades herself once.' She turned her gaze to Ben. 'Now, young man, take good care of my daughter. She is very precious to this family. Her happiness is foremost in our minds. When she spoke of you it was obvious to me that she was set on having you as her escort to the ball, and also desired to get to know you better. So you may take her to the ball, and you may also meet her between now and then.'

Ruth had relaxed as her mother was speaking. Now, as she thanked her, she was grateful too for the revelations she had made about herself. Ruth had always known her mother as someone who was kind and understanding, firm but fair, but had always thought of her as being prim and proper also. She knew little of her mother's younger days and had never realised that she could once have possessed something of the independent spirit that lurked within Ruth herself. She felt a new affinity with her. Even if the desired relationship with Ben

Coulson came to nought, at least meeting him had brought her a new understanding of her mother and Ruth felt closer to her for that.

'Thank you, Mrs Holmes,' Ben broke in. 'I assure you, your daughter will be in safe hands.'

'I am grateful for your reassurance, Mr Coulson. And I myself hope to get to know you better. Now, I am sure you young people don't want to sit here chatting to me.'

'Mrs Holmes, it would give me great pleasure to do so.'

Georgina gave him a small smile. 'I've told you, Mr Coulson, flattery will get you nowhere. Now, off with you.'

Rising from his chair, Ben said, 'It is rather chilly, Miss Holmes, but shall we walk?'

'I would like nothing better, Mr Coulson. I have missed the fresh Whitby air while I have been on the Continent.' Ruth went to her mother and kissed her on the cheek. 'Thank you,' she whispered. Reaching the door, she paused and looked back. 'I shan't be long.'

Her mother gave a dismissive wave of her hand which expressed her unspoken words, Take as long as you like. I was your age once.

'You have an understanding mother, Miss Holmes,' remarked Ben as they left Grape Lane to cross the bridge. 'She is a fine lady. I think my mother would have been like her.'

'Do you still miss her?' There was a sympathetic tone in Ruth's voice.

'I do.' Regret clouded Ben's expression. 'My sisters are helpful and understanding but no one can replace a mother.'

'I suppose so, but you would know whereas I do not. I am glad you think highly of my mother. I believe she likes you.'

'Good. That is one barrier we needn't break down.'

'Your reputation is widespread, Mr Coulson. My father might be less easily won over.'

'As I said to your mother, rumours have a habit of attracting untruths. I'll have to prove that to your father in due course.'

They reached the west side of the river.

'Where shall it be, Miss Holmes, the cliff top or the West Pier?'

'The cliff top,' she replied without hesitation.

A group of people were coming towards them as they climbed the rise in Flowergate and Ben automatically took hold of her arm to guide her past them. Ruth found herself approving of his gesture which, though casually performed, gave her a sense of security. She made no attempt to draw away once they had an open pathway before them.

They turned into Skinner Street and soon reached the cliff top. Ruth breathed deeply of the sharp breeze here. When they had left the buildings behind and were alone, she stopped. 'I love to feel the wind in my hair so I shall throw convention aside and remove my bonnet.' She looked at Ben with doubt in her eyes. 'Unless you disapprove?'

'My dear Miss Holmes, please take whatever liberties you desire.' His eyes conveyed his approval of her decision.

'Mr Coulson,' she returned firmly, 'if formalities are breaking down between us then I wish you would call me Ruth.'

'There is nothing I would like better, for with that suggestion comes the implication that you approve of me?'

'I do, and indeed I will until such time as you give me cause not to.'

'I will never do that, Ruth.' The sincerity in his voice was matched by the look in his eyes as they met hers.

In that meeting a bond was sealed as if this was a moment of destiny, a time that had been preordained. They both felt something drawing them together as if their pasts had been shaped for this moment, one that would be forever imprinted on their hearts and minds. Their future was being forged in the blossoming of love between them.

Words were not needed. Ben reached out and drew her towards him. Ruth came willingly, her eyes inviting. There was adoration in his, expressing the depth of the love that he felt for her. He leaned towards her upturned face and met her lips gently with his. Neither drew away. Their kiss lingered, heightening the expression of their love for each other.

As their lips finally parted still their eyes held each other.

'Ruth, I'm sorry,' he started clumsily.

She smiled. Was this the practised rake his reputation had promised? She put her fingers to his lips to halt his words. 'I'm not.'

'I shouldn't have presumed . . .' he stumbled on, only to be stopped again.

'Why not? I would have even if you had thought me forward.' A chuckle started in her throat, her lips twitched in amusement. 'Why are we apologising when we both wanted this to happen?'

Ben grinned and shook his head. 'I don't know.' He started to laugh at his own awkwardness, and it was infectious. Ruth laughed with him and the bond between them was deepened.

Their walk on the cliff was idyllic. They were lost in their own world, intent on getting to know each other. They talked of their interests, their families, she of her year in France, he of his life in Whitby and of the voyage that had turned him against whaling, the decision that had so antagonised his father.

'That might be one thing about you that will not sit well with my father and brothers, but Mother and I will win them over,' Ruth told him.

'And I'll use all my powers of persuasion to get them on our side,' Ben reassured her. There was nothing more sure in his mind now than that one day he would ask her to marry him, and would not rest until she had promised to do so. He wondered if many people knew Ruth for a bold, adventurous girl, willing to cast convention aside in her desire to draw as much from life as she could?

She in turn wondered how this kindly young man could have been so misjudged. His behaviour was far more thoughtful and courteous than she'd expected from the rumours about him, but if there was only a mite of truth in some of them then life with him would certainly be spiked with excitement.

*

Rachel Holmes had left her bedroom door ajar so she would not miss her sister's return. For the last hour she had attempted to read *The Vicar of Wakefield* but her mind was too restless. There were moments when she read the same sentence two or three times without really appreciating its significance. She knew Ben Coulson had called on her mother and was aware that Ruth and he had left the house together. Shortly afterwards her mother had gone out too, leaving her alone except for the servants.

With the lively mind and vivid imagination of a seventeen year old, Rachel missed little. After seeing what had passed between her sister and Ben when the *Water Nymph* had sailed and linking that with this morning's events, she reckoned she was not far wrong in guessing that Ben Coulson was interested in Ruth. Could her sister reciprocate that interest? She had been surprised when she had seen them leave the house together. It must have been with her mother's permission. Surely she knew of Ben Coulson's reputation? Why, only two weeks ago Sally Egremont had told Rachel he was supposed to have defended the reputation of a lady of low repute.

The alleged incident was driven from her mind when she heard the front door open and close. She put down her book, failing to place a bookmark in the page she had reached, and listened for footsteps on the stairs. Her sister's. Rachel knew her tread. The steps reached the landing and moved in the direction of Ruth's bedroom.

Rachel rose from her chair beside the window, crossed the room and paused beside the door. She listened intently, and when she heard her sister's door close, stepped outside. She hurried quickly along the corridor, tapped lightly on the door and, without waiting for an answer, impetuously entered the room.

'Ruthie, is he as bad as people make out? Does he break every girl's heart? Was he terribly forward? Did he try to kiss you?' Rachel's words poured out.

'You, young lady, should not take notice of the mischievous

gossip your ill-informed friends pass on to you,' responded Ruth haughtily. 'Nor should you believe the tittle-tattle you carefully contrive to overhear. Nor should you speculate merely because two people have gone for a walk together.'

Rachel assumed a hurt expression. 'Oh, Ruthie, don't get on your high horse. I'm only interested because it's you.' She dropped her pretence of remorse and asked excitedly: 'Did he kiss you? I'm told he kisses all the girls the first time he takes them out.'

'Stories, Rachel, mere stories,' replied Ruth indignantly, hanging her coat in the wardrobe as if that would put an end to this questioning.

'He did, didn't he?' Rachel believed persistence always paid off.

'We went for a walk.'

'I know, but what *happened*?'

'We talked.'

'You did more than that, I can tell. You're blushing.' Her remark brought a heightening of the colour in Ruth's face. 'There, I knew it!'

'I'm saying no more,' snapped her sister. Turning to her dressing table, she picked up a brush and started running it through her hair.

Rachel was beside her in a flash, looking into her face with a satisfied grin. 'Ah, that confirms it.' She started for the door, pleased with the knowledge she had gained.

'Rachel!' The sharp tone of Ruth's voice brought her to a halt. The sisters faced each other. 'You little know-all!' Her voice became icy as she went on: 'If you tell anyone of this, I'll tell Mama that I saw you kissing Jeremy Wilshaw.'

'That was only a peck on the cheek!'

'It could be made to sound like a kiss.'

'Ruth, you wouldn't?' There was a touch of entreaty in Rachel's voice now.

'I will if you persist in sticking your nose in where it's not wanted.'

Rachel's lips tightened. She was cornered.

'One secret kept for another?' Ruth raised her eyebrows quizzically.

Rachel hesitated then agreed.

'You like him, don't you, sis?' There was genuine interest in her voice now. She and Ruth were close. The teasing was over. They could talk now in the full confidence of sisterly secrets never to be told.

'I do, and I'm sure he likes me.'

'Then beware of Alicia Campion,' warned Rachel. 'She has her mind set on Ben Coulson. That isn't a rumour, it's a fact. You've been away so wouldn't know that they were often seen together.'

'This isn't just gossip?'

'No, it is not.' Rachel emphasised her words so that Ruth could be in no doubt of the sincerity of her statement. 'You have a rival, Ruth, a serious one.'

Two days later Alicia Campion was still smarting from the treatment she had received from Ben Coulson down on the pier. She stared at herself in the mirror of her dressing table. The fingers of her right hand began to beat an irritated rhythm. Surely he could not have fallen for that bitch Ruth Holmes? And *she* had better not get any ideas about him. Ben was Alicia's had been since they were children. She had always dreamed of one day becoming Mrs Ben Coulson but had never forced herself on him; let him have his fling before he settled down, as settle down he would one day. She would see to that. Maybe the time had now come when she should make her feelings known, show him what he would miss if he turned his attention elsewhere? An invitation to accompany him to the ball would be an admirable indication that they shared an interest in one another, but as yet that invitation had not come. She would see that it did. May as well strike now. Ben's sister Sarah could be the excuse.

Alicia rose from her seat, went to the wardrobe and took out her cloak. She draped it round her shoulders, fastened the clasp at her neck, grabbed a bonnet and hurried from the room. She tripped quickly down the stairs, paused to adjust her bonnet in the mirror near the front door, and left the house.

She hurried down the long front garden and, in spite of the climb that left her a little breathless, was soon outside the front door of the elegant stone house that Sam Coulson had had built to his own specifications in 1789. It was in the row known as New Buildings. Alicia had always admired the three-storey house of five bays with its fine view across Whitby. She knew Sam had built it to outdo her own father who had modelled his house on elegant but more modest lines in Bagdale earlier that year.

'Is Miss Sarah at home?' she asked when the maid opened the door.

'Yes, miss.' The girl stood back and, as Miss Alicia Campion was a frequent visitor, directed her straight to the smaller drawing-room.

Sarah looked up from the letter she was writing at the dainty oak desk that stood close to the window. 'Hello, Alicia.' She laid her quill down and stood up to greet her friend with a kiss on each cheek. Of the same age, the two girls had been close all their lives. 'Do sit down. Will you take some chocolate?'

'That would be welcome.'

Sarah went to the bell-pull and, when the maid appeared, ordered the drink.

'Are we having our usual ride on Saturday?' Alicia asked when Sarah had taken a seat opposite her.

'Of course. Last week Ben told me he had ordered the horses to be here as usual at ten.'

'Good.' He had done so before the *Water Nymph* had sailed and so before he had met Ruth Holmes. Alicia knew him to be a man of his word; he would not break a prior arrangement. 'I'll look forward to it.'

'I love the ride along the cliffs beyond Sandsend and returning on the beach – can we do it again? Unless, of course, you'd rather it be elsewhere?'

'No. That makes a wonderful ride.' Alicia wouldn't have minded where it took them so long as Ben was with them.

The chocolate arrived and the friends enjoyed a chat while savouring the drink. After a while Alicia asked, 'Is Garth Ford taking you to the ball?'

'Yes.' Sarah knew her friend was fishing. 'Don't get ideas about us. We're just good friends who enjoy each other's company on occasions like this. Is Ben taking you to the ball?'

'I don't know. He hasn't asked me yet.'

'What?' Sarah was surprised. She had always regarded theirs as a natural match and one that she was sure the two families would approve of. 'Then I must arrange for you and him to be alone during our ride on Saturday. If I gallop off, don't follow me!'

'I surely won't.' Alicia gave her friend a knowing smile. And no doubt Ben will be too much of a gentleman to leave me, she added silently.

Alicia stirred in the soft luxury of her feather bed. The early-morning light spilled across her pillow and brought her awake. Immediately thoughts of the morning ride, of being with Ben, flooded her mind. She glanced towards the window but could not tell from her position what the weather promised. She slid quickly from her bed and crossed the room to the window. When she found a clear sky and light breeze, she breathed a sigh of relief. The signs augured well for a fine day.

She glanced at the carriage clock on the mantelpiece. Seven o'clock. There was time to slip back between the sheets, snuggle down with thoughts of what it would be like with Ben beside her. After her imagination had run riot she marshalled her thoughts to concentrate on which of her two riding habits she would wear, though there was little doubt about it – she would wear the one she had bought last week specifically to impress Ben. Her thoughts drifted to him again.

Ten minutes later, she threw back the bed clothes and half an hour later, after her painstaking toilette, she slipped on a

36

plain morning dress and went down for breakfast.

Her father and mother were already taking a leisurely meal and greeted their daughter with loving smiles. A few minutes later her younger sisters, Griselda and Dorothea, arrived, breaking off an animated conversation as they entered the room.

'Riding this morning?' Griselda asked, directing a glance at Alicia.

'Of course. It's Saturday and not raining,' she answered a little testily, as if annoyed that her usual Saturday morning routine should be questioned.

Griselda gave Dorothea a surreptitious wink and directed the conversation towards their mother and father. Alicia took little part in it, content to let her mind dwell on Sarah's ruse to leave her alone with Ben during the forthcoming ride.

Finishing her breakfast, she excused herself and hurried to her room. Her pulse raced with excitement as she took her riding habit from the wardrobe. She held it at arm's length, eyed it critically and then nodded with satisfaction.

Alicia slipped the navy blue velvet skirt over her head and drew it tight around her slim waist. She slid her arms into the waist-length matching jacket, and viewed herself in the full-length mirror. She piled her hair on the crown of her head and pinned it firmly into place. On top she arranged a small green velvet cap, its jaunty curve adding a dashing note to her habit. She appraised herself once more in the mirror and put the final touch to her appearance by pinning a marcasite brooch in the shape of a whale to the left breast of her jacket.

She arrived at the Coulson household a few minutes early and found it as busy and full of life as ever. It was not always the easiest of households for whenever Sam was at home there was a certain tension here, especially if Ben was around at the same time. Then, though open hostility was rare, it was clear that father and son did not see eye to eye.

Today Sam had already left for the office from which he directed the Coulson empire. Saturday or not, there was always work that needed to be done and he had no time for what he regarded as the frivolities of life. Alicia sometimes envied Sarah and Dina with no mother to oversee their behaviour. The strong personalities inherited from their father were tempered by the gentleness of their dead mother. They would not hold back from making their views known yet were aware of the value of a demure ladylike request which it would be churlish to refuse. Spending so much time with them when younger, Alicia had thrown off her own childhood shyness and had learned from them when and how to assert herself. Her own family's simplistic and less adventurous attitude to life sometimes irritated her. There was a whole world beyond the house in Bagdale, beyond Whitby, and she was determined to explore it one day. With no brothers, she knew that her father's business, or at least part of it, would become hers. Maybe when the time was right she could persuade her sisters to sell their shares to her. Then, with Ben beside her, there was no telling what they could achieve. And she was sure he would be with her. She would see to it that he was, and that he returned the love that burned for him in her heart.

Sarah and Dina were hurrying down the stairs, laughter on their lips, when Alicia was admitted to the house. They slowed their rush and negotiated the last few steps with their eyes fixed on her.

'Alicia, you look so smart,' said Sarah admiringly as she held out her hands to her friend.

Alicia took them and they kissed each other's cheeks.

'Divine,' said Dina in mock ecstasy.

'Indeed she is.' These words of agreement came from the top of the stairs and made them all look up. 'Alicia could capture any man's heart.'

'Flatterer,' she returned, in her mind silently adding, But there's only one I want and mean to have.

Ben came slowly down the stairs. He knew he was making an impression and revelled in his ability to make hearts flutter.

Alicia's did when she took in the elegance of his light brown short jacket and matching trousers cut tight towards the calves and tucked into the top of tan riding boots of the finest leather. He'd chosen a yellow waistcoat worn over a white shirt, at the neck of which he had tied a yellow silk cravat.

He came to Alicia, took her hand and raised it to his lips. 'A new outfit, Alicia? May I say how becoming it is.'

'Thank you, Ben.' She was pleased he had noticed.

'A drink before we leave, or would you prefer to go now?' he asked, glancing from her to his sister.

'We'll go now,' replied Sarah. 'No point in spending time indoors on such a nice morning.'

Ten minutes later they were proceeding at a walking pace to the top of the West Cliff. They passed the new buildings that were springing up everywhere as the port's prosperity increased. Once they had left them behind they reined their mounts to a halt to admire the view that never failed to draw their admiration. Sea with hardly a ripple in it reflected the blue of the sky. The breeze was too lazy to disturb its tranquillity. Ahead of them the cliffs swept down to the shoreline. They glimpsed some of the cottages at Sandsend, nestling around a cutting that ran inland, a small community of fishermen and their families who tended to keep to themselves except for the occasional visit to Whitby. Beyond the village the cliffs soared again to form a formidable coastline that had claimed many an unwary ship.

The trio of riders set their horses into a trot. A few minutes later, relaxed in their saddles, Alicia and Ben were caught unawares when Sarah shouted, 'Race you to the cottages!'

She had already gained the advantage before they responded. And that was increased when Alicia, sensing this was the ruse Sarah had spoken of, held back a fraction more. Realising that she had not responded as readily as he, Ben checked his horse so that she could catch up with him.

'She outsmarted us,' he called, and, knowing the strength of his sister's horse and her ability as a rider, added, 'We'll not catch her now.' Nevertheless he urged his horse into a gallop and Alicia could do no more than follow suit. Earth flew beneath pounding hoofs. She thrilled to the strength of the horse beneath her as she matched Ben's pace. Sarah glanced over her shoulder and gave a laugh of triumph when she saw the gap she had opened up and knew it would widen even further when she urged her mount for greater effort. This was the sort of ride she enjoyed and she was enjoying it even more today when she reckoned she was doing her friend a good turn. The space between them increased. When she reached the cottages, a glance behind her told her that she was out of sight of Alicia and Ben. She turned her horse alongside the stream and rode inland.

Reaching the cutting a few minutes later, Ben and Alicia drew their mounts to a halt. Breathing hard from the exertion, they looked around but saw no sign of Sarah.

'Where's that sister of mine got to?' snapped Ben. He had expected her to be waiting for them.

'She'd be in sight if she had gone straight ahead.' Alicia pointed out. 'She must have gone up there.' She indicated the track beside the cottages.

'You there,' Ben called to the group of folk who stood in front of the nearest cottage, staring curiously in their direction and clearly wondering why these riders should intrude on their privacy. The fisherfolk of Sandsend eyed any stranger with suspicion until they knew them better. 'Did a young lady just ride this way?'

The tone that came back was friendly enough, for Ben and Alicia had been recognised as folk who regularly rode by and were always ready with an amiable remark.

'Aye, sir, she rode yon way.' The speaker indicated the track that ran inland.

'Thanks,' Ben acknowledged the information. He turned to Alicia. 'Sarah could be anywhere. There are several tracks she could take once she reached the top of that rise. It will be hope-less to try and find her.'

'But hadn't we better try?' Alicia made a token protest but

smiled to herself at the way Sarah had engineered the situation. 'Will she be all right?'

'You know my headstrong sister. She can certainly take care of herself. I don't think we need worry about her. Come on, it's too nice a day to miss our ride on yon cliff.'

They crossed a shallow stream and set their horses at the climb to the cliff top. They allowed the animals to make their own pace but nonetheless they were breathing heavily when finally brought to a halt close to the cliff edge with its mesmerising view.

Waves broke gently in a line of foam along the strand in the direction of Whitby. The West Pier, with its stone lighthouse marking the entrance to the river, stretched like a pointing finger into the sea. Directly below them deep water broke quietly on the jagged rocks.

'Let's walk and give the horses a rest,' suggested Ben. He swung from the saddle and went to help Alicia.

The way this situation was developing could not have been better had she planned it herself. She slid into his arms and felt their strength as they supported her. She raised her face expectantly. He gazed into her eyes. Her heart beat faster, then she felt his fingers relax and he eased himself away from the hands that had gripped his arms. 'Which way?' he asked casually.

Alicia was puzzled and annoyed. This was not the usual Ben Coulson. He would never before have missed such an opportunity to kiss her, and of late those kisses had held a passion that had led her to believe there was something special between them. She was on the point of letting her annoyance show but controlled herself. That would only sour the atmosphere and she wanted Ben to be at his most receptive. 'I'd like to see the view further on, where the path turns back slightly and you get a view of the magnificent cliffs rising towards Boulby. It has a special memory for me.'

'Special?' asked Ben as they started to walk.

'Yes, surely you remember? It was where you first kissed me.'

He laughed. 'I'm flattered that you remember.'

'Of course I remember. A girl always remembers her first kiss.'

'Probably because I wasn't very good at it,' chuckled Ben.

'Oh, you've improved all right, but to me there was something special about that first time. You see, Ben, I think I had always loved you, ever since childhood. I'd longed for you to kiss me, and then you did.'

'Now we *are* getting serious.'

'Love is a serious thing.'

'I know it is, more so now than I have ever done.' The tone of his voice coupled with the distant look that had suddenly come in to his eyes set alarm bells ringing in her mind.

She stopped and grasped his arm, turning him to face her. 'What do you mean?' she demanded, her face clouding with anxiety.

He hesitated. Alicia was a lifelong friend. They had grown up together in the closeness of their families. As they had moved into their adult years Alicia had encouraged a more intimate relationship. Ben had been flattered by her attention. Now, even though he'd cast his eyes elsewhere, he maintained his old respect and admiration for Alicia. She'd turned a deaf ear to the rumours that thrived around him, believing that he would always come good. She'd also believed that she held his love. He, too, once thought that their future would be together, but now he had met Ruth Holmes. He had never before experienced the profound feelings she awakened in him. He only wished there was some way he could break the news to Alicia gently.

'There's someone else,' he said quietly.

'What?' Alicia's eyes widened in astonished disbelief and her query was laced with incredulity.

He gave a nod, confirming his statement. 'It's true.'

'You can't be serious? You and I . . .'

'I know, Alicia, we have been close all our lives, but I never really knew I could feel love for a woman until now.'

'Of course you did,' she replied with an impatient snap to her voice, 'or you wouldn't have paid me the attention you did.'

'True, we were close, but it is only recently that I've experienced real passion – believed in a love that could go on forever.'

'Infatuation!' she dismissed this sharply.

'No.'

'How do you know?'

'I just do. I knew instantly it was something special.'

'What sorceress has woven her magic spell on you?' Alicia sneered.

'No sorceress. And she did not set out deliberately to do so. She was just being herself, but there was magic in it for me. I knew immediately that she was the one I wanted to spend my life with.'

'But who . . .?' Alicia cut her words short as enlightenment dawned on her. 'Ruth Holmes!' The words came out in a tone of disbelief but she knew she was right. 'You hardly know her,' she protested.

'But I know I'm in love with her.'

'Balderdash!' snapped Alicia. 'How could you be?'

'It's something I can't explain. You would recognise it instantly if it happened to you.'

'It has, but mine is a love that has grown over the years. My love for you is solidly based on deep feeling, admiration, and the desire to make you happy.'

Ben frowned in embarrassment, wanting to spare her further heartache. 'Please, Alicia, try to understand. I like you a lot. Maybe there was a time when I thought you were the girl I wanted to marry but . . .'

'There you are,' she interrupted. 'I knew it! How can you have changed so after just that meeting on the West Pier? Because that was the time you meant, wasn't it? It must have been. She's been in France the past year. You didn't know her before that. Or did you? No, you couldn't have. Ruth Holmes

43

was never in our circle, and would never associate with the other type of girl you have frequented.' She glared at him. 'It is her, isn't it?'

'Yes,' he answered reluctantly.

Anger surged through Alicia. Her eyes smouldered. 'That prim and proper bitch!' She gave a grunt of disgust. 'Roguish Ben Coulson tied down by her? Because that is what will happen. She'll have you tied, tethered and hobbled. You are making a grave mistake, Ben. You'll soon realise it and miss then what I could give you.'

She stepped closer to him, forcing the anger from her voice and replacing it with a note of seduction. 'I'll not tie you down, Ben. You can sow your wild oats where you like, but you will always come back to me because you know I can give you a better time than anyone else.' Her voice had become husky. She reached out to slide her hands up to his neck but he stepped back from her with a gesture that said he was not tempted.

Alicia's eyes filled with fury. 'Damn you, Ben Coulson, damn you! When your romance collapses, don't think you can come running back to me and take up where we left off. I suppose you'll be taking her to the ball?'

'Yes, I am, with her mother's permission.'

That just shows you what she's like,' sneered Alicia. 'Did you ever have to ask *my* mother's permission?'

'No, but our families have been friends for so long, a lot is taken for granted between them.'

'It is, and our lives are none the worse for that.' Alicia made one last effort to retrieve the situation. She looked pleadingly at him. 'Ben, don't throw your life away. You and I could have the world at our feet. We know each other's ways so well. I love you, Ben. Don't do this to me.'

'I'm sorry, Alicia. I had hoped you would understand and that we could always remain friends.'

'Friends? Be second best? I don't think so, Ben. You have just killed any prospect of friendship between us, though I suppose for the sake of our families we will have to make a pretence of it.' She gave him a withering look, swung away from him and hurried towards her horse.

'You'll find someone else, Alicia,' he called after her.

She stopped and turned back. 'I won't.' Tears streamed down her face.

'You will. Someone better than me.'

'I couldn't find anyone better.'

'You will. You'll fall in love and know then how I feel now.'

Alicia did not reply. Still with tears flowing down her cheeks, she left him staring after her as she rode away, giving vent to her anger by putting the animal into an earth-pounding gallop. Reaching Sandsend, she turned the animal on to the beach and rode at the shoreline, sending the water splashing as if to cleanse her mind of the hatred now focused on Ruth and Ben.

Halfway to Whitby she slowed the horse to a walking pace and finally to a halt. She sat quietly, allowing the peace of the day to seep into her. She must compose herself. No one must see Alicia Campion at less than her best.

When she reached the Coulsons' house Sarah was already there. She had been watching for her friend and came out to meet her.

'Where's Ben?' she asked, surprised to find Alicia alone.

'Somewhere behind.'

Sarah sensed this meant that something was wrong but made no enquiry except to verify that Ben had invited Alicia to the ball.

'He's not taking me,' she replied tersely.

'Why not?' Sarah could not hide her astonishment.

'He's taking Ruth Holmes.'

'What?' She was even more surprised by this. 'I'll see about that!'

'No, Sarah, please. Leave it.'

'I can't.'

'You must. Please don't cause any trouble. Ruth is his choice. Leave it at that.' The pleading in Alicia's eyes convinced her friend. 'It goes deeper than the ball, in fact. But what happened today is between Ben and me.'

'But we'll still be friends?'

Alicia held out her arms. 'Of course we will.' They found comfort in each other's embrace.

'And you'll still go to the ball?' asked Sarah.

Alicia had regained her composure. 'I certainly will. I'll show Ben I'm not short of a beau.'

'Who will it be?'

'I can always tempt Warren Laskill.'

Sarah smiled. Ben's best friend. 'That will put my brother's nose out of joint.'

'That's the idea. And I only hope he'll realise what he's missing by staying with Ruth Holmes.'

The ball had started when Alicia, escorted by Warren, arrived at the Angel. She had easily manoeuvred him into proposing that he should escort her once she had indicated she had not been asked by Ben. Wanting her entrance to be noticed, she managed to linger among people in the vestibule until the music stopped, then, taking Warren's arm, walked into the main assembly room. They pushed the double doors open with a purposeful sweep as if announcing their arrival. The action certainly drew attention to them and that in turn brought gasps of admiration and whispered comment. There was not one person in the room who could deny the elegance of the couple who paused just inside the room while letting their imperious gazes sweep round it as if seeking someone. Alicia had primed Warren over the impression she wanted to make, and, though he'd disapproved, he'd agreed to comply with her wishes.

'Over here,' whispered Alicia, putting a little pressure on his arm.

They set off across the room towards Ben and Ruth.

Speculation had run rife when people had seen Ben and Ruth together after he'd been expected to be Alicia's escort. Groups of onlookers around the room pretended to be deep in conversation when all the time their attention was on the coming confrontation.

'Good evening, Ben,' said Alicia. She deliberately ignored Ruth.

'Good evening, Alicia. Hello, Warren.' He turned to his companion. 'Ruth, though you may know my friends by sight, may I introduce you to Alicia Campion and Warren Laskill?'

'I am pleased to meet you, Miss Holmes.' Warren bowed graciously.

Alicia drew herself up and gave Ruth a look of disdain but did not speak to her. She sensed that Ruth felt intimidated by her elegant clothes, something that she had deliberately set out to do by wearing a dress of bright scarlet with black trimmings and jet accessories.

Ben seethed at Alicia's attitude to Ruth but kept his composure. 'I hope we shall all have a pleasant evening,' he offered.

The music was starting again.

'We certainly should,' said Alicia. 'Let us begin it the right way by having this dance together, Ben.'

Refusal was on his lips but he deemed it wisest to agree and escorted Alicia on to the floor.

'Shall we?' Warren asked Ruth graciously.

'Thank you.'

'May I say how elegant you look,' he said as they fell into step.

'Thank you. But not so elegant as Miss Campion.'

'She is more flamboyant, but that does not necessarily mean more elegant.'

'You are just being kind.'

'Not at all. And I'm quite sure that in Ben's eyes no one can outshine you.'

'You are a good friend of his, I believe?'

'Yes.'

'He has a certain reputation . . .'

'Don't believe all you hear. I'll not deny he lives life to the full at times. We have shared many an escapade together, and we both like a wager, especially at cards. But I have detected a lessening of his interest since he met you.'

'What?' Ruth gave a little laugh of disbelief. 'I can't have influenced him that much – I've only known him a short while.'

'Nevertheless, you have. I would say he's very much in love with you.'

'But what about Alicia?' She glanced in the direction of Ben and his partner.

Warren followed her gaze. He saw they were in deep conversation.

'So you've a new conquest.' Ben made his comment sound like a criticism.

'Don't be like that, Ben. I had to find someone to escort me.'

'And you chose the ever-faithful Warren.'

'I thought you'd prefer my choosing your best friend rather than a total stranger.'

'You please yourself. Who you are with or what you do is no concern of mine.'

'But *you* concern *me*.'

'There is no need for you to be concerned.'

'But there is when you take up with the likes of Ruth Holmes.'

'No matter what you say or do, the situation is as I explained it to you. I love her and I always will.'

Alicia's lips tightened. Her eyes blazed with fury. She would have moved away but Ben held her tight. 'No, you don't, Alicia. We finish this dance like good friends and will remain so for the rest of the evening. I will not have a scene, and I will not have anyone's pleasure spoiled by you. Don't show yourself up.'

The emphasis on those last four words made Alicia think. That was the last thing she wanted to do. Besides, there were other ways to win Ben Coulson for herself.

Chapter Three

Seaton Campion, sitting in his office overlooking Whitby's river teeming with the commercial life of the port, stared at the figures on the papers laid out across his desk. No matter how he surveyed them, running his eye down that column and up the next one, viewing that total then turning his attention to another to find a mistake, they always threw back the same message: You made some very bad investments.

He sighed as he leaned back in his chair, trying to find a way of reversing the disaster that was confronting him. He glanced out of the window. The frenzy of activity on the quays, along the river and in the shipbuilding yards, seemed to mock him. He had always been very much a part of it but faced losing those connections for good if he was forced to sell his assets to settle his losses. Only he knew the seriousness of his situation. To all outward appearances he still ran a sound business built upon solid foundations, one that commanded the respect of Whitby's commercial community and was known for fair treatment of its employees. He cursed himself for having been persuaded to make some investments with London firms when he had been visiting the city two years ago. He had been persuaded by glib talk and by the fact that the promoters had promised him a fortune. He had agreed, on request from the London agents, to keep the arrangements to himself, otherwise they had said the value of the stocks could fall. He had planned to use the profit to benefit his Whitby enterprises and help the people of his beloved town.

Instead, the figures spread across his desk revealed the depth of his folly.

How could he retrieve the situation without his family knowing, and without losing all credibility before Whitby's commercial community? To borrow money would put him at the mercy of the bankers and, though they would be discreet, he would face anxious and undesirable times. He had never borrowed, even when he was first building up his business. If he did so now he would step into an alien world, one he had always sworn to avoid.

Should he turn to his old friend Sam? He would be only too eager to lend Seaton the money, but he would want his pound of flesh. Friends since they were youngsters maybe, but in their commercial enterprises they were rivals, and accepted that. Sell out to Sam? There was a possibility. He knew his friend cast envious eyes on his business, especially certain aspects of it in which Sam had no real foothold. He saw them as valuable adjuncts to his own assets. The combination of their interests would make him the most powerful trader in Whitby. But Sam would not be expecting such an offer and might be suspicious of the motive behind it.

Surely there must be another way?

Seaton sat staring at the papers on his desk, wishing the figures would rearrange themselves to present a more satisfactory picture.

He was still bemused when, ten minutes later, a rap on the door startled him. In near panic he shuffled the papers together and thrust them into a drawer before he shouted, 'Come in.'

His clerk appeared and announced, 'Mr Coulson to see you, sir.'

'Show him in,' replied Seaton even as he thought, Think of the devil and . . .

'Seaton, I hope I'm not interrupting anything?' Sam came bustling into the room.

'No, nothing.' Seaton rose from his chair.

Their handshake was firm, born of long association.

'I thought you were in London, Sam,' commented Seaton as he indicated a chair to his friend.

'I decided to return early. I obtained, quite by accident, some information I should act on immediately.' Sam's smile expressed satisfaction at knowledge his friend did not have. He spread his hands. 'And here I am.'

'What has this to do with me? Or have you come to gloat over your latest coup?'

'Now, do I do that?' Sam feigned hurt. 'I'm here, Seaton, because you are part of my plan. I would not want you to miss out on what could be a highly profitable enterprise for you.'

'And not for you? I don't believe that, Sam. Your words seem to hint at a partnership, something we have always avoided. Partnerships can mar friendships.'

'But this is so good, we must not let it . . .'

Seaton began to give a dubious shake of his head.

'Hear me out,' pressed Sam.

He eyed his friend and raised a warning finger. 'Don't count on anything from me.'

'Ah, but I shall have to, and I think when you have heard what I have to say, you will want to take the opportunity that presents itself.'

'All right. I'll listen.' Seaton's curiosity was roused. He knew Sam too well not to recognise that he was revelling in the knowledge that he had and would most certainly use it to his own advantage.

'Well, I heard of a new firm setting up in London to import the best wines from Spain. It is the undertaking of two ambitious young men. They were in Spain with their wives when they met, found that they both had a common interest in wine and, after talking to the growers there, realised that there was a shortage of exceptionally good wines being imported into England. They hit upon the idea of forming a company to do just that. They were shrewd enough to test the possible market when they returned to England. When I met them, they were dining at the same inn as I was, finalising the details and about to embark on finding someone to import the wine for them. I told them to look no further. That though I was a merchant who traded widely, I had little knowledge of the wine trade. But I said that I knew someone who had, and had made the importing of wines from the Continent a speciality of his business.' He gave the briefest of pauses and then added with a proud flourish, 'You, Seaton.'

'Why are you doing this?' He could not ignore the suspicion in his mind. If this deal was so good, why hadn't Sam kept it to himself? He could have set up the necessary arrangements and said nothing.

Sam seemed to have read his mind when he said, 'Seaton, you have all the necessary contacts and arrangements with warehouses for storage in Spain and in England already in place. I saw that as essential to making this enterprise a success. I talked at length with the two partners and they can see that an understanding with you would benefit their prospects immensely. I have got them to promise to do nothing for two weeks, by the end of which you can have more details to consider though personally I don't think you need more than my recommendation. Possibly we could arrange a meeting.'

'Ah, but you have not mentioned where you fit in. Sam, you and I have known each other a long time. We know each other's ways. You don't do anything unless you profit by it. We have an understanding that we will never interfere in each other's trading. That resolve has served us well, and kept us and our families the best of friends. So why this change of heart?'

Sam leaned back in his chair and fixed his gaze on his friend. He did not want to miss one tell-tale reaction to what he was about to say.

'I was dining one evening and had either the fortune or misfortune, whichever way you want to view it, of overhearing a conversation at the next table. I was not eavesdropping, merely pricked up my ears when I heard the name Whitby mentioned. The drift of the conversation led me to believe that the gentlemen concerned were trying to locate someone living here. I introduced myself and informed them that I was from Whitby, offering to help them. They exchanged guarded looks which made me wonder if I had stumbled on some underhand game. Naturally my curiosity was roused even further.

'They invited me to join them and then began a subtle questioning about trading prospects in Whitby and the prosperity of the trading community here. They were discreet in mentioning no one by name but I surmised by the way they phrased their enquiries that they were trying to ascertain the credit of someone who was in their debt for a considerable sum. It was obvious that they were anxious to obtain their money and that they would stop at nothing to retrieve it.

'I tried to play down their suspicions and to reassure them that I knew of no one in Whitby's commercial fraternity who would not honour his debts. In following up that reassurance, one of them let slip the amount owed. I made no comment, reassured them again and took my leave. As I paid my bill and collected my coat and hat, I enquired who the gentlemen were. The next morning I visited my London banker and arranged with him to pay the debt anonymously. That afternoon I collected the receipt and a note from Messrs. Wendover and Bicker exempting the original debtor, you, Seaton, from all further claims.' As he was speaking Sam drew an envelope from his pocket. He tossed it on the desk so that it landed in front of his friend.

Seaton's gaze left him and came slowly to rest on the envelope. His heart was beating faster and yet he felt no anxiety. His mind raced with all manner of thoughts but one predominated. He experienced an indescribable feeling. He felt numb yet elated, like a prisoner let out of prison. The future that only a few moments ago had seemed dark and ominous, had had the veil drawn from it.

'Why did you look into this matter?' Seaton asked quietly.

'There were little things that the two men mentioned, and I recalled that you had been to London some time ago. Though I did not know with any certainty that I was right, I was prepared to follow my hunch. I could not see my dear friend left in a position where ruin or even worse was threatened. These men were prepared to go to extreme lengths.'

Seaton nodded. He picked up the envelope, opened it and withdrew the two sheets of paper that freed him. Or did they? He gazed at them with mixed feelings. Was it possible they might only enmesh him in a yet more tangled web?

He looked up and met Sam's eyes. 'Why did you pay my debt?'

He sensed a hint of suspicion in Seaton's tone. His friend expected a catch and was right to do so. Anyone sensible would do the same. Sam spread his hands and put on an air of innocence. 'Because you are a lifelong friend who I did not want to see in serious trouble over a little indiscretion.'

'Hardly little,' returned Seaton glumly. 'And I've only exchanged one debt for another. You'll want repaying and I cannot do so now.'

'I know that, Seaton, but at least you know I won't inflict the gravest sanction for non-payment.'

'But you will want something out of it?'

'Oh, Seaton, don't be so suspicious. As I say, you are a friend, and what are friends for but to help each other?'

Seaton could tell from the ingratiating tone that had come into his voice that Sam had something in mind. 'And what help do you want from me?'

'Well . . .' Sam paused and pursed his lips thoughtfully. He wanted to engage Seaton's full attention by making him wonder, just a moment longer, what was coming. 'I have just mentioned a possible lucrative deal we could make in the Spanish wine trade. I haven't the knowledge you have or the means of putting it into operation immediately. I would have to set it all up and that would take time. The young men I mentioned are anxious to be operational as soon as possible.'

'You want me to do this in exchange for these two pieces of paper?' Seaton pointed at the documents lying on the desk.

'Important pieces of paper,' Sam emphasised.

'But if I set this up for you, I can see my own wine trade suffering or even being lost.'

'No, no, Seaton.' Sam put on a hurt expression. 'I have no

intention of running you out of the wine trade. I want you with me as a partner. That debt there can be repaid any time. You and I will go into this new enterprise on, say, a sixty-forty basis after expenses have been paid.'

Seaton hesitated over his answer even though he knew he could do nothing but agree. After all, it offered him an unexpected escape from a dilemma that had seemed horribly pressing a few moments ago. 'There is just one thing, Sam. No one must know of the indiscretion from which you have generously rescued me.'

'My lips are sealed.'

'No one,' Seaton insisted.

'No one,' his old friend returned just as emphatically.

Seaton knew that when it came to secrets, Sam was a man of his word. He relaxed in his chair.

'Then we are partners in this venture?' Sam pressed him.

'We are. I only hope this partnership will never mar our friendship.'

'Why should it? Besides, we won't let it.'

'Good.' Seaton felt that an enormous weight had been lifted from his mind.

Sam gave a little nod of approval, then added in a half-casual manner, 'Oh, there is one other thing.' He paused and saw suspicion come over Seaton's face again. He gave a little laugh. 'Relax, friend, I'm not going to scupper our arrangements! All I'm asking is that Martin be put in charge of this new wine trade.'

'But he's in the Arctic.'

'I know. You bring it into operation now and keep it running until he returns. Then you hand over to him.'

'I thought Martin always saw himself as a whaler?'

'Oh, he inherited that much from me, but he sees his real future lies in running the firm. I spoke to him about it before he sailed. He agreed, and I must say enthusiastically, to be involved much more. He is therefore giving up any active part in whaling. This wine enterprise will give him a good introduction to the more commercial aspects of running a firm such as mine.'

Seaton held back his reply momentarily, and then nodded. 'Very well.'

Sam smiled. He leaned back in his chair. 'You know, Seaton, I'm sorry you have no sons to whom you could pass on the firm you have built up.'

'Now hold on, Sam,' cut in Seaton harshly. 'You're not going to use those two pieces of paper to get me to sell out to you.'

'Hackles down, Seaton. I'm not suggesting that, I'm sympathising with you. If I had wanted to, I could have used them by now. I wouldn't have waited until we'd set up a new deal. It was never my intention to use them to ruin you by taking over your firm. Trading in Whitby wouldn't be the same if you weren't here. Besides I know that, though you have only daughters, Alicia takes an interest in your business. She is a young woman of strong personality who knows her own mind. I can see she would be a great prize to a like-minded man, and he of course to her.'

Seaton began to nod slowly. He was seeing where this was leading but wanted to hear it from Sam. 'You don't usually hold back when you have something to say. Out with it, Sam.'

His friend's eyes narrowed knowingly. 'I think you've guessed it. Aren't I right in thinking a marriage between Martin and Alicia would ensure the survival and expansion of both our firms? Not a takeover, an amalgamation. Not immediately, in trading terms. That would only come when you and I decided to quit the fray, leaving both businesses as one in the capable hands of Martin and Alicia. Until then we can both continue to operate independently, but work closely in certain enterprises such as the Spanish wine trade. We would eventually be partners in the most formidable trading enterprise in Whitby, one that could hold its own against rivals anywhere in the land.'

'Long a dream of yours,' commented Seaton.

'Aye, and now, with your cooperation, within my grasp.' His glance at the two sheets of paper on the desk and the unspoken meaning behind it was not lost on Seaton.

'And if I don't agree, those two pieces of paper will be used against me and you will exact your pound of flesh?'

'No, Seaton, I would not be so inconsiderate for the welfare of you and your family, nor for your reputation in Whitby. We have come a long way together. I owe you and your parents a great debt for the kindness that changed my life so long ago. No, Seaton, I would not ruin our friendship by greed.'

'But you would hold me to ransom with the words and figures on those papers?'

'I wouldn't put it like that. Let me say only that I will tear them up on the day that Martin and Alicia marry – a union that would benefit us both.'

'But suppose they refuse?'

'When I told Martin I wanted him ashore and that this was to be his last whaling voyage, I also suggested he should think about marriage. I believe he would not be averse to marrying Alicia. And apart from its being beneficial to the future of our two firms, it is an ideal match. After all, they have known each other all their lives.'

'You have Martin's agreement but Alicia may not be so willing,' Seaton pointed out.

'Oh, come now, Seaton, daughters do tend to obey their fathers.'

'You yourself have said that she has a strong personality and knows her own mind.'

'True, but I am sure you can be most persuasive.' Sam paused and then added meaningfully, 'Let us hope you are, for the sake of your firm and its future.'

Alicia had just started up the stairs when her father came out of the drawing-room. 'Ah, Alicia, I thought I heard you come in. I would like to see you in my study at eight after our evening meal. And not a word to your sisters.'

'Yes, Father,' she replied without displaying any curiosity in her tone though her mind was busy trying to find a reason for his wish to see her alone. She continued up the stairs, un-fastening her pelisse as she did so.

By the time she tapped on the study door at eight o'clock she had reached no conclusion. The evening meal with her parents and sisters had proceeded just as normal.

When she entered the room she found her father standing with his back to the fireplace, facing the door, and her mother sitting beside the fire. Alicia's heart gave a little flutter. If Mother was here this was a serious matter indeed.

'You wanted to see me, Papa?'

'Yes. Please sit down.' Her father indicated a chair opposite her mother's. He waited until Alicia was settled before he went on, 'We have something serious to discuss with you.' His tone was grave. This was very different behaviour from his usual light-hearted ways. 'I have asked your mother to be with us because over the years I have come to value her wisdom. She and I have spent much of the time since I came home from work today discussing the matter with which I am going to acquaint you.

'Two years ago I was persuaded, during a visit to London, to make some investments. They looked good and there was the promise of substantial profits. Regrettably, the investments went wrong and I found myself badly in debt. To redeem it myself would have meant selling the business that I had built up so diligently. That would have reduced our circumstances significantly. We would have had to leave this house and no longer be able to move in the social circles we have hitherto enjoyed. Apart from that there would have been the stigma of my failure and misjudgement to live with.'

He paused and Alicia, who had been listening intently in shocked silence, took the opportunity to speak.

'Father, you seem to indicate from your use of words that the problem has been solved, yet still you look grave. Please explain why?'

'The problem has not finally been solved. There is a chance of a solution, but that depends on you.'

58

'Me? How could that be?' She glanced at her mother but found no enlightenment in her grave expression.

'Mr Sam Coulson has been in London recently and by accident heard of the matter – I don't need to go into details of how or what transpired, only to say that he repaid the debt.'

'Then everything is all right?'

'Not quite. I still owe that money, not to the people in London but to Mr Coulson.'

'But being such a close friend, he will not press you. He will give you time.'

'That is true, but the debt is still there and with it hanging over me, he sees an opportunity to expand some plans he has in mind.'

'And what might those be?'

'He wants to set up in the Spanish wine trade, making use of my knowledge, organisation and connections.'

'I still don't see what this has to do with me?'

'After Martin's return from the present whaling voyage, he will comply with his father's wishes to take a more active part in the firm ashore. Sam wants him to be in charge of this Spanish wine trade. He also believes it would be advantageous to both our firms if you and Martin were to marry.'

For a moment Alicia thought she had not heard him correctly but then the words hit home. She looked in amazement from her father to her mother and back again. She swallowed hard. This couldn't be happening to her. Her parents had always encouraged her to make her own decisions and had shown by their own relationship how love between partners mattered. Her love was for Ben, not Martin. Since that day on the cliffs when Ben had declared his love for Ruth she had toyed with the idea of coming between them, but now? Even as these thoughts were pursuing each other she heard her mother speaking.

'Alicia, my dear, nothing has been arranged, but please hear your father out.'

'There's some sense in what Sam says. Of my three daughters you are the only one who has shown interest in my business.

I have always envisaged you taking it over eventually. I know some folk would frown on a female running such an enterprise in what is considered a man's world. I also know that female intuition and advice in many cases play an unseen part in the commercial world. There is no reason why at times they cannot come to the fore. That is why I have encouraged your interest for I knew you would do me proud, and I also knew you would look after the interests of your sisters when I left the firm to the three of you. Marriage to Martin Coulson would put the whole situation on a much sounder basis. The two firms would continue to operate independently until Sam and I retire, leaving their eventual amalgamation in the capable hands of you and Martin.'

She dampened her lips. 'And if I refuse, Mr Coulson will force you to repay the debt?' There was a touch of contempt in her voice and Seaton sensed it. He knew she wanted to add another comment, 'Call him a friend?' but out of respect for him she did not.

He tried to ease her disquiet. 'Sam saved my reputation, he has saved our living, saved us all from near poverty . . .'

'Only if I agree to his plan,' said Alicia in a non-committal tone.

'I know this has come as a shock to you but think carefully on it,' put in her mother. 'So much hangs upon your decision.'

'Doesn't my happiness count for anything?' she cried, feigning disillusion.

'Would you be happy if we were all close to destitution? Could you live with that?' When Alicia made no comment, her mother continued, 'Couldn't you be happy with Martin? You've known him all your life, are already great friends. You'd want for nothing as his wife, and I'm sure you would be able to play your part in running a firm that will become one of the most important in Whitby. Doesn't that sound better than the hardships that could otherwise face you and your family?'

Alicia bit her lip. Anxiety choked her. She loved Ben but . . . what of the future?

Hardship . . . could she really face that? Could she forego the comfortable living she had been used to? Could she really condemn her parents and sisters to a strange new life that would tear at their hearts, all for the sake of winning Ben when it was no longer certain that she could do so? His rejection of her had awoken her desire for revenge. Maybe this marriage could be used to that end as well as to spare her own family from suffering. She looked at her mother and saw the anxiety in her eyes, the hopeful expectancy in her face.

'Think about it, Alicia,' said her father. 'There is so much at stake. The decision has to be yours; after all, you will be making a lifelong commitment. Whatever you decide, you must regard it as the right decision and never look back with regret.'

Alicia's eyes blurred. How could she hurt these two gentle, generous people?

'Would you like time to—?'

Alicia halted her father's question. 'No, Father, I would not. I will marry Martin.'

She sensed the tension drain from the room. Her father relaxed, no doubt offering up a silent prayer that his daughter had not decided otherwise. Her mother smiled with relief and uttered a quiet, 'Thank you, Alicia.' There were tears in her eyes as she stood up and came to her daughter with arms outstretched. Alicia rose to meet her. Mother and daughter held each other in an embrace that expressed their love for each other, the mother's including gratitude, the daughter's bowing to the needs of the family.

When they turned to see Seaton's smile of approval, he said, 'Please do not mention any of this for the time being, not even to your sisters. There are things to arrange with Sam, and Martin returns in two months.'

Chapter Four

The *Water Nymph* sailed within sight of the pack ice under half sail. The season was drawing to a close; soon signs of the coming winter would be evident. Whale-men always hoped to be long gone from the Arctic by August, sailing for less dangerous seas. Linger too long here and there was always the chance that a sudden deterioration in the weather could catch a vessel out with the danger of being iced in.

Eric Coulson had fitted in well on his first voyage. He'd sought no privileges as the owner's son, for he had been warned by brother Martin that Captain Holmes would not give him any. A willing hand, not shirking any job that came his way, eager to learn and unashamed about seeking advice from anyone, he soon became popular with a crew who at first had muttered about a second owner's son being on board. They had put him through it during the first four days, but he had dealt with each 'test' without complaint so that they had soon tired of trying to embarrass him and came to accept him as one of them. He had taken to life on a whale-ship, become caught up in the frenzy of the hunt and thrived on it. This he knew would be his life. He was alert to everything that would help him to that end, hoping to gain promotion as soon as possible.

Now he stood with his brother at the rail, eyeing the vast ocean for the sight of a tell-tale spout that would indicate whales. The hold was three-quarters full and they both knew, as did the rest of the crew, that Captain Holmes did not like returning without a full ship. He had all the available crew on the lookout, for he was sure that they would sight more whales and get in a last profitable hunt before they must turn for home.

'The men are chuntering among themselves,' commented Eric. 'They reckon we should be on our way home by now and to hell with the Captain's obsession.'

'I know,' replied Martin.

'Shouldn't you say something to him?' asked Eric.

Martin gave a laugh of derision. 'What, and bring his wrath down on me? He's a good captain but you've seen how he rules this ship with a rod of iron. He's master and what he decides is not for us to question.'

Eric knew his brother was right and realised it was better not to raise the matter again even though tension among the crew began to mount throughout the next three days. The weather held fine but there were those among them, men with several whaling voyages to their credit, who said they could sense a deterioration coming before too long.

Their murmurings and uneasiness vanished on the fourth day when the cry came from the masthead where the Captain had stationed two lookouts: 'There she blows! There she blows!'

The mood immediately changed into one of excited anticipation.

'Whither away?' The Captain's stentorian tone boomed across the deck.

'Port bow, a mile!'

'Ten degrees port!' Holmes called to his helmsman.

'Aye, aye, sir. Ten degrees port.' He swung the wheel.

'Make ready!' The Captain's next order sent men scurrying to their allotted boats.

Eric watched as he had done whenever the boats were made ready and launched earlier in the voyage, each time wishing he was a member of one of the crews. But he was a greenhorn. Maybe next voyage.

Captain Holmes was in the grip of subdued excitement. Even though he had completed many voyages he still felt a thrill when whales were sighted, especially at times like this with spout after spout rising on the cold air. He had been right. He had 'smelt' whales three days ago and had held on in order to fill the ship. His decision was now vindicated. He kept his eyes fixed on the rising spouts, measuring the distance with care. He did not want to scare the whales but needed to heave to in a position that would give his boats the best chance of a kill.

His orders rang out firmly but in subdued tones. Sails were trimmed and the ship's head was brought near to the wind so that she was making no headway.

'Away all boats.'

Eric watched, admiring each crew's skill and coordination. This moment always thrilled him. Boats dropping down, pushed from the side of the ship, oars into the water, backs bending, boats cleaving through the sea.

He concentrated on the boat in which his brother was the harpooner, the man in charge but relying on the boat-steerer to get him close enough at the right moment for the kill. How Eric wished he was in that boat . . .

Rowing bow oar, Martin bent his back as willingly as any man as he watched the boat-steerer, the only man in the boat who could see the spouts.

'Heave, lads, heave!' Meredith, the boat-steerer, eager to have his boat first on the whales, called for greater effort. 'Bend 'em . . . bend yer backs!'

Martin increased the pace and the rest of his crew matched him. They drew ahead of the other boats. Their bow cut through the gently undulating sea. The conditions could not have been better. This was their lucky day. All thoughts that the weather could soon be taking a turn for the worse had vanished in the excitement of making more kills to fill the hold.

In spite of the sharp air they were soon sweating in their heavy clothing, but oblivious to the discomfort. Hands were clamped to the oars, muscles strained with exertion, chests heaved air into tight lungs.

Martin resisted the temptation to look over his shoulder. To do so would break his concentration and that could have a fatal effect on their speed and manoeuvring. Surely they must be nearing the whales? Then he saw a gleam of excited anticipation come into the boat-steerer's eyes. He knew they must be close to their quarry.

'Ease, lads, ease.' Meredith's voice was low now. Their pace slackened until he gave them the signal to stop rowing. Quietly they shipped oars. The boat glided on, its motion gradually slowing.

Martin stood to take up his position in the bow. Other harpooners were doing the same in their boats but he was the first to seize his harpoon. His boat-steerer had skilfully brought him close to a whale. Martin's action as he turned was almost instantaneous. He firmed his grip round the harpoon. He swung, his back bending and releasing like bowstring. The harpoon arrowed through the air towards its target. It struck and gripped.

'Stern all!'

Immediately the men at the oars propelled their craft away from the whale and its enormous flukes that could shatter a boat and kill its crew.

Similar actions were taking place around them. The sea heaved as whales sought to escape the men determined to hold them and get alongside to use their lances for the kill.

But the whale Martin had struck thought otherwise. Its fury made it sound. Down it went. The rope ran out fast from its tub, its speed around the bollard in the bow making the wood burn. Martin grabbed the pitcher filled with water for such an emergency and threw the liquid over the bollard. Steam rose as he scooped more water from the sea and doused the bollard time and time again. Five lengths of line were run out before it slackened. No more rope was taken. The tension heightened among the men. The calm around their boat, where there had recently been fury, was uncanny. Then, with no further evidence of activity, the men were galvanised into action, taking up the slack in the rope and coiling it back into its tubs. Martin concentrated his attention on the sea immediately in front of them, trying to interpret the signs from the rope and to distinguish movement below. He wished he had eyesight that could pierce the depths.

He stiffened. 'She's rising' His voice was low but it reached every man in the boat.

They cast fearful glances at each other and at the sea around them. Where would the whale strike the surface? Under them to toss the boat high in the air, spilling them into the swirling icy waters? Nearby, to cause a maelstrom from which they might or might not escape? Suddenly they had their answer. It blasted through the surface close enough to the boat to set the water swamping it.

'Bail!' Martin yelled. It was an order he need not have made. The crew knew that if they were to remain afloat they had to be rid of that water. Backs were already bent to the task. Others were hauling in the rope quickly so that the slack would not become an impediment.

The whale's flukes rose high and then lashed down on the sea with a terrifying impact. Water foamed and heaved around them but the sailors battled the pandemonium, managing to keep the sturdy craft afloat and stay attached to the whale.

Desperate in its desire to shake off its attackers, the whale tried another tactic and ran. The rope tightened. As it dragged the boat through the sea its crew could only hang on and hope that the whale did not run too far before tiring. The boat bounced across the sea, sending spray flying to saturate the crew even more.

On and on it ran, taking them further and further away from their fellow crew members who were still engaged in their own battles with their strikes or else triumphantly towing their catch back to the *Water Nymph*. Soon boats and ship were lost to sight but the whale did not seem to have any inclination to give up. Worry began to crease foreheads. Apprehension began to grip minds. Why didn't Martin use the axe and free them from this onward rush which would soon be fraught with the additional danger of being lost?

A few minutes more and they detected a slowing. Relief came over the men. Now they might get their chance. It seemed even more likely when they saw the whale stop running. Still

Martin gave no order. He allowed the boat to lose momentum and drift. When it too had come to a stop he gave the signal to pull on the rope and so edge them slowly and carefully towards the whale. Nearer and nearer. The men were tense as they moved in for the kill. Martin picked up a lance with which he would strike the final fatal blow. He positioned himself, perfectly balanced, in the bow. Closer and closer. Tension heightened. Any moment Martin would strike to make a sure kill.

That certainty was blasted away when the whale that had but a moment ago appeared so harmless ran again. The sudden action, with its element of surprise catching the men unawares, caused havoc. One man cracked his head against the thwarts, another let out a yell when he felt his arm break on impact with the gunwale.

Once again they bounced across the waves, bruised and battered, desperately trying to regain some control. Martin, who had managed to keep his balance, yelled order after order that seemed impossible to carry out in the confusion. But some stability was established while the whale continued its run.

'Ice!' The yell came from the boat-steerer. 'Ahead!'

All eyes turned to seek it, anxious to know how far away it was. The whale was momentarily forgotten in their dread of its menace.

'Hell, she's running for the ice!' The realisation of what the whale intended penetrated everyone's mind.

Panic gripped them.

Martin realised his responsibility as skipper of this boat. The lives of his crew would depend on his decision. He was accountable for their safety, but also to his captain. They needed to add to the stock of blubber they would take home, and he was fast to a whale with all the possibilities that brought – a kill, increased profits for his father, and a boost to the business that he was destined to inherit. And this was to be his last whale hunt. He must extract every possible thrill and triumph. He must win! He could not let a whale outsmart him. He weighed the distance from the ice. There was still time to outwit and kill his last whale.

He called the men into order then shouted, 'Lucas, report damage to Wilf and Joey.'

'Aye, aye, sir,' Lucas, the only crew member with a smattering of medical knowledge, was already examining Wilf. It took him only a moment to see that the blow to the head had been a bad one. The cut was deep and Wilf kept drifting in and out of consciousness. He turned his attention to Joey whose face was screwed up with pain from his broken arm. Lucas assessed the damage as easily as he could in an open boat skidding across the waves behind a whale. He didn't like what he saw. He scrambled forward to report his findings.

'Not good?' asked Martin.

'We should get them back to the ship.'

Martin nodded. 'Soon.' He eyed Lucas and added, 'Make them as comfortable as you can.'

'Aye, aye, sir.' Muttering to himself, Lucas scrambled back to the two men. 'Not bloody easy in this cockleshell fast to a bloody whale!' But there was more than that worrying Lucas. He had seen the lust to kill in Martin's eyes. He had only seen it once before. On that occasion, only action by the second-in-command that cost the harpooner his life had saved the rest of the boat crew. Lucas glanced around. He saw no one who would risk such a drastic measure against Martin, knowing that if someone talked they would all face the terrible wrath of Sam Coulson. He could only hope that Martin would soon realise their peril and swallow his pride before the whale dragged them to their doom.

Martin's eyes narrowed. They were nearing the ice. His whole body was charged with tension, heightened by his hunger to make one last kill. He saw a slackening in the rope. The whale was slowing. Did it too fear the ice?

'Haul in!' he called.

Eager hands grabbed the rope. Backs bent willingly, fired

by the keen desire to be away from this place and to have their ship in sight again.

The whale stopped. The men hauled faster. Suddenly the rope was torn from their hands. The whale was running again. Curses flowed in exasperation. How much longer was this going on? Why didn't Coulson cut the rope? There were injured men who needed attention.

'She's turning!' Martin's call brought some measure of relief and every man was thankful that the whale seemed to have decided against diving under the ice. They were still aware that she could change her mind but every second took them further away from that danger. But now there was an added worry; they were going further and further away from the *Water Nymph* too. It would be a long hard row back. They only hoped Captain Holmes had ordered the flensing to stop so that he could bring his vessel in search of the boat that hadn't returned.

Ten minutes later, with the crew growing more and more nervous, a voice called out, 'Cut the bloody rope!'

Martin turned sharply. His eyes blazed with anger. He had recognised the voice and was going to let the man know it. 'I'm in command here, Lucas. Challenge me once more and I'll have you in irons when we get back. I'll cut the rope when we've made the kill, and not before.'

Anxious glances passed between the crew to accompany their rebellious mutterings.

Lucas glanced around his mates. He sensed they wanted someone to speak up. He had already been admonished and threatened by Martin but firmed his resolve, swallowed hard and spoke up. 'Sir, please cut the rope. We've injured men. They should be back with the ship.'

Martin swung round, maintaining his balance in the swaying boat. His eyes narrowed with threat. 'That sounds like mutinous talk, Lucas. I've already warned you.'

But Lucas was determined not to be browbeaten again. He sensed he had the men behind him. No one in his right mind would have allowed a whale to tow them this far from their parent ship.

'The *Water Nymph* is long out of sight. We might never find her again.'

'That's a slur on my ability to navigate us back to her!'

'Slur or not, I'll tell thee summat else – this whale's not going to be killed. Let it go and let's get the hell out of this godforsaken ocean.'

Martin set his lips tight. 'I'll say when.' The iron in his voice showed he would tolerate no further disagreement. He turned his back on the crew to stand in the bow, emanating an aura of authority that would not tolerate challenge.

Lucas exchanged meaningful looks with Bob who rowed second oar. Bob realised Lucas had spotted something behind him and half-turned to follow the direction of Lucas's gaze. A knife lay on the thwart close to Martin but within Bob's reach. He drew Lucas's meaning but looked at him doubtfully with a slight shake of his head, letting his eyes move to Martin's broad shoulders before looking back at Lucas again. Lucas gave him an encouraging nod. He saw some of the apprehension disappear and gave further encouragement with several quick gestures.

Bob bit his lip as he tried to pluck up courage to perform an act that most certainly would bring Martin's wrath down about his ears and set even worse in motion when they reached the *Water Nymph*. He glanced at Lucas who urged him on with small motions of his arms. A quick survey of the rest of the men told Bob that they were all aware of Lucas's intention and in their eyes he saw silent approval. He knew they depended on him. He swallowed hard, inched himself into a better position to take the knife and eyed the harpoon-man one more time.

Martin, eager for a kill, was still engrossed in watching the whale. Bob reached out slowly. The knife seemed tantalisingly far away. He drew a deep silent breath, forcing himself on. His movement was swift, uninterrupted, as he swept up the knife and brought it down across the rope, severing it neatly.

70

For one moment the scene did not change, whale and boat remaining in position. Then the gap widened, but it was only when the severed rope flew past Martin that he realised what had happened. There was a moment of disbelief, then realisation that the whale was escaping and there was nothing he could do about it hit him hard and brought all his fury to the surface. He swung round, barely keeping his balance in the becalmed boat. He saw Bob still with the knife in his hand.

'You damned fool!' he snarled as he lashed out with the lance he had been holding for the kill.

Bob saw the flash of its blade. He threw up his arm for protection as he tried to sway out of the way. The lance slashed his arm above the elbow, driving deep towards the bone. He yelled in pain and collapsed into the bottom of the boat.

'Captain Holmes will hear of this,' shouted Martin. He realised Bob must have had the backing of the whole crew. 'You'll all be in irons when we get back, and tried for mutiny in Whitby!'

They knew his threat was no idle one and that, with his father's backing, they would be condemned even before they were tried.

'Get your oars out!'

Men fumbled to do as they were told. Oars clattered into their rowlocks.

'All of you,' snarled Martin. He would show no mercy 'You've a good arm Bob, so has Joey, and Wilf doesn't need his head to row.'

There were protests, particularly from Bob whose arm gushed blood.

But Martin would have none of it. He slipped into his position of rowing bow oar. Oars dipped into water but the regularity of their strokes was missing now and the rhythm could not be found.

'Damn you, row together,' yelled Martin.

Hostility tightened the men's postures. Belligerence charged the Arctic air. But they knew their only chance of survival was

71

to find their ship as soon as possible, and to do that they realised they must work as a team, no matter how they resented Martin Coulson for getting them into this situation. They tried their best to get a flowing motion into their rowing but it was not easy with injured men fighting pain. Progress was slow. Although they eventually settled into some sort of pattern it bore no resemblance to their progress when they had set out from the *Water Nymph* in the exuberance of the hunt.

After ten minutes a tinge of doubt settled on Martin. Were they rowing in the right direction?

'Boat-steerer!' he called

'Aye, aye, sir?'

'Take her ninety degrees starboard.'

'Aye, aye, sir.' Meredith leaned on his long steering oar and brought the boat round on to the new heading.

Martin reckoned they should now be making for the pack-ice away from which, surprisingly, the whale had towed them. If he could sight that and run along the edge of it he felt sure they would find the ship and all would be well.

After half an hour, with the men, especially those who were wounded, feeling exhaustion coming on them and still no sight of the ice, Martin was thinking he had miscalculated. He could sense antagonism heightening among his crew. The battle in his mind as to what further action he could take was suddenly interrupted by a shout from the boat-steerer.

'Sir!'

In that split second Martin's hopes soared. Had his look-out sighted the *Water Nymph*? Then his hopes were dented when the man continued, 'Don't like the look of them clouds.'

'Stop rowing!' Martin's command brought relief to the crew even though they knew it would be only for a few moments. He turned to see what had captured the boat-steerer's attention and felt his body drained of any resistance when he saw the dark ominous clouds spilling over the horizon with awesome rapidity. They and the rising wind heralded vicious seas, greedy for victims.

Dejected, he drew himself up purposefully. The men must not become aware of his true feelings. He scanned the sea, still hoping that he would catch a glimpse of a sail that would mean rescue and safety. But there was none. A vast ocean of icy water mocked him.

'Take oars!'

The men moaned. Someone muttered, loud enough for all to hear, 'What's the use? We can't escape what's coming.'

'Row!' roared Martin, mustering all the authority he could.

Realising they would have to try to run with the storm, Meredith had started to bring the boat on to a new course. Now the men would have the terrifying sight of dark bubbling clouds and a hostile sea, driven by a strengthening wind, heading for them like a black devouring monster.

Martin watched the gathering storm, blaming himself letting his judgement be obscured by that overwhelming desire to take one last whale and leave the trade as a hunter second to none. Instead he had imperilled not only his own life but those of his crew. He should have returned to the ship when his men had suffered injury; instead he had inflicted a terrible wound on Bob whose one-armed rowing was now faltering even more.

He must do all in his power to bring them through the ordeal that was bearing down on them, must make amends when they reached Whitby. Whitby! It seemed so far away.

They felt the proximity of the storm in the undulations of the sea.

'Ship oars!' Martin's voice boomed above the howling wind.

He and Lucas had little difficulty in doing so then, realising that their wounded companions were faltering turned to help them. Martin, whose oar was already on board, reached past Bob at second oar. His grip closed on the wood and he started to pull the oar on board. The boat was taken high by a vicious upward thrust of the sea. Martin lost his balance. The oar swung from his grasp and caught Bob across the chest, sending him overboard into the raging sea. Martin grasped the gunwale, staring in unbelievable horror at the spot where the man had

73

disappeared. If there was a moment when the crew froze in disbelief it was gone in a flash as the screeching wind and pounding sea reminded them that deadly danger stalked them.

Another wave broke viciously against the tiny boat. Martin realised that Meredith was having a battle to keep the steering oar manageable. He stumbled towards the stern, contesting the violent movement of the boat, to lend Meredith a hand. He slumped beside the boat-steerer and gripped the long oar.

No one knew where they were being driven by the storm. They would cope with that dilemma when they had to. For now it was purely a question of survival, of outliving this tumult that threatened their lives. Water poured into the boat as it was tossed high then driven downwards to what seemed like the bottom of the ocean. Men bailed as best they could and somehow the tiny craft stayed afloat.

But the storm would not be denied. Hurling the boat down towards the bottom of a trough, the sea gave it a final twist. Martin and Meredith fought to keep it on an even keel but in the moment before they won a cry rent the air and to their horror they saw Joey thrown into the maelstrom. Meredith automatically reached out with his left hand as if he could pluck his shipmate back. Then his face creased in a terrible grimace as the thought of telling Joey's mother of her son's fate when he got back to Whitby. He realised the absurdity of that thought as another enormous wave pounded down on them.

Lucas, holding on to the thwart beside Wilf who lay in the bottom of the boat crying out obscenities in his delirium, looked up as the wave hit them. The boat was tossed around. How it kept afloat Martin and Meredith never knew but when the wave had cleared them they saw that they were alone in the boat. They gazed at each other in disbelief.

'You and I must fight it through!' yelled Martin in encouragement.

The next five minutes were an eternity to the two men. They lost count of the times their lives flashed before them amid the whirlpool of water and the banshee cry of the wind.

'It's easing!' Meredith yelled.

Martin did not believe him for a few moments then he too sensed a slight slackening in the wind and with it a lessening in the height and ferocity of the waves. They were becoming more manageable. Both men drew heart even though they were being driven relentlessly on by the wind and a strong-running sea. They began to wonder if they would ever see the *Water Nymph* again, and with it their last chance of survival.

'Hurry that flensing!' Captain Holmes paced the deck, cajoling the men to greater effort. This late in the season the weather could turn nasty and then the ice would start to move. The last hunt had been successful. There was jubilation among the crew for it meant they would have a nearly full hold. One more whale would do it and Martin Coulson, last seen fast to one, was still out there. With that whale flensed and on board they would be able to head for home. So the men worked willingly to have their present kills out of the way before Martin returned.

Flensing knives flashed, cutting away the blubber, spades eased it from the meat, huge strips were hauled on board to be cut up and stowed in barrels for the voyage home. In spite of the cold, the effort made the men sweat, but, eager to be finished, they ignored the unpleasant feeling and remained oblivious to the blood and grease that made standing on the whales and walking on the deck precarious.

Captain Holmes, alert to every movement of his men and every motion of his ship, kept a watchful eye over the whole scene. Orders and advice marked his authority over the operation but concern began to trouble him. Where was Martin Coulson and his crew?

'Parsons, get aloft!' the Captain's voice rang across the deck.

'Aye, aye, sir.'

Parsons, a lithe man of twenty-three with five years sailing in the Arctic behind him, had no need to question the purpose of going aloft. It certainly wasn't to search for whales. The barrels were filling rapidly. He knew he was there to sight the one whale-boat that had not returned and also to keep an eye on the weather. He climbed the rigging rapidly to the top-gallant mast, the position used by a lookout. Settling himself as comfortably as possible, he swept the expanse of sea with a quick search. Nothing but undulating waves was his first impression. Then he began a more meticulous probe, hoping that his first sweep had missed what he desired to see. His heart sank a little as he completed the search. Only the endless sea. But he would continue to look.

On the deck Captain Holmes waited in the hope that Parsons would give a positive report before the flensing was finished.

Actively forking blubber into the shoot that took it to the men below deck, Eric Coulson was aware of the Captain's order sending Parsons aloft and guessed the reason for it. He had become increasingly concerned for his brother, though in his hero-worship he believed Martin to be invincible. He was a survivor, was sure to return. Eric, like the rest of the crew, knew that he had been fast to a whale that had run. He was certain that his brother would win the contest and return triumphant with the catch that would finally fill the ship. And on his first whaling voyage Eric would bask in his brother's glory and success.

Time drifted on. The last of the blubber had gone below deck, the final carcass had been cast adrift. The *Water Nymph* idled on an ominously calm sea. The men began to fidget. They did not like it. Unease began to permeate the ship. They had expected to be gone by now. Instead they waited expectantly for a shout from the mast-head. When it came it was not what they wanted to hear.

'Storm brewing!'

The call hit the men like a slap in the face. A buzz of alarm swept through the crew.

'Whither away?' shouted Captain Holmes.

'Port bow!'

Captain Holmes swung on to the ratlines and climbed until he had a better view. What he saw disturbed him. Dark clouds were massing and moving in their direction. He could see the distant ocean disturbed by the wind, the first gusts of which began to reach him. Soon its present liveliness would become a fury and it would propel the sea into raging turmoil. He switched his attention to the ice a mile on their starboard side. It stretched in both directions as far as the eye could see. It presented no danger at the moment but this gathering storm could change that. His mind was in a turmoil. He had six men somewhere out there. They needed finding. But he also had the ship and its crew to think of. How long dare he wait? If he got underway, how far dare he search? He climbed down quickly to the deck. His orders rang out. Men climbed to set the sails. The helmsman brought the ship so that they could run before the storm.

Eric froze. He had read the Captain's intention. Surely he couldn't leave the boat and its crew to such a horrible fate? Fear set his heart racing, banishing the numbness that held him. Galvanised into action, he raced across the deck towards his Captain.

'Captain Holmes! Captain Holmes! You can't leave them!' His eyes were wide with dread and defiance.

'Get back to your station!' snapped Holmes in a voice that warned of the consequences if he was not obeyed instantly.

'You can't!' yelled Eric.

Holmes's eyes narrowed. 'One more word of defiance and you'll suffer dire consequences.'

Eric stood his ground. 'But my brother's out there.'

'I know who's in that boat.'

'Then search for them.'

'Who's in command here?'

Eric was silent. Tears began to stream down his cheeks. What had he to do? He must try and save his brother.

'You've got to find them!' There was anguish in his voice now.

'I'll decide what's best for this ship and my crew.'

'But—'

'Stop!' The command in Holmes's voice cut Eric short. While seething at a crewman's defiance, which he could not tolerate without losing his authority over the others, he deemed a short explanation was warranted to the young son of the owner on his first expedition. 'Is it to be six men and the possibility of losing this ship if we try to find them, or do I choose the safety of the majority and getting this ship and its cargo safely back to Whitby? You answer me that dilemma.' His voice resumed its harshness again, his eyes flared with anger. 'Now get back to your post!'

Eric's lips tightened. All reason fled. 'Murderer! Murderer!' he yelled.

'Harrington! Welsh!' the Captain called to the two nearest sailors. 'Take this man below deck and lock him up.'

'Aye, aye, sir.' Acknowledgement came from both men simultaneously. They stepped beside Eric, each grabbing one arm, and forced him across the deck.

'Murderer!' he yelled over his shoulder. 'My father will hear of this . . .'

Ten minutes later the storm hit the *Water Nymph* and Eric's last threat was dismissed from the Captain's mind as he concentrated all his skill on ensuring their survival.

Chapter Five

'Whale-ship! Whale-ship!' David Bunch, an idle youth who spent most of his time mooching on the cliff top near the ruined abbey, was galvanised into unusual animation at the sight of a sail breaking the horizon. Gifted with a sharp knowledge of Whitby ships and exceptional sight, one which would have served him well if he had had the intelligence to go to sea, the words sprang to his lips even though there was no one near to hear him. But that was not the case when a few minutes later, still shouting, he raced through the churchyard, past the old parish church and down the one hundred and ninety-nine steps to the town.

The information soon ran before him as it was taken up by others to resound through the entire port, turning everyone's mind from what they were doing. Carpenters laid down their saws and chisels; fishermen mending nets dropped them on the ground; housewives cast aside their spoons and mixing bowls, snatched up their baby or grasped their youngest by the hand, and called to the older ones to come quickly and follow; clerks laid down their pens, swung from their stools and left the ink on the ledgers to dry itself. Folk streamed from house, workplace, office, shop or inn, work and pleasure forgotten. A whaleship had been sighted! One of their own was home. Which one? Who would be the first to identify it? Were there others close behind? Whitby had sent four ships to the Arctic, were they all safely home? Had the catch been good? Were they full? Would it mean money in their pockets to contest the winter?

People speculated as they streamed through the streets. Some to the quays and staithes to win closer contact with the ship as it entered the river; others to the clifftops for an early sight and hopefully to see the vessel that carried their own menfolk home from the rigours of the Arctic and the dangers of the whale-hunt.

Alicia was on her way to her father's office where at her own instigation, readily accepted by him, she was learning more details of his business, when she heard the cry.

She felt a tightening in her stomach, apprehension in her mind. The moment that had occupied her thoughts during the last few weeks was here, but she had not yet decided whether she truly welcomed it or not. Martin would be home and the obligation she had agreed to would have to be faced. How she wished it was Ben she would be going to!

Ben heard the news as it swept from the street through the ropery to his tiny office at the back of the building from where he conducted his other trading activities and speculations.

He pushed himself from his chair, grabbed his hat and shrugged himself into his coat as he strode to the door. Though he was not given to the sea himself, he always gained a thrill from watching the whale-ships return. It was part of Whitby life, and few folk would miss the excitement of welcoming home these sailors whose aura of hunters, adventurers and explorers gave them a special standing in the community. Besides there were his brothers to welcome home, and now he would be taking a special interest in the arrival of Ruth's father and brothers also.

He hurried across the bridge to the east side of the river and joined the throng heading for the Church Stairs. Reaching the top and passing quickly through the churchyard, he made for the place on the edge of the cliff where he and Ruth had arranged to meet when the cry heralding the return of the whale-ships disrupted Whitby life.

The crowds were already thickening and he slowed his step, straining to catch sight of the girl he loved. His heart raced a little faster when he spotted her and he was pleased to see that she was looking around as if searching for him. Then she did.

Their eyes met and in that moment no one else mattered. It was as if in that moment of union they were completely alone. Her concern at not seeing him disappeared into a warm smile of unspoken pleasure. He raised his hand and inclined his head to the right where there were not so many people. Ruth slipped through the crowd to meet him.

'You beat me then,' Ben said, smiling down into her flushed face.

She slid her hand into his. 'Let's walk along the cliff,' she suggested. 'The ship won't be here for a while.'

He needed no second bidding. 'Anyone identify her yet?'

Ruth gave a slight shake of her head. 'No.'

'Wait a moment.' He stopped and drew a spyglass from his inside pocket. He moved to a position from which he could see the ship and levelled the spyglass towards it. 'The *Wanderer.*'

'Abel is safely home from his first voyage to the Arctic!' There was a measure of relief in Ruth's voice.

'She's the only one in sight,' commented Ben as he slipped the spyglass back into his pocket. He took her hand again and they continued their walk, rapt in the joy of being together.

Far below a gentle sea broke quietly against the foot of the soaring cliffs. A symbol of their future? But each knew that this sea could equally well be turbulent and vicious, threatening the foundation on which they stood.

The path dipped into a hollow. When they reached the bottom of the gentle slope Ben stopped and gently turned Ruth to him. His firm hands took her by the waist and drew her closer. His lips met hers and in her response he felt her love.

'Ruth,' he whispered, 'we've known each other six months. They've been the happiest of my life. I cannot put off asking you this any longer – will you marry me?'

Her eyes brightened. 'Oh, Ben, yes. Yes!'

He held her tight. 'You have made me very happy.' Their lips met again and in their touch there was all the promise of a wonderful future together, one in which only their love would matter.

'Can we wait until Father returns before we make any announcement?' Ruth asked. 'I'm sure Mother would say that if you were to ask her. I know you have charmed her since the ball. I think you will have an ally in her.'

Ben gave a wry smile. 'Win the approval of one parent and you are well on the way to winning the other. Of course we'll wait before telling anyone else. It's our secret until your father returns. Come on, let's see if the *Water Nymph* is in sight.'

Eager anticipation was in every step as they hurried along the clifftop towards the crowds. There was a buzz of excitement among the folk who lined the cliff, and they could sense it rising from those who thronged the quays and staithes as well.

They stopped. It was clear that there was bone at the masthead of the *Wanderer*, a sign that her hold was full of blubber, a good catch that would put money in the pockets of Whitby folk. They saw two more vessels in the far distance. It was a good sign if the four Whitby whale-ships arrived home the same day. Hopefully the fourth was not far behind. Ben drew his spyglass from his pocket and trained it on the distant vessels.

'The *Hunter*.' Ben drew on his knowledge of the set of the vessels to identify them. He knew their peculiarities with an expert's knowledge drawn from a love of ships, though he had no desire to be a sailor. He trained his glass on the next ship. 'The *Sunset*.' He conveyed the information with some disappointment in his voice. 'There's bone at both mastheads,' he added, as if that was some consolation for not identifying the ship they wanted to see. They watched the three ships pass between the piers and make their way upriver to quays convenient to the try works where the blubber would be boiled to produce the oil vital to Whitby's economy. Ruth was pleased that all her brothers were safely home but that joy was subdued a little by the fact that her father's ship still had not come into view.

Some of the crowds had hurried to the quays to greet their loved ones. Wives anxious to greet and appease the urges of their husbands and escape their own loneliness; fathers and mothers wanting to welcome sons; siblings eager to greet their brothers with whom they would share a joyous homecoming and then instantly be at loggerheads over some trivial matter; girls eager to take coins from unattached sailors. All gathered close to the ships as they were tied up. Those left on the cliffs hung around hoping to catch sight of the fourth whaler then began to drift away. Ruth, although anxious to greet her brothers, lingered a while in the hope of sighting the *Water Nymph*.

Ben sensed her anxiety. He slipped a comforting hand into hers. 'I'm sure your father will be all right. Because he isn't with the others doesn't necessarily mean something's happend. Let's go. One of your brothers might have news of him.'

The quays where the whale-ships had tied up were still crowded with people who, eager for contact after nearly six months' separation, reluctantly let their menfolk complete their docking procedures. Those men needed no cajoling from the Captain and his mate to finish their work quickly. They were keen to experience the comforts of home again.

'There's Edmund,' called Ruth, spotting her brother on the deck of the *Sunset*. She called and waved and in a moment received a response.

He came quickly to the gangplank and down on to the quay. 'It's good to see you, Ruth.' He hugged her to him.

'And you,' she replied, then concern took over. 'Have you any news of Father?'

Edmund eased her back a little so that he could look into her eyes and reassure her. 'Last we saw of him he was sailing west, close to the ice. I suspect he hadn't a full ship and had smelt whales somewhere.' Worry flickered in her eyes at the mention of ice and he hastened to reassure her. 'He was in no danger.' He felt the tension that had come to her body drain away at his reassurance.

Ben had noted that Edmund cast a glance in his direction. It carried curiosity. What are you doing with my sister? And a warning. Be careful how you treat her. Ben knew the protective Holmes brothers were back. He would have to tread lightly, but he was sure that Ruth's charm would alleviate any suspicions of a man known only by his exaggerated reputation.

'Edmund,' she said, turning towards Ben, 'you know Ben Coulson?'

'Aye,' he replied abruptly, eyes still asking questions of Ben. He held out his hand. 'Glad you're back safely.'

There was still hostility and a warning in Edmund's quick clasp and muttered, 'Thanks.'

'Seems you had good hunting,' said Ben, casting a glance at the masthead.

'Aye.' Edmund clearly thought there was no need to be more forthcoming. He turned to his sister. 'I'll be free in twenty minutes. I'll see you home.'

Ben wondered whether that was a dismissal to him.

Ruth read it as such but she was not going be ruled by her brother and let him know it. 'Ben has promised to do that.'

Edmund's response was a reluctant grunt. He cast one more look at Ben in which he could only read a warning. 'You have a reputation. Don't fool with my sister.'

Ben's smile was such that it told Edmund he had read the warning and did not like being threatened. 'She'll be safe with me,' he replied.

Edmund made no response but said to his sister, 'See you later then, Ruth.' He strode back up the gangplank with vehemence that told her he was annoyed with her for associating with Ben. She smiled to herself, wondering what her brother would have said if he had known that Ben had just proposed to her and she had accepted.

'Let's greet my other brothers,' she said.

They walked to the *Hunter*. Daniel saw them before they saw him and was on the quay to meet them. His reactions were almost identical to Edmund's, but when they reached the *Wanderer* Abel was bound up in his own excitement at having returned from his first whaling voyage. His broad smile embraced both his sister and her escort. It did not matter if he was Ben Coulson. Abel as youngest son was least likely to bear animosity to anyone courting his sister. He was very close to Ruth, and in his young mind worshipped her and recognised she did not wish to be swamped by her elder brothers' over-protectiveness.

His tongue ran away in his desperation to tell his sister all about the voyage. Ruth laughed loudly at the rapture on his face as he recalled seeing his first whale killed.

'Steady on, Abel,' she cried, trying to calm his desire to tell her everything at once. 'I'll hear about it some other time. I'm so pleased that all went well for your first voyage.'

'Oh, it did! It did.'

'You know Ben Coulson,' she said.

'Of course.' Abel grinned at Ben. 'Sorry to let my tongue run away with me like that.' He held out his hand to Ben who took it and smiled back.

'I'm glad you're home safely,' he said, taking an instant liking to the youngest brother. He was pleased, for he realised he might need all the allies he could muster within the Holmes family. Get on friendly terms with Abel now and maybe he would influence his elder brothers. 'You'll have to tell me all about it sometime.'

Abel, delighted at this interest, replied with enthusiasm, 'Oh, good, I will. Better get back on board now.' He gave his sister another hug and ran up the gangplank.

'Someone's happy,' commented Ben with a smile. 'A very different reception from the cold ones I received from your other brothers.'

'Take no notice of them, they'll soon come round. Else they'll have Mother to contend with.'

'Maybe I have an ally in her, but they might well have the support of your father,' commented Ben as he was drawing up what might be lines of battle in his mind.

'And she can be equally formidable if she wants,' offered

Ruth. 'When Edmund and Daniel realise the strength of the love between us, they'll give us their support.'

'Should we tell them now?'

'I'd rather wait until Father gets back. Edmund and Daniel will have no case to make if we get his approval.'

They waited expectantly for the last cry of 'Whale-ship!' to resound through Whitby's streets. With each successive day a feeling of anxiety began to spread through every house in Whitby. Three whale-ships were home, but where was the fourth? The life of the port went on but it seemed as if it was doing so in a muted fashion; excess noise might cause people to miss the shout they all wanted to hear, though they knew that missing it was highly unlikely.

Even so it seemed to catch them unawares when it did come.

Immediately the town bubbled with new-found hope. Whatever people were doing they stopped. Soon the streets were full of folk as they poured into the open and made their way to the vantage points they preferred. There was relief and happiness in their banter. The whale-ship they were beginning to think had been lost was home. It must be given a special reception.

Ben hurried up the Church Stairs and quickened his step when he spotted Ruth ahead of him.

She first knew he was beside her when he slipped his hand into hers. Their eyes met and he saw relief in hers, and she support for her in this long-awaited homecoming. After the steep climb they headed for the cliff edge, neither speaking as they recovered their breath.

Ben drew his spyglass from his pocket. A moment later he verified what they were longing to know. 'She's the *Water Nymph*.' The news ran through the crowds on the cliff top like a prairie fire. Someone with a prearranged signal transferred that news to those who crowded the staithes and quays along the river. The sense of relief over the whole town was palpable.

'She's not full. There's no bone at the masthead,' commented Ben.

'Doesn't matter so long as she's safely home,' replied Ruth.

The joy that hung over Whitby began to evaporate as the vessel approached the piers and people realised her crew did not demonstrate the good spirits that were usually evident in men safely home from the trials and tribulations of the Arctic. The pall of silence that hung over the ship was read as a sign of tragedy.

Ruth's hand tightened on Ben's as she scanned the crew. She felt relief when she saw her father close to the helmsman.

'Where's Martin?' Ben's voice was low. Bewildered, he added, 'He's not there.'

Ruth had been running her own gaze across the ship, and she too could not see Ben's brother. 'Maybe he's below deck.'

'No sailor would miss sailing into his home port.'

'We must get down to the quay,' urged Ruth, starting to turn away from the cliff top.

The cry of 'Whale-ship!' caught Alicia unawares. Since the arrival of the other ships a few days ago, Martin's homecoming and what it meant for her had drifted to the back of her mind. Now it was back into prominence. Although he would not know of her acceptance of the arrangements, she decided she should be on the quay to greet him. Her thoughts were mixed as she hurried to cross the drawbridge before it was opened for the returning vessel to pass along the river.

Joining the people cascading on to the quay to watch the *Water Nymph* berth, she sensed the joy fade from the lively atmosphere that had been generated with the first news that the *Water Nymph* was home. Word that Martin Coulson's crew were missing had been passed from the ship to those folk on the piers and had travelled from lip to lip like a grassland fire.

A chill gripped Alicia's heart. Martin lost! The horror of his dying in the icy Arctic wastes numbed her, and yet she recognised a tiny flicker of relief that her unwanted marriage would not now take place. But what would happen instead? What now of her father's debt?

*

Ben and Ruth were at the *Water Nymph's* berth when word preceded it that Martin's crew had been lost.

'Oh, no!' Ruth whispered, full of pity. Could she really know how Ben was feeling at this news? Her heart reached out to him. Knowing he would need all her support in these moments of tragedy, she wanted to give him all the love she could.

Ben felt weak, as if the life was being drained from him. He felt numb, yet his mind cried out for this news not to be true. He knew that Ruth must be suffering from shock as well. There was a moment when the world stood still, when they felt as if they were outside all feeling, looking on to a scene that made no sense.

Then Ben started. 'My God, Eric!' he gasped, seeing his young brother on deck. What must he be feeling? He started for the gangplank. Eric saw him and rushed to meet him. He reached the quay and, with tears streaming down his cheeks, flung himself into his brother's arms. Ben enfolded him in an embrace that tried to comfort and give strength.

Ruth moved silently beside them. She searched for a word of comfort but could not find one adequate to ease the sorrow the brothers must be feeling, especially the younger one who had been so close to the tragedy that must have haunted him throughout the long voyage home. She knew her father must be suffering too. Knowing he would want comforting, she wanted to go to him but waited.

Eric suddenly looked up into his brother's face. 'He left him! He left Martin!' Each word was like an arrow meant to pierce with deadly accuracy. Its intent was never in doubt.

Ben's mind raced. Eric's accusation could be directed only at one man – the Captain of the *Water Nymph*! What had happened in the far lonely wastes of the Arctic?

'Hush, Eric.' He wanted no further accusations voiced now. If there was anything behind what his brother was implying, it must be said in private.

'He did!' insisted Eric.

'Later,' said Ben firmly.

'But . . .'

'Not now!' Though Ben's voice was quiet, its tone was authoritative. 'You must go back on board, Eric. Finish your work. We'll talk later at home.' His instruction was firm. He eased Eric away. His young brother cast him a pleading look which said, Don't make me do this.

'You must be brave.' Ben gave a little nod of reassurance that said, I am suffering too so don't make it worse for me. Do as I ask.

Eric licked his lips and nodded his understanding. He turned away and walked towards the ship. Captain Holmes was coming down the gangplank.

Ben held his breath, hoping that Eric would not do anything foolish. He breathed a sigh of relief when he saw his brother take no action but to step aside and then climb the gangplank when it was clear.

Ben glanced at Ruth. Her face had drained of colour. It was ashen. Her eyes were unseeing but held an expression as if the troubles of the future, were visible before her.

Captain Holmes's face was wreathed in sadness. Loss weighed heavily on him. No Captain liked to lose one crew member, let alone six. As the type of man he was, Gideon Holmes felt it was his ultimate responsibility to see all his crew home safely. In this he had failed. But what choice had he had?

Ruth read all these emotions. Her heart went out to him. He looked older, as if the weight on his shoulders had been hard to bear and was now, with the homecoming, becoming even heavier. She knew her father would not settle until he had seen the families of the men who had been lost. And even after he had done so life would be hard to bear, with the memories of what had happened haunting him until he could find peace of mind again in the hostile Arctic. He'd need to return there at least once in order to purge his memories of what had happened on this voyage.

'I must go to him.'

Neither spoke as father and daughter embraced each other.

Four people came to stand beside them. Captain Holmes held out his arms to Daniel, Edmund, Abel and Rachel in turn. They embraced him, offering their comfort and support. He looked to his wife, standing close by, waiting to add her love to theirs.

Ben, hurting from his own loss, felt as if he was intruding on a family's private emotions. He started to turn away.

'Son.' Captain Holmes's quiet voice halted him.

He stopped and swung round. 'Sir?'

'I'm sorry.' Captain Holmes paused, bit his lip, then went on with slow deliberation. 'Martin was fast to a whale. It ran. The ice was threatening. I had to make a decision I did not like. I'll be reporting the full facts to your father.'

Ben nodded. 'Sir.' He accepted the Captain's brief explan- ation and would never question that decision. He cast a quick glance at Ruth and saw that she had read his acceptance and was glad he laid no blame on her father, in spite of Eric's outburst. In her eyes he saw thanks and love.

As he walked away he saw his sisters, Sarah and Dina, hurrying from the quay in the direction of their father's office. He realised his father would know the terrible news before he was able to break it himself and set off after them.

He had only gone a few steps when he felt a touch on his arm. He turned to see a solemn-faced Alicia, sympathy in her eyes.

'Oh, Ben, I am so sorry.'

'Thanks, Alicia, it's tragic but we'll have to get over it. I must go to Father.'

She nodded. 'I understand. Ben, if there is anything I can do, any help I can give to any of you, you only have to ask.'

'Thanks, Alicia. I must go.'

As he turned her hand found his and squeezed it, expressing her hope that he would come to her for comfort.

When he walked into the building housing his father's office Ben felt the heavy pall of mourning. The unusual silence that enveloped the place had charged the rooms with sorrow. He walked carefully along the corridor as if his footsteps were an affront to the silence. The door at the end stood slightly ajar without allowing him to see into the room. He paused in front of it and then, with his will charged to meet his father, pushed the door slowly open.

He was not prepared for what he saw. Sam Coulson was sitting in his chair, an arm round each of his daughters who knelt beside him with tears streaming down their cheeks. That did not shock Ben. But he had never seen his father cry before, not even when he'd watched his wife's coffin lowered into the ground. The lack of feeling he saw that day, through his own tears, showed Ben how deep the estrangement between his parents had become. He realised now that the loss of Martin must be the first tragedy his father had allowed to touch his emotions. And that emphasised to him what a hard man his father had become.

Ben stepped forward towards the group. His sisters glanced at him in abject sorrow, without saying a word. His movement startled his father and Ben saw him jerk as if trying to throw off a mantle he did not want his son to see. Sam straightened, let his arms slip from his daughters in a way that was a signal for them to rise. They scrambled to their feet and Sam stiffened his back. His tears had disappeared even though he had not wiped them away.

'Son, this is a sad day.' He made no effort to hold out his arms to Ben, and he knew that even this tragedy had not completely broken down the barrier that had grown between them. That might happen when his father realised Ben was now his eldest living son.

'Indeed it is, Father. I have seen Eric.'

'How is he?'

'Shocked, naturally. It will have been a terrible voyage home for him.'

'Aye, it will. I hope he is taking it like a man.'

His comment drew no response from Ben who had decided that he would say nothing about Eric's outburst on the quay.

He hoped his brother would have reconsidered his accusation. Maybe he had assumed too much at the height of the tragedy.

Sam glanced at his daughters who were standing to one side, dabbing their eyes with lace handkerchiefs. 'Stop your snivelling, girls,' he said harshly. They were startled by the change in him from the man who had been offering them the comfort of his arms a few moments ago. 'Life has to go on.'

'That may be true, Father, but we can't help but mourn our brother,' Ben put in quickly in defence of his sisters and offering his approval of the tears he had seen in his father's eyes.

If Sam recognised it as such he showed no sign when he said, 'We do not need to make spectacles of ourselves. Time will not stand still, and work will not stop because Martin is no longer with us. I suggest that we all behave with decorum over the next two or three days. No doubt there will be a memorial service for the men who were lost. See that you do not disgrace your brother's memory on that occasion by over-reacting.'

Sarah and Dina had silenced their sobbing. They bobbed their father curtseys and rushed from the room.

'Don't be hard on them, Father. They loved Martin,' said Ben. 'Let them weep.' He almost added 'you did', but thought better of it. His father would not welcome such an observation.

'Don't you criticise me, boy. I understand them. It behoves you to respect your brother as much as they do.'

'I do, Father. But I shall miss Martin.'

His father gave a grunt that carried with it his misgivings about Ben's statement. 'That's as may be, but there's one thing –' he fixed his eyes on his son with a penetrating look '– I do hope. That is that you have learned a lot from him and can follow adequately in his footsteps, though you may never be able to fill them as head of the Coulson firm. You'd better learn to do so, for now you are the eldest son and even though we don't see eye to eye, I expect you to follow me as Martin would have done. See that you mend your ways.'

Words sprang to Ben's lips but he held them back. His

father's statement had jolted him. He was now the eldest son with all that that entailed. Sam had just reminded him of his responsibilities towards the Coulson family. One day he would be its head and would be expected to look after his sisters, if ever they needed help, and see that his brother did not want. He would have to see that the firm his father had created continued to thrive for the benefit of the Coulson family. Ben began to feel the burden of it on his shoulders.

His father eyed him for a moment longer, wondering what was going on in his son's mind. When he received no response he said, 'We'll talk of this another day.'

Ben welcomed the dismissal. He wanted time to think.

As he closed the door to the office behind him, the front door burst open. Eric strode in with an agitated purposeful step. His hair was dishevelled as if he had not bothered to put his cap on for protection against the wind. His eyes contained a wildness that Ben did not like to see there.

'Where's Father?' Eric's demand was automatic.

Ben grabbed his arm, halting him. 'Be careful what you say.'

Eric knew that Ben was referring to his outburst on the quay. 'I know what I saw and heard,' he rasped.

'Don't make accusations you can't prove,' snapped a tight-lipped Ben.

Eric shook his arm free, glared at his brother, flung open the door and slammed it behind him, a gesture that implied that Ben would not be welcome during what was about to take place.

Ben stiffened. He reached out for the door handle but stopped. If he followed Eric he would do no good. He could not refute what his brother would say. He turned away with a sigh.

Startled by the sharpness of the intrusion, Sam sprang to his feet when he saw his youngest son. Anxiety swept over him upon seeing Eric's contorted face. He came from behind his desk, arms held out to his son, an unusual gesture for Sam Coulson. Eric ignored them. He did not want comfort. Time had passed. After the initial shock, when his whole world seemed to have caved in, he realised he could seek justice for what had happened to his brother only by accusing Captain Holmes. Facing Sam, he did not hold back.

His gesture of stopping three yards in front of his father and not seeking solace in his arms brought Sam to a halt too. He let his arms fall to his sides, his mind grappling with the expression on his son's face. It was so mixed he could not imagine what was going on in Eric's mind.

'Father, he let Martin die!'

The words rang in Sam's mind. He hardly dared consider the implication behind them. He stared at his son, trying to make sense of what Eric was saying. 'Who did? What do you mean?' His eyes narrowed beneath a frowning brow.

'Captain Holmes!'

'What?' Sam was astounded by this accusation.

'He did, Father. He did!'

There was such conviction in his words. Sam, though he was shocked by what his son was suggesting, forced himself to assess this situation calmly. He must listen to all Eric had to say. He could not ignore his son even though he would soon be getting a report from the Captain of his ship, the man in authority who would have recorded what had happened in his log.

'Steady, son, steady. These are serious words.'

'They are true!'

'Sit down and tell me exactly what happened.' Sam held a chair out for his son.

Eric dampened his lips, a gesture that made Sam wonder if he was trying to pluck up courage to make his accusation again.

Sam returned to his own seat. He leaned back in it and eyed his son with a grave expression. 'Before you say any more, consider carefully what it is to be. Behind the words you have uttered so far lies a dreadful accusation. You must be sure it is the truth and that you can substantiate it. Can you?'

Eric bit his lip and did not reply.

Sam leaned forward on his desk. He saw that the firey

emotion in his son was subsiding. 'All right. Just tell me what happened, slowly and carefully.' He leaned back in his chair again, a gesture intended to make his son feel more settled.

Eric swallowed hard. 'He left Martin.'

'Begin at the beginning. You were hunting whales?'

'Yes. We had seen other ships leaving but our hold wasn't full. You know Captain Holmes has a reputation for smelling out whales so, although the crew were getting uneasy due to the lateness of the season and the fact that we were in sight of the ice, Captain Holmes continued to sail west.'

'And was he right about smelling whales?' Sam prompted when his son paused.

'Oh, yes, he was right enough. We came across a great school. All boats were launched. Everyone made a kill.'

'Including Martin?'

'Well, he was fast on and the whale ran. We lost sight of him but Captain Holmes didn't bother at first. He was concerned with getting the whales flensed as quickly as possible.'

'Quite right.'

'Yes, but . . .' Eric hesitated.

'What?'

'A storm was brewing. We should have stopped flensing and searched for Martin's crew.'

'Instead Captain Holmes continued flensing?'

'Yes.'

'Did he get all the blubber aboard?'

'Yes. But he still made no effort to find Martin.'

'The storm hit you?'

'Yes. We did not get the brunt of it but it was bad. We rode it out successfully.'

'And after the storm?'

'It had affected the ice pattern, and with the wind that followed the ice was on the move.'

'Was it endangering the safety of the ship?'

'No, not then. But Captain Holmes thought so. He left without making any attempt to search for Martin and his crew.'

'Are you sure he did nothing?'

'Yes. I pleaded with him but he ignored me, and when I persisted he had me taken below deck.'

'What?' Sam's anger was beginning to quicker. He could picture the whole scene that had led to the loss of his eldest son, the heir who was to carry on the Coulson dynasty and through whose marriage to Alicia Campion Sam would own the biggest commercial company in Whitby.

'I was confined for three days, by which time we were well away from the Arctic. Captain Holmes lectured me on the seriousness of my outburst. He said he supposed it had stemmed from the shock of losing my brother and therefore he would overlook the matter, especially as it was my first voyage to the Arctic.'

'You said no more to him?'

'No. I thought it wise to keep quiet until I got home and saw you.'

'Good. Did you voice your opinion to anyone else?'

'Some of the crew overheard my outburst.'

'Did any of them voice an opinion?'

'No. I reckon they were afraid to say anything. Captain Holmes rules with a rod of iron.'

Sam nodded. He knew of Holmes's reputation at sea. 'You told no one else?'

'I saw Ben on the quay.'

'You told him?'

'I only said that the Captain had left Martin.'

'What was Ben's reaction?'

'He warned me to be careful about what I said.'

'Quite right.' Sam was going to say no more to Eric about that, but wondered why Ben had not said anything so far. 'You mustn't say a word to anyone else, not even your sisters. This is a serious matter which I will deal with in my own way. Now, let us go over this once more so that I am certain of the facts.'

Eric once again related what had happened and how he had viewed the situation at the time.

'You are perfectly sure that Captain Holmes could have searched without endangering the ship?'

'Yes.'

Sam nodded. 'All right, Eric, thank you for telling me. It is good to have you back, though I'm sorry your first whaling voyage ended like this.'

Eric squared his shoulders. 'It won't put me off, Father. I want whaling to be my life.'

'Good man. With such determination you'll be a successful captain one day.'

Sam felt proud of his youngest son as he watched him walk from the room. He wished Ben had had that attitude instead of shirking the trade after only one voyage.

When the door shut, Sam found all his emotions about the loss of his eldest son come together in deep anger at the man whom he judged, from Eric's words, could have saved Martin. His lips tightened into a thin line and he beat his fists on his desk. 'Why? Why?' his mind screamed. Curses on the head of Captain Holmes sprang to his lips and thoughts of revenge burned deep into his mind. Holmes would pay, and pay dearly.

He sat upright in his chair and then, his mind made up, slammed both hands down on his desk and started to push himself from his chair. He heard footsteps in the corridor. There was a light tap, the door opened and a clerk announced, 'Captain Holmes to see you, sir.'

'Show him in.' There was a touch of irritation in Sam's voice that caused the clerk to give Captain Holmes a silent grimace of sympathy at having to face Mr Coulson in such a mood.

A few moments later, with his cap neatly held in the crook of his arm, Captain Holmes walked into the room.

'Holmes.' Sam's voice was cold. He had remained standing and he extended no hand in welcome to his captain.

'Sir.' Gideon gave a slight inclination of his head to accompany his greeting. 'I am sorry that I come with such terrible news. It quite overshadows my report of an almost full hold.'

'Tell me what happened,' said Sam curtly.

'It is all in there, sir,' replied Gideon, holding out his log book.

Sam took it and tossed it on to his desk. 'I'll read it later. I want to hear things in your own words, which no doubt will expand on what is written and therefore give me a better basis on which to form my judgement and apportion blame.'

'I don't think there is any blame to mete out,' replied the Captain stiffly.

'I will be the judge of that.'

Captain Holmes summed up the attitude and words of his employer and knew that Mr Coulson had already been given one version of the incident, no doubt by his son Eric. Knowing what that would have been, Gideon realised it would not have gone in his favour. He must be careful what he said now. It would be the truth, but words could be twisted. He must be very careful how he used them.

'We were sailing in good weather . . .' he began, only to be halted by Sam.

'This could take some time. We had better sit down.'

Gideon noted that his employer did not offer him a glass of Madeira as he usually did at the end of a successful voyage.

When they were seated he took up his story again. Sam listened carefully. The general pattern was as Eric had told him. That, coupled with the fact that he had made a preconceived judgement, set his anger rising as the Captain's story went on. He fought to keep it under control, determined not to show his fury for he believed the cold anger that came with menace to be much more telling and effective.

'Captain Holmes, were you concerned for the crew of the whale-boat commanded by my son?'

'As much as I am for all members of my crew.'

'And how much is that?'

'As if every member of the crew was my own son.'

'Would you have searched for your own son?'

'Not if it would have endangered the lives of any other members of my crew.'

'Did it in this case?'

'In my opinion, yes.'

Sam nodded and pursed his lips thoughtfully for a moment. 'I might come back to that point, Captain Holmes, but tell me, do you set any regulations for the boat crews?'

'Yes, sir, I do.'

'And what may they be?'

'They must not go out of sight of the ship.'

'You rely on having your ship near enough the whales so that it won't be necessary?'

'I do. You know my reputation as . . .'

'I do indeed,' Sam interrupted. 'What if a boat is fast to a whale and is towed out of sight of the ship?'

'No crew should ever be towed out of sight of my ship. If it appears that they will be, they are under strict instructions to cut the rope and let the whale go.'

'Even if they should be fast to a whale that would make a full ship? You also have a reputation for never returning without your hold being full unless it is not a good season.'

'No matter how much I wanted that whale, they should cut the rope. Not to do so endangers the rest of the crew, for it means that we might have to search for them. That is made perfectly clear.'

'So this crew disobeyed your orders?'

'It is a regulation rather than an order. There are always exceptional circumstances when a regulation may be overlooked or breached.'

Sam nodded thoughtfully. Was Captain Holmes seeking to excuse his own actions? 'Did you instigate a search when this crew went missing?'

'I could not do so immediately. Firstly, we were in the middle of flensing when we became aware that one crew had not reported back. I sent a man aloft but he could see no sign of the boat.'

'Should you not have searched then?'

'And let the rest of our kill go? If we had done so, and within

99

a few moments had sighted the boat, we would have lost a valuable cargo. Besides, there was still a chance that it might reappear. I kept a man aloft, hoping for a sighting. We had finished flensing and were casting off the carcasses intending to sail in the direction in which the boat was last seen when the lookout reported an approaching storm. We had to prepare to ride it out.'

'Obviously you did that successfully. Then you searched?'

'No.'

Sam looked at Captain Holmes in disbelief. 'No?'

'The lookout reported a shift in the ice. I looked for myself and realised that we were in danger of being trapped. As much as I regretted it, I had to take the decision to sail for home.'

'You left six men to perish?' There was accusation in Sam's cold tone.

'And maybe saved the lives of the rest of the crew, the ship and its cargo,' replied Gideon pointedly.

'How much time before that ice would have become a real menace?'

'Who can tell? A shift in the wind can speed disaster or remove it.'

'And you did not think you had time.' A note of disgust tinged the hostility already evident in Sam's voice. His eyes narrowed. 'At that point I think you were frightened, Captain Holmes.'

Gideon sprang to his feet. With colour rising on his face, he glared at his employer. 'Don't you dare call me a coward, Mr Coulson!'

Sam was on his feet too. 'I'll call you what I like, Holmes. I also accuse you of grave misjudgement. When that boat did not appear you should have stopped the flensing and searched for it.'

'It is easy to say so in hindsight,' snapped Gideon. 'And remember, all my crews were told to cut the rope once at a distance from the ship. I encouraged them to do so.'

'You are saying my son disobeyed orders?' Sam voice rose with fury.

'I am saying he did not follow our usual practice; either that or something happened that we do not know about. Once he had failed to cut the rope, the whale could have taken the boat anywhere. The storm was one of the most vicious I have encountered. It was highly unlikely that an open boat would outride it.'

'So you assumed that was the case and that its crew had perished? You left without searching?'

'The ice, Mr Coulson . . . remember, I told you about the ice? To search after that storm would have yielded nothing and heightened the possibility of our becoming trapped.'

'In other words, you did nothing.' Sam's voice was cold. 'And your negligence cost the life of my son. You left him to die. Well, Gideon Holmes, I no longer want you as a captain of one of my ships.'

Though he had sensed this coming the dismissal was still something of a shock, but Gideon would not protest or beg. He drew himself up, glared at Sam and said in a quiet but telling voice, 'As you wish. There are plenty more out there.' He started for the door but stopped when Sam spoke.

'There is not one Whitby ship will employ you, Gideon Holmes. I'll see to that!'

The icy menace in Sam Coulson's voice left no doubt in Gideon's mind as to the outcome of this interview. It sent a chill through his heart. He did not reply but turned and walked from the room.

Chapter Six

Georgina Holmes turned from the fire she had been stirring and held out her arms to her husband when he walked into the kitchen. Her initial greeting had been made on the quay in the public gaze; now she must offer him more intimate consolation in the privacy of her home. She naturally associated his grave expression with the loss of six of his men.

He came to her and found comfort in her arms and in the closeness that he had missed so much.

'I'm so sorry, Gideon,' she said with quiet sympathy.

He gave a slight nod in reply.

'The moment I heard the cry of "Whale-ship" I laid your clean clothes out on the bed and prepared your favourite – beef and Yorkshire puddings. They'll be ready in twenty minutes. The family made themselves scarce for our first minutes together.' She eased him gently away but still held him. The words faded on her lips when she saw the despondent expression in his eyes. 'What is it, Gideon?' she asked, her curiosity tinged with alarm.

'Sam Coulson has relieved me of my command.'

'What?' Disbelief replaced the joy that had shone in her eyes but a few moments ago.

'There's worse.'

Puzzled, she waited for him to explain.

'He swore that he would see I never got a Whitby ship again.'

'Why? Does he blame you for what happened?'

'Aye. In spite of my explanation, he says I should have searched.'

'And should you?' She held him with a gaze that said she

wanted the truth though she had never found him out in a lie.

'If I had, the whole crew could have been endangered.'

'Then you made the right decision.'

'He doesn't see it that way.'

'He wasn't there.'

Gideon gave a quirk of his eyebrows signalling that that did not come into Sam's reasoning.

'All owners trust their captains and so should he, no matter what the circumstances,' Georgina protested.

'Maybe, lass, but he's my employer.'

'But he can't get you banned from every Whitby ship.'

Gideon gave a little grimace that contradicted her. 'Sam Coulson has a lot of power in this port and can make it very awkward for anyone who goes against him.'

'But he . . .'

Georgina never got to finish her sentence. The door opened to admit the rest of the Holmes family. There was additional sympathy and love in the kisses of Ruth and Rachel, and in the handshakes of Daniel, Edmund and Abel.

'Gideon, go and get changed. We'll talk over the meal.' Georgina took charge of the situation. She wanted no more to be said on the matter until the right moment when everyone was settled.

When they were seated at the table the talk was rather muted as the children realised that this was not the time to ask their father questions. Instead he gained information on his sons' voyages, though even that was not given with the usual enthusiasm. The children imagined the subdued atmosphere to be connected with the loss of the whale-boat and its crew and were not aware of the consequences of this until their mother spoke after they had finished their apple pie. 'Gideon, I think it is time to tell them.'

They all looked askance at her and then turned their eyes questioningly on their father.

He cleared his throat and told them what had happened between himself and Sam Coulson. Their immediate disbelief gave way to cries of outrage and protests. When he assured them that Sam Coulson really did blame him and meant what he said, the seriousness of the situation cast a gloom over them but in a few moments there was determination among them to combat the consequences of Coulson's threat.

'Father, if we move quickly, get you signed on with another owner, we can outsmart Mr Coulson.' Daniel was on his feet.

Gideon hesitated.

'Come on!' Edmund urged as he sprang from his chair.

Gideon glanced at his wife. She gave several sharp nods that helped to emphasise the approval in her eyes.

Gideon, though, was not at all sure that this would work. He had sensed that Sam Coulson would do all he could to prevent him from finding another position as captain of a ship out of Whitby, but he knew, for his family's sake and for his own, he must try.

'I'm coming too,' said Abel who was already heading for the door.

Gideon could not deny his youngest who, having accomplished his first whaling voyage, was now as much of a man as his brothers.

The four men left the house together.

'Do you think Mr Coulson will carry out his threat, Mother?' asked Rachel.

'I have no doubt he'll try,' she replied. When she glanced at Ruth she saw her lips tighten with worry, and the concern in her eyes was bordering on tears. 'Rachel, will you start the washing up? I want a word with Ruth.'

Rachel started carrying the dirty crockery into the kitchen. She made no protest at being singled out for the task for she guessed that her mother wanted to advise Ruth about her relationship with Ben Coulson in the light of this new development.

Georgina led the way into the front room, the best one that was set aside for visitors and special occasions, a quiet place that was used only when required.

Georgina raised a questioning eyebrow. 'Well?' she said softly without any hint of her own view of the changed circumstances.

Ruth bit her lips. Her face creased with unease. 'Oh, Ma, I don't know. What will Father say?'

'He'll be opposed to any relationship with a Coulson, you can bet on that.'

'But this has nothing to do with Ben,' Ruth protested.

'Maybe, but he's a Coulson. Though your father is a tolerant man, being blamed for what happened and relieved of his command won't endear any member of the family to him.'

'Maybe I could get Ben to make his father see reason?'

Georgina gave a doubtful smile. 'I don't think Sam Coulson will take any notice. Besides Ben will now be the eldest son and Sam will expect him to assume the responsibility that goes with that.'

'But Ben does not see eye to eye with his father,' Ruth pointed out, hoping that she could salvage something from the situation.

'So it is rumoured, but don't forget, lass, blood is thicker than water. My advice is to tread carefully, think hard about your relationship with Ben and your feelings for him. How, in the present circumstances, it might affect this family.'

Ruth nodded. Her eyes brimmed with tears.

'Come here, love.' Georgina held her arms out to her daughter.

Ruth came to her, welcoming the comfort it brought. She let tears flow but in a few moments, determined to control them, straightened and wiped her eyes as she said, 'You won't tell Father about Ben?'

Georgina gave a wan smile. 'No, lass, I won't. Now, let's go and help Rachel with the dishes.'

Gideon threw off his doubts and matched the determined stride of his three sons as they crossed the bridge to reach Bagdale on the west side of the river where merchants and ship-owners and sea captains had built their homes on the wealth acquired from the booming port.

'Mr Morris?' queried Daniel.

'Good choice,' agreed Edmund. 'He has interests in three ships.'

They turned through a gateway and walked single-file along the narrow path, climbing towards the house. As he approached the elegant building Gideon felt a sense of regret. If things had gone well and the boat-crew had not been lost he and Georgina would be discussing their promised move to this side of the river. Now, unless he was successful in finding another command, they would have to drop that idea. Could he possibly evade the threat Sam Coulson had issued?

When the door opened to them the maid showed surprise at seeing four men, one of whom made the polite request, 'May we see Mr Morris?'

'Is he expecting you?' the girl asked.

'No. But we would like to talk with him.'

'I'll see if he will receive you. Whom shall I say is calling?'

'Captain Holmes and his three sons.'

'Wait a moment.' The maid turned back into the house, leaving the door slightly ajar. She returned to open the door wide and say, 'Mr Morris will see you.'

They found themselves in an elegant room furnished so that each piece of furniture was not challenged by another. The wallpaper was in a delicate shade of green with a small motif of roses. A marine painting hung on each wall. Two tall sash windows overlooked the front garden.

Georgina would love this, thought Gideon. The thought was interrupted by Mr Morris. He rose from a wing-chair set to one side of the fireplace, laid his book down and stepped towards them. He held out his hand to Gideon. 'Captain Holmes.'

Gideon gave a little smile. 'I think we've known each other long enough to dispense with the formalities, Josh.'

'Aye, I suppose we have.' His grip was firm, friendly. Gideon drew hope from it. 'I was sorry to hear of your loss.'

'It happens,' replied Gideon.

Josh's welcoming glance at the brothers embraced them all. 'Boys.'

Each of them returned the greeting politely with, 'Mr Morris.'

He looked at Gideon. 'A delegation like this is unusual. What do you want of me?'

Daniel stepped forward. It had been agreed that he should make the initial enquiry. 'Mr Morris, we are here to see if you have a ship for my father.'

They'd expected an expression of surprise. It did not come. Their hearts sank.

'I'm afraid not.'

'Your *Dancing Lady* is at her quay. I hear that Captain Forbes has resigned his command and you haven't engaged anyone yet.'

'You certainly have your ears to the ground, Daniel, but I'm afraid I cannot appoint your father.'

Reading what lay behind that statement, Daniel bristled.

Gideon, knowing his son well, laid a hand on his arm to restrain any outburst. He looked hard at Josh and said quietly, 'So Sam Coulson has got to you already?'

He grimaced. 'I'm sorry, Gideon. I'd employ you any time, but I daren't risk Sam's wrath. You know he has the power to destroy me. Cross Sam and you can be in real trouble. In my case, I'm about to close a deal in which he is a part. If he chose to pull out, it would ruin me.'

'He's threatened you so soon?'

'Aye. Runner came with a note. Likely he'll have contacted all the ship-owners hereabouts.'

Gideon sensed anger in his boys. He didn't want that erupting, and besides an outright confrontation would do no good. His lips tightened. 'I understand. Come, boys.' They started for the door. Gideon stopped to look back. 'Some day, Josh, Sam's going to reap what he sows.'

'I hope you find a ship, Gideon.'

He and his sons left the house.

'Where now?' asked Edmund when they paused at the gate.

'I think it's going to be a forlorn attempt,' said their father quietly. 'You heard Mr Morris, Sam Coulson's contacted all the ship-owners in Whitby. It's what I expected.'

'Father, we can't give up,' cried Abel. He couldn't visualise his father without a ship.

'We're not going to,' said Daniel.

Gideon was sure that the conviction in his son's voice would be dashed before the day was out.

So it proved. After trying five more ship-owners even his sons had to agree that the position looked hopeless. Despondently they decided to go home.

When they walked into the house Georgina and her two daughters knew immediately that the men had failed in their quest. Gloom settled over the gathering as the men related their story.

'I didn't know Mr Coulson wielded such power in Whitby,' said Ruth.

'He's a hard man. Over the years he has made it his business to see that he has a hold over those people who are likely to be of use to him, and with the knowledge he has he can turn the screw whenever he wants. If people are making a good living it does not behold them to go against Sam Coulson.' Gideon let his gaze meet that of each of his sons. 'I'm just afraid you too might find yourselves without a ship.'

'I thought that might be the case after what he's done to you,' said Daniel. 'We'll find out tomorrow.'

Ruth had little sleep that night. Her father without a ship was unthinkable. She turned the problem over and over in her mind. She viewed it from all angles, but whichever one she chose she always encountered an obstacle. Could she enlist Ben's help? But that would mean her father would know of their relationship which could lead to trouble. But need he know? As Ben came into her thoughts she realised that he was now heir to the Coulson empire. Could that give him a greater influence to

108

change his father's attitude or would he have to follow the path laid down by Sam? If it was the latter then the position was truly hopeless. If he couldn't or wouldn't help then she wanted nothing more to do with him. It was with her heart aching at this thought that she dozed off. It was not for long, however, for shortly afterwards she was awakened by the light of a new day.

As she dressed, thoughts of the previous night ran through her mind. She came to the conclusion that, because of her feelings for Ben, she must ask him to intervene.

Sam Coulson waited impatiently for the door of the Campion residence to open. When it did so, his request was sharp. 'I want to see Mr Campion, tell him that Mr Coulson is here.'

'Yes, sir.' The girl, quaking at the formidable aspect Sam presented and the ill-tempered snap in his voice, forsook all the procedures she had been taught and scurried away to do his bidding. She came back a few minutes later to find the visitor, lips tightening with frustration at the delay, tapping his walking stick irritably on the step. 'Come this way, sir.'

Sam stepped into the hall and removed his hat while he waited for the girl to close the door. He thrust both hat and walking stick at her. She took them, fumbled and almost dropped them as she turned to show him to a room on the right.

He strode past her, expecting to find Seaton there. When he saw the room was empty he swung round but before he could pose his question the girl said, 'Mr Campion will be with you in a few minutes,' and rushed away, closing the door quickly behind her.

Four minutes, that seemed interminable to Sam, passed before the door opened to admit his friend.

'Good morning, Sam.'

'Good morning.' His words came out as a grunt of irritation at having been kept waiting.

'I'm sorry about Martin. I hope you will accept the condolences of all my family?'

'Yes, yes,' he replied rapidly as if the matter was over and done with. 'There are things that must be seen to, Seaton. Martin's death means our plans will have to be altered, and there's no time like the present to get them settled.'

A chill gripped Seaton. Was Sam going to call in his debt? 'So soon, Sam? Don't you want to observe a period of mourning?'

'Martin died in the Arctic. Of course I mourn but I do it privately in my own way. And I get on with life.'

Making money and expanding your empire, thought Seaton. 'But . . .'

'No buts, just hear what I have to say.'

Seaton nodded.

'As I told you, Martin agreed to the marriage I proposed before he sailed. You got Alicia to agree. Now it can't happen.'

Knowing Sam, Seaton could guess what was coming. 'You have another proposal?'

'Yes. Ben is now my heir so Alicia will have to marry him,' he replied matter-of-factly, as if there was nothing else to consider.

'You have given no thought to their feelings?'

Sam gave a dismissive wave of his hand, as if they weren't worth considering. 'Ben will do as I say. You see that Alicia does. You know the consequences otherwise.' He started for the door, leaving Seaton staring after him. 'No time to stay talking,' Sam called over his shoulder. 'Let me hear from you when you have spoken to your daughter.' He strode from the room, picked up his hat and stick in the hall where the girl had put them and left the house.

Seaton said nothing to his wife and Alicia about Sam's early visit before he left for his office. He wanted time to think about the proposal and the possibilities of finding an escape from this blackmail attempt. He regarded it as little better than that.

The Holmes family were subdued when they gathered for breakfast. Any attempt at conversation was overshadowed by everyone's recognition that their lives had changed. As much as they tried to believe that everything would turn out right, they had been made to recognise the power that Sam Coulson wielded in Whitby and the speed with which he could employ it.

Ruth had made a resolve about her own course of action. She could not voice it but must wait for the right moment to leave the house so that she could engage Ben's help.

'Father, is there anything you can use to prove that you did nothing wrong by not searching for the missing boat?' Daniel asked hopefully.

'Son, I've racked my brains,' said Gideon with a slow shake of his head. 'There is nothing. The position is made worse by my having had Eric Coulson on board. He accused me in front of all the crew and that made them think there was something in what he said. He's obviously voiced his opinion to his father and Sam Coulson is more than likely to believe his own son.'

'Can't you get some of the crew to speak up on your behalf?' suggested Abel.

'Do you think they would after they hear what Sam has done to me? They too could be out of a job and facing hardship for their families. They'll know they can't change Sam's mind so they'll keep quiet.'

Edmund scowled and set his chin with determination. His eyes were afire with resolve. He slammed one broad fist hard into his palm. 'Maybe some of them can be persuaded.' The meaning behind his action and words was not lost on anyone around the table.

It was Georgina who spoke first, her voice full of an authority that had to be listened to. Its tone carried a warning to anyone who did not heed her words. 'There'll be none of that, Edmund!' Her eyes swept to her other two sons. 'And that goes for you as well. There'll be no violence to try to solve our problem. Nothing was ever resolved that way. It will only lead to bitterness and that will be followed by remorse and regret. Mind you heed my words.'

*

Those words were very much in Ruth's mind as she hurried along Grape Lane and crossed the bridge to the west side. So engrossed was she in the hope that Ben would be the one to answer their dilemma that she was hardly aware of the crowds that thronged the streets and the bridge. Life was going on around her as normal and none of these people knew the problems and worries that beset her mind.

She pulled her cloak a little closer to her as she felt the cold wind blowing up the river, sending the water into dancing ripples. It seemed bleaker today. She glanced upstream and saw the *Water Nymph* lying idle at her quay as if no drama had been played out during her mission to the Arctic. She bit her lip with regret for the begging she must do, though she hoped that would only be in her first words and Ben would soon be persuaded to help.

She turned into Skinner Street and entered the building where she knew he conducted his business. She was immediately assailed by the smell of hemp and the clatter of machinery. Two men, caps on their heads, stained aprons around their waists, shot a glance in her direction when they were aware of the door opening. A third man paused in coiling some rope and, on seeing her, laid aside his task and came to her, surprise showing on his face that a lady should venture into these premises.

'Good day, ma'am,' he said politely, touching the peak of his cap with his right forefinger.

'I would like to see Mr Coulson,' she said firmly.

There was no mistaking her determination not to be put off. The man replied without hesitation, 'Follow me, ma'am.' He led the way to some wooden stairs, paused at the bottom and turned to her, saying, 'Careful on these stairs, ma'am, they are a bit rickety.'

Ruth nodded and followed him up the stairs, supporting herself with the wooden handrail that also served for protection from the drop on her left.

They reached a small landing. He knocked, paused and

opened a door. 'Lady to see you, sir,' he announced, and stood to one side so that Ruth could enter the room.

Ben was surprised. He was not expecting anyone, least of all a lady. He sprang from his chair when he saw her.

'Ruth, what are you doing here?' His eyes widened with surprise.

'I needed to see you.'

The door closed. He came to her and took her hands in his. He knew immediately from her response that something was wrong. 'What is it, Ruth? You are troubled.' As he was speaking he led her to a chair. 'Sit down, tell me and let me help.'

He waited for her to be seated and then perched himself on the edge of his desk.

'I only hope you can,' she said with a tremor in her voice.

'You know I will do all I possibly can. What is it?'

'It's apparent that you do not know what your father has done.'

Ben looked mystified. 'I know he is troubled and shaken by the loss of Martin and his crew, as we all are, but I do not know to what you refer.'

'Your father blames mine for what happened.'

Ben gave a little grimace of disgust as he offered an explanation, 'You heard Eric's outburst on the quay. He must have gone to Father with the same story, and Father's listened.'

'It's worse than that. He's dismissed my father from his command.'

'What?' The astonishment on Ben's face convinced her that he did not know.

'And there is worse. He's told Father that he will see he never commands another ship out of Whitby.'

'He couldn't!'

'He has. Father and my brothers have visited all the ship-owners in Whitby and not one of them would engage him. Your father acted fast and apparently made it obvious that he could ruin anyone who went against him.'

Ben was so taken aback that he did not know what to say.

'It will kill my Father if he cannot follow his trade,' Ruth went on. 'He can't be blamed for what happened. I'm here to ask you to get your father to change his mind. Please, Ben.'

He tried to hide his doubts about his own influence. He knew from personal experience that his father was a headstrong man who could be ruthless. He had been like that with Ben over his refusal to sail a second time. His attitude to someone outside the family, whom he blamed for the loss of his eldest son, was proving even more ruthless. 'I'll do what I can,' he replied, hoping that his tone would convince Ruth of his support. 'I don't condone what he has done, believe me. He must ascertain the true facts of what happened.'

'Will he get that when the crew of the *Water Nymph* believe that the consequences would be disastrous if any of them supported my father? He's more likely to believe his own son than the men.' The hopeless tone of her voice tugged at Ben's heart and mind.

'I'll try to get more of the story from Eric. It was his first whaling voyage. The shock of losing his brother would be all the harder to bear and would no doubt influence his reaction.'

'We do need your help, Ben. There is no one else to turn to.' Her face creased with anxiety. She was on the verge of tears.

'I'll do all I can, Ruth. Don't give up hope.'

She left, still not wholly convinced that the future held anything but disaster.

When she had gone Ben sat for a while pondering how he could get an unbiased opinion out of Eric and then how he should approach his father.

Realising that Sam would be at his office and that Eric was likely to be at home, Ben left his work and hurried to the house in New Buildings. He was thankful to find his brother there and came straight to the point. 'Eric, tell me what happened in the Arctic.'

Eric frowned. He did not want reminding, but from the way

114

his brother pressed him thought it was out of a genuine desire to know what had happened aboard the *Water Nymph*. He explained how the crew had believed it was time to be leaving the Arctic but said Captain Holmes insisted on staying because he wanted to return with a full ship.

Knowing Holmes's reputation for smelling out whales, Ben said, 'And he proved to be right?'

'Aye, but it delayed us.'

'Then what happened?'

'All the boats made a kill, with the exception of Martin's. He was fast to a whale that ran. So intent were we on the flensing that at first no one noticed he was no longer in sight. Captain Holmes sent a man aloft but he saw no sign of the boat. I believe Captain Holmes was thinking of a search until the lookout reported a change in the movement of the ice.' The thought of those moments when the ship turned away came back vividly to Eric. His voice rose, its tone hot with anger. 'Holmes could have stayed! He left Martin and his crew to perish. He's a murdering bastard! He ought to be made to pay!'

'Hold on, Eric. Be careful about making accusations. Remember, it was your first voyage to the Arctic. You'd had no experience of its ice and weather conditions. Captain Holmes had. I'm sure he would have searched if the *Water Nymph* had not been seriously threatened.'

Eric gave a grunt of derision. 'You weren't there! Who do you believe, your own brother or an incompetent captain who thought only of his safety and not that of his men?'

'But maybe that's just what he *was* thinking of? He had more than the crew of that whale-boat to consider.'

'Are you trying to make excuses for him? Don't you grieve for the loss of your own brother?

'Of course I do but—'

'There's no but about it!' Eric stormed from the room, disgusted that his brother appeared to be defending Holmes.

Ben stood thoughtfully by the fireplace. There were two sides to any story, each purporting to be the truth which usually lay somewhere in the middle. What was the truth here? If only he knew. The banging of the front door shook him out of his disturbing thoughts. Eric had left the house. So must he, to face his father.

Though greetings came his way as he hurried to his father's office, Ben merely returned them automatically. With his usual bonhomie missing, people assumed that the loss of his brother was preying heavily on his mind. It was true but in a different way from how they supposed.

He did not wait for the clerk to announce his arrival but went straight in to see his father.

Sam looked up from the figures he was analysing. Though Ben had been determined to plunge in with a criticism of his father's attitude to Captain Holmes, he was forestalled by his father's words. 'Ah, Ben, I'm surprised to see you here but now that you are, I can tell you what I was proposing to say this evening.'

Puzzled by his father's amiable attitude, as if no differences lay between them, Ben held back what he had planned to say. Following a friendly gesture from Sam, he sat down on the opposite side of the desk.

'Now that we no longer have Martin with us, you are my eldest son and heir. I hope that you will assume those responsibilities and that we can say goodbye to our differences. When you arrived I was studying the provisions in my will. I'm going to change it so that you all receive a share of what Martin would have inherited, and I will make over to you the shares he had in the business. In return I would like you to take more of an interest in it and become active in its running.' He held up his hand to stop Ben speaking. 'Hear me out before you say anything. As you once pointed out to me, you were not made for the sea. I wish I had respected your opinion at the time.'

Ben was stunned by this admission from his father, but as Sam continued had some idea why it had been made. 'This whaling voyage was to be Martin's last. He and I discussed this before he sailed. I wanted him to take a more active part in the business ashore. As much as he liked sailing aboard the whale-ships, he agreed.'

'I had no idea,' replied Ben, his head awhirl with this information and the fact that his father was casting aside all their differences and welcoming him to work alongside him.

'You couldn't have,' Sam agreed amiably. 'Martin and I only spoke about it shortly before he sailed. We were to say nothing about it until he returned.'

Wondering why, Ben raised one eyebrow.

'There was a very good reason for this. I've always nurtured the idea of having the strongest and most influential trading firm in Whitby, with a base that could widen even more as world trade expands.'

'And haven't you already?'

Sam gave a snort. 'I may have a strong company but there are those who would rival me. There is one such firm, operating in certain branches of trade where I do not operate. That firm and the trade it would bring with it would make me almost unassailable.'

'And what firm is it?' asked Ben when his father paused.

'Campion's.'

'What? Uncle Seaton's company?'

Sam nodded. 'Aye, that's the firm I want.'

Ben was amazed and puzzled. His father and Uncle Seaton, as the Coulson children had called him since childhood, were lifelong friends. The Campion firm could be no threat to Coulson's. Or did his father know something that he didn't? Rumours generally circulated around the trading fraternity in Whitby but nothing regarding these two firms had reached Ben's ears recently.

'I tried to buy Seaton out, but he wouldn't sell,' Sam went on. 'There had to be another way. I hit on an idea and put a proposal to Martin before he sailed. It linked up with my suggestion that he should give up going to sea.'

'And that was?' prompted Ben, his curiosity rising even further.

117

'Seaton has no sons to inherit his firm. It will go to his three daughters. Alicia, is the eldest and the one with the business acumen, so she will be the one who runs the business when her father retires. My proposal was that Martin should marry her, and he agreed.'

Ben was astounded. He knew marriages were sometimes arranged but had always regarded this as an audacious move to satisfy ambition without any thought for the feelings of the participants.

'What about Alicia? What was her reaction?'

'I spoke to Seaton after Martin had sailed. He agreed to my proposal. There is no need for you to know why, but he did.'

His father's remark made Ben suspicious. He knew Sam was not averse to using underhand methods, but had no time to consider this further as his father was continuing.

'I will just say that Alicia was in full agreement.'

'But now this scheme has fallen flat because of Martin's death?'

'Not exactly. I have suggested to Seaton that you should marry Alicia. I am sure she will agree.'

'Me?'

'Aye, lad. You are now taking Martin's place as successor to this firm so I expect you to do what he would have done.' Sam's tone had hardened in the certainty that he would be obeyed.

Ben knew that tone. It had raised rebellion in him in the past and now he could feel his defiance rising again. Protests rose to his lips but were never uttered. Discretion ruled. Reveal his relationship with Ruth Holmes now and his father would explode. The consequences would be dire. This was not even the time to plead for mercy for Captain Holmes. He needed time to think, to form a strategy, and then must wait for the right moment to make his defiance public.

'Very well, Father.'

His compliance, so easily given, surprised his father but he made no comment except to say, 'Good,' as he leaned back in his chair with a look of satisfaction on his face. 'You can see why we did not make any announcement until Martin returned. Now, of course, it doesn't matter when we do it. I think we will have to wait a respectable period to mourn those who were lost, however. I'll seek Seaton's opinion.'

And from what you've told me he'll dance to your tune, thought Ben. I wonder what hold you have over him?

Chapter Seven

'You're home early,' remarked Grace Campion when her husband walked in during the afternoon. Worry immediately assailed her, not only because of his unusually early arrival but also because of his serious expression.

'Is Alicia at home?' he asked, ignoring her remark.

'She's in her room. I sent her to have a rest. I think she was shocked by the news about Martin. After all, she was expecting to marry him.'

'Griselda and Dorothea?' put in Seaton quickly to pre-empt the questions he knew must be forming in his wife's mind.

'Visiting friends.'

'Good. Ring for some tea and ask Alicia to join us.'

'What is it, Seaton?'

'All in good time, just do as I say. I will join you in a few minutes.' He left the room, leaving his wife worried and curious.

She rang the bell and when the maid appeared, asked her to order some tea and then to tell Miss Alicia that she was wanted in the drawing-room

A few minutes later her daughter appeared. 'What is it, Mother?' she asked as soon as she entered the room.

'Your father is home and wants to speak with us.'

At that moment the door opened and two maids appeared bearing trays set for tea. They put them down and arranged the cups on a convenient table between the two settees that faced each other in front of the fireplace.

'Shall I pour, ma'am?' one of them asked.

'I'll do it, Abigail,' replied Grace.

The maids left the room. For something to do, Grace poured

the milk into the cups and put a spoonful of sugar into her husband's.

Alicia was silent. It had been a shock, yet something of a relief, to learn of Martin's death. He had been a lifelong friend though they had never been especially intimate. She had not shared the closeness with him that she had with Ben. She would have gone through with her father's wishes if only to prevent Sam Coulson from calling in her father's debt, but her proposed marriage to Martin did not include the element of attraction that a marriage should, so she found herself heart whole now that it would not take place. But what would happen with Sam? Would he call in his debt and shatter their lives?

Before she had time to ponder those questions the door opened and her father walked in.

'I had a visit from Sam Coulson early this morning,' he announced. 'I did not mention it before because I wanted to think about what he said. I've explained to you both how I came to agree to the marriage between Alicia and Martin to which you, Alicia, thankfully agreed. With the loss of Martin, Sam came to me with a new proposal.' He looked closely at his daughter. 'As Ben will now be his heir, he wants you to marry Ben. If you will agree to this, the rest of our agreement stands. I've tried to find another way to appease Sam but I cannot and therefore I am going to have to agree, but it is up to you, Alicia.'

Her mind was already racing. She wanted to shout 'Yes! Yes!' but had to keep her excitement under control. She could not let her parents be aware of her overwhelming joy. Ben, the man she wanted to marry, the man who had rejected her even though she had declared her love for him, would be hers! But what of him? Did he know of his father's proposal? And if so, had he accepted it?

'Does Ben know about this?' She had to put the question.

'He didn't when Sam spoke to me this morning, but he hinted that Ben would do as he was told.'

121

Alicia made no comment but wondered if he would indeed obey his father. He was headstrong, and had defied his father in the past. Would he do so now? There was a lot at stake. If he didn't agree, Alicia was sure he would lose his inheritance. But the loss of a brother might have engendered a more filial feeling in him. If it had, would Ruth Holmes continue to occupy a place in his heart? After all, her father had been in charge of the ship from which Martin had been lost.

'Well, Alicia, what have you to say?' her mother prompted.

She hesitated a moment then said, 'Of course I will, we can't let Mr Coulson ruin our lives.' She could sense the relief in her father and mother. 'When will it be?' she asked.

Seaton smiled. 'We hadn't got as far as arranging that. We did not know if you would agree. I have to see Sam with your decision first.'

They settled down to enjoy their tea.

'Any other news today, dear?' Grace asked.

'I heard that Sam is blaming Captain Holmes for Martin's loss and has dismissed him.'

'That's rather harsh, isn't it?'

'He's blaming Holmes for not searching. I don't know all the circumstances but I hear Sam has taken it so seriously he has threatened any fellow ship-owner with ruin if they engage Holmes.'

'Will they comply?'

'You know Sam, he can be ruthless.'

Alicia had sat quietly through this exchange. She foresaw that Ruth Holmes would no longer be a rival. Ben dare not reveal his relationship with her or he would feel the full weight of his father's anger. A relationship with the daughter of the man who had caused Martin's death would now be out of the question. Ben was hers and Ruth Holmes but a memory to him.

The future was settled. Their lives could go on as usual. They enjoyed their tea.

As he replaced his empty cup, Seaton stood up. 'It is still early, I'll go and give Sam his answer now. There is no sense in delaying.' He looked at his wife. 'When do you think the marriage should take place?'

'There will be a lot of things to see to: consultations with the vicar, the reception, Alicia's dress, bridesmaids, guest invitations . . . oh, dear, there is so much to do, I can't see it taking place before Christmas.'

'Oh, a Christmas wedding would be delightful,' put in Alicia.

'Think of the weather,' warned her father.

'It might be better to wait until spring,' her mother suggested.

Alicia nodded thoughtfully. 'Maybe you are right. But we should have some sort of celebratory party.'

'That would be most agreeable,' said Grace, 'but there should be a mourning period of six months.'

Alicia pouted, an expression that her father was just in time to see. 'Your mother is right, Alicia.'

'But if we had it here, just for the two families, say in four weeks, who would know?' she protested.

'Sam wants this marriage, so maybe he would agree. It's not as if Martin died at home,' said Grace. 'By the time of the party it will be almost two months since he was lost.'

'I'll see what Sam thinks,' said Seaton, 'but I won't press him. I don't want him to feel we are not sympathetic to him in his loss.'

Seaton knew he would still find his friend at work in his office.

'Ah, Seaton, come in.' Sam rose quickly from his seat when his clerk announced Mr Campion was here to see him. 'We meet again so soon.' He indicated a chair to his visitor.

'There is no need to waste time when I have an answer from Alicia for you.'

'No need at all,' agreed Sam. 'I sincerely hope her answer is positive?'

Though he left out the words 'for your sake', Seaton knew they were implied but chose to ignore the inference.

'It is. She has agreed to marry Ben. Have you spoken to him?'

'I have,' returned Sam. 'As I said, he'll do as he's told. Besides, I'm sure he sees life in a different light now that he is aware of his greater responsibilities as my heir. So I think you and I should drink to the future.' He went to a glass cabinet, took out two glasses and a decanter of Madeira. He poured the liquid and brought a glass to Seaton who stood up to receive it.

Sam raised his glass. 'To Alicia and Ben and the continued friendship of our two families.'

Seaton acknowledged the toast, and after they had each taken a token sip they sat down again.

'We think a spring wedding, but Alicia would like a cele-bratory party soon, say in a month's time? We pointed out to her that there should be a respectable period of mourning. She suggested we should keep the party to just our two families then no one else need know what it is really about. Grace and I said it would have to be your decision. If you decide in favour, Grace says we could hold it at our house and it will stay a very private affair.'

Sam had listened carefully. He remained bound up in his thoughts for a few moments longer. The sooner this betrothal took place the better; the nearer he would then be to his aim of controlling the biggest mercantile enterprise in Whitby.

'I appreciate your thoughtfulness about the period of mourning. While the loss is heavy in my heart, it is not the same as if Martin had died at home. There is not the immedi-ate impact. Besides, I've always thought that our observances relating to death are overdone. We cannot stand still because a wife, a mother, a daughter or a son has left us.' He gave a small pause. 'So let us have this meeting of our two families to celebrate an even closer union between us. Alicia has suggested a month from now – should we say four weeks on Friday?'

'I'll mention it to Grace but I'm sure that will be possible.'

'It should be a very special occasion, Seaton. One on which you will see me tear up those documents you saw on my desk . . . documents I'm sure you would not like anyone else to see. They shall be my engagement gift to Alicia. But I will still hold you to our partnership in the Spanish wine trade and have the documents drawn up to be signed that very night.

'However, there is one other thing. I would prefer that not a word of this should get out until after the party. I have some business nearing fruition and if word got around that our two firms will soon be working closely together, it would be injurious. So please tell your family to keep all this to themselves.'

'Consider it done,' replied Seaton.

Sam smiled and raised his glass.

Sam walked home a very satisfied man. Things had gone as he had planned except that Ben had taken the place of Martin. He had not always agreed with his second son's mode of life and had been angry at his refusal to sail with the whale-ships, but maybe he had misjudged Ben's capabilities. Maybe the additional responsibility he faced now would be the real making of him.

At home Sam sat in the drawing-room with the door ajar. He wanted a word with his son as soon as he heard him come home. He had not long to wait. On hearing Ben enter the house, he called to him. When Ben appeared, Sam told him to shut the door. 'I have some news for you. Seaton lost no time in making my proposal known to Alicia and she has agreed to marry you.'

Ben was taken aback. Things had moved faster than he had expected. He did not know what to say but discerned that this was not the time to disclose his feelings for Ruth. There must be another way out of the corner into which he had unwittingly been driven. He had not even started to contemplate this when his father announced, 'Mrs Campion is arranging an engagement party just for the two families four weeks on Friday.'

'So soon?' was all a bemused Ben could utter.

'Why not? If Martin had survived this is exactly what would have happened, so why shouldn't it now that you have taken his place? Oh, and by the way, no word of this engagement must get out before the party, so don't breathe a word until after the event.'

Ben shrugged his shoulders in a gesture of acceptance. His mind was racing. He had no doubt that Alicia, after her declaration of love for him, was pleased with the way things had worked out. She would be aching to tell her friends. Thank goodness for the restriction! Only four weeks to solve everything! He must see Ruth, and the sooner the better. Thankfully he had come home early. It was only five o'clock and there would be plenty of daylight yet in which to meet if only he could get word to her.

When he left the drawing-room he went to find Sarah. Relief flooded through him when he saw her coming up the front path. He hurried outside to meet her.

'Sarah, I want a favour from you.'

She looked at him curiously, wondering why there was such urgency in his tone and expression. 'If I can.'

'Walk with me.' He took her by the elbow and turned her back towards the gate. He said no more until they were away from the house.

'I want you to get a message to Ruth Holmes.'

Sarah stopped. 'What?' She frowned. 'You want me to go to her house?'

'That's right.'

'From what I've heard today, a Coulson won't be welcome there.'

'I know, but I think there would be less hostility to you.'

'What's this all about?'

'Let's keep walking.' He started off and she fell into step beside him. 'I can't explain but I need to see Ruth urgently.'

'Why can't you explain?' she asked, hurt that he did not trust her.

'Believe me, Sarah, I would if I could. You'll understand one day. Please trust me and just accept what I have said.'

'All right. You must be very keen on her,' she commented.

'I am. Sarah, I love her.'

'You'll be defying Father, wanting to marry the daughter of the man he blames for Martin's death. If you do, the consequences could be catastrophic for you. He'd cut you off without a penny and see that you got no help from anyone in Whitby, just as I hear he has warned people from employing Captain Holmes. Think carefully on it, Ben. I know you liked Alicia once and I thought you and she—'

'I know,' he cut in. 'But then I met Ruth.'

'The day you watched the *Water Nymph* sail?'

'Yes.'

'I thought there must be more to it when you took her to the ball instead of Alicia. I know you have been seeing her since then. I'd thought you might be ready to make an announcement. Maybe it would have been better if you had.'

'Ruth wanted to wait until her father came home. We did not expect such a tragedy to affect our lives.'

'Of course you didn't, but now you've got a terribly awkward situation to deal with. What can I do to help?'

'Give me your understanding, and get a message to Ruth for me.'

'I'll do what I can.'

'Get word to her to meet me at the West Pier in a few minutes.'

They had reached the bridge, two figures in earnest conversation who raised no curiosity in any of the folk hurrying about their business in the late-afternoon.

'What if she isn't at home? I couldn't leave a message.'

'Let's hope she is.'

Sarah started across the bridge and Ben headed slowly towards the West Pier, his mind in turmoil as to how Ruth would take this news.

Sarah considered her brother's quandary. Would love or loyalty to the Coulson family prevail? If he chose the latter, could he come to love Alicia? Once she'd thought he did, but that was before Ruth came on the scene. Could that love for Alicia be revived and strengthened, bringing the two families closer? If his love for Ruth prevailed, what would happen to the Coulson empire? Sam would be sure to denounce him. Eric, capable in some ways, did not show the ability or the sense of responsibility needed to run the business. Much hung on Ben's decision, even Sarah's own future and that of Dina.

By the time all these questions had risen in her mind Sarah found herself in Grape Lane. She paused. What should her tactic be to get the message to Ruth? A decision made, she walked firmly to the front door and rapped hard with the whale-shaped knocker. The door was answered by a maid who looked enquiringly at her.

'If Miss Ruth Holmes is at home, will you tell her that there is a young lady who wants to see her and that I will be waiting at the end of the street? You must deliver this message to her personally so that no one else hears it.'

The girl was mystified by the unusual request, but her responsibility was not to question, only to do as she was told. She should be wary about passing on such a message but this lady was well-dressed and had a kindly face. 'I'll see what I can do, ma'am.'

Sarah took that for a sign that Ruth was at home.

The maid started to close the door.

Sarah spoke up. 'Tell no one of this visit. Miss Holmes will want it that way and she will know if you speak of it.'

'Yes, ma'am.' The girl closed the door but not before noting which direction Sarah took.

She strolled to the end of Grape Lane. In a few minutes she saw Ruth hurrying towards her.

Ruth's face was troubled, she was clearly wondering who had sent such an unusual request. Her features brightened with relief when she saw Sarah.

'It was you?'

She nodded. 'Yes. Ben wants to see you. He asked me to deliver the message, thinking it unwise for him to come to the house or even be seen near it.'

'That was thoughtful of him. I'm sure Father and my brothers would have been angry had he appeared.'

'He is waiting at the West Pier. I'll walk with you.' They started off. 'I'm so sorry for what has happened, Ruth. I want you to know that the loss of Martin weighs heavily on our hearts but neither I nor Dina condone what Father has done. And I think you know that Ben doesn't.'

'I thank you for your support. I don't know if he told you that I went to see him, to ask if he could try to get your father to change his mind. I expect that's what he wants to see me about now. I hope he's been successful.'

Sarah made no comment to this but said only, 'Ruth, if you don't mind my asking, and you don't have to answer this question if you don't want to, do you love my brother?'

'From the moment I saw him that day on the quay,' she replied without hesitation.

The statement was made so positively and with such sincerity that Sarah knew it to be the truth. She also realised that she herself hoped that love would survive the trails and tribulations that must lie ahead if they declared their love for each other publicly.

Ben stopped his nervous pacing when he saw them and hurried to meet them. He shot his sister a look of appreciation and then gazed with love and concern in his eyes at Ruth. 'Thank you for coming.'

'What is it, Ben? Has it to do with what we talked about earlier?' There was hope in her voice.

Before he answered Sarah spoke. 'Do you want me to wait?'

'I'll see Ruth home,' replied Ben.

His sister said her goodbyes and started back.

'Let's walk,' said Ben, taking Ruth's hand and setting off at a strolling pace along the stone pier.

'Why have I a feeling that this is something terribly serious?'

'Maybe because it is. Even more so than getting my father to rescind the blame he places on yours.'

'What could be more important than that?'

'You and me.'

She stopped and looked hard at him. 'Ben Coulson, say what you have to say.'

'Ruth, my father and Mr Seaton Campion have arranged a marriage between Alicia and myself.'

'What?'

'It's true.' He went on to explain the reasons as he knew them.

'So this is just to fulfil your father's ambitions,' snapped Ruth indignantly. 'Have you agreed?'

'No.'

She detected that this one word did not tell everything. 'But you've raised no objection?'

He looked embarrassed.

'You would have done if you truly loved me,' she declared firmly, withdrawing her hand from his and making no attempt to disguise the fact that she was bitterly hurt.

'Ruth, I do love you, more than anyone else on this earth.'

'Then why didn't you declare it when your father arranged this marriage? Or is it that you see your own future being wrecked if you announce your love for Gideon Holmes's daughter? For be sure if you do, your father will cut you off without a penny.'

'Ruth, hear me out, please.' He took her hand in his and gripped it firmly. There was pleading in his eyes. 'Believe me, I wanted to tell him about you, but I knew it would spoil my chances of getting him to change his mind about your father. If I agree I could use this marriage as a lever to get him to reinstate your father. I would say I would not marry Alicia unless Father agreed to do so.'

She was stunned, staring at him in amazement, admiring him for the sacrifice he was willing to make. But it also meant she would have to make one too. 'You would do that for my father?'

'No, for you. I know how much he means to you.'

'Ben Coulson, I love you, not just because of what you are prepared to do but because you are you. You are not to do that!

I want you and I'm going to have you. And besides, my father would never agree to our sacrificing our love for his sake.'

'Thank you.' He took her in his arms and kissed her. 'I love you, Ruth Holmes. The future will be ours. But you know what it will mean. Even if you can persuade your family to let you marry a Coulson, we'll be near poverty at first until the ropery and my other assets can be made profitable.'

'I have faith in you, Ben. I want nothing more than to be with you, no matter what the circumstances.'

'With that love between us we'll overcome anything.'

'What happens now?'

'Say nothing yet to anyone, not even your family. I'll see how the situation develops.'

'Are you sure?'

'Yes.'

'Don't let it get out of hand.'

'Trust me, I won't.'

They let the situation lie there and it was not mentioned again as Ben took her home. At the corner of Grape Lane she stopped and said, 'Better not come any further, Ben.'

'As you wish, my love.'

Chapter Eight

Ben was surprised to find his father still at the breakfast table when he entered the dining-room the next morning. He had always known Sam to be an early riser, away to the office before the rest of the family had appeared or, at least, were crossing the hall as he was leaving the house. Ben had expected him to be gone this morning. He really did not want to have any sort of dealings with him today. Worries had woken him on more than one occasion during the night or had haunted his dreams and he still had much to think about.

'Good morning, Ben.' The light tone of his father's voice surprised him, almost catching him off guard. This was quite alien to the usual attitude he displayed towards the son who had disappointed him.

'Good morning, Father,' Ben returned automatically as he sat down and reached for the teapot.

'I purposely waited for you. Though you have shown little direct interest in my business, I have no doubt that you know something of what I do to earn the money that keeps you and your brother and sisters in such style. Now, as my heir, you are going to have to get to know it in more detail. I thought it best for you to start right away.'

A maid appeared, having been alert for any of the family coming into the dining-room. Before she could take Ben's breakfast order the rest of the family arrived. The maid was pleased for it meant that this morning the meal would not drag on and she would be able to get on with her other work sooner than usual. She took their orders and left.

Ben could see questions forming in Sarah's eyes but knew

she would not voice them until they were alone.

'I'm glad you are all here,' said Sam, settling himself more comfortably in his chair. 'I have an announcement to make. Prepare yourselves for a party at the Campions' four weeks on Friday.'

Dina's and Sarah's eyes brightened with excitement. They were always ready to enjoy such occasions.

Eric frowned and put a note of objection in his voice. 'Should we be attending a party so soon after losing Martin? Shouldn't we be observing the proper period of mourning?'

His father adopted a gentle tone for his reply. 'Eric, we mourn Martin, and it is right that we do, though I believe we attach too much importance to timing such observances. Life must go on, it is for the living. The world does not stand still because of one person's death. My enterprises must continue, commerce won't grind to a halt, because we have lost Martin. We can still mourn in our own private ways. You can all buy new mourning clothes on my account. I think this party, which is just for our two families, should mark the end of our mourning. When I tell you the reason, I think you will understand.'

Now Sam's daughters and youngest son were even more curious.

'The party is to celebrate the engagement of Alicia to Ben.' The atmosphere in the dining-room became charged with astonishment, excitement and questions. Sam called for quiet so that he could add a warning. 'No word of it must get out before the party. This is of vital importance. I cannot emphasise that strongly enough. If it does, a great deal of hard work will be ruined and certain opportunities lost. There is no need for you to know exactly what is involved. Mr Campion has agreed to this and will tell his family to honour it too.'

Congratulations came in Ben's direction. He was the only one who read much more behind Sarah's words, for in her gaze at him he saw the questions she wanted to voice. So this is why you needed to meet Ruth yesterday. You couldn't tell me because of father's embargo. Why has he made it? Do you

133

know what lies behind it? What did you tell Ruth? She loves you and you love her. And Alicia – she has got who she wants, but do you want her?

Ben wanted to tell his sister so much but knew it would have to wait. Now he had to accompany his father to the office.

Immediately he saw Ben's clean plate and empty cup, Sam stood up. 'It's best if we are away.' He cast his gaze across the others. 'Have a pleasant day.' He strode to the door and Ben, with a rueful look at Sarah, followed him.

They shrugged themselves into their redingotes and collected their high-crowned hats. Ben stood at the front door while his father picked up his stick. They left the house, making their way down the hill to Baxtergate which was already alive with people. The shops were busy and the air was filled with the smells of baking, spices and leather, all mingling with the tang of salt drifting in from the sea. Noise abounded with shopkeepers calling their wares, and the scolding words of mothers directed at children who consistently refused to behave themselves. The whole cacophony was overlaid by the screech of seagulls that became more prominent in Coulson ears as Sam and Ben neared the bridge. The birds wheeled and floated lazily on the currents of air then swooped down to the deck of a ship or swept across the water to grab a tasty morsel. The tide was in, filling the river on which craft of various types plied their way between the two riverbanks or headed for positions at the quays and staithes. Much activity was centred on two merchant ships that were taking on cargoes destined for London and the Continent.

Sam paused on the bridge to admire the *Water Nymph*. 'Thank goodness she came to no harm.'

Though the words were said half to himself, Ben caught them. They brought a surge of hope that made him voice his next question: 'Then you believe Captain Holmes did the right thing?'

Sam stiffened. He had not considered what could be inferred from his remark. 'Certainly not, Holmes should never have left Martin and his crew.'

Ben's hopes sagged. 'But that could have endangered the *Water Nymph* and then she would not be lying safe and sound at her quay now.'

Sam glared at him. 'Are you trying to make excuses for Holmes? He should have kept a sharper lookout when he saw the whale towing Martin's craft away from the ship. He should have sent another boat-crew to help or else gone himself. It was sheer negligence on his part and I'll hear nothing in his favour. He cost me a son!' With that he turned and continued across the bridge.

Ben stared after him for a moment, then, with a heart heavy at the prospect of being unable to carry good news to Ruth, he followed.

'Good day, sir,' chorused the two clerks, looking up from their ledgers which were open on high sloping desks in the first room to the right in the building that housed the offices of Coulson and Sons, Merchants.

The second door was also open. Seamus Telford always had it that way until Mr Coulson arrived so that not a moment would be wasted. He heard Mr Coulson return the clerks' greeting and was on his feet in the doorway by the time Sam and Ben reached it.

'Good morning, sir. Good morning, Mr Ben.'

'Good morning, Seamus,' Sam returned as he swept past his manager. Sam had recognised Seamus as trustworthy when he had first engaged him in the expanding firm twelve years ago. His faith in this small, rotund man who stood just five foot three inches had been well-founded. Seamus was a loyal servant who could take on additional responsibility when necessary. Sam admired his efficiency, and the order he had brought to every aspect of the firm so that it always ran smoothly.

Ben followed his father into the main office. He was familiar with it, having visited it from early childhood, though with the rift between father and son during more recent years his visits had ceased. Now that he found it just as he remembered it, a touch of nostalgia tightened his chest.

They were shedding their coats when Seamus came in. He had been surprised to see Ben accompanying his father. He had heard raised voices coming from this very office when Ben had refused to sail with the whale-ships ever again after his first voyage. Now he was back and taking off his coat as if he meant to stay. Were father and son on amiable terms again with their differences forgotten?

'Ah, Seamus,' said Sam as he took his place behind his desk, 'it was my intention that once the *Water Nymph* returned Martin should forsake the sea and take on additional responsibility ashore. Alas that was not to be. Now Ben is heir to all this he will become involved as his brother would have done. I want you to pass on to him as much knowledge of the firm and its workings as you can.'

'Very good, sir.' He turned to Ben. 'And might I welcome you to your new position? I am sure that, from past visits here, you are reasonably familiar with what the firm does and how it works. You will be less familiar with developments during the last few years, but that can soon be rectified. I wish you every success and hope you will be happy here. If there is anything you want to know, do ask. I am at your disposal.'

'Thank you, Seamus. I am sure we will get on famously,' returned Ben, his outward demeanour bright and eager, knowing he must hide from outsiders and his father any private unease.

'Then you can start right away. Leave those papers with me, Seamus,' Sam indicated the sheets that he had brought with him, 'and sort out the office next door for Ben.'

'Yes, sir.' Seamus handed over the papers and glanced at Ben with a look that meant, Follow me.

The two men left the office and Seamus led the way to the next room.

Ben found it very similar to his father's, though here all the furniture and decorations were new. He realised that his father had had it prepared for Martin. For one moment Ben was filled with apprehension. He felt he was stepping into a dead man's shoes. Would he be able to fill them adequately? No sooner had that question posed itself than he realised that if a life with Ruth were to materialise it would be irrelevant, for his father would not tolerate him in this building nor even his own home.

'Sir, is this suitable for you?' Seamus interrupted his thoughts.

'Perfectly.'

'If you would like anything changing, please let me know.'

'Thank you, Seamus. Now, my father seems keen for me to get started. Where do we begin?'

'Well, I suggest that I explain the trading that is underway, the contracts that have been signed and which ships we will be using. You will need to know if we are exporting and importing goods that we have bought or whether we are merely acting as shipping agents.'

'I know we used to do both in the past. Since my disagreement with my father . . .'

'I was always sorry about that, Mr Ben.'

He gave a dismissive wave of his hand. 'It is over and done with,' he said, but in his mind foresaw an even bigger rift opening up. 'So,' he went on, 'do we still do both?'

'Oh, yes. We have expanded both methods of trading. Our newest enterprise is an agreement with Mr Seaton Campion to deal as one in high-class Spanish wines.'

Ben raised an eyebrow. This was a surprise to him. Uncle Seaton had always prided himself on having exclusive rights to dealing in high-class Spanish wines coming into Whitby. It was something he'd jealously guarded. How had his father persuaded him to share this trade? What had Sam used to prise open the door to what Ben judged to be a highly profitable enterprise?

'This is certainly a new venture for my father. I thought Mr Campion had exclusive rights?' commented Ben.

'It was a surprise to me too. I don't know how it came about, but trading agreements have been signed and sealed.'

'Good. Does this mean we will ship more wine, and if so have we customers who will buy it?'

137

'The quantity will depend on the harvest and its yield. We will have no trouble in selling. Mr Campion brings his usual customers with him and I know your father has some ideas about expansion and shipping on, but what they are I don't know.'

Trust Father to grasp this opportunity, no matter how it had come about. Was it linked to the proposed marriage between Alicia and Martin into whose place he had had to step? Ben was left to ponder.

His day was full, most of it spent with Seamus except at midday when his father took him to dine at the Angel so that he could parade his son as an important new participant in the firm of Coulson and Sons. He wanted the other merchants and ship-owners who used the Angel to know that, in spite of his loss, there was another young man who would step into his shoes one day.

On this first day Ben's eyes were opened to the extent of his father's business. Since their rift his cognisance of the business had been limited but now he began to realise what a shrewd manipulator his father was, and that he had sailed very near the wind on several occasions. It made Ben wonder about the deals his father had cited as the reason not to mention the proposed marriage until after the party.

Even as information flowed to him from Seamus, Ben's mind continually drifted to Ruth and the problem facing them.

Gideon Holmes also faced a situation in which a decision about the family's future would have to be made. As they were all involved he and Georgina had decided to raise the matter when they were all together at breakfast.

'You have all realised that I am not going to get another position as a captain sailing out of Whitby,' said Gideon. 'Sam Coulson has seen to that. And I doubt if anyone would dare sign me on even as a deckhand.'

'Why don't we leave Whitby?' put in Daniel, the conviction in his voice showing that he was certain this was the solution.

Edmund and Abel added their agreement. It was obvious to Gideon and Georgina that the boys had been discussing the future between themselves. Rachel nodded her approval. Georgina noted that only Ruth appeared to show no reaction to what was being said.

Gideon held up his hand to stop the discussion. 'Your mother and I have considered that. It was one thought that came immediately to mind. While it does seem to be the obvious solution, it would also give the impression that we were running away and thereby condoning Sam Coulson's opinion that I was to blame for the loss of his son and the other members of that crew. We are not prepared to do that.

'Besides, although your mother and I came originally from Hull, Whitby has become our home. We do not want to leave it. If all had been as normal following a successful whaling voyage, we would now have been discussing another matter – a move to the west side of the river.' He smiled when he saw the surprised looks on the faces around the table. 'For some time it has been your mother's desire to move to a better position, to a house with views across the town. Before we sailed I had promised her that when I got back we would seriously consider it. With no adequate source of income we cannot do so now but I am determined to fulfil your mother's dream. How I will attain it I do not know, but one day I will.'

Silence descended on the room. Everyone agreed with Gideon that the move their mother had long desired was well-merited, but it was unclear how it would ever come about now.

Georgina was the first to speak. Her eyes were damp. 'Thank you, Gideon.' He could not mistake her sincere love and belief in him as her eyes met his.

'Edmund, Abel and I will get jobs ashore to support you and our sisters until another alternative is found.' Daniel's suggestion received nods of agreement.

'That is most generous of you all,' replied Gideon, 'but I won't have it. You are sailors at heart and are particularly drawn to the whaling trade. I will not have you forfeit that and the possibilities of promotion. You have your own lives to lead. Your mother and I discussed various things I could do and the one which we think holds the best promise is for me to become a fisherman.' He gave a little laugh when he saw doubt in their expressions. 'It's what I started out as in Hull before I graduated to the whaling trade.'

'Then let us stop here and help you,' put in Edmund.

His father shook his head. 'No. I want you to follow your own ambitions and I know they rest with the whale-ships. You must not give that up. I will buy a one-man boat and keep to inshore fishing, or maybe try and find two partners.'

'If we stayed, we could sail with you.' Abel's words were full of youthful enthusiasm.

'Son, that would cost more money, money that we do not have.'

He looked a little dejected but accepted his father's point.

'I advise you to get signed on for the voyages that I am sure the whale-ships will be doing to the Baltic for timber before winter closes those ports.' He glanced at his daughters. 'Girls, support your mother with understanding. Times will be a little hard until I can find a boat and a market for the fish I'll catch.'

'Ben, I'm going to Newcastle for a few days to see if we can expand our collier trade. I see more and more coal being needed in London; more ships will be wanted, and we build them in our shipyards here in Whitby. More ships mean more ropes. While I'm away, consider bringing your ropery fully into our business. It could be much more lucrative than having to deal with separate contractors.'

Ben nodded thoughtfully but made no comment. He could see the ropery would be an asset to his father's business, but it was vital to his own plan to marry Ruth. The ropery would be their only means of income, apart from a few minor investments, for his father was sure to cut him off without a penny.

'You are in charge while I'm away,' Sam went on. 'Seamus

tells me you are a quick learner, but if there is anything you are doubtful about, ask him.'

'I will. Are there any negotiations pending that I should know of?'

Sam pursed his lips as if he was considering something and then shook his head and said, 'No.'

Ben figured from his hesitation and the way he drew the word out that something had sprung to his father's mind, so decided to fish for the unspoken information. 'What about the deals you hinted at when you requested that the engagement be kept quiet until after the party?'

'You needn't worry about those.'

'But supposing something does come up? I could easily make a slip if I'm not aware of what they are. Knowing will put me on my guard.'

Sam considered Ben's reasoning. He supposed that could happen. 'All right, but you must keep this strictly to yourself. The only other people who know are the three people concerned and Seamus.'

'Seamus?' Ben allowed an expression of surprise to cross his face.

'Yes. He has been with me a considerable length of time and is entirely trustworthy. I pay him well and he would never wish to jeopardise that. In briefing you, he has not mentioned these pending negotiations?' Sam did not wait for an answer, he knew it already. 'There, that is proof of his loyalty.'

'So, are you going to tell me?'

'You know Blacket and Rose?'

'Yes. They trade in alum.'

'Wadworth and Worthy?'

'Also alum traders.'

'Aye.'

'Are you trying to buy them out?'

Sam did not answer his question immediately. 'Who is the biggest dealer in the alum trade?'

'Uncle Seaton.'

'Correct. Now, if Blackett and Rose, and Wadsworth and Worthy, were to get to know that Seaton and I are close to amalgamation, even though it is to be through marriage, they would see that their supplies along with Seaton's alum would make us the most powerful force in that trade. It would set more value on their companies and they would expect me to pay more for their wares. Not knowing of the link with Campion's, however, the price they will take will be less, so I stand to gain by keeping the news of your engagement quiet. The negotiations will be completed before that date. I have a meeting to finalise and sign the agreements a week before your engagement becomes public knowledge.'

'There is not likely to be any query before then?'

'I have put my proposition to both firms and it is only a matter of signing as far as I can see. I don't expect any queries.'

'What if they pull out at the last minute? How will that leave Uncle Seaton?' Ben paused then added quickly, 'I suppose he knows?'

'No, he doesn't. I wanted to keep these deals as close to my chest as possible. The negotiators for the two firms know the whole thing will collapse if word gets out and then they will lose what appears to them a lucrative deal.'

'And Uncle Seaton?' Ben pressed again. 'This looks as if you are moving more and more into his territory. I thought you had an unwritten agreement with him that you both followed certain trades and never impinged on each other?'

'That was long ago. Times change,' was the only comment Sam made. He pushed himself from the table, stood up and glanced at his son. 'You look after things, Ben, it will all be worth your while.'

'When are you leaving?'

'I'm sailing in half an hour on the *Lady Anne* bound for Newcastle.'

'I'll come and see you off.'

'No, Ben, coming to the quay to see me sail is a waste of time and time is money. Yours will be better spent at the office.

I worked late yesterday and have left information with Seamus about some negotiations I'd like you to see to. And you may as well start to put the transfer of your ropery to Coulson and Sons in to motion.'

Ben nodded, knowing it was not good pointing out that his offer to accompany him to the ship was a gesture towards a closer relationship. His father left the room. Ben shrugged his shoulders. What did a closer relationship matter when that would soon be shattered when he announced he was going to marry Ruth Holmes?

Should he have done so before his father left for Newcastle? His lips tightened. That was not really the way he wanted to do it, for he knew it could bring his father's wrath down not only on him but also the Holmes family. There had to be another way, a situation in which a fait accompli was created. That could only mean marriage before the party without anyone knowing, but there wasn't time for them to fulfil the conditions necessary for the banns to be read, even at a distant church so that their families would not know.

Ben tried to solve the dilemma as he walked to the office but was no nearer a solution by the time he was saying, 'Good morning,' to the clerks and Seamus.

As the manager followed Ben into his office, he said, 'The weather looks set fine for your father's voyage. I hope being on board ship will make him relax for a while. He puts in such a lot of work. Maybe bringing you into the firm will take some of the load from him.'

'Before he left he told me he had been working late yesterday and has left some things for me to see to.'

'Yes, I have them here.' Seamus laid some papers in front of Ben. 'The easy matter I have placed on top. It is the documents I have had drawn up regarding the transfer of your ropery to this firm.'

Ben raised an eyebrow. 'You've got on to that quickly.'

'Your father mentioned the possibility and told me to see that the necessary papers were ready before he left for

Newcastle. I did that with Broadbent the attorney whom your father told me to contact for this particular transaction because he would deal with it quickly.'

I'm not surprised, thought Ben. Broadbent knows which side his bread is buttered on. But those documents would require his signature and he was not about to deal with that immediately. He glanced at the papers, and those referring to the ropery he laid to one side. He looked up at Seamus who was standing beside him. 'These?'

'There is a small firm of jet makers in Flowergate that went under the name of Jepson, Jet-workers. Your father heard they were in difficulties and, thinking he might be able to take the business over at a bargain price, looked into the situation. He found that the firm was owned by two brothers and a cousin, and that there had been certain irregularities in the book-keeping which was looked after by the cousin.'

'How did my father find this out?'

'Ah, Mr Ben, I don't know. I may be trusted with most things but there are still certain aspects of his affairs your father does not reveal to me.'

Ben nodded. 'Go on,' he prompted.

'Your father approached the brothers with this information and suggested that they should prosecute their cousin. They would not, as it would bring shame on the family and a term in prison for their relative. Your father suggested that the only way for them to come out of this situation without further embarrassment was to allow him to pay off the debts incurred by their cousin, and that if he did that he would expect them to sell him the firm. Eventually they agreed and those papers in front of you refer to the settling of the debts and the transfer of the firm. Your father would like you to see to everything related to them.'

'Very well. Thank you, Seamus.'

The manager left him. As the door closed Ben leaned back in his chair, rested his elbows on the arms of the chair, and stared thoughtfully at the papers. Trust his father to learn of these things and profit from other people's misfortunes.

After five minutes, during which his mind skipped between the work in front of him and thoughts of Ruth, he flicked his fingers over the documents relating to the jet works. Irregularities? He wondered what they were. It really was no concern of his. His father had completed the transaction and had merely left him to finalise it. Ben started to peruse the papers but could not get the thought out of his mind that his father had used this knowledge for his own ends. There was nothing illegal about it but it did not rest easy with Ben and he began to wonder if there were any other such situations that his Sam Coulson had taken advantage of to build up his empire. And that turned his mind to the deal his father had made with Uncle Seaton. Had there been any irregularities there? Surely not? He knew his 'Uncle' as being beyond reproach; a man highly respected within the Whitby community and in trading circles beyond. Ben also knew he was proud of holding the exclusive rights to a lucrative trade in certain high-class Spanish wines. So why had he agreed to let Sam into that business? Curious, Ben rose from his desk and went to the manager's office.

'Seamus, what do you know of my father's venture into the Spanish wine trade? It was something he had never considered until recently.'

Seamus gave a slight shake of his head. 'I don't know any of the details. Your father conducted all the negotiations with Mr Campion himself. I've never seen any documents relating to that side of the venture.'

Ben pondered that information. It seemed strange that Seamus knew so little about it when he was otherwise very well-informed.

'It appears to have been generated shortly after he came back from London earlier this year. Do you know why he was there?'

'I know he went to see some London merchants about the sugar trade but I don't imagine the deal with Mr Campion arose from that.'

'I suppose not,' commented Ben. 'Were there no documents at all?'

'Oh, yes, but they are straightforward agreements that establish a firm called Whitby Wine Importers with Mr Sam Coulson and Mr Seaton Campion as shareholders. There were also agreements with the London firm of Johnson and Flanders that Whitby Wine Importers had the exclusive rights to ship special wines from Spain for Johnson and Flanders.'

'May I see them?'

'Certainly, sir. I'll bring them to you in a few minutes.'

Ben was thoughtful when Seamus had left the room. Had something else arisen during that visit to London that no one else knew about? Ben's enquiring mind was starting to get the better of him. He really must curb his curiosity and imagination.

Seamus brought the documents and left him to peruse them. He saw that they were all signed and witnessed correctly. He could see nothing untoward about them and yet he could not help wondering why Uncle Seaton had gone into this partnership. The only reason Ben could think of was that his father had established contact with the London firm and persuaded his friend to consider a deal that would prove particularly lucrative. He was still surprised that Seaton Campion had agreed, for until now both men had kept their trading only on 'friendly rivals' terms. This deal seemed to speak of something else. But what? Did his father know something that he was able to use to persuade Seaton to comply? Irregularities? Ben dismissed that idea. Uncle Seaton ran an above-board company, but the word stuck in his mind.

Later that day it persisted so strongly that Ben threw aside the papers on which he was working. He was sure that he had heard that word somewhere before but in a different context. Where, and to what had it related?

He left the office. Work could wait. It would only confuse him when he had more important personal matters to see to. He must find a solution quickly.

He crossed the bridge to the west side of the river and headed for the pier, oblivious to the activity around him as the word 'irregular' crowded his mind again. Was it trying to tell him something? By the time he turned for home he was no nearer to answering that question.

'Ruth, come and sit down, I think we should talk.' Georgina, who had kept an eye on her daughter during this past week, seized her opportunity when they were alone in the house. Gideon had gone to look at a boat he might purchase for fishing. His sons, who would be sailing to the Baltic in two days' time, had gone with him. Fortunately Sam had not extended his vengeance as far as their future employment, which was one blessing. Rachel was visiting a friend. They sat down side by side on the sofa in the drawing-room.

'You are looking peaky, are you not feeling well?' Georgina enquired.

'I am perfectly well, Mother.'

'Then I can only conclude this has something to do with Ben Coulson.'

Alarm flickered in Ruth's eyes as she looked up at her mother. 'You haven't told Father?'

'No, I haven't. Nor shall I until the truth of what happened in the Arctic is known. To mention the name Coulson to him now would be like showing a red rag to a bull. Though he loves you very much, I dread to think what his reaction might be if he found out that you have been seeing Ben Coulson.'

'Oh, Mother, what can I do? What really happened in the Arctic may never be known.'

'I think it might be wise for you to go to your aunt's for a while. The change of air would do you good and you would have time to think your problem out. A separation would help you to see where your love truly lies.'

'Mother, I know where my love lies, it is with Ben,' replied Ruth a little testily. 'And I don't need a change of air or scene.'

Georgina raised her hands in a gesture of retreat. 'All right, love, it was only a suggestion. Forget it. But if ever you change your mind, I'll write to your aunt.'

'Thank you. Sorry I snapped.'

Georgina gave her daughter a sympathetic smile and said, 'Come here.' She held out her arms to which Ruth came willingly, gaining comfort and a feeling of security from the embrace. 'Love can hurt. Be sure you and Ben love each other enough to face your father when the time comes.'

Those words haunted Ruth over the next two days. She knew she loved Ben with all her heart, but did he love her as much? He had said so and had asked her to marry him, but could he keep to that under the pressure he must now be experiencing? She must see him. Time would fly even faster as the day of the engagement party drew nearer.

Ben was troubled by the same thought, that time was speeding by too quickly. He wanted to able to tell Ruth that he had found a solution to their problems but that seemed to be eluding him.

He had left the documents relating to the acquisition of the jet works on his desk untouched. He really must check them again and visit the Brothers Jepson to finalise the signing. As he fingered the papers the word 'irregularities' crept into his mind again. He started. Why had it done so? Was it trying to tell him that there was something wrong about this deal? He scanned the papers quickly. No. Everything was correct. He recalled that he had wondered where he had heard the word before. Why was that concerning him?

For one moment he stiffened. Enlightenment can come in strange ways. His whole body tensed with realisation, then relaxed as his mind told him that what he had recalled had no bearing on the present situation. But maybe it did . . . He had to find out. Ben leaped to his feet and left his office. He paused at Seamus's room to tell him he was going out and may not be back for the rest of the day.

He lost no time in donning his coat and hat, and left the building at a brisk pace. He kept that up until he reached the

Church Stairs. The climb slowed him a little but his determination to see the Vicar, once the daily morning service was finished, urged him on. He arrived at the top of the steps breathless and needed to stop to ease his heaving lungs before he entered the church.

Realising that the service was almost finished, he sat down in a pew at the back of the church. With his mind occupied with the question he would put to the Vicar he hardly heard the intoning of the prayers. He became aware that the small congregation was leaving and that he had not even noticed the Vicar preceding them. He rose from the pew, knowing he would find the clergyman outside acknowledging the worshippers who had attended his service. He waited until the last one had left.

'Ah, Mr Ben Coulson, I've never seen you at my morning service except on Sundays. I hope this will be the start of weekday visits.' The cleric was rubbing his skeletal hands together as he spoke and his deep sunken eyes seemed to reproach Ben.

He ignored the jibe and instead said, 'Some weeks ago you gave a sermon on marriage.'

The Vicar broke in before Ben could say more. 'Yes Yes, indeed. A sacred institution that should never be taken lightly.'

'I seem to recall that you mentioned irregular marriages . . .'

'Indeed I did. I was referring to the practice prior to 1754 when marriages could be conducted anywhere by anyone and did not need witnesses. In fact, all that was required was the consent of the couple themselves.' The Vicar paused in his explanation and asked, 'Why do you ask me this?'

'I came across some documents relating to the family of a person with whom we are dealing.' Ben's mind had raced to provide what he hoped was a plausible explanation. 'There was mention of a marriage and the words used were what you have just said "by consent of the couple".'

'Was there a date on this document?'

'Yes, 1798.'

The vicar looked shocked. 'If this was legitimate then it could only have taken place in Scotland.'

'Scotland?'

'There may, or may not, be a reference to a place somewhere in the document where this marriage had taken place. Probably it would be Gretna Green or Coldstream, the two most likely places for such marriages to occur. Lord Hardwick's Marriage Act of 1753 made such weddings illegal, but his Act did not apply to Scotland. I was therefore preaching against these irregular marriages because people from England do cross the border to take advantage of the situation. Hardly a desirable way in which to enter the holy estate of matrimony.'

Ben's mind started racing at this information. He had not remembered details of the sermon, he never did, for the monotonous drone of what he called a parson's voice always lulled his mind away from what was actually being said so that he never remembered anything, except for the odd word that stuck in his mind. It was most peculiar how he had remembered the word 'irregular', and to have had the association revived by Seamus's reference to it regarding the jet deal. But he was thankful that the parson's sermon had lodged in his mind, for it had led to an escape from his predicament. A solution. He wanted to dash off, find Ruth, swing her into his arms and tell her their problem was solved.

'Thank you, Vicar.' Ben made his departure swift. He wanted no more sermonising by that monotonous voice.

As he strode down the Church Stairs almost at a run he had to remind himself that all was not solved yet. He and Ruth could get married, but what repercussions would it have on their families, maybe even people beyond their families, and on their own lives? Were they both prepared for what it would bring? Ben reminded himself of the intense love he felt for Ruth. If she felt the same for him, surely their love would conquer everything? If they were married no one could do anything about it, and if it raised problems they could always be solved.

He headed for the office but turned away to walk by the

river. To go inside would stifle him. He needed space to think and plan. A journey to either of the places mentioned by the Vicar, and back, would need two overnight stops. He could easily find an excuse to be away from home, but what about Ruth? It would not be so easy for her. If they were to elope in this way they could make no announcement beforehand. And could they ever return to Whitby afterwards? So much now depended on Ruth.

Chapter Nine

Ruth had not heard from Ben for three days and was worried. She found it more and more trying to go through everyday life as if nothing was troubling her and to hide her feelings from her father and her siblings.

She was alone in the house, her mother and sister having gone to visit friends; her father was still looking for a suitable vessel, and her brothers were somewhere on the high seas. Ruth was sitting in the drawing-room where, for appearances' sake, she had a book on her lap The words meant nothing, her mind occupied with thoughts of Ben, but the sound of the doorbell pierced her thoughts. She was thankful that she was alone when a maid came in bearing an envelope.

'This has come for you, miss.'

Ruth's heart beat a little faster. 'Who brought it?'

'The young lady who called the other day, miss. She said I was to give it to you when you were alone. I knew you were, so I said it would be delivered immediately. She said in that case she would wait on the bridge to see if there was an answer.'

'Thank you.' Ruth waited until the maid had gone before she opened the envelope. With trembling fingers she withdrew a sheet of paper and read the words quickly. She jumped to her feet and shoved the paper and envelope into the pocket of her dress as she crossed the room. She grabbed her coat and bonnet and left the house. A few minutes later she was approaching Sarah who, ignoring the people who hurried past her, was watching the river traffic.

'Hello, Sarah,' she said quietly. 'Thank you for bringing the note from Ben.'

'He told me if you got the note immediately I should wait to see if there was an answer.'

'Do you know what it says?'

'No. That's something between you and Ben.' She turned a serious expression on Ruth. 'Look, I love my brother and I like you, but under the present circumstances I can only see your relationship heading for disaster.'

'You can thank your father for those circumstances,' replied Ruth testily.

'I am not taking sides in this,' replied Sarah.

Ruth raised her hands in surrender, and nodded. 'There is no need for us to quarrel.'

'Very true.' Sarah pressed her hand in a mark of affection. 'Ben asks me to meet him as soon as possible. Is he at home?'

'Yes.'

'Then I shall walk with you and continue beyond to the West Cliff. Tell him to come there.'

'Very well.'

They walked together to New Buildings where Ruth left Sarah. On the way she had eyed the houses, especially that belonging to Sam Coulson, with a little envy, for she recalled her father telling the family that it was her mother's dream to move to this side of the river. How quickly lives can be changed. She cast such thoughts from her mind in anticipation of seeing Ben again.

She had neared a point where the path started to run along the cliff edge when she heard his footsteps. She stopped and turned to await the man she loved.

He was breathing hard when he reached her and took her into his arms without any preamble, holding her tight as if from this moment on he would never let her go.

She felt safe in his arms as love for him welled in her heart. She looked up at him and gave a little smile. 'Is that excitement in your eyes because you have seen me or because of something else?'

'Both!' He laughed and kissed her with an eagerness that told her he had much more to say.

'What have you to tell me?' Ruth asked impatiently.

'Let's stroll.' He took her arm and they fell into step. Ben told her quickly how they could get married if they went to Scotland and waited for her reaction. It did not come immediately. She had to try to get it clear in her mind even though the promise of marriage to Ben Coulson was strongly to the forefront of her thoughts. 'Well?' he prompted.

Ruth stopped. He turned her to him and looked hopefully at her, pleading with his eyes for her to give him the answer he wanted.

'Yes, Ben Coulson, I'll marry you in Scotland.'

Joy came into his face. He swept her into his arms and kissed her with a passion that sealed all his wishes for their future and the happiness he was determined to bring her.

A few moments later he eased her away and looked at her with troubled eyes. 'You are sure? The repercussions, not only for us but for others, could be devastating, especially if we come back to Whitby.'

She frowned. 'I know that. I don't want anyone to be hurt because of us, but that is a risk we'll have to take. And I certainly want to come back to Whitby. If we don't we'll be cut off from our families for ever, and I don't want that, do you?'

Ben shook his head. 'No, I don't. Things will be extremely difficult but I'm prepared for that. I'm sure all will be well in the end.'

'So what are we going to do?'

'We can't announce anything before we leave.'

'But that means the plans for your engagement party will go ahead.'

'Yes. I propose we make that our wedding party.'

She gave a laugh of incredulity. 'What?'

'It's the only way. We will have to time things to perfection. I propose we go to Coldstream. It is just over the border and will mean a better journey north for us than having to cross the Pennines. I'll hire a postchaise of two horses with a postillion.

I've already worked out my reason for leaving Whitby. I will be visiting some ship-owners in Shields in connection with supplying their ships with ropes. But how are you going to explain your absence from home?'

Ruth smiled at the concern on his face. 'You see that as a real stumbling block. Well, let me tell you, quite innocently my mother has played into our hands. She suggested that I was looking peaky and should consider visiting my aunt in King's Lynn for a few days. I refused. I did not want to be far from you. Now I can take up that suggestion.'

The troubled light in Ben's eyes vanished. 'Perfect.' He laughed as he saw how everything could drop into place. 'You must arrange to go to your aunt's by coach. The first leg will end at the Black Swan in Coney Street, York. I will be there and have booked rooms for us as brother and sister for the night. That will be our story as we travel together to Coldstream. I will have hired a postchaise and postillion to leave York the next day and drive us north. We will stay at a suitable inn that night and continue our journey the next day. The following day on the way back we shall stay the night at a different inn as man and wife. We'll arrive in Whitby the next day in time for the party and to announce that we are married.'

'You have it all worked out.' There was pleasure and admiration in Ruth's voice.

'Since talking to the Vicar and seeing the possibilities, I have given it a lot of thought. My main problem was the reason for your absence but you have just solved that. You will have to take the coach a week today. Time is getting short.'

'Oh, Ben, I hope nothing goes wrong.'

'It won't, love, it won't.'

Ruth waited a day before approaching her mother. She needed that time to control her excitement so that no one would guess that something was afoot. She did not want her shrewd mother to think her peaky look was disappearing.

'I think that is a good idea,' Georgina agreed with her

daughter. 'The change will do you good and give you chance to come to terms with what has happened and assess your own standing with Ben.'

Ruth knew at what her mother was hinting – that it might be better if she doused any hope of a relationship with Ben Coulson – but she made no comment.

'I'll write to your aunt,' her mother continued.

'Mama, please don't bother. We got on so well in France that Aunt Celia said I could go any time, but I will write to tell her when I will arrive. It will look better coming from me.'

'You'll go by ship?'

'No.'

'But it will be much more convenient, you can sail directly to King's Lynn.'

'You know I am a poor sailor.'

'If you go by coach it will mean staying a night in York and I don't like to think of you being . . .'

'Oh, Mother,' cut in Ruth, a touch of irritation in her voice, 'I will be perfectly all right. I'm sure the coachman will see me safely established in the inn in York if you have a word with him when you see me off.'

'Very well. When will you go?'

Ruth pondered the question. She did not want it to appear as if she had already worked out the details. 'Next Monday, I think. I'll go and write to Aunt Celia now. It will give her chance to reply if it is not convenient.'

Ruth went to her room but did not write that letter. When she left the house a little later she carried an empty envelope – a pretence that she was going to send a letter to her aunt by the next coach carrying mail to York for onward dispatch.

The following morning as he walked to the east side of the river and the building that housed the offices of Coulson and Sons, Ben had much to think about. His father would be home in a few days and he needed to have various aspects of the business concluded or at a stage where progress was evident.

156

Two ships had sailed to the Baltic for more timber. He had decided it would be a purchase for themselves to sell on rather than being chartered as a transport for a timber firm. He had already, over a tankard of ale, sold half the cargo before its arrival and felt sure that before his father's return he would have sold the rest. This was a new venture for Coulson and Sons, selling timber in their own right. Seamus had been doubtful about the new departure but Ben had insisted, spurred on by the fact that he wanted to prove his ability to his father even while he was planning to foil Sam's scheme for merging with the Campions.

He reached the bridge and automatically paused to view the activity on the quays upstream of the bridge, but his mind was not fully on the scene. His father's words when he had told him of the arranged marriage to Alicia crept into his mind – 'Seaton agreed, there is no need for you to know why,' and again, 'I will just say that Alicia was in agreement.' Ben was troubled. What was it he needn't know? Agreement was the word used but it sounded as if there had been pressure applied by someone, and that must have been his father. But what pressure? What knowledge did his father possess that could influence Seaton into an arrangement that involved the marriage of his daughter?

As he continued his walk Ben pushed these thoughts aside by allowing his mind to turn to the necessary arrangements for his elopement with Ruth.

'Good morning, Mr Ben, I've had an early caller this morning,' said Seamus as he came into Ben's office to hand over the documents and figures on which the clerks had been working yesterday.

'And who might that be?'

'Charles Seymour.'

Ben gave a grimace. 'That young upstart. Looking for a bargain, I expect.'

Seamus smiled to himself. Young upstart? He was three years older than Ben. 'He'd heard we were importing timber to sell on and wondered if he could buy from us. Said he had a market.'

'Typical! Wants to play the middleman so he doesn't even have to do any handling.'

'He said he'd be in the White Horse at ten if you're interested in a deal.'

Ben nodded. 'I might go along and see what he has to say.'

'I'd be a bit wary.'

'I will. Thank you.'

Seamus hesitated and cleared his throat as if there was something he wanted to ask. 'Mr Ben, er, I wonder if I may be excused for the rest of the day? My wife has heard that her sister in Ruswarp is not well. She would like to visit but wants me to accompany her.'

'Of course, Seamus. You have nothing that can't wait until tomorrow?'

'Nothing, sir.'

'Very well. I hope you find your sister-in-law not too indisposed.'

'Thank you, sir.'

When the clerk had left, Ben sorted through the papers that the manager had brought him. There was nothing that needed his immediate attention though one letter from a merchant in Hull, seeking a ship to carry goods to Rotterdam, caught his eye and made him wonder why a Hull merchant sought a Whitby ship. He looked at the quoted dates again and as there was no immediate action required, put it to one side. Maybe his father knew this merchant. It could wait until his return. For now he would like to sell the rest of the timber that would be due in Whitby in a couple of days. He would like to complete that deal before his father returned. Maybe he shouldn't deride Charles Seymour's interest. He wondered if they had dealt with Seymour before. He should have asked Seamus before he left.

Ben pushed himself from his chair and went to the office occupied by the two clerks.

'Do you know if we have had any dealings with a Mr Charles Seymour?' he asked.

Both young men looked thoughtful and then replied with a slow shake of their heads: 'No.'

'Of course, sir, we have only been here just over a year, maybe there would be something before that,' one of them added.

Ben looked thoughtful for a moment. 'Let me have the sales ledgers for two years before you started here. Bring them to my office.'

'Yes, sir.' They slipped from their stools and made for a large cupboard.

A few minutes later they entered Ben's office, each carrying a large thick leather-bound ledger.

'Ah, good. Just place them on that table.' He indicated the large oak table that stood against one wall.

As they were doing so one of them said, 'One of these ledgers is the present one but there is an overlap into the previous year. The other contains transactions before that.'

'Thank you.'

When the clerks had left Ben rose from his chair and went to the table. He looked at the dates on the books and decided that, as he did not know exactly when the clerks had started using these books, he would work back from the present. He flicked through the recent pages quickly, admiring the neat handwriting. It was obvious that both men were particular about the presentation of their work and took a pride in its neatness and legibility. A change in the presentation would be obvious and would indicate when the men had started. If his father had had any dealings with Seymour it would obviously be before the change in the writing style. He turned the pages faster.

Suddenly he stopped. Something had caught his eye. He turned back two pages. Yes, he was right. An entry in different writing! It stood out from the neatness of the rest of the page and had been what could only be described as pushed in. Whose writing? His father's! The size of the sum surprised him. What on earth had his father paid for? There was no indication. Only the name of the recipient, a firm by the name of Wendover and Bicker.

There was no indication of who or what they were or what the payment was for. It must have been something substantial. And why had his father made the entry himself? Why not pass on the information to the clerks so that it would appear in the proper sequence of payments? It might be that Sam had not wanted anyone else to know of it and had waited until the entries had passed beyond this page before inserting the mysterious item himself. But why enter it at all? Ben supposed the transaction must have been paid for out of the firm's funds and would be needed to balance the accounts at the end of the year. There must be a secret behind it, something that his father wanted kept hidden. He wondered if an invoice had been filed to support the payment?

Ben went to the clerks again. 'Will you look out the invoices for April the fifth, sixth and seventh this year?'

Ten minutes later one of the clerks arrived with the appropriate folders for those dates. Ben perused them quickly but there was nothing to support that substantial entry. As he handed the papers back to the clerk he asked, 'Have you heard of the firm of Wendover and Bicker?'

The clerk looked thoughtful for a moment then shook his head. 'No, sir.'

'We keep correspondence files under the names of individual firms, so if there was any filing of letters from or to that particular firm you would have known?'

'Yes, sir. Unless it was prior to our coming to work here.'

'This would have been last April.'

'I suppose it's possible that the manager filed it without us knowing, but that is extremely unlikely because he likes us to handle such things in case we are asked for them afterwards.'

Ben wondered if his father might have filed something, though he suspected that was unlikely too. He did not voice that query, but said, 'Just check in case Seamus opened a file without your knowledge.'

'Yes, sir.' The clerk left to return a few moments later with the information that Ben was expecting. 'There is nothing under the name of that firm, sir.'

'Thank you.' The clerk turned back to the door. Ben stopped him. 'I would like you to keep this enquiry of mine to yourselves. Don't even mention it to Seamus. I am considering a transaction with this firm and wanted to know if we had dealt with them before. I would like to keep the possibility to myself until I am much clearer about it.'

'Very good, sir.'

Ben pondered the knowledge he had gained, flimsy though it was. There had been some dealing with the firm's money that his father wanted no one to know about, but at the same time wanted to be a legitimate transaction before the end of the year. There must be some supporting documents somewhere. Could his father have taken them home? That was a possibility but Ben had never been aware of any such work being conducted at home. Could there be documents at the bank? There was only one way to find out.

Ben stepped outside and hurried to the premises of Simpson, Chapman & Co. in Grape Lane. His request to see Mr Chapman took him straight to the latter's office.

'Good day, Ben.' Mr Chapman rose from this seat behind his desk and shook Ben's hand with a welcoming grip. 'I hear you are going into the business under your father's wing.' He indicated a chair and resumed his own seat.

'Yes,' replied Ben. 'At the moment I'm in charge while he is away.'

'I hope everything is proceeding to your satisfaction and that you are not here with any complaints?'

'None at all, Mr Chapman. Everything is satisfactory. I'm here with an enquiry.'

The banker inclined his head as he asked, 'What might that be? I'll do what I can to help?'

'I'm looking for some papers that are important to a transaction I am near to closing but I cannot find them in the office. My manager is away today so I cannot ask him, and the two clerks have not heard of the firm concerned. I wondered if my father might have deposited any documents or letters with you?'

'Yes, my boy, we do keep documents for clients. They know that they are safe under our locks and keys. And we do have some left by your father.'

'These would have been deposited earlier this year.'

Mr Chapman nodded thoughtfully before he replied, 'Yes, I do recall that he brought a sealed envelope in. There was only his name written on the outside and no reference to its contents.'

'So I could not tell if it is the one I want?'

'Not from the outside.'

'May I have it?'

'Ah.' Mr Chapman looked doubtful. 'I was afraid you were going to ask me that.'

Ben frowned. 'Is there some reason why I can't?'

Mr Chapman dampened his lips in a gesture that seemed to indicate that he did not relish what he had to say. He liked Ben Coulson, wished that he himself as a young man had had the happy-go-lucky attitude that this youngster displayed. But he also knew that many of the rumours that stuck to Ben were exaggerated and that he had a serious side to him and a shrewd brain. He only wished Ben's father would recognise it. Maybe he had now that he was involving the young man more closely in the firm. 'I had instructions from your father that the only other person who could have this envelope, if ever the need arose, was your brother Martin for, as I understood it, he was to become your father's second-in-command when he returned from the Arctic.'

Ben spread his hands in a gesture of understanding that at the same time emphasised his request. 'Sadly Martin will never need to look at the contents of that envelope. Wouldn't you say that that instruction now passes to me as the eldest living son?'

Mr Chapman pursed his lips and gave a little nod. 'I suppose there is something in what you say, but could we not wait until your father's return?'

'If that envelope contains the documents I am looking for I need them to conclude an important transaction, the closing date of which is before my father returns.'

Mr Chapman knitted his brow. He was in an awkward situation. He would have liked Sam Coulson's authority to act but there was something in what Ben said, he had taken Martin's place.

'Look, Mr Chapman, I understand your reluctance to—'

Chapman held up his hands. 'That is no reflection on you, dear boy.'

'I'll look at them here, if that will ease your mind, then they need not go off your premises.'

'Well, if that will satisfy you?'

'It will.'

Mr Chapman rose from his chair. 'I'll be back in a moment.'

When he returned he was carrying a metal deed box. He placed it on the desk in front of Ben who stood up as Mr Chapman unlocked it. He lifted the lid and took out an envelope from the top of a small pile. 'That is the envelope in question. The other contents have been here much longer.' He handed the envelope to Ben.

'Thank you.' He felt a tremor of excitement run through him. He sensed he was on the verge of something important, yet there was nothing written on the outside of the envelope to lead him to believe this. 'May I?' With a quick querying glance at Mr Chapman, Ben reached across the desk for a metal letter opener. The envelope was slit open before Mr Chapman could raise any objection, though the banker saw no reason to do so.

Ben extracted two sheets of paper and unfolded one. His eyes scanned the page quickly. What he saw staggered him but he concealed his surprise from Mr Chapman. He perused the paper a little more slowly and confirmed that the information that had made the initial impact was correct. The paper was a receipt from Wendover and Bicker for the amount he had seen entered in the ledger. But across the bottom left-hand corner his father had written, 'Relating to a debt incurred by Seaton Campion'. He forced his trembling fingers under control and opened the second sheet of paper.

The words leaped out at him. He could hardly believe what

he was reading. He must absorb the sense more carefully. He looked up at Mr Chapman who had busied himself sorting some papers behind his desk. 'Do you mind if I study these more carefully, Mr Chapman?'

'Not at all, my boy.' He indicated a chair at a small table that stood next to the door.

'Thank you.'

'I hope you have found what you want?'

'They are a help,' replied Ben as he sat down.

'Take your time. You won't be disturbing me.'

Ben looked at the receipt. The note, in his father's handwriting, clearly made this a receipt for a sum he had paid to settle a debt incurred by Uncle Seaton. He stared at the paper, realising that this gave his father a hold over his old friend. Sam had told his son of his ambitions to expand the firm, and that to achieve them he wanted to acquire Seaton's or else conduct a merger. His father need have done nothing in this matter. Once he was in debt Uncle Seaton would have had to sell, but that would have left the Campion family in dire straits. At least this way Sam Coulson had saved them from that. Maybe the friendship they had shared since boyhood and the esteem and admiration that his father had for Seaton stood for something. But was there more behind his father's action? Maybe he had used it as a means to enter the high-class section of the Spanish wine trade that had once been Seaton's exclusive in Whitby. Ben turned again to the second sheet of paper.

It was headed, 'Copy of an agreement between Sam Coulson and Seaton Campion, dated this day the fifth of April 1803'.

Ben read slowly.

'Seaton Campion agrees to repay to Sam Coulson the sum stated on the attached receipt unless within the next eighteen months his daughter has married Sam's eldest living son. On the occasion of the marriage Sam Coulson agrees to forego that sum and renounces all claims to it from that day.'

The document was signed and dated by both parties.

For a few minutes Ben continued to stare at the paper, the

words drilling into his mind, then he read them again more carefully. What had he stumbled on? Questions formed in his mind. Answers came, but could he be sure he was right?

He reasoned that somehow his father had found out about Uncle Seaton's debt. How that had occurred was not evident, nor what the debt was for. It was evidently with a London firm. Maybe it was about to foreclose when his father had learned about it, possibly during his visit to London earlier in the year. It must have been, because the date on this document was shortly after his father had returned.

Ben realised it put his father into a position where he could eventually control both firms, maybe not directly but certainly through his son, and yet make it appear a philanthropic gesture towards an old friend. He had possibly used the settling of the debt already to get a part of Campion's Spanish wine trade. His offer to renounce all claims to repayment of the debt would be overwhelmingly tempting to Uncle Seaton and had no doubt contributed to his persuading Alicia to marry Martin. Ben figured she must know the reasons behind the arranged marriage. Her father was too much of a gentleman to force her into a marriage she may not want. But, knowing Alicia as he did, he realised that because of her devotion to her family and her delight in their station in life, she would not want their prospects altered so would agree. But marriage to Martin was not to be.

The words 'eldest living son' confronted Ben. His father had been cautious enough not to mention Martin by name. He had covered a scenario in which something happened to Martin between the signing of the document and the marriage, and Ben was now 'the eldest living son'.

The facts whirled in his mind. As they did they seemed to say that if he married Ruth, the lives of Uncle Seaton, Aunt Grace, Alicia, Griselda and Dorothea would be shattered. Eric could not be considered for this marriage – the term used was 'eldest living son'. Besides, he did not have any desire for a life ashore. If the marriage failed to proceed his father would foreclose, even if it was with reluctance. Ben saw that a family he held dear would face a life of poverty unless he married their daughter.

He folded the papers slowly and replaced them carefully in the envelope.

Mr Chapman noticed him do so and wondered what the young man had discovered that made him look so thoughtful.

'I am finished with these, Mr Chapman.' He stood up and crossed the floor to hand the banker the envelope.

'Before you go, I want you to witness that I have sealed the envelope.' Mr Chapman opened a drawer of his desk and took out some wax. He lit a taper and held it so that it melted the wax which he allowed to drop on to the envelope in such a way as to seal it. 'There,' he said with satisfaction, and met Ben's eyes. 'If your father comes and requests that envelope he will know it has been opened as it is now sealed differently.' There was a query behind the statement.

'From the nature of the contents I think it is extremely unlikely that he will, but if he does I will take full responsibility and you can tell him so. But, Mr Chapman, I would ask you not to draw his attention to it, nor to the fact that I have visited you on any other matter but to ascertain our standing with you financially. The information I have gained from those papers will help me conclude a transaction but I would rather my father knew nothing about it until I am ready to divulge it myself. I am hoping it will surprise him and show him that the firm of Coulson and Sons is dear to me.'

'My lips are sealed, my boy. No one will know the real purpose of your visit.'

Ben shook hands and left the premises. As he walked back to his office he was haunted by the thought that by marrying Ruth he would be condemning the Campion family to a life of distress.

Chapter Ten

Ben tossed and turned. Troubling images spun in his mind. His father's face smiling in sardonic triumph, Uncle Seaton, levelling accusations at Ben himself in despair. Finally a girl standing with her back to him. She turned slowly and, with a smile of triumph on her face, beckoned. He moved forward, drawn by the promise she extended – and it was Alicia! His mind cried her name, not in desire but in rejection. She heard and wept. In her tears was bitter reproach. Her fine clothes fell away and she was left in rags, her expression condemning him for what he had done.

Ben tossed and turned to escape but succumbed to her need for a saviour from the life that threatened her. He cried out. Whatever the word was he saw shock on Alicia's face before she was enveloped in a mist, but not before she looked back at him in condemnation. For a moment there was blackness. It cleared slowly and in its place he saw Ruth holding her hand out to him in a gesture of love. He reached out but could not touch her. Laughter seared his mind but it was not Ruth's for in it there was hatred for what he had done. A voice whispered so that no one else could hear: 'There is only one way to salve your conscience and I am that way.' Ruth was gone. The laughter remained along with the words, 'Desert me and you'll never rest easy.'

The horror of the nightmare stalked Ben's mind, bringing his sweating body upright in bed. He stared wide-eyed at the moonlight seeping into the room past the swaying curtains, but there was no wind. He sank exhausted on to his pillow and wiped his hand over his face. He lay for a few moments then swung out of bed to pour himself some water. He sighed and shook his head as if to try to make sense of his nightmare.

He slept fitfully for the rest of the night and was not sorry when it was daylight.

Ben was thankful his father was not due back until tomorrow, for he would not have relished any conversation at breakfast. Being alone gave him time to reflect on his nightmare. He concluded that it told him that if he followed his heart it would bring misery to Alicia and her family. Could he have that on his conscience? If he had, would he never rest easy as the voice had threatened? If he could not do so he would bring misery to Ruth. That he did not want. But wouldn't he bring misery on her if he did not marry her? It was Ruth he loved. Whichever girl he married it would bring misery on the other.

But had this nightmare been brought about by his surmise that Alicia was aware of the part she was playing in his father's schemes? He had to find out what she knew.

Knowing him to be a close family friend, the Campions' maid ushered Ben to the drawing-room when he requested to see Miss Alicia.

'I'll tell her you are here, sir,' said the servant as she closed the room door.

A few moments later Alicia hurried in. 'This is a pleasant surprise, Ben.' She held out her hand to him as she crossed the room. He took it and she offered her cheek for a kiss. 'I thought maybe we would not meet until the party next week. I've missed seeing you, but now . . .' She left the inference that they would spend the future together unspoken. The lightness in her tone faded when she received no response. 'Is something wrong, Ben?'

He held back a moment but then, deciding that there was no use in being evasive, came straight to the point, 'Alicia, do you know why this proposed marriage was arranged?'

She was taken aback by the directness of the question.

'Why do you ask?'

'You were to marry Martin but—'

'That was not supposed to be known until he returned from the Arctic. Who told you?'

'Father.'

Alicia's lips tightened. 'What else did he say?'

'That as it could no longer be, I was to take Martin's place. Do you know what lies behind this?' Alicia did not answer. 'You do, don't you?' he pressed.

'Do you?' She countered question with question.

'My father did not say but while he has been away certain facts have come to my notice. They give me reason to believe that this marriage was arranged to save your father.'

'How much do you know, Ben?' The dejection in her voice now told him that she knew the truth. He saw no reason not to tell her all that he had learned. As he divulged his knowledge he saw alarm and worry in her face.

When he had finished Alicia was close to tears, but she bit her lips and nodded. 'What you have learned and deduced is true. No one beyond your father and my family were to know.'

The strength of pleading in her tone indicated to Ben that she did not want him to divulge his knowledge. 'I promise you I won't say a word, Alicia.'

She gave a wan smile. 'Thank you, Ben. So nothing will ever come out. When we are married those papers will be torn up as an engagement present. Provided your father keeps his word, no one need ever know of my father's indiscretion. You'll see that he does, won't you, Ben?'

He looked at her pityingly. 'I will, Alicia, I will, though I must say, for all his shortcomings, my father is a man of his word. I don't think you need fear that he will dishonour Uncle Seaton after the debt has been paid, even in this way.'

'Thank you, Ben.'

'You do know about the Spanish wine deal?' She nodded. 'And you realise that these two things have given my father a substantial stake in your father's business.'

'Yes, but they have been friends all their lives, your father would do nothing injurious to that friendship. Isn't it evident from the fact he paid my father's debt?'

'Yes, but he has used it to his advantage.'

'It is only natural that he wants something in return, and getting it through business harms no one. In fact, it will benefit both families.'

'I will tell you this, but please say nothing to anyone. My father is about to move into the alum trade. He will, I feel certain, seek to join that to the trade in alum your father already handles. They're combining in the wine venture, and this will be next, I'm sure of it.'

'Surely,' broke in Alicia quickly, 'that shows he has my father's best interests at heart.'

She sounded so convinced that she was right that Ben held back from contradicting her.

She gave an amused little laugh. 'Isn't it strange how things work out? You and I were meant for each other. I always thought so from childhood. You hurt me when you rejected my declaration of love for you, that day on the cliffs, and told me you were taking Ruth Holmes to the ball. Even though you went on seeing her after that, I always believed it was only infatuation and that one day you would come back to me.'

Ben wanted to stop her but he couldn't.

'Then I was told that I was to marry Martin. I was devastated, but when I learned the reason I knew I could not turn my back on my family and condemn them to a life of poverty. So I agreed. But I always hoped it would bring you and me closer. Now Martin is lost and I've found that all my dreams have come true. It is you I must marry. So I save my family *and* get the man I have always wanted. Always loved.'

Alicia rose from her seat as she was speaking and came to him. She put her hands on his shoulders and looked deep into his eyes. 'I promise you, Ben Coulson that I will make you happy and one day you will look back on your infatuation with Ruth Holmes as only a slight interruption to your love for me.'

She hugged him tight and his arms reluctantly came around her waist in a reciprocal gesture.

*

As he left the house Ben chided himself for not being strong enough to tell her that he would not go through with the marriage. But how could he shatter a world of comfort and condemn old friends to a life that would destroy them?

His mind was in uproar. Go through with the marriage to Alicia and all would appear well, with a settled future for her and her family. But it would bring heartache to Ruth. Her life would be shattered. She may find love somewhere else but he knew, from the intensity he had witnessed in her, that he would always be in her heart just as she would be in his. Could he inflict such devastation upon her? Could she free her mind of him and build another life for herself? Could he do so with Alicia? Doubt assailed him in waves. The future in one form or another swam in and out of his confused mind. Could it take care of itself? No, it depended on decisions made in the present, and a big decision faced him now. Should he undo the plans he and Ruth had made?

He stopped, aware that the wind was plucking at his hat. He reached up and settled it more firmly on his head. It was only then that he became aware he was on the West Cliff. He looked around. How had he come to be there? He had not been aware of where his steps were taking him. But here he was, in the very place where he had asked Ruth to marry him. Why was he here? He sensed her beside him and her name came to his lips. 'Ruth, help me.' Words formed in his mind 'Be true to yourself.' His problem and its various solutions pounded in his brain. He cried out for help again. Ruth faded into the mists of his mind and he was left to face his own question: 'Where does your heart truly lie?'

He answered without hesitation. 'With Ruth.'

'Then follow your heart.'

Two days later his father was back. Niceties were exchanged quickly with his daughters and youngest son and then he asked, 'Is Ben at the office?'

On being told that he was, Sam left the house and hurried

through the streets, acknowledging greetings without stopping. The clerks and Seamus were soon aware that he was back as he strode into the building and along the corridor to Ben's office.

He went straight in without knocking and the impact of his entrance startled Ben who was making the final alterations to two documents.

'Father!' He jumped from his chair and came to shake Sam's hand. He needed to have everything between them on the most amiable of terms.

'Ah, Ben, my boy. Has everything gone well?' Sam threw down his stick, dropped his hat on a chair and swept his coat from his shoulders. 'Come to my office and tell me all that has been happening.' He was out of the room before Ben could say any more.

'Did your visit to Tyneside prove successful?' he asked as he followed his father.

'Indeed it did. We have a lucrative deal to ship coal from Newcastle. We'll need to buy or hire two colliers. I see that some are nearing completion in Sanderson's shipyards. We might think about buying them. I have some figures provided by the Newcastle merchants. We'll go over them together and then see if we can make a profit with those two ships.'

'Very good, Father. We had better do that as soon as possible, today or tomorrow. On Saturday I too am going to Newcastle.'

His father raised his eyebrows in surprise as he sat down behind his desk. 'What's this about?'

'You wish to bring my ropery fully into Coulson and Sons?'

'Yes. I had hoped that you would have done that while I was away. I told Seamus to have papers drawn up ready for you to deal with. Hasn't he done so?' A touch of annoyance had entered Sam's voice.

'Oh, yes, he did, very efficiently, but I had to put them to one side. You see, I didn't mention it before you went away as I wasn't certain what was going to happen, but I had a deal in the offing to supply rope to a shipbuilding concern on the

Tyne. If it were to materialise, I wanted it to be completed before we took my ropery business into Coulson and Sons.'

'Quite right, Ben.' His father nodded his approval.

'The matter developed further while you were away,' he went on, pleased that his father was accepting the explanation. 'It has reached a stage where it requires me to go to Tyneside to complete the arrangements.'

'Good, good.' Sam looked proudly at his son. 'Now what else has been going on while I have been away?'

Ben gave an account of his stewardship. His father expressed delight and approval. It made him think that maybe he had underestimated his son. Maybe Ben was not so irresponsible as he had imagined.

Once the details had been discussed, Sam leaned back in his chair. 'You say you are going to Tyneside – when?'

'I'll have to go on Saturday.'

'Before the engagement party?'

'I'll have to otherwise I could lose the deal.'

'Well, be sure you are back in time. It's an occasion of great importance to me and to your Uncle Seaton.'

'Have no fear, I certainly will be.' Ben gave a chuckle. 'It's just as important to Alicia and to me. I'll be there.' He put such conviction into his voice that his father had no doubt that he would be.

Ben returned to his office. He picked up the papers he had been scrutinising when his father had arrived, smiling to himself as he fingered them. They referred to a transaction to supply ropes to a firm in Newcastle. The space for the firm's name had been left blank and they had not been dated, but they were authentic enough to fool his father should he have asked to see them. Ben folded them and slipped them into his pocket.

'One more time, Sarah. Please?' Ben had cornered his sister the day before he was due to leave Whitby.

'This gets riskier every time. I told you I would take no more messages to Ruth.'

'Please.' There was desperation in his tone and in his expression.

'There's every chance that one of us will be caught. If I meet Captain Holmes, I dread to think of the consequences for Ruth. Or us for that matter.'

'He won't be about. He's busy every day with getting a boat for his fishing venture.'

'Are Ruth's brothers still away?'

'Yes.'

'What about her sister Rachel?'

'Ruth has some hold over her. I don't know what it is but, even if she knows about our meetings, she won't say anything. Besides she will probably be visiting a friend.'

'So her mother is likely to be the only one at home?'

'Yes. Or she might be out. She is sympathetic to Ruth in any case.'

'She knows about you two?' Surprise widened Sarah's eyes.

'Well, she knows only so much, not about you arranging the meetings.'

'Thank goodness for that.'

'You'll do it then, Sarah?'

'What is so desperate about it this time?'

He tried to play down his eagerness. 'Nothing.'

Sarah snorted with disgust. 'You don't fool me, brother. There's something in the wind.'

'Look, I'm going to Newcastle on business tomorrow. I want to see Ruth before I go.'

She was still not altogether satisfied with Ben's explanation. She could read her brother and now he was trying to play down his original eagerness. 'Does Father know you're going to Newcastle?'

'Yes.'

'A week today is the party at the Campions? Have you told Ruth about that?'

'No.' Ben realised that if he said yes his sister would regard the need for this meeting with suspicion.

'What?' Sarah gasped with astonishment. 'You *are* playing with fire. You can't play with people's emotions like that. Get her told. I'll take the message for you, but tell her about next Friday.'

'Thanks, Sarah.'

The note was duly delivered to Ruth without anyone else knowing and forty minutes later she met Ben on the West Cliff.

As he watched Ruth hurry to meet him he was so struck by her appearance and the charm that seemed to flow from her that his heart and mind reassured him he had made the right decision.

No word was spoken as they took each other into their arms and held on as though neither would let the other escape. Once again Ben felt justified in the path he had chosen. The future was theirs to take and mould to their liking whatever the circumstances they found themselves in. Nothing could break the love that existed between them.

As he eased her from him, so that he could look into her eyes while still holding her close, he said, 'Are you all prepared for Monday?'

'Yes.'

'Will you pretend you have had a letter from your aunt?'

'No. That is too risky. Mother might ask to see it. I made out that if I didn't hear from my aunt I would take it that she was expecting me. Of course, I never will receive a reply.'

He nodded. 'Good. And you know what to do on Monday?'

'Yes. Take the coach to the Black Swan in York.'

'Right, and don't worry, I'll be there. I am leaving tomorrow. My father thinks I am going to Newcastle on business.'

'Did he mention the party again?'

'Just to say I had to make sure I was back in time.'

A serious expression came over Ruth's face. 'You are sure?'

'Sure that we'll be back in time? Of course we will'

'Not that. Are you sure that you want to go through with this?'

'Of course, my love. Nothing could stop me.'

'Irrespective of the dire consequences we will have to face?'

'I'll face them as long as I have you by my side.'

'And so will I,' she added gently.

Their lips met. Their love and future together were sealed.

Ben found the wind freshening and was thankful that he'd decided to travel in his winter coat. He passed his valise to his left hand and pulled his top hat more firmly on his head.

As he reached the Angel one of the boys who worked there recognised him and ran to meet him.

'You're travelling on the coach, sir. I'll take your luggage,' the boy called brightly with a broad smile.

'Thank you, Jim,' said Ben as he handed over his valise. 'You've been studying the passenger list?' he added with a smile and an approving nod.

'Yes, sir. It pays to know who's travelling.'

'And you watch out for those you know will give you a tip,' grinned Ben.

'Nothing wrong in that, sir.'

'Nothing,' agreed Ben. 'You've a sharp brain, young Jim. One day you'll work for me.'

'I'd like nothing better, sir,' he replied with enthusiasm.

As they were speaking Ben had been fishing a coin from his pocket. He flipped into the air and Jim, as one who had practised this skill often, plucked it from the air without altering his stride.

'Thank you, sir.'

They reached the coach and the boy heaved the valise up to a man who was stowing the luggage.

'There's hot punch for travellers travelling on this cool day. Follow me, sir.'

As they walked to the building Jim asked, 'Going to York, sir?'

'Aye, and on to Newcastle.' Though he did not anticipate any enquiries being made about his journey, Ben thought it best to make this false information public knowledge.

'Have a good journey, sir.' The youth ran off, no doubt to see if there was anyone else who would part with a coin for his help.

Ben sipped at his punch and felt its warmth course through him. He sauntered to the door and watched the activity around the coach. Two men were making the final adjustments to the harness while a boy stood at the head of the two leading horses. Another who had been making sure that the inside of the coach was ready for passengers emerged and hurried into the inn. Adjustments were being made to the luggage, and the coachman responsible for the speed of the journey and safety of his passengers was making his final inspection. Two groups of people stood to one side. Ben eyed them, picking out who he thought would be accompanying him in the coach, when a voice at his shoulder drew his attention.

'Ah, Mr Ben, travelling today.'

'Aye, Jed.' He glanced at the rotund red-faced landlord of the Angel. 'You do us well.' Ben raised his cup, acknowledging Jed Crowther's thoughtfulness for the comfort of his passengers.

A boy appeared with a tray on which rested more cups of warm punch. He crossed the cobbles to the two groups who gratefully accepted the steaming liquid.

'As I said, you look after your customers,' said Ben, indicating the scene before them.

'Pays off in the long run, as you'll know. From what I hear your ropery business is thriving because you oblige yours.'

'It is,' agreed Ben.

'It must have been taking more of your time. You haven't been in for your usual evenings of cards lately. The others are wondering why?'

Ben gave a little laugh. 'Tell them I have work to attend to.' He saw Jed raise a quizzical eyebrow. 'You just said yourself that my business is thriving. It doesn't do that without my attention.'

Jed laughed. 'True, Mr Ben, but I happen to know you have a very capable manager.'

'Aye, that is true, but there are other things besides the daily business to see to. I'm off on such a mission now to Newcastle.'

Jed's laugh grew stronger.

'I'll tell your fellow card players that Ben Coulson is becoming a real businessman.' He suddenly became more serious. 'Maybe you're having to now that you're Sam's heir.'

Ben gave him a noncommittal 'Maybe' in return. He wanted no more questions so thrust the empty cup into Jed's hands, said, 'Thanks for that,' and walked off towards the coach.

The other passengers were making their final farewells. The groups split up and Ben saw that he was to be accompanied by two couples whom he judged to be married. He was proved only half-right for two introduced themselves as a brother and sister who had been visiting friends in Robin Hood's Bay. The other man introduced himself as Captain Beecher, late of the Green Howards, a landowner in the Esk Valley. He and his wife were travelling to York to visit her family. Ben did not take to him. There was a certain arrogance about him that was reflected in what appeared to be the shyness of his wife, though Ben reckoned that she was in reality a browbeaten woman. He took to the brother and sister whose names he had gathered were Harry and Rose Slingsby.

When he introduced himself as Ben Coulson he was immediately confronted by Captain Beecher with the question, 'Is your father Sam Coulson?'

'Indeed he is,' replied Ben sharply, not liking the tone of the man's voice.

Having had his reply, Captain Beecher immediately took Ben to task. 'I say, he was very hard on Captain Holmes, dismissing him for something he had no control over and then blackening him with every ship-owner in Whitby so he could not get another command.'

Ben was taken aback by the strength of this man's disapproval. His hackles rose. Though he agreed with the Captain up to a point he could not sit by and let his own father be maligned by this man. 'And what do you know of it, being a military man?' he asked testily.

'Maybe more than you think,' replied the Captain with a supercilious sneer. 'I have been in the timber trade for five years dealing in trees from my estate. I have recently been asked by a firm in York for timber which I thought would be better coming from one of the Baltic countries. I knew the whalers went to the Baltic for this trade after returning from the Arctic, so I went into Whitby a while back where I came into contact with Daniel Holmes, whom no doubt you know or know of. It doesn't matter how I met him but the result was that he is making enquiries about the timber I want. In the course of our conversation the story of his father's voyage to the Arctic came out. I must say I consider your father is a blackguard for what he did.'

'Sir, I'll have to ask you to mind your tongue,' snapped Ben. 'You should not make such accusations without having the full facts.'

'And what are they? Do you know the truth or are you only prepared to listen to the Coulson side of the story? It's shameful to deprive a man and his family of a living as your father has done.'

'If there were not ladies present I would give you—'

'Please, gentlemen,' broke in Harry Slingsby. 'I have no knowledge of what this dispute is all about but I do not think this is the place or the company in which to pursue your argument. I ask you, for the sake of the ladies, to abandon this dispute immediately.'

Captain Beecher puffed out his cheeks, glared at Harry and then, indignant that his behaviour had been criticised, spluttered, 'Very well then. Ladies, I apologise. The matter will be dropped, but I must say one last thing to this young . . .' he gave a slight hesitation as if reluctant to use the next word '. . . gentleman.' He looked malevolently at Ben. 'When I return the day after tomorrow, I will make it my business to see Daniel Holmes and tell him that I met you on this coach.' He gave a sharp nod, as much as to say, that is that, and lapsed into silence with his own thoughts.

Annoyed that this confrontation had led to the possibility of his presence on the coach being divulged to Daniel, who might link it with his sister's visit to her aunt, Ben closed his eyes momentarily in despair.

He apologised to the ladies who fell into conversation with each other, though under the glare of her husband Mrs Beecher did little of the talking. Ben showed interest in Harry's story. He was from Selby, south of York, where his father was a wool merchant. Harry was following him into the same trade. As they drove into York, Ben and Harry exchanged addresses, having in mind that Ben's connection with shipping might mean a lucrative deal for both parties in the shipping of wool to the Continent.

By the time they reached York the weather had deteriorated and a light rain had set in. This made their partings quick. Captain Beecher's farewell was curt while his wife's was simpering, as if she dare not express what she really felt. Ben got the impression that she did not condone her husband's earlier attitude towards him. They were soon greeting a member of Mrs Beecher's family who had come to escort them to their final destination, a house in Bootham.

The Slingsbys' goodbyes were much more amiable and contained a promise from Harry that he would keep Coulson's in mind when they were next handling wool destined for the Continent. Brother and sister then lost no time in seeking the shelter of the family carriage that had been sent to meet them for their onward journey to the family home.

Ben hurried into the Black Swan where he found his valise had already been deposited. He slipped a coin to the youth whom he had seen handling it from the coach.

'Ben Coulson,' he introduced himself to the stout man behind a counter that ran along a wall to the right of the main door. 'I trust you can let me have a room for three nights?'

'I certainly can, sir. I hope your journey was not too trying and that your stay with us will be to your liking. I'm the landlord of these premises, John Aimies. Anything you want, sir, call for me.'

'There is something. My sister will be arriving from Whitby by coach on Monday. She would like a room for the night. Will you reserve one now?'

'Certainly.' He scanned a list that was placed conveniently at one end of the counter. 'She can have room fourteen. You will have number twelve.' He took a key from the wall behind him and, when he turned, the youngster who had brought Ben's valise in and had remained close at hand stepped forward to take the key.

The boy pointed out the public rooms and then took Ben upstairs. He surveyed the room that was to be his home for a couple of nights. He had been given a good-sized one and was thankful for that. He felt he needed space, did not want to suffer the sensation of being hemmed in, as if the world was conspiring to close him off from Ruth and their future together. The wardrobe, chest of drawers, two armchairs and dressing-table did not overcrowd the room. The bed, with its pristine white sheets and colourful bedcover, looked inviting. The wheels of the future had been set in motion and, now that they had been placed firmly on a particular course, he felt a sense of relief. Nothing should go wrong unless something happened to prevent Ruth leaving Whitby.

He toyed with the plans he had made as he freshened up after his journey and had to be stern with himself to stop anxiety creeping in. No one could know that he and Ruth were meeting in York and that neither of them was bound for the destination they had indicated to their families. Now, he must see about a postchaise.

'Ruth, you're sure you have everything you want?' Georgina Holmes asked as she watched her daughter fasten her valise.

'Yes, Mother.' Ruth hoped she was successfully hiding the anxiety and guilt she felt. She hated not being truthful with her mother and father but she dare not risk one little hint of what she was doing slipping out. She was on her guard and hoped it didn't show.

'You've got the figurine I'm sending your aunt carefully wrapped so it won't break?'

'Yes, Mother.' She closed the final fastening on her valise.

'I'll take that for you,' said her mother, and took it by the handle. 'You bring your coat and hat.'

When Georgina had left the room, Ruth picked up her coat and bonnet. She paused at the door and looked round the room. Sadness began to envelop her. This was probably the last time she would see the place that had played such a big part in her life. A room in which she had grown up, in which she had come through girlhood into womanhood, a room full of memories and of dreams, and now one of those dreams was about to be fulfilled. She cast one more glance around, strengthened her resolve not to give way and went downstairs.

'Lass, thee does look bonny.' Gideon looked up from the paper he was reading when his daughter walked in.

'You waited, Father?' Her appreciation was in her eyes and voice.

'I had to see thee off. The fish will wait. Your Mother and I will see you to the coach.

'And I'm coming too,' said Rachel, her voice catching on these last words as she came into the room.

Ruth wanted to protest but she knew it would be unkind to do so. She would much rather have gone from home and quietly remained unaffected by thoughts of their prolonged parting.

'Your brothers will miss you when they get back from the Baltic.'

'When will that be?' she asked for something to say.

'Most likely in a couple of days if the weather holds. It looks as if it is settling down again after the wind and rain of the last two.'

'Best be going,' said Gideon, taking Ruth's valise.

They left the house and headed for the bridge. Their chatter was strained, an attempt to occupy time and mind before a parting they would all feel, none more so than Ruth. As they crossed to the west side of the river she felt a tightening in her chest. The next time she crossed this bridge she would be Mrs Ben Coulson. She was so carried away by the thought that she almost cried out but stifled her reaction and made a desultory remark to a comment by Rachel though she hardly knew what it was. Her heart beat a little faster as they neared the Angel.

The horses were already harnessed to the coach, and were being soothed by two stable-boys. The coachman was making his usual checks and passengers were assembling near the coach door.

'Ah, there's Mr and Mrs Dobson, they must be going to York to visit her sister. You'll have someone you know travelling with you,' said Georgina brightly, thankful that her daughter would not have complete strangers as travelling companions.

Ruth's heart sank. The last thing she wanted was to see anybody she knew. Too many questions might be asked. She must truly be on her guard for she knew Emily Dobson to be an inquisitive chatterbox who could make five out of two and two.

At that moment Emily spotted Georgina and broke away from the people she was speaking to.

'My dear Georgina,' she cried with a great sweep of her arms. 'Are you travelling with us? How delightful.'

She smiled at Emily's over-exuberance. 'No. It's Ruth who is going to see her aunt in King's Lynn.'

'Oh.' Emily Dobson quickly hid her disappointment. 'That will be just as delightful.' She leaned forward conspiratorially to Georgina and said quietly, though making sure that the others could hear, 'Thomas and I will see her safely to York. King's Lynn, you say? She'll have to stay the night and catch the coach for Doncaster tomorrow then change there to another for King's Lynn. We'll see she gets accommodation in York, and if the time is convenient we'll see her on to the coach she'll need for Doncaster.'

Ruth's heart sank even further. Her mind went numb and she was hardly aware of her mother thanking Mrs Dobson profusely and saying how wonderful it was to know that her daughter was in safe hands. Rachel caught her sister's eyes. Knowing how fussy Mrs Dobson could be, Rachel raised her eyebrows in sympathy. Ruth grimaced in reply.

The call came for passengers to board the coach. She said her goodbyes, keeping her emotions firmly under control, though she nearly broke down when her father, his hands on her shoulders, looked her in the eye and said, 'Don't stay away too long, lass, we'll miss you.'

'I won't.' The words almost stuck in her throat. She had to turn away quickly and get into the coach to stop the tears coming.

Once all the passengers were settled, the coachman cajoled the horses to take the strain and set the vehicle on its route to York. Shouts of goodbye were called, hands were raised to wave farewell and a safe journey.

There were three other people on the coach none of whom Ruth knew, but Mrs Dobson made sure that Ruth sat next to her and that she soon knew who the other passengers were. She dominated the general talk and was not averse to interrupting a conversation between others if she caught wind of something that she decided needed her observations or opinion. She constantly gave the impression that she knew people they knew. But when she turned her attention to Ruth it was to quiz her about her father and what he was doing now that Sam Coulson had sacked him.

'Dreadful man, dreadful,' she commented, and pulled a face of disgust, though no doubt she would be as nice as pie if she was in Sam Coulson's presence. 'Your father has been very tolerant in accepting Coulson's behaviour. You know, traits are passed down or at least rub off on other members of the family. I mean, look at you, your sister and brothers, all showing signs of being like your parents. Now Sam Coulson's family . . . I ask you! That Martin wasn't everyone's idea of a likeable person, did some rum things from what I hear, and as for that other son . . . what's his name? . . . Ben. He's a wild one, a wastrel. If his father makes him his heir now Martin has gone, he'll soon be through what his father has made. Though I hear not all Sam's deals have been above board. Maybe it'll be easy come, easy go. You know, Ruth, you are better off not associating with the likes of that family. And you know . . .' Emily Dobson went on and on. Ruth felt like screaming at her. She tried to close her ears to the unsubstantiated never-ending chatter. The only relief she had was when Mrs Dobson chose to muscle in on other people's conversations.

Ruth directed her mind to the quandary that faced her. What would Mrs Dobson think and deduce when she saw Ben meet her? How could they get over the fact that he would already have booked her a room? And what about tomorrow if Mrs Dobson came to carry out what she thought was a good deed seeing Ruth off on the southbound coach?

Her heart thumped with anxiety as the coach rolled through York to the Black Swan. It came to a halt amidst much bustle and activity around the inn. Passengers were helped from the coach, luggage was unloaded, the horses unharnessed and led away. Once the coach was clear, four youths swarmed over it to have it spick and span for use tomorrow.

Ruth looked around expecting to see Ben but he was nowhere to be seen. Her heart missed a beat and anxiety gripped her. Where was he? He had said he would be here. In a way she was thankful that he wasn't, otherwise he would not have escaped the sharp eyes of the lady who was beginning to fuss over her, but she wanted him here, wanted to know that everything was arranged for them to proceed to Coldstream.

'You see to our luggage, Mr Dobson,' Emily said, using the term she always did for her husband even in the privacy of their own home. 'It keeps him in his place' she would tell her close friends. 'I'll see that Ruth gets a comfortable room.'

She bustled into the inn with Ruth following reluctantly in her wake. 'Now, my good man,' she boomed as she approached the counter, 'I hope you have a nice room in which you can accommodate this charming young lady. She'll be here for one night as she is going on to King's Lynn tomorrow. Tell me what time the coach leaves and I will be here to see that she gets a comfortable seat.'

John Aimies had met this type of person before and did not think much of them, always full of their own importance and trying to appear what they were not. He could see the young lady was embarrassed and sympathised with her for having such an obnoxious mother then experienced relief when the lady said, 'I am Mrs Dobson and this young lady is Miss Holmes, the daughter of a friend of mine. I was coming to York to visit my sister and I reassured her mother that I would see that she had suitable accommodation.'

'She will have that.' He called out to the boy who was hovering near the door. When he came forward he handed him a key. 'David, Take this young lady to room ten.'

'I'll come and see if it is suitable,' said Emily.

'Really, there is no need, Mrs Dobson. I'm sure it will be perfectly all right.'

She started to insist but then, much to Ruth's relief, Mr Dobson appeared at the door and said, 'Your sister and her husband are here.'

'Oh.' She turned to Ruth. 'Are you sure, my dear? I did promise your mother.'

'I will be perfectly all right, Mrs Dobson. Thank you for your help.'

'A pleasure, my dear. I'll be here in the morning to see you safely on your way.' She looked at the landlord. 'What time does this young lady's coach leave?'

'Eleven, ma'am.'

Mrs Dobson nodded. She started to turn away when the landlord asked, 'Was there another young lady on the coach?'

'No.'

'Oh. I was expecting a Miss Coulson.'

'Thank goodness she wasn't! Wasn't that a blessing, Ruth? That would have been most awkward.'

Ruth's heart was racing. How far could this go? She glanced at the landlord and caught his eye. Her little shake of the head, and pleading look to say no more, were thankfully interpreted by him.

He said quickly, 'I suppose something happened to prevent her travelling. Ah, well . . .' He gave a resigned shrug of his shoulders.

Mrs Dobson's mind was diverted when she saw her husband waving frantically from the doorway. 'I'll see you tomorrow, Ruth.' He bustled to the door from where they could hear her berating her husband for his impatience.

Ruth turned to the landlord and raised her eyebrows. 'I'm sorry about that.'

John smiled, 'That's all right, lass. At first I thought she was your mother. Thank goodness she wasn't!'

'That would indeed be horrible.'

They laughed together, the first light moment in her day.

He eyed her with a fatherly smile. 'I think perhaps you are two young ladies travelling as one on that coach? One of those ladies has had a room booked for her already by a young gentleman.'

'Yes I am that person.'

'A Miss Coulson?'

'Yes. But really I am Miss Holmes.'

'Oh.'

'And I thank you for saying no more when I caught your eye.'

'That's all right. I gathered there was something you didn't want her to know.'

'That's right. Now tell me, is Mr Coulson here?'

'Yes, he arrived on Saturday and made the reservations. He has ordered a postchaise for tomorrow morning to leave at ten. He was around here until he saw the coach arrive. I was busy then and didn't see where he went.'

There was the sound of someone hurrying down the stairs. 'I'm here.'

Relief swept over Ruth and she rushed to meet Ben at the bottom of the stairs. They hugged each other tightly, a gesture that told John Aimies that these two young people were very much in love and that there must be a very good reason for the subterfuge in which he now found himself involved, rather to his delight after his encounter with Mrs Dobson.

'I nearly died when I saw the Dobsons getting out of the coach with you. I made myself scarce but not before I realised they were not staying here. Then I went to my room and watched for them leaving,' Ben explained.

'Thank goodness you did.' Ruth went on quickly to tell him what had happened with Mrs Dobson and how their subterfuge had nearly been uncovered when John Aimies had mentioned that he was expecting a Miss Coulson to arrive on the coach. 'Fortunately he got my signal before he said any more.'

'Mrs Dobson doesn't know I'm here?'

'No.'

Ben heaved a sigh of relief. 'So all is well.'

'Not exactly. She insisted that she will be here in the morning to see me safely on the coach for Doncaster.'

Ben slapped his forehead in exasperation. He looked sharply at John who had been taking all this in. 'What time does that coach leave?'

'Eleven.'

'And our postchaise will be ready for ten?'

'Yes.'

'Then we will be an hour out of York before she appears.'

'I'll arrange for you to start half an hour earlier and then you certainly will be.'

'Thank you for all your help, landlord.'

'But what do you want me to tell the lady when she arrives and you, young lady, are not here?' asked John, eyeing Ruth quizzically but with a smile that told her he would take care of the problem.

Chapter Eleven

'Good day, ma'am.' John Aimies greeted Mrs Dobson in a friendly manner, though his thoughts ran, Can't the battleaxe smile on such a beautiful morning? He glanced at Mr Dobson, who had trotted in behind her, and assumed that was the position he always took up.

Mrs Dobson gave him a sharp nod. 'Where is the young lady I have come to see safely on the next step of her journey?'

'Young lady, ma'am?' John knew very well who she meant but wanted to play hard for information.

'Yes, yes,' snapped Mrs Dobson irritably. 'The young lady who arrived with us off the coach from Whitby.'

'Oh, that one. Another young lady arrived later I thought you might be referring to her.'

'No, of course not.' She half-turned to her husband. 'I expect that was the Coulson girl, though how she got here I can't imagine.' She turned back to the landlord. 'I'm talking about Miss Ruth Holmes, you remember her?'

'Of course, ma'am. You should have mentioned her name at the start.'

Mrs Dobson tightened her lips at what she took for criticism. She glared at John and said, 'I've mentioned it now, so please have Miss Holmes called or else she will miss her coach.' She glanced towards the door through which the sounds of the coach being prepared penetrated the building.

'I'm sorry, ma'am, I cannot call her.'

'Cannot? What do you mean, or are you being obstructive?'

'I am not being obstructive, ma'am. I cannot call Miss Holmes because she is not here. She left early this morning.'

'What? That can't be right.' Mrs Dobson was indignant. She was not going to be fooled by this man who did not seem to know who his betters were. 'Call her this minute.'

John was enjoying this but kept a straight face. 'Madam, what I say is true, she left early this morning.'

'But she was to get this coach.'

John spread his hands. 'I'm afraid she won't be doing that.'

'Where did she go? She's supposed to be going to see her aunt in King's Lynn.'

'Oh, she'll be doing that, ma'am, but not for a couple of days. She went to see friends in York and sent word to me that she will be staying with them and will get the coach on Friday.'

'But I shan't be able to see her on to that coach. We are going back to Whitby on Thursday. Her mother never said anything about friends in York. I didn't know the family knew anyone in this city.' She drew herself up and shot a glance at her husband. 'Come along.' She strode towards the door.

Mr Dobson gave the landlord a look of despair that had a touch of amusement in it as if he had just thought of something. He leaned towards John and whispered quickly, 'That's something she's missed. She'll blame everyone for not telling her. I'll never hear the last of it.'

'Close your ears, sir.'

'There's no one better at that than I.' He winked at John and scampered after his wife.

John shook his head sadly as he watched him go, then grinned as he thought, Maybe he has a better life than she thinks. I hope so. Then his mind turned to Ruth and Ben. He had taken to them and, after the accidental revelation that they were not brother and sister, had guessed what they might be up to though he had not queried it. It wasn't his place to do so. He had seen many couples, married and not married, pass through the Black Swan and reckoned he could tell when two people were truly in love. The couple he had seen off earlier in the postchaise fitted that category. He wondered how they were faring and where they were.

*

190

'Are you comfortable?' Ben asked with concern.

Ruth laughed. 'How many more times, Ben? I'm perfectly comfortable,' She snuggled closer to him as if to emphasise her contentment. 'And I'm immensely happy.' She half turned her head to look at him so that he could read the truth in her eyes.

'Mr Aimies did us well with this postchaise.'

'And with the postboy,' Ruth added eyeing the man who was riding the left-hand horse and keeping both under his control with an efficiency born of experience.

'True. I heard Mr Aimies giving Greg instructions to look after us well and see that we got the best accommodation. It appears that Greg has done a north run on a number of occasions and knows all the best hostelries.'

Ruth gave a little chuckle, one that revealed she was amused by her own thoughts. 'I wonder how Mr Aimies got on with Mrs Dobson this morning?'

Ben laughed. 'I think between us we cooked up a plausible story that Mrs Dobson will have no reason to question.'

'It was useful that she had told me when she was returning to Whitby,' said Ruth. She frowned. 'I wonder if she will call on Mother?'

'Well, if she does immediately on her return, your mother will only have one day's worry. We'll be back the next day.'

Ruth gave a little shudder.

'Anxious about that?' he asked.

'Aren't you?'

'I suppose so.' Ben drove the mood of seriousness away. 'Let's not think about it now. Think only of the moment.'

They both made a resolve to do so and for the rest of the journey did not consider the future.

They relished in sharing the experience of their journey. They saw large, well-kept houses where the land was farmed well, and others where the land was poor and its owners barely scratching a living. In run-down villages barefoot children ran alongside the postchaise for a few yards, staring up at them with eyes wide with curiosity and admiration. Young men and women, living on the edge of poverty, glared with sullen envy, making Ruth feel uncomfortable and in need of reassurance from Ben. In contrast they saw well-dressed ladies pass in phaetons and gigs, and young men and women of about their own age enjoying an exhilarating ride when they let their mounts have their head.

About midday the postillion guided the horse on to a flat expanse of grass and brought the postchaise to a halt. He swung to the ground, tethered the horses and came to Ben. 'Sir, we'll stop here for some lunch?' Ben looked around. There was no sign of an inn.

Greg smiled. 'Don't worry, sir, Mr Aimies had an excellent picnic made up for you.' He glanced at Ruth, 'Can I help you down, miss?'

'Thank you.' She took his proffered hand and stepped lightly to the ground. 'You have chosen a place with a wonderful view.'

'It is, miss. It is one I like. We are looking along the valley of the River Wear. If you excuse me, I'll get the picnic.' He moved to the back of the vehicle and a few moments later appeared with a large hamper which he placed on a flat stone. He opened it to reveal bread, cold mutton carefully sliced, cheese, butter, apples, a jar of home-made plum jam and a bottle of French wine.

'This is delightful.' observed Ruth light-heartedly. It seemed to her symbolic of her new life. She and Ben were eating together in the open with neither family knowing where they were. The break had been made and now they were no longer 'running away' but journeying together. It made their future seem more settled somehow.

They enjoyed the picnic, commenting on the quality of the food, the pleasant weather and the wonderful view. Once they were finished the postillion quickly packed everything away and, after seeing his passengers comfortably ensconced, mounted his horse and set the chaise in motion. He kept to as brisk a pace as the roadway would allow but made good time in spite of the sections that slowed him down to a cautious speed. Daylight was beginning to fade when they reached the outskirts of Morpeth and Greg manoeuvred the chaise to a stop in front of a three-storeyed inn. Immediately the glass-panelled door swung open and a youth in a smart livery ran down the steps to help Ruth from the chaise.

'Good evening, ma'am,' he greeted her brightly in an accent that almost made his words a mystery to Ruth, but she inclined her head and smiled in return. 'And to you, sir,' he added as Ben stepped down beside them. 'You require accommodation?'

'Yes,' replied Ben as he glanced round to see their postillion instructing a young man about the care of the horses and the chaise.

'Follow me, sir, ma'am.' He set off towards the door of the inn.

Ruth and Ben followed and entered a square hall. A staircase swept in a graceful curve to the next floor. A dark oak chest stood at the bottom of the stairs and a matching table was placed against the wall opposite. Brass plates and bed-warmers hung on the panelled walls. The whole was lit by four large candelabra and several oil lamps hanging in brass brackets attached to the walls.

'Good day, sir.' A slim middle-aged woman, smart in her black dress trimmed with white lace, greeted Ben pleasantly.

'Good day,' he returned. 'Would you have a room for my sister and one for myself?'

'Indeed, sir.' The woman cast a quick glance at Ruth standing in the middle of the hall taking in her surrounding appreciatively. She called to the youth who had escorted them into the inn and handed him two keys. He picked up the valises and Ruth and Ben followed him up the stairs. On the first landing he turned to the right. He stopped at the second door, unlocked it and said, 'Your room, miss.' He stood to one side to allow Ruth to enter.

She cast a quick glance round the room and was delighted

to find that it reflected the good impression she had gained in the hall.

'Splendid,' she said.

'Your key, miss.' The youth handed it to her and turned to Ben. 'I'll show you to your room now, sir.'

With, 'I'll see you soon, Ruth,' he followed the youth from the room to a room four doors along the corridor.

Ben found himself in similar accommodation to Ruth's. He tossed the boy a coin. He caught it and expressed his thanks then added, 'If there is anything you or your sister want, let me know. Andy it is, sir.'

'Thanks,' replied Ben.

'Leave your boots out, sir. I'll return them clean in the morning when I bring you some hot water for shaving. Let me know what time you would like it.'

'I will.'

He left and Ben set about washing off the grime of travel and changing into a clean shirt, fresh trousers and jacket. He examined his appearance in the mirror. Satisfied, he went to see if Ruth was ready. He opened the door to her room when he heard her say, 'Come in.'

Ben stepped inside and came to a full stop, his only movement being to close the door quietly behind him without turning round for he was transfixed by the sight of Ruth standing beside the foot of the bed. The subdued pastel colours of her simply styled cotton dress complemented her complexion. Her slim form was emphasised by the close-fitting skirt that flared only slightly from the high waist. She had taken her hair from her neck and piled it on top of her head.

'You look beautiful,' whispered Ben. He came to her and took her hands in his. 'Thank you for agreeing to be my wife.' He kissed her on the cheek.

As he moved back she gave a little coquettish inclination of her head. 'I think you can do better than that, Ben Coulson, or have you used up all your kisses on other girls?' She reached for his hand and guided him to her. She kissed him and let her lips linger on his in a way that left no room for doubt about her love for him. He loosed their fingers and swept his arms around her waist. They hugged each other, escaping into a world that was only theirs.

When they stepped apart Ruth smiled. 'It's a good job the maid did not return. She would have wondered what was happening between brother and sister.'

'They have provided you with a maid?'

'Yes, Amy. She came just after you had gone to your room and was very attentive, laying out my clothes and helping me with my hair. She took my travelling clothes away and said she would bring them back in the morning all freshened up. Oh Ben, thank you so much for choosing to travel by postchaise.'

He smiled and held out his hand. 'Should we go down?'

She nodded but held his hand tight to prevent him from going to the door. She returned his smile and kissed him. 'Now we must be brother and sister,' she said as she loosened her hold and stepped back for him to open the door.

It was in that role that they enjoyed a glass of Madeira in front of a crackling log fire before going to the dining-room, where they found two elderly couples and a single man already engrossed in their dinner.

After the meal they returned to the fire and exchanged a few pleasantries with the other guests until, tired by the anxiety of their elopement, the excitement of the journey, and the excellent meal, Ruth excused herself and retired to bed. Ben, in his role of brother, deemed it wise to stay a little longer and engage the guests in further conversation before he decided it was time for him to retire.

Ruth had expected that on sinking into the comfort of the soft feather bed she would soon be asleep, but her mind deemed otherwise. Tomorrow loomed before her with the prospect of an irregular marriage ceremony. She bit her lip, regretting that she and Ben had not been able to marry openly with their families around them. She would especially miss her mother and was sad that she would hurt the one person who knew of her love for Ben and had offered no criticism, only words of caution. She eventually fell asleep thinking of him and what the future held for them both.

Ben too had regretful thoughts but he pushed them aside by concentrating on his love for Ruth and wondering how he should deal with their arrival in Whitby.

Ruth slipped from the bed and crossed to the window. Her eyes swept the sky and she was pleased to see it was almost clear; the few clouds visible were thin and high. Light from the east heralded a new day, one that she knew would be fixed in her mind forever. She crossed her arms about her and hugged herself. With joy filling her heart she spun around and flopped on to the bed. At that moment there was a tap on the door. After a pause it was edged tentatively ajar.

'Miss?' The voice was low as if it did not wish to disturb her.

'Come in,' Ruth called, recognising Amy.

The maid was dressed in a freshly laundered apron on top of a gingham dress. 'Good morning, miss,' she said brightly. 'I hope you slept well?'

'I did, Amy,' replied Ruth, pushing herself from the bed. 'Oh, you've brought my clothes.'

Amy was laying them down carefully on the bed. 'I hope they are to your liking, miss.'

'You look to have done a wonderful job,' remarked Ruth appreciatively.

'Thank you, miss. Can I do anything else for you?'

'I don't think so, thank you.'

'Call me if so.'

Further along the corridor, Ben was appreciating the hot water that Andy had brought him. A few minutes later he was expressing his delight at the high polish on his boots. He was adjusting his jacket when there was a light tap at the door. He crossed the floor quickly and opened it.

'Good morning, Ben.' Ruth greeted him quietly but with a sparkle in her eyes.

'Good morning,' he whispered as he glanced quickly both ways along the corridor. Seeing no one, he gave her a quick kiss on the cheek. 'I hope you have a wonderful day.'

'You to,' she replied.

He stepped into the corridor and took her elbow gently, a gesture that outwardly held no more than brotherly affection, and guided her down the stairs.

They entered the dining-room and were shown to the table they had occupied the previous evening. Not knowing when they might eat again, they enjoyed a substantial breakfast. When they had finished they were on their way to their rooms and had reached the bottom of the stairs when Greg appeared from a side door.

'Sir, when would you like the chaise?'

'As soon as you have it ready.'

'Will ten minutes be all right?'

Ben glanced questioningly at Ruth who nodded.

'We'll be ready then,' said Ben.

'Very good, sir.'

Eager to be at their destination, impatience made the journey seem longer than it was. The postillion managed to keep a brisk pace and surprised Ruth and Ben when he slowed the horses and brought them to a stop. He slipped from the saddle and ran back to them.

'Sir, the River Tweed is a short distance ahead. The place you want is the toll house just over the bridge and technically in Scotland.'

'Thank you, we'll drive on in a few moments.'

Greg walked back to the horses.

Ben turned to Ruth. 'You are sure you want to go through with this?'

'As sure as I am of anything.'

He kissed her lightly. 'I am too.'

'Just let me get straightened.' Ruth sat up, adjusted her dress, patted her hair into place and put on her simple bonnet, tying it under her chin.

Ben flicked some dust from his jacket and awaited her word. 'I'm ready.'

He called to Greg who mounted his horse again. The chaise rolled towards the stone bridge that spanned the river carrying the road into Scotland. Ruth gripped Ben's hand tightly.

They rumbled over the bridge and saw on their right a one-storey cottage. An elderly man stepped out of the building and held up his hand to stop the vehicle.

'There's a toll to pay,' he said, coming to Ben.

'Yes,' he acknowledged. 'There's also a ceremony we'd like you to perform.'

The man's eyes flicked from Ben to Ruth and back again. 'You want to marry?' He was already working out what he could charge. This couple must be fairly well-to-do, travelling independently in a postchaise.

'Yes, we do,' replied Ben.

The man nodded. 'Come inside then.' He waited while Ben got to the ground and helped Ruth from her seat. 'You'll be returning immediately to England?'

'Yes.'

The man nodded again and called to the postillion, instructing him where to leave the chaise.

'Will you be wanting documentary proof of this marriage? It isn't necessary but some people like proof that they are married, especially if they are returning to their families.'

'We would like that,' replied Ben.

'Whenever I get that request, I always like the document to be signed by yourselves and two witnesses. It makes it more authentic.' Without seeking Ben's approval he called to the postillion, 'Come inside when you've settled the horses. You are to be a witness.' He turned to Ben and Ruth next. 'The other will be my wife. Follow me.' He headed for the door and they fell into step behind him.

They were taken into a plain room, not very big but light-ened by the whitewashed walls. There was the minimum of furniture, a central pine table with two chairs of similar material facing it on one side and a single chair on the other.

The man indicated the two chairs to Ruth and Ben who, with a tentative glance at each other, sat down. He went to the door and shouted, 'Mrs McCabe! Get thee here!' At this point the postillion appeared and was ushered into the room. The man indicated for him to stand behind Ben. A tall woman, as thin as her husband, came into the room. She looked with searching eyes past a sharp pointed nose at Ruth and Ben as if passing judgement on to their suitability to marry, but did not utter a word. The man had gone to the chair behind the table but had not sat down. He cleared his throat. About to say something, he appeared to think better of it and said, 'This is my wife, Mrs McCabe. I am Mr McCabe.' He heaved a great sigh as if the weight of the world had suddenly been thrust upon his shoulders and the ceremony he had been asked to perform was a burden to him. He raised his eyes heavenwards implying that he was seeking help from above. His eyes narrowed sharply as he cast a glance over Ruth and Ben before saying a deep sonorous tone, 'We will begin.'

The voice remained resolutely sonorous throughout the ceremony. Twenty minutes later Ruth and Ben were back in England, a piece of paper nestling in Ben's pocket that proved they had undergone a ceremony, performed by A. McCabe, witnessed by F. McCabe and G. Houseman, at which they had agreed to be husband and wife.

The sadness that had come over Ruth during the ceremony, when she had realised that all her girlhood dreams of a church wedding, surrounded by family and friends, would never be fulfilled, lifted when she saw the intense happiness on Ben's face.

His smile was warm and loving as he said, 'Happy, my love?' She gave a little nod, but the way in which she vehemently delivered it told him all he needed to know.

Lost in their own world they knew little of the journey until the chaise slowed and stopped. They looked beyond their immediate surroundings and saw that the postillion had brought the vehicle on to a broad sward of grass from where there was a view across a gentle valley through which a tree-lined river meandered its way.

Greg came up to them. 'I thought you might be ready for something to eat, ma'am.'

Ruth savoured that word: Ma'am. No longer Miss. Now she was Mrs Ben Coulson. There was something satisfying about it. 'That would be pleasant, but where?' She glanced across the open landscape. 'With all that was going on we never thought to order anything at the inn.'

'I enquired, ma'am, and when they told me nothing had been arranged, I asked them to provide us with something.' He looked at Ben. 'I hope I did right, sir?'

'Of course you did, and thank you for thinking of it.'

During the course of their stop Ben informed the postillion that they wanted to be in Whitby at six-thirty the following evening, deposited near a certain house, not a minute before nor a minute after. Greg informed them that they would stop for the night in Durham where he knew there was an inn the equal of the one they had stopped at going north.

So it proved and Ruth and Ben, as a newly married couple, revelled in the luxury. It was a night when nothing else was of consequence but their closeness. The past was gone, the future did not matter. They were lost in a love that transcended time. They were together and that was all that mattered.

After the bliss of waking together had brought its own joys, harsh reality began to impinge as time relentlessly ticked away.

Ready to go to breakfast, Ben asked, 'Are you worried about today, love?'

Ruth hesitated then said quietly, 'Apprehensive.'

Though he had similar feelings he tried to bolster her confidence. 'Don't be, love, we have each other.'

She gave a wan smile, trying to muster the belief that everything would be all right, but that did not answer the question that posed itself: How can it be? But whatever the outcome it would have to be faced. She forged a steely determination within herself.

*

Alicia, half-awake, stretched the rest of the sleep out of her and brought her mind to focus on the joy that today would bring – betrothal to the man she wanted. She snuggled into the luxury of her feather bed, imagining that she was sinking into it with Ben's arms around her.

She tightened her lips in irritation. Why hadn't she insisted on a Christmas wedding? Why had she agreed to wait until spring? But what was done was done. Today was today and she would enjoy it, counting every passing minute with excitement, deciding which dress to wear, surveying the mouth-watering food, trying to guess what was in the parcels sent by both families. She would also savour the relief in her father and mother as Uncle Sam tore up the loan agreement, an action that would release her father from debt. But most of all, she was anticipating being with Ben. She hugged herself. 'Oh, it is going to be such a wonderful day!'

'Where has that damned boy got to?' How many times her father had voiced that question Sarah did not know. Sam's annoyance mounted as time passed and still Ben did not appear. His father had expected him home earlier in the week. Sarah had tried to calm him by reminding him that Ben had gone on a business trip and that there could have been some snags that had delayed him.

She grimaced at Dina and Eric as their father paced the hall and looked at his watch for the umpteenth time.

'It's time we were going. Where the devil is he?' From the snap in Sam's voice the family knew his anger was rising and that it would be better to say as little as possible in reply.

But Sarah ventured to try and calm him. 'Maybe he'll go straight to the Campions'.'

Her father uttered a grunt of disbelief. 'Irresponsible! I thought he'd changed his ways, seems he hasn't.' He tightened his lips, shook his head in disgust and said, 'I suppose we'd better go though it seems stupid arriving without the one person who should be there.'

'He might be there already,' Dina suggested.

'He should have been here to go with us.' Sam tightened his lips, grabbed his hat and stick and stormed from the house.

His family followed closely, hoping that their suggestions would prove to be right. They did not demur at the pace their father set, for the air was sharp, rain threatened, and they would be pleased to seek shelter as soon as possible. Sarah thought the weather suited her father's mood. She was beginning to have her doubts about Ben turning up and, knowing Ruth was not in Whitby, was even starting to think that the two of them might be together.

When they reached the Campions' they were ushered in quickly by the maid.

Hearing their arrival, Seaton and Grace came from the drawing-room to welcome them.

'Where's Ben?' asked Seaton, with a glance that embraced them all.

'He's not here then?' Sam shied away from the question with one of his own.

Seaton looked surprised. 'Should he be?'

'He's been on business in Newcastle. Said he would be back for tonight, but hasn't arrived. I thought he might have come straight here.'

'He hasn't.' Seaton gave a shake of his head. Doubt crept into his eyes. 'Newcastle, you say? If that's the case he's not likely to reach Whitby tonight.'

'He could have hired some reliable means to get here. He said he would.' Sarah tried to sound reassuring.

'I hope you are right,' said Seaton. 'Well, we are doing no good standing here. Come into the drawing-room and have a glass of warm punch.'

They all filed into the room where greetings were exchanged with Alicia, Griselda and Dorothea.

'Alicia, you look so pretty,' exclaimed Sarah. 'I do like your dress.'

'I'm so glad. I thought maybe it was too plain.'

'No, no. It's the height of fashion, especially as it is white and so slim-fitting with no adornment.'

'Except the pearls around my neck.'

'Which complement it perfectly.'

As they had been talking, Alicia kept glancing at the doorway. 'Where's Ben?' she asked eventually when he did not bring up the rear.

'A little late,' put in her father quickly.

Though he was seething, Sam realised that Seaton did not want to disturb his daughter so offered an explanation. 'He had some urgent business in Newcastle. Thought it might result in some delay but assured me he would be here. We are a little early. He knows we were invited for half-past six.'

Alicia said nothing.

Seaton quickly organised some punch which was accepted with forced alacrity. Ben's absence was creating an uneasy atmosphere. Conversation was staccato and forced, delivered as if they shouldn't be making a sound lest they miss his arrival. Though they did not want to be seen to do so, each of them kept giving surreptitious glances at the clock on the mantelpiece. The minute hand moved on, drawing nearer and nearer to the half-hour. Each person in the room became more and more tense.

It was half-past six. Sarah had her eyes fixed on her father. He pulled his watch from his pocket as if to check that the Campions' clock was right. She saw him scowl and knew that both timepieces matched.

'Ben did know it was six-thirty for seven?' Grace's quiet voice almost startled everyone.

Sam's 'Yes' was sharp.

'Well, then, he still has time.'

'I suppose so,' Sam agreed somewhat reluctantly. 'But he should have been home to come with us.'

At that moment a postchaise was coming to a halt a short distance from the house.

'You are sure you want to go through with this?' asked Ben.

'It will have to be faced some time,' replied Ruth. 'If we don't do it now we cannot go to my family. They think I am in King's Lynn, but your father is expecting you tonight and shouldn't hear of our marriage from anyone else. Nor should Alicia. We should face them now, no matter what the result is.'

Ben nodded. 'You are a wise young lady, and I love you for it.' He stepped out of the chaise and helped her to the ground.

'I've written a note for the landlord at the Angel. He will give you accommodation for the night, Greg.'

'Thank you, sir.'

'Please wait there until I contact you tomorrow.'

'Yes, sir.'

Ben was taking precautions in case the most obvious course was to leave Whitby after they had faced their families.

The postchaise moved away. Ruth watched it for a moment, recalling the happiness to which it had taken them. She gave a quiet sigh of regret, took Ben's arm and said, 'Let's go in.'

'More punch, anyone?' put in Seaton to relieve the tense atmosphere.

Before anyone could answer they heard the distant ringing of a bell. Tension evaporated, glances of relief were exchanged.

'This must be him now,' said Grace.

They all turned to face the door. Seaton and Sam were relieved for different reasons. Seaton would soon be free from debt; Sam would soon have within his grasp the empire he had always dreamed of. Grace was thankful that all her preparations for this party could now get underway. Griselda and Dorothea were looking forward to having a handsome brother-in-law. Dina and Eric were relieved that they would not feel any more of their father's wrath over Ben's prolonged absence. Sarah felt some relief that Ben had arrived, though she could not dispel a niggling little doubt about the reason for his late arrival. Alicia felt the anxiety that had gripped her depart. Ben was here. In a few moments, with the announcement of their engagement, he would be hers. Her future would be as she had always wanted it.

Even though nobody was speaking, a buzz of excited anticipation filled the room. When the door opened it vanished, replaced by utter disbelief. Everyone stared at the couple who came in. Any word that could have been spoken was lost in the explosion from Sam.

'Get that Holmes woman out of here!' His face had gone red and dark with rage. 'What the devil do you mean by bringing her here? You know damned well this is a special family occasion.'

Ben drew himself up. 'Yes, it is a special occasion. And Ruth is not a Holmes, she is my wife.'

A shocked silence filled the room. Minds were numb. This couldn't be happening. It wasn't true.

Only Sarah really grasped what had happened, for she knew a little more about the relationship between these two people than any of the others did. The journeys to Newcastle and King's Lynn had been a cover for what Ben and Ruth really intended. Her heart sang with joy for her brother. Good for you, Ben, you followed your heart. Be happy, she thought. All these feelings were pushed aside, however, in the outburst that followed.

'She's what?' Sam glared at the newcomers ferociously.

'Ruth is my wife,' replied Ben calmly, and tightened his loving hold on her hand.

'She can't be. You've had no time—'

'I have a document, signed by the minister, confirming our marriage. Two witnesses signed to prove it also,' replied Ben firmly. 'We were married in Scotland.'

'Scotland? An irregular match!' stormed Sam. 'That won't be recognised here.' He believed he had found a loophole that would enable him to disregard this marriage.

'What you mean is that irregular marriages are no longer permitted in England, but that is not the case in Scotland. The fact that we have committed ourselves to each other is enough, but I made sure we had written evidence of the marriage also. You can do nothing about it.'

Sam's anger had been mounting all this time. Veins stood out in his neck. All around him there was chaos. Seaton could see his whole world collapsing, with a furious Sam demanding his money back. Grace saw poverty staring them in the face if Alicia's marriage did not go through. She knew she could never cope with that. Griselda and Dorothea were astonished. In spite of Sam's mounting anger that she knew could have devastating consequences, Sarah was inwardly calm. There was nothing her father could do to reverse this. Eric fumed, grim-faced. What the devil was Ben thinking of, marrying a Holmes? How dare he? Serve him right if he felt the full blast of Father's wrath. Dina showed no outward reaction but it was Alicia, a lifelong family friend, she really felt sorry for. She glanced at her and was shocked.

Alicia's face had drained of colour. Her eyes stood out in disbelief and her whole body was taut. When comprehension of what had happened finally dawned, the disbelief in her eyes changed to hatred. Ben had betrayed her. She had taken his promise to be at the party for confirmation that they would marry when all the time he had been planning to elope with Ruth. She felt weak but kept a grip. She would remain in control of herself. She would not give him the satisfaction of seeing her give way under the shock he had inflicted on her. He had never had any intention of marrying her, and saving her family. He had chosen this bitch instead, didn't care what happened to them.

Her ice-cold words cut sharply through Sam's tirade.

'Damn you, Ben Coulson. I hope you and this bitch,' she looked contemptuously at Ruth, 'rot in misery.' Alicia drew herself up proudly but it took all her strength to keep her emotions under control and sweep imperiously from the room.

Everyone was taken by surprise by her reaction, but as the door swung shut Grace and her two other daughters were jolted out of their stupor and went after her. They found Alicia holding on to the banister rail, her body racked by silent sobs. Grace laid a comforting arm around her shoulders and, with Sam's tirade growing fainter behind them, the four women walked up the stairs.

'You want horse-whipping, boy, marrying the daughter of the man who killed your brother.' Sam's voice was jagged with anger.

'My father did not kill your son, Mr Coulson.' Ruth's tone was quiet but firm.

Sam glared at her. 'I'm not talking to you, girl. No doubt you lured my son away. Well, as far as I am concerned, *you* do not exist.' His words lashed at her but she accepted them calmly, not taking her eyes off him.

'Don't you speak to your daughter-in-law like that,' snapped Ben.

'Daughter-in-law?' Sam gave a contemptuous laugh that added more vitriol to what he thought of her. 'Not likely. Because, Ben Coulson, you are no longer my son! Now get out of here and don't let me set eyes on you again. Don't ever contact any of my family again.'

Ben's lips tightened. He had expected to feel the full blast of his father's wrath but it was a shock to be severed from his family. In that moment he saw sympathy in Sarah, indifference in Dina, and a sneer implying 'you got what you deserve' from Eric. He was about to say something when his father lashed him with his tongue again.

'Don't ever come begging from me, you'll get nothing. I don't want a son with no honour. You promised to marry Alicia.'

'I did not!' rapped Ben. 'You all assumed that. Nobody ever asked me outright how I felt about it. You put me in a dilemma and thought I would see it your way. Well, I chose the course my heart chose. I followed my love.'

'Love?' Sam sneered. 'You mean that bitch ensnared you, thinking you would be a good catch.' His eyes fixed on Ruth. 'Well, see if you like the poverty you have reaped. Now get out of here!'

Ben's eyes narrowed. 'Don't talk to my wife like that! One day you'll be sorry for it.'

Sam laughed. 'Sorry?'

There was such derision mixed with contempt for Ruth in his voice that Ben, anger in his eyes, started towards his father, but Ruth laid a restraining hand on his arm.

'Let us leave quietly,' she said.

He hesitated, and then feeling the pressure on his arm turned to her and nodded. They started for the door.

Sarah shot a glance at her father and then, daringly, reached the door before them. She opened it and as they passed, whispered, 'Be happy.'

Ruth smiled a thank you. Ben mouthed it, thankful that there was at least one member of the family who would not refuse them a blessing.

Chapter Twelve

When she stepped outside the Campions' house Ruth turned up the collar of her coat. They had been inside only a short while but in that time a distinct chill had come into the air. Or was that feeling the result of the hostile reception they had just faced? Though it was no more than she had expected, there had been a last lingering hope that things may not be as bad as she had anticipated. But they had been and anger at their reception had left her numb. Was this an omen for her future life with Ben? She moved closer to him, seeking reassurance from his presence. She wanted to hold his hand, to feel the love in his touch, but could not for Ben carried their valises, one in each hand.

'What do you want to do, love?' he asked.

'I think we can do nothing else but go to my parents,' she replied. 'But how do you feel about that?'

'It can be no worse than facing my father. I'm sorry about his attitude to you.'

'You have nothing to be sorry for, Ben.'

The activity around the port was subdued. At this time of the year people chose to be inside, even more so this evening when a wind blew from the sea, rippling the water of the river, sweeping round corners and along the narrow streets, seeking out every nook and cranny. Those people who were abroad hurried home or to friends', while others made for shelter in the inns and sought solace in tankards of ale.

Ruth and Ben crossed the bridge and turned into Grape Lane. They stopped at the door with the brass whale for a knocker. A glance of apprehension passed between them. Ben placed the valises on the ground and reached for the knocker. He paused then, with a nod of approval from Ruth, rapped it hard on the door. A few moments later it opened. Light from a lamp on the wall close to the door flooded on to their faces.

'Miss Ruth!' The maid expressed astonishment at seeing her.

'Hello, Harriet.'

The maid moved to one side and Ruth stepped into the narrow hall followed by Ben.

'Hello, Harriet,' he said with a friendly smile, not knowing when he might need an ally among the servants.

She bobbed a curtsy, trying to fathom the fact that Miss Ruth was here when she'd thought her to be in King's Lynn. Not only that, she was accompanied by Mr Ben Coulson! Harriet's thoughts started to race. She knew of Captain Holmes's trouble with Mr Sam Coulson. Oh, my, now there could be even more trouble!

'Where is everybody, Harriet?' Ruth's query broke into the girl's thoughts.

'Oh.' Realising she was still holding the door open, she closed it quickly and replied, 'In the dining-room, miss, they've just started their meal.'

'Is everyone there?'

'Yes, miss.'

Ruth exchanged a look with Ben that said this might be more formidable than they'd expected. As well as her father's hostility, there was certain to be antagonism from her brothers.

Ruth took off her bonnet and coat and indicated for Ben to do likewise. She thought that appearing without their outdoor clothes would impart a semblance of normality. Harriet took the garments and was about to move to the dining-room door when Ruth whispered, 'We'll announce ourselves, Harriet.'

'Very good, miss.' She scurried away to dispense with the clothes and hurry to the kitchen with this news that had her all of a flutter.

Ruth patted her hair, smoothed her dress, drew a deep breath and opened the door.

Conversation came to a sudden halt. A hush filled with disbelief descended on the room and everyone's gaze passed beyond Ruth to Ben, standing just behind her.

'Ruth!' Georgina broke the silence. Though she had immediately guessed something of the situation on seeing Ben, she automatically put the query, 'What . . . where . . .?'

Her words broke the paralysis that had gripped Gideon. 'What's he doing here? Get him out.' His voice was icy cold, eyes narrowed and charged with fury.

Ruth's three brothers started to rise to their feet, visibly hostile to this man they regarded as an unwanted intruder.

Their movement stung a response from Georgina. She knew she had to act now to keep this situation from getting out of control. 'Sit down!' The authority in her voice would brook no rebuttal. Her sons hesitated and looked to their father, but Georgina caught his eye and he would not go against his wife. He signalled with his hand and his sons sat down slowly and reluctantly, without diminishing the atmosphere of hostility.

Gideon met his wife's gaze. 'Well?' he asked.

'It is obvious that Ruth has not been to her aunt's. She could not be walking in here at this time if she had. I want to hear what she has to say.' Georgina looked at her daughter.

'Maybe I should explain,' said Ben, but before he could go on Ruth had laid a hand on his arm in a gesture that said, Let me.

'Mother, Father, Ben and I were married yesterday,' she said, emphasising the last three words so that no one could be under any misapprehension.

Then came a moment when the world seemed to stand still. Georgina gasped, though it was what she had half-expected when Ruth had walked in with Ben. Daniel, Edmund, Abel and Rachel were speechless. How could their sister do this? Gideon was the one who spoke for them all when he thundered, 'What?'

'Ben and I were married yesterday,' Ruth repeated calmly.

'You can't be!'

'We are, sir, and I have a paper in my pocket to prove it,' said Ben.

Gideon glared at him. 'How can you—?'

'We went to Scotland.'

'Damn you, what have you done?'

'Sir, I have married your daughter because we love each other.'

'You hadn't the decency to seek my permission,' Gideon fumed, 'and I know why. You knew you wouldn't get it after what your father did to me and to this family.' He turned his eyes on Ruth. 'What were you thinking of, daughter?'

'I love him, Father.' The emotion in her voice left no doubt in anyone's mind that she was genuinely in love.

'But why did you consent to marry him this way?'

'Sir, there was no time to pursue the normal course as we would have wished, even though we might have had to battle for your permission.'

'No time?' asked Georgina in a hushed voice, though instinct told her that the immediate thought that had come to her could not be right.

'There is indeed a good reason for our doing what we did,' said Ruth. 'Ben will explain.'

'Does your father know about this marriage?' asked Gideon.

'Yes, sir, he does. We went to see him first. You will understand why if you will allow me to explain.'

Gideon was not sure that he wanted to hear this explanation. He sensed the hostility still seething in his sons and knew it would only take the slightest nod from him for them to throw Ben Coulson to the dogs. But he saw a look in Georgina's eyes that said, Don't you dare.

She spoke up. 'We will hear what you have to say, but first, I don't suppose you have eaten?'

'No, Mother, we haven't.'

Georgina rang the bell and in a few moments Harriet appeared. 'Please set two more places between me and Rachel. We will have enough soup here,' she said, glancing in the tureen that was on the table in front of her. 'I am sure that there will be enough to follow to satisfy everyone.' Georgina had taken charge. She glanced at her sons. 'Two more chairs.' They may do it reluctantly but she knew this was the way to ease the situation. Having heard that Ruth and Ben had already been to the Coulsons' she knew that the meeting must have been stormy. Now, if they wanted to keep their daughter's love, it was up to them to try and understand her actions, and the first step on the way to an easier relationship was to share a meal.

As they ate, Ben explained. 'Sir, I fell in love with your daughter when I first saw her, and then I took her to the ball.' Gideon nodded. 'I saw her occasionally after that, then came the tragedy in the Arctic.' The mention of that set anger mounting in Gideon but he saw his wife raise a warning finger and held back the retort that came to his lips. 'Sir, I did not condone my father's reaction. The events of that voyage also had an effect on my life, though I did not know it immediately.' Ben paused. He glanced quickly around the family sitting at the table. Though they were eating he saw from their expressions that their attention was fixed on what he was saying. 'I would like a promise from all of you that what I am about to tell you will not go beyond these four walls?' They stopped eating and looked up from their plates. Wondering what was so important that it had to remain a secret, they gazed directly at him.

Gideon grunted and gave a little nod.

'You boys, and you, Rachel?' Georgina's voice was hard, demanding that they agree and warning that she would be hard on anyone who broke such a promise. When they had made it she looked at Ben. 'You have our word.'

'Thank you, Mrs Holmes, and the rest of you. Apparently before the whale-ships sailed, Martin had promised my father that he would marry Alicia Campion on his return. My father and Mr Campion had made an agreement but no one else was to know of it until Martin returned. I need not go into the reasons for this. I knew nothing of it at the time, but when

Martin did not return my father told me about the understanding and said that I was expected to step into my brother's place. But I was in love with Ruth.'

'Did you not refuse your father?' demanded Daniel.

'There were reasons why I could not. Shortly afterwards I discovered why this arrangement had been made with Mr Campion. I did not like what was likely to happen to him if I did not comply so I held back from a direct refusal.'

'And kept my sister in limbo?' snapped Edmund in disgust.

'There were good reasons,' said Ruth, springing to Ben's defence.

'I needed time to think things through, find a way out of the dilemma I was in. Please believe me, there were good reasons why I could not act in the normal fashion. An engagement party for Alicia and me and our families had been arranged for this evening. I had to take action before that. Ruth and I could not go through the normal channels. If I had told my father I would not marry Alicia, he would have found some way to force my hand. The only way was for Ruth and me to marry secretly, and that meant a marriage in Scotland where irregular marriages are allowed. So that is what we planned and what we did, arranging it so that we would be back here to walk in on the party and make our announcement.'

'And so your father could do nothing about it,' said Georgina thoughtfully.

'Exactly,' replied Ben. 'All I hope is that the consequences for the Campion family will not be drastic.'

'Why should they be?' asked Daniel.

Ben raised his hands in apology as he said, 'I cannot divulge what I discovered to be the reason for the arranged marriage.'

'No doubt some dubious deal made by your father,' grunted Gideon.

'Sir, I will not deny that there were commercial considerations behind it.'

'Thought so.'

'But,' Ben went on as if he had not been interrupted, 'in

defence of my father, I must say that the chief motive was to help someone. I can say no more than that.'

'Thank you for being frank with us,' put in Georgina quickly. She did not want any more prying questions. They had to take Ben on trust.

'All right, young man,' put in Gideon reluctantly, his voice losing some of its hostility but none of its authority. 'What's done is done. It is not the marriage I would have wished for my daughter, so see you treat her right or else you will have not only me to answer to but all this family.'

'Sir, I love Ruth deeply. She will always be in my heart and have all my consideration. She will know happiness with me.'

'See that she does.' Gideon looked at Ruth. 'You want my blessing?'

'Father, nothing would please me more at this moment.'

'You are very precious to me, as are all my children. If they are happy so am I. I want nothing more than that, but it may be hard to achieve. If it makes you happy that I give my blessing to this marriage, then I do.'

The tension that had hovered around the table vanished. Ruth jumped to her feet and went to her father, flung her arms around his neck and kissed him.

'Thank you Father, thank you so much.' There were tears in her eyes as she straightened and went to her mother and kissed her.

'Be happy, Ruth,' said Georgina quietly.

'I will,' she whispered.

Gideon stood up. He eyed Ben and allowed any last glimmer of hostility in him to drain away. Ruth wanted his support and approval and he was prepared to give it, for her sake and the sake of his family. He held out his hand to his son-in-law.

Ben, almost unable to take in this unexpected gesture and the reversal of Captain Holmes's attitude, rose slowly to his feet. He reached out and felt the strong, firm grip of his father-in-law. It was a signal to the rest of the family. Reluctance to accept Ben was erased from the minds of the three young men and their sister. Daniel, Edmund and Abel shook hands with him and then hugged Ruth. Rachel kissed Ben on the cheek. 'I'm pleased you are my brother-in-law,' she said softly.

'And I'm pleased to have you as my sister-in-law.' He gave her a broad smile and winked.

'I think a glass of Madeira to toast the bride and groom is in order,' said Gideon. 'See to it, Abel.'

The youngest son jumped to his feet and soon had a glass placed before everyone.

Gideon stood, raised his glass and proposed the toast.

The atmosphere eased and chatter flowed around the table. Ruth and Ben told them of their journey to Coldstream, described the ceremony and the journey back to Whitby. When they had left the dining-room and settled in the drawing-room, he was soon in possession of the facts regarding Captain Holmes's future.

'We did not want to leave Whitby. As your father has blocked any chance of my finding employment on a local ship, I have decided to take up fishing again though it is many years since I followed that trade. My sons wanted to join me but I insisted they remain employed on the whale-ships and in their winter work,' explained Gideon.

'Their financial contribution plus my husband's receipts from his last voyage have enabled us to keep this house and still employ the maids and a cook,' put in Georgina, 'but we will have to review the situation before long.' She paused. 'We shouldn't be talking about such mundane matters on this day. Let us leave them until tomorrow. I expect you have no accommodation to go to?'

'I was going to get us a room at the Angel,' said Ben.

'There is no need to do that. There is Ruth's room. I'm sure you will manage in that and we'll talk again in the morning.' Georgina glanced at her daughter. 'Does that meet with your approval?'

'Yes, Mother.' She smiled her thanks.

'That is a very generous suggestion, Mrs Holmes, and I thank you.'

'You must stay as long as you like,' added Gideon.

'I don't want to be any trouble, sir. I will sort my affairs out as soon as possible.'

After Captain and Mrs Holmes decided it was time to retire and leave the young ones, Ben got into conversation with Daniel and learned that he, with his brothers and sisters, had wanted the family to move away from Whitby so that his father could get command of another ship but that his parents had refused, believing that if they did people would think Gideon was admitting responsibility for what had happened in the Arctic.

'I hope that some day he can prove his innocence,' Daniel concluded, 'though how I don't know. In the meantime I trust he can make a success of fishing. Until then we will continue to contribute to the family's upkeep. His first priority is to find a boat and two partners.'

It gave Ben a lot to think about when he and Ruth went to bed.

When she walked into her room, Ruth experienced a strange feeling. The last time she had stood here she had looked back thinking she would never sleep in this room again. Here she was so soon afterwards, but with one enormous difference. The room that had been exclusively hers she was now to share with a man. In a way it seemed he was intruding on a world where he had no place. She pushed that thought away. He was her husband, had every right to share this room. She heard the door click shut behind her, turned and saw him watching her. She held out her arms, smiled and said, 'Welcome, my love.'

He came to her and when her arms enfolded him he felt at home. Their future would begin from here. It was there for their taking. His arms slipped round her waist. 'I love you, Mrs Coulson,' he whispered, looking deep into her eyes and seeing there the same response. Their lips brushed, came together again, lingered. A passion that needed to be satisfied flared between them.

By the time Grace Campion and her three daughters reached the top of the stairs Alicia had, with steely determination, resumed control of herself. They reached her room.

'Stay with her for a while,' Grace said, looking at Griselda and Dorothea, 'I must return to your father and the Coulsons.'

'Yes, Mama,' they both said together.

Alicia stiffened. 'I'm all right, Mother. I'd rather be on my own.'

Grace looked doubtful and hesitated for a moment. Then her knowledge of her eldest daughter prevailed. 'Very well, but call for your sisters if you need them. They'll be in their rooms.'

'I will, but I'll be all right.' Alicia opened her door and slipped inside, letting the door shut quietly behind her. She heard her sisters' footsteps pass down the corridor and her mother hurry down the stairs. With a deep sigh Alicia leaned back against the door. She stood for a few moments trying to bring recent events into perspective. She felt choked. Crying might bring some relief but if she did it would mean that Ben was triumphant, and she was determined that would not be so. Her eyes narrowed as she pushed herself away from the door. Crossing the room to the stool at her dressing-table, she eyed herself in the mirror and vowed, 'One day, Ben Coulson, you'll pay for this and regret what you have done!'

An atmosphere of shock still lingered in the drawing-room when Grace returned. With Sam continuing to rail against Ben, the rest of his family stood around in the embarrassing position of not knowing what to do. Seaton looked perplexed. He wished Sam would calm down. What had happened, had happened. Sam's fury could not undo that. Marriage? There was still Eric, but he would not wish to encumber Alicia with a young man whose only interest was the whale-ships. Surely Sam would not push that union when he wanted a son who could participate

218

in the business ashore? Even if he did, Seaton felt sure that his daughter would refuse but with no marriage to a Coulson his position could be precarious, especially if Sam called in his debt which he had every right to do

'I'll see that Ben pays for this, Seaton, and you can be sure . . .' Sam stopped when he saw Grace. His voice was a little calmer when he made his apology. 'I am devastated by this. I'm sorry, Grace. I don't know what else to say.'

Seeing he was going to try to go on, she raised her hand to stop him. 'I think it is best if no more is said now. In the light of tomorrow things may look different. We will be able to look with cool minds on what is to be done, though I can see no way of dissolving Ben's marriage.'

'Maybe we should go,' Sarah suggested, glancing at her father for support.

'I think it would be best,' he agreed. 'Seaton, we'll talk tomorrow.'

When the door closed behind the Coulsons, Seaton Campion was left nervously wondering what tomorrow would bring.

On the way home, lost in his morose thoughts, Sam did not speak. Recognising their father's mood Sarah and Dina exchanged knowing looks, while Eric was lost in his own pleasure at the thought that Ben had got what he deserved. Now he himself would inherit the bulk of his father's fortune after his sisters had been provided for. Maybe all his talents were directed where his heart was – sailing the Arctic, hunting the whale. Well, he could continue to do that even after the Coulson empire became his. Maybe he would not be as smart as Martin and Ben would have been in charge but he knew enough to be able to keep track of what a competent manager was doing.

'Penny for them?' Dina's prod startled him.

He had been allowing his thoughts to run ahead of themselves. 'Oh, noth . . . nothing,' Eric spluttered.

Sarah gave Dina a wink which raised a smile from her younger sister.

When they reached home Sam tossed his hat, coat and stick on to a chair in the hall and went into his study without a word. Eric bounded up the stairs and disappeared into his room.

Dina paused outside Sarah's door. 'Talk?' she asked.

Sarah knew her sister well enough to realise that Dina had some questions she thought Sarah could answer. Besides, didn't they always share thoughts and gossip? 'Why not?'

They slipped into Sarah's room and, once they had discarded their outdoor clothes, flopped on to the bed and twisted themselves into comfortable lounging positions, Sarah with her back cushioned by her pillows and Dina propping herself on one elbow so that she could observe her sister's reactions.

'Well?' said Dina.

'Well, what?'

'Come on, Sarah, you weren't as shocked by the appearance of Ben and Ruth as the rest of us. What did you know?'

'I was,' replied Sarah.

'Oh, come on, I know you and your reactions.'

Sarah gave a little shrug of her shoulders. 'Well, I knew that Ben and Ruth had been seeing each other in spite of Father's hostility to Captain Holmes. Then the day before Ben supposedly left for Newcastle, I arranged a meeting between him and Ruth.'

Dina's eyes widened. 'You did?'

'Yes. Then he went to Newcastle, and Ruth a couple of days later to King's Lynn. Now there was nothing in that to suggest they were together, but when Ben was late returning from Newcastle, I began to wonder.'

'And you were right. Do you approve?' There was eagerness in Dina's voice as she awaited her sister's opinion.

Sarah looked as if she was considering her words. 'I do. I like Ruth.'

'I thought you'd support a family friend?'

'Well,' Sarah gave a little shake of her head, 'I think Ben will be happier with Ruth than he would ever have been with Alicia.'

'I hope you are right. Do you know why Father and Uncle Seaton arranged a marriage between Alicia and Ben, and why Ben must have agreed though he never meant to go through with it?'

Sarah shook her head. 'I don't, but I suspect there was some commercial reason behind it.'

'But why did Ben let it go this far?'

'I can only surmise he had a very good reason. Can you picture Father's reaction if he had refused?'

'Can't I just!' Dina laughed. 'And imagine if Ben had told him that he was going to marry Captain Holmes's daughter!'

'Exactly. Ben and Ruth took the only way open to them.'

'Will you defy Father and still see them?'

'I'm not going to lose touch with the brother I love even though I'll have to do it discreetly.'

'Keep me informed, won't you?'

'Of course, and we'll see him together.'

'As long as he stays in Whitby.'

'I don't think Ruth will want to leave, not when her parents have chosen to stay here.'

'I wonder what Ben and Ruth will do?'

'He does have the ropery.'

Dina sat up on the bed, drew her knees up and hugged them. 'Isn't it romantic, being whisked away like that without anybody knowing and coming back married? Father doesn't approve of Rowan so I think I'll have to persuade him to do the same as Ben.'

'Don't you dare, Father will be apoplectic,' said Sarah, then laughed when she saw the teasing twinkle in her sister's eye.

'What about you, Sarah? Not over Tim yet?' As soon as she had said it Dina regretted recalling his tragic death at the Ravenscar alum workings. 'I'm sorry, sis, I shouldn't have . . .'

'That's all right,' broke in Sarah. She gave a small regretful shake of her head as she said, 'No, there's no one special yet, though Ryan Bennett has sent a note inviting me to a concert being held at Mulgrave Hall.'

221

'Oh, you must accept, Sarah, you must. Mr Bennett is that eligible young man who has recently moved to live with his aunt there, isn't he? When did you meet him?' The excited curiosity in Dina's voice brooked no evasive words from her sister.

'He was attending that exhibition of paintings in the Angel that Ben and I went to. We were introduced, we chatted, he was charming – and I thought no more about it until two days ago when this invitation arrived.'

'Oh you must accept, you must!' cried Dina. 'I'm so pleased for you.'

'But I don't know whether I'm over Tim yet.'

'You can't live the rest of your life in the past. Tim wouldn't want you to live on a memory.'

Sarah nodded slowly. 'I suppose you're right.'

'Of course I'm right.' Dina jumped from the bed. 'Dream of Ryan tonight.' She hugged her sister and left the room.

Sam, still furious at what had happened, cursed as he slammed the study door behind him. He stirred life into the fire to help to drive out the cold that had gnawed his bones as he walked back from the Campions'. He crossed the room to the sideboard and poured himself a large whisky, dragged a chair in front of the fire and slumped into it. He held his glass so that the flames lit up the amber liquid, stared at it for a moment and then took a drink. He let his arms rest on the chair and stared morosely at the flames.

How could Ben do this to him? Sam's idea of getting his hands on Seaton's business was now as far from being realised as ever. No, it wasn't. He could still demand it in exchange for Seaton's debt . . . but though he was ruthless in business, he did not want to foreclose in order to gain what he wanted. If he did it would destroy a friendship that had lasted from boyhood and make a mockery of the gratitude he'd felt towards Seaton's father and mother for accepting him into their lives. To demand repayment from their son and so condemn him and his family to near poverty would sit heavy on Sam's conscience even though he was a hard man. That was not the way he wanted it. It was not the way he had planned it. Why had life given him such nasty kicks? First the loss of his beloved Martin, and then betrayed by Ben. What was he going to do about it?

He sat there until he shivered, the fire but an ember in the grate and the decanter more than half-empty beside him. He was no nearer an answer. He cursed and hurled the glass into the fireplace where it shattered into a thousand pieces. He pushed himself from the chair, wobbled, breathed heavily for a moment and staggered to the door. He opened it and stood for a moment, listening. Silence hung heavily over the house. It felt like the silence of defeat.

Sam crossed the hall unsteadily but found support on the banister and negotiated the stairs without mishap. Reaching his room, he undressed, leaving his clothes scattered where he had dropped them. He crawled between the sheets but sleep did not come easily. With thoughts of Ben and Martin haunting his mind, he tossed and turned, cursing the son who had thwarted his plan.

He awoke to a wintery sun sending daylight streaming through his window. Sam stirred with a low moan and twisted round so that he could see the clock on the mantelpiece. Nearly nine o'clock! Good heavens, why hadn't anyone called him? Annoyed, he threw back the bedclothes and swung his feet to the floor. He stood up swiftly, a man who could take his drink and feel no ill effects the next morning. Downstairs he found his three children already sitting at the breakfast table.

'Why didn't someone wake me?' he asked irritably.

'We didn't know what time you came to bed,' explained Sarah. 'We thought you might prefer to have your sleep. I instructed the maids that you should be left.'

Though he appreciated his daughter's thoughtfulness he snapped, 'As I have told you before, time is money.'

With Alicia's wakening there was no escape from the numbness that had gripped her last night. Then, feeling as battered and bruised as if she had taken a beating, she had crawled miserably between the sheets, buried her head in the pillow and cried silently until she fell asleep in the small hours of the morning. Now, realising that it had not been a bad dream, she cursed Ben Coulson and renewed her vow that one day he would pay for the hurt and humiliation he had brought her, and Ruth Holmes, as she still regarded her, was included in that resolve. With a future objective firmly in mind, Alicia strengthened her determination to hide her disappointment and get on with life. The course that would take depended very much on Sam Coulson and his attitude to the debt her father owed. Alicia judged that he would not make a direct demand immediately. He would not want to ruin their long friendship, nor would he want to appear the hard-hearted creditor, demanding his pound of flesh. That tactic could rebound on him and lose him friends among the local trading fraternity by whom her father was held in high respect.

But she was smart enough to realise that behind this proposed marrige, first to Martin and then to Ben, lay an attempt to gain some of the assets of her father's company. What would Sam do now? Propose a marriage to Eric? She shuddered at the thought. She would protest if it came to that, but might she be forced into it to protect her family's way of life? There must be another way out of this dilemma. Could she find it and through it hurt Ben? And what would he do . . . disowned by his father, his inheritance lost? She was sure his father would not relent and whatever vengeance Sam wreaked on his son, she would rejoice. Maybe she could play her part too.

When Ben woke the events of yesterday flooded back to him. His father's attitude had been expected, but the generosity of understanding extended by the Holmes family was more than he had hoped for. He glanced at Ruth. She was still asleep, the expression on her face one of tranquil contentment at the way things had worked out. Ben drew strength from that and focused his own thoughts on what they should do. When his wife stirred ten minutes later, to jolt his mind back to the present moment, he had formed a possibile plan for their future.

Ruth moaned and stretched. Her arm fell across Ben. She started and came wide awake with a small amused laugh. 'Oh, it's you. I wondered where I was.'

Ben hugged her. 'It's me, Mrs Coulson, and I love you so very much.' His kiss expressed the urgent need of his body and she responded with an equal desire that neither of them wanted to end.

When she lay back on her pillow, they held hands. They lay in shared quiet, still bound by the love they had experienced.

Eventually, Ruth broke the silence.

'What are we going to do, Ben?'

He turned to raise himself on one elbow so that he could look into his wife's face, brought his forefinger gently across her brow and down her cheek to her lips. 'Don't look so solemn, love. Frowning mars the face I love.' He leaned to her and brushed her lips with his.

She met his eyes and smiled. 'There is our future to consider, Ben.'

'I know. I was awake before you and lay for a while looking at you with love and determination to make things right for us. I've thought of two things. As you know, I have a ropery. I also have some investments in one or two Whitby companies that I can sell. We can buy a house and live off the proceeds of the ropery. The second proposal, the one I like best, is that I sell my investments *and* the ropery, and with the money go into partnership with your father.'

'What?' Ruth sat up and turned to him. 'You mean, you and he would become fishermen?'

'Well, your father will know more about it than I do – Daniel spoke of his possibly taking two partners. I could be one of them.'

There was a thoughtful pause then Ruth flung her arms round his neck. 'That sounds wonderful, but you have no experience of fishing whereas Father has from his younger days.'

'He can teach me.'

'But . . .'

He stopped her. 'No buts until we have put the proposal to your father.'

'Let's suggest it now,' cried Ruth excitedly, and flung back the bedclothes.

Ben caught her by the arm and in the same movement swung her round to face him. 'I love you when you are excited.' He pulled her to him, kissed her and laughingly said, 'What are we waiting for?'

Ten minutes later they burst into the dining-room expecting to find the family all present but there was only Ruth's mother.

'Hello,' she said, and then gave a puzzled frown. 'Oh, you look disappointed?'

'Where is everyone?' asked Ruth.

'Edmund and Abel have gone to see about a winter voyage, Rachel's in her room, and your father and Daniel have gone to Robin Hood's Bay intending to buy a coble.'

'Oh, my.' Ruth glanced at Ben with alarm.

'Why, what is it?' Georgina, wondering what had caused this anxiety, looked from one to the other, seeking an answer.

Instead Ben asked her, 'How long have they been gone, Mrs Holmes?'

'About half an hour. Is something the matter?'

He did not reply but turned to Ruth. 'Don't worry love, I'll hire a horse at the Angel when I dismiss the postillion, and get after them. They're on foot?' He glanced at Mrs Holmes for verification. She nodded. 'So I'll catch them before they get to Robin Hood's Bay. You explain to your mother.' With that he rushed from the room.

Within ten minutes Ben was riding out of the Angel yard and once clear of the town put the animal into a gallop along the track to the tiny fishing village of Robin Hood's Bay, five miles along the coast. He felt sure that Captain Holmes and his son would have taken this well-trodden route and was relieved to find he was right when he saw two figures ahead.

The sound of pounding hooves had them turning round to

see who rode with such haste. They exchanged glances of curiosity when they recognised the rider.

'Now what's up?' said Daniel.

'I hope there's nothing wrong at home,' commented his father.

Ben did not let up his pace until he hauled on the reins to bring the animal to a swirling halt close to the two men. He quickly settled the horse and said breathlessly, 'Thank goodness I caught you before you got to Robin Hood's Bay.'

'Why, what's wrong?' asked Captain Holmes.

'Sir, I have a proposition to put to you.'

'Proposition?' Gideon cast a glance at his son and saw he was equally curious.

'Yes, sir. You are proposing to buy a coble?'

Gideon nodded.

'Are you thinking of a three-man boat?'

'Aye. Maybe two men and a lad.'

'Then let me be the other man, unless Daniel has changed his mind about staying with the whale-ships?'

Both men were surprised by this proposal. 'Daniel hasn't changed his mind.'

'Well, I'm sure we'll soon find a third partner if we don't get a lad.'

'Hold on a minute, you're moving too fast for me. Let's hear what you've been thinking.'

'Well, sir, I'll sell my assets and put them into a boat with you, maybe get a better one than you had been thinking of – but you know more about suitable craft than I do.'

'Aye, no doubt both Daniel and I do, but you become a fisherman?' Captain Holmes shook his head rather doubtfully.

Daniel gave a little laugh that carried a hint of derision. 'Ben Coulson fishing? Now *that* would be something. Bobbing about on the water every day when he ran from the sea after one whaling voyage.'

Ben stiffened. 'Maybe I don't relish the sea, but I'll tell you this, Daniel Holmes, I'll work alongside you and match your effort if you throw in with us.'

'Done!' Daniel held out his hand.

Ben grasped it to seal their understanding before Daniel's father could protest quickly enough to stop it. But he did raise one objection.

'Daniel, you want the whale-ships. This isn't the way to achieve your ambition to become a captain.'

'Father, one season away from the Arctic won't hold me back. It will enable me to see that your new enterprise is on course – apart from which, I just could not miss seeing Ben Coulson heaving his guts out over the side of our boat!' He chuckled at the thought.

'All right. That's that then.' Gideon shrugged his shoulders in resignation and held his hand out to Ben who took it to seal their bargain. 'This is a generous offer but we will put it on the usual footing, So I think we should return to Whitby, talk this over and plan accordingly.'

'Yes, sir. If you don't mind, I'll ride ahead. I'd like to get one or two matters settled there before we do so.' With that Ben swung into the saddle and as he sent the animal forward, called over his shoulder, 'See you at Grape Lane.'

Gideon and Daniel watched him for a few moments and then began to retrace their steps towards Whitby.

'Is this going to work, Father? He really has no experience of the sea,' said Daniel doubtfully.

'He is a determined young man, and full of character. I'll be surprised if he doesn't surprise you.' Gideon chuckled. 'He certainly tricked you into a partnership, but if you want to pull out, I'll persuade him to let you.'

'I made a pact, I'll stick to it.'

They walked on a while then Captain Holmes stopped, threw back his head and let out a loud peal of laughter.

Daniel, trying to comprehend what had amused his father, stopped. 'What is it?'

'Just a thought. It's a right turn up for the book. A Holmes and a Coulson going into partnership. What will Sam think?'

Chapter Thirteen

Ben lost no time in reaching Whitby. He returned the horse to the stables at the Angel and hurried to the east bank of the Esk. The building he entered was Holt's Ropery where, much to his relief, he found the owner, Mr Welburn Holt, in his office. The gentleman, in his late-fifties, looked surprised when Ben walked in but his greeting was welcoming.

After they shook hands he indicated a seat. 'Sit down, young man.' Mr Holt resumed his seat, leaned back in his chair and cradled his hands over his rotund stomach. 'Well, I don't suppose you are here to sell me that ropery of yours, so what is it that—'

'That is exactly why I am here,' cut in Ben.

Welburn Holt sat up in astonishment. 'I don't believe it. After all the times I've made you an offer, you just walk in here and say you want to sell?'

Ben smiled. 'That's right. The sooner we close this deal the better.'

Welburn's eyes widened but his brain was telling him to question Ben's motive when so many times before he had been adamant that he would not sell. 'What's made you change your mind?' he asked warily.

'I need the money.'

Welburn gave a small smile. 'Well, I suppose that reason is as good as any. Although you want this transaction completed quickly, I would like to see your premises again.'

'Very well, Mr Holt, let us away.' Ben jumped to his feet.

Again Welburn was surprised by the urgency of Ben's actions. He came from behind his desk, obtained his hat and coat and led his visitor outside.

'I'll tell you about the assets connected with the ropery as we go. It will save time,' Ben offered.

'Very well. Tell me about your stock in hand, the orders you are at present fulfilling and contracts which you are negotiating.'

By the time they reached the ropery in Skinner Street, Welburn Holt was in possession of all these facts. Ben gave him a quick tour of the building. Mr Holt liked what he saw and heard. He made Ben an offer which was immediately accepted, leaving Welburn wondering if he could have obtained the business for less. However, both men were satisfied and shook hands to cement the deal.

Ben called his staff together and told them he had just sold the business to Mr Holt. 'I'm sure you will find him a good employer,' he concluded.

'I do not intend to make any changes.' Mr Holt informed them. 'This business will fit neatly in with my present one. I'll come and have a word with each one of you.'

As the men went back to their jobs, Ben said, 'Mr Holt, will you see to the necessary documentation as soon as possible? Leave it at my bank, Chapman's. I'll sign the contract, and then if you could deposit the money into my account there I would be grateful.'

'Certainly, Ben.' Welburn was curious and fished for information. 'You are in a bit of a rush with this one?'

'I have good reasons,' he replied.

Welburn raised his hands in apology for prying. 'Sorry, Ben.'

'That's all right, Mr Holt, it was only natural you should wonder, but I don't want to tell you any more at this moment.'

Welburn nodded. 'Now, will you introduce me to your workers?'

'Mr Holt, my foreman will do that. I would like to but I need to be away. Please forgive me?' Without waiting for Welburn's reply Ben shouted for his foreman, shook hands with Welburn and was off.

*

After waking up later than usual, with yesterday's events still on his mind, Sam Coulson was not in an amiable mood when he reached his office. At his curt 'Good morning', the two clerks raised their eyebrows at each other. They would have to tread carefully today, better keep out of Mr Coulson's way as much as possible.

Sam continued his way down the corridor, snapping, 'Seamus!' as he went even though he knew his manager would be waiting just inside his office as usual. As Sam passed, Seamus fell into step behind him. His 'Good morning, sir' went unanswered.

In his office Sam flung his coat and hat on to a chair. Seamus as usual placed some papers on his desk ready for his attention.

'Mr Ben not with you today?' he queried for something to say when Sam seemed reluctant to speak.

'Does it look like it?' Sam snapped, then after a brief pause said, 'He won't be in ever again.'

Seamus stared at him, hardly able to believe what he had heard. If the worst had happened why was Mr Coulson here? Surely he would have stayed at home? 'I'm sorry if . . .'

Seamus's solemnity irritated Sam. 'It's not that,' he snarled. 'My son Ben ceased to be recognised as such from last night.'

'Oh,' Seamus floundered.

'We have nothing more to do with him. I don't think he'll dare set foot in this office again but if he does just get him out.'

'Yes, sir,' muttered a mystified Seamus. 'Er . . . the document I drew up about bringing his ropery into your firm, I put it on top of some others to remind him to sign it.'

'He's not likely to sign it now,' rapped Sam tersely. 'Forget it. Tear it up!'

'Yes, sir.' Seamus started for the door, deeming it best to get out of the way when his employer was in this sort of mood.

'Wait!' The sharpness in his tone brought Seamus to a halt.

'Sir?' The manager turned to find Sam looking thoughtful.

231

'Leave it on his desk.'

'Yes, sir.' Seamus returned to his own room.

Sam went to his chair behind the desk and sank into it slowly. He sat staring at the papers Seamus had left but not really seeing them. His mind was working overtime with a new scheme. He started to go through the papers on his desk but, while he was able to deal with them, his mind was really occupied with Ben's ropery.

An hour later he pushed himself to his feet, put on his coat and picked up his hat. He went to the office he had allocated to his son. The papers drawn up concerning the transfer of Ben Coulson's ropery to the firm of Coulson and Sons were lying there. The words 'Coulson and Sons' glared up at Sam. He cursed the fact that all his dreams had been shattered by that incompetent fool Holmes. Martin gone. Ben's audacity in marrying Holmes's daughter. His plans in ruins. There was only Eric to fulfil the role of husband to Alicia and heir to the Coulson empire. But he would never fill it as Martin would have done, or even as Ben would have. Nevertheless Eric was now the heir. Maybe he would turn out more accomplished than Sam expected. With a good manager, he could probably cope. Sam must fix that, but first things first – the ropery.

He glanced through the document that had never been signed. Could he get Ben to sign it now? Surely his son owed him some compensation for ruining his plans. Could he make Ben see that?

Sam put the document in his coat and left the office in the hope that he might find Ben at work. His steps were determined and fast. He wanted this settled, the ropery would be a useful addition to his other businesses.

He went straight to Ben's office but found it empty. Sam's lips tightened in exasperation. Maybe his son was elsewhere in the building. He set off to look and headed for the voices he could hear.

'Welburn Holt! What are you doing here? Have you seen my son?' Sam demanded suspiciously.

'Hello, Sam. Yes, I've seen him. He left a little while ago, had no more interest in this business.'

'What do you mean?'

'He's sold it to me.'

'What?' Disbelief thundered in Sam's voice.

'It's true,' replied Welburn. 'Ask my manger here.' Welburn emphasised the word 'my'.

Sam glanced at the man standing a few yards away.

He nodded. 'It's right, Mr Coulson.'

'Damn him.' Sam could not bring himself to say, 'That son of mine.' He felt this was another blow to his plans.

'It fits in nicely with my ropery. Ben came to me wanting a quick sale.'

'I'll bet he did,' snapped Sam, disgust in his voice. He swung on his heel and hurried from the building.

Welburn watched him go. 'Well, well. Trouble between father and son clearly brought this sale about,' he commented to himself.

Ben hurried back to Grape Lane pleased with the news that he would be able to impart to the Holmes family. On his way he called at Chapman's Bank in Church Street, instructed Mr Chapman to sell almost all his investments in various business and also to accept payment for the ropery from Mr Holt.

'Did you catch Father and Daniel?' were Ruth's first words when Ben entered the house.

'Yes. They should be here soon. I rode back before them as I had some transactions to see to before they got back.'

'What have you been up to, Ben Coulson?' asked Ruth suspiciously.

'You'll have to wait until they return. It concerns us all.'

Ruth was impatient to know but all her wiles and charm could not persuade him to tell her first. Then she heard the door open. 'Here they are,' she cried eagerly.

A moment later the door to the drawing-room opened and Gideon and Daniel walked in.

'You got back then,' said Gideon, looking at Ben, then laughed at the remark and added, 'That's pretty obvious, isn't it?'

'Sorry I left you,' he apologised, 'but I want you all to hear what I have to say.'

'I'll get Mother,' said Ruth, and left the room to find her.

When they returned and everyone was seated, Ben started by saying he wished Edmund and Abel and Rachel were here but that he would tell them later. He went on explain what he had done.

'But you have given up a trade you know for something you don't,' Gideon pointed out.

'I know, but this way I feel I am doing something to atone for my father's misjudgement of you.'

'Son, there's no need but if that's the way you want it then I am grateful to you.'

'I am not experienced in fishing, but you tell me what is required and what to do and I'll try not to let you down.'

'Well, it's many a year since I used a coble for this purpose but I was brought up with them before moving on to merchant ships. Once learned, never forgotten. Daniel has more recent experience of fishing, though that was before he signed on the whale-ships.'

'Aye, that it was,' said Daniel. He grinned at Ben. 'We'll make a fisherman of you and maybe give you a liking for the sea.'

'Right,' said Gideon, 'if we three are agreed, we'll explain a few things to you, Ben.'

'Yes, sir.'

'We'll cut out that sir for a start. We're all equal in this boat as you'll see when I explain the arrangements.'

'Ruth,' broke in Mrs Holmes,' I think we can leave the men to it. We'll see Cook about this evening's meal.'

When they had left the room, Gideon started his explanation. 'We'll get a three-man boat and work it on a share basis. The three of us are putting equal money into this venture so we'll divide the week's earnings into four.'

'Four?' queried Ben. 'Why four?'

'One for you, one for Daniel, one for me and one for the boat.'

'The boat?' Ben was still puzzled. Living in Whitby he shouldn't be this ignorant but he had never been one for the sea. Now he was facing a whole new way of life and was determined to make a go of it before he returned to the world of commerce, as he was determined to one day.

'Aye,' put in Daniel. 'Normally whoever owns the boat gets the fourth share for its upkeep but, as we are all equal owners, we say the fourth share is the boat's.'

Ben nodded. 'I understand. What about a boat? You were going to Robin Hood's Bay for one, why there? Can't we get one in Whitby?'

'Aye, we can. We were going to Robin Hood's Bay because the Bay men have one of the biggest fleets along this stretch of coast. I thought I might get a second-hand one cheap there, but as it's now a family affair, with more of our own money available, we can get a new one in Whitby.'

'I suggest we go to see Mr Gale first,' said Daniel

'There's no time like the present,' Ben pointed out.

'Right,' said Gideon, 'let's go.'

After he had informed his wife that they were going out, the three men made their way the short distance to Church Street where they confronted Adam Gale with their request.

They walked into an open shed where two boats were under construction, one in an advanced stage, the other only just begun. Planks of beech and larch were stacked against the walls. Wood shavings and sawdust littered the floor. Ben sniffed the air, relishing the smell of wood.

Adam Gale, a man in his late-fifties, face lined from years of concentration on a craft he loved and at which he excelled, looked up from the clinker-built boat on which he was working. He pushed his cap back and rubbed his forehead as he said, 'Good day, Captain Holmes.' He nodded at Daniel. 'Daniel.'

Then took in Ben and added with a touch of surprise in his voice, 'Mr Coulson.'

'Good day to you, Mr Gale,' said Ben pleasantly. 'And, please, it's Ben.'

Adam did not reply but looked at Gideon who could not miss the unspoken query in the boat-builder's eyes.

'You'll hear soon enough, Adam,' said Gideon. 'Ruth and Ben married a few days ago so he is one of the family now.'

If Adam was surprised he hid it, though surprised he was for he knew, as did all of Whitby, about Sam Coulson's treatment of Captain Holmes. 'I heard tell of no wedding.'

'It took place out of Whitby.'

Adam nodded, giving the impression that what other people got up to was no concern of his. 'Well, what can I do for you, Captain Holmes?'

'Adam, we've known each other long enough for you to drop the Captain. Besides I don't command a ship any more. Now, we three want a coble. Is that one that you're working on spoken for?'

Adam gave a little grimace. 'It was a special order but the person concerned has had to pull out. I was going to finish it off and put it up for sale. If you want it, it's yours.'

'I don't doubt your work, Adam, you have a reputation second to none in Whitby, but let's have a look at her and explain a few things to Ben.'

'It's a three-man boat,' Adam started, then stopped to give them a querying look. 'Are you three sailing her?'

'Aye,' replied Gideon. 'We've gone into partnership.'

'Ain't heard tell of you having any experience of fishing, young man? Adam peered at Ben.

He laughed. 'How right you are, Mr Gale, but I'm a quick learner and I reckon in Captain Holmes and Daniel I'll have two good teachers.'

'Reckon you will, young man, reckon you will.'

'This is a beautiful-looking boat, Mr Gale,' said Ben. Living in Whitby, he had seen plenty of cobles before but, not being much interested, he had never taken a lot of notice of them and had never seen one under construction. Now that he was to have a share in one he knew it would behove him to learn all he could about them. He listened intently as Mr Gale explained that the boat had no keel.

'Instead it is built on what is called a ram plank. That is joined to the vertical stern which as you can see gives the boat its sharp-rising stern. Towards the stern the ram plank flattens out but then tilts up slightly, so . . .' here Ben noticed a change in the tone of Mr Gale's voice. It was as if he was describing something he loved and admired dearly '. . . we get this beautiful curving shape from bow to stern.'

'I see the slope of the stern comes from the shaping of the plank, but why is it flat, Mr Gale?' asked Ben.

'So that it can withstand being beached stern-first in a heavy sea, and because of that we strengthen it at the stern.'

As the lesson continued Ben noticed Gideon and Daniel looking over the boat, examining it carefully. When they realised that Adam was coming to the end of his lesson, one which he had been delighted to give for Ben had shown such interest, they strolled over to the pair of them.

'We think we should have it, Ben,' said Captain Holmes. 'That is if you agree, and we can get the right price from Adam.'

'You know more about it than I do,' he said, 'so whatever is good enough for you is all right for me.'

When they had settled on a price and shaken hands on it, Adam Gale asked, 'What colours do you want it painting, and when do you want it launching?'

'Colours?' Captain looked at Daniel and Ben.

'How about white with two red stripes?' put in Ben.

'That's all right with me,' agreed Daniel.

'Red and white it is, Adam,' confirmed Captain Holmes. 'Launch date? As soon as possible. I'd like to do some winter line fishing, and we have to ensure that Ben is seaworthy before that. He'll need a lesson or two.'

Adam nodded. He eyed the boat, assessing in his mind what

still had to be done and how quickly he could do it. He could divert the two men who were working on the second boat as that was a speculative build, not to order. 'Two weeks today, if that is all right by you?'

'We are in your hands, Adam. Two weeks today it is.'

Once outside the boatyard the three men stopped and grinned at each other as Gideon said, 'Here's to a profitable partnership.' Their handshakes sealed their agreement. 'Let's get home and tell the ladies.'

Their news was greeted with delight, especially by Georgina who was thankful that her husband now had an occupation that, though far from being as prestigious as skippering a big vessel, would keep him in touch with the sea and would also show Sam Coulson that he was not bowed down by the insults and accusation made against him. She was more than grateful that Ben had come forward with his offer to make this a family enterprise.

Once they were alone Ruth flung her arms round her husband, hugged him tight and thanked him for what he had done. 'I hope it all works out, Ben.'

'It will, love. We'll make it work.'

'Word will soon get round Whitby. I wonder what your father will think to it?'

Ben shrugged his shoulders. 'It doesn't matter what he thinks.'

Sam Coulson was still in a foul mood when he reached his office after leaving the ropery. Seamus and the clerks sensed it as soon as he walked in and knew they would have to tread carefully. They were thankful when he went straight to his office.

After throwing off his coat and flinging it, with his hat and stick on to a table, he slumped into his chair. Tight-lipped, he stared at the papers on his desk. He cursed fortune who seemed to have turned her back on him. But had she? Didn't you make your own fortune? Of course you did. All his life he had determined his own. Fortune smiled on those who helped themselves and he had done just that. Oh, there had been setbacks, there always were, but he had surmounted them. He could and would do it again.

But how could he achieve his aim of gaining influence over Seaton's firm? Call in the debt and he would get the lot. It was tempting but he couldn't bring himself to ruin a friend. There must be another way to achieve his aim? But how?

Recalling Seaton, Sam remembered he had said he would see him today. His friend must be worrying about the possible outcome of that meeting. Sam must go to reassure him at once. He donned his outdoor garments again and left the office.

Deep in thought, he was hardly aware of the bustle and activity of this leading port in which he had made his fortune. He had recently added an alum enterprise and a jet workshop to his expanding empire and there could be diversification. The ropery would have fitted in very nicely and put him in a position to challenge other rope manufacturers. He felt doubly betrayed by Ben. How could his son do this to him? Well, Ben had made his bed and he must lie in it.

As Sam rounded a corner two urchins in chase collided with him, sending him reeling against a wall. The breath was knocked out of him, his hat tumbled from his head and he lost his grip on his stick. The shock was dispelled a few moments later by the sound of a voice asking him if he was all right. He looked round and saw a middle-aged lady showing concern. A man Sam took to be her husband was picking up his hat and stick for him.

'Thank you. Yes, I'm all right,' he spluttered.

'Little beggars,' said the woman indignantly. 'Run off they have. Not bothered if they hurt you.'

'Can we be of any assistance?' the man asked, handing Sam his hat and stick.

'No. You have both been very kind and I am obliged. I think my mind was elsewhere otherwise I might have avoided them.'

'Well, we'll bid you good day, sir,' said the man. He raised his hat and the couple continued on their way.

Sam straightened his coat, gave his hat a brush with his hand, replaced it on his head. As he turned from the wall a notice caught his eye. He paused and read it, giving himself time to gather himself together. It announced that in two days' time a production of *She Stoops to Conquer* would be performed in the theatre in Scate Lane. Having regained his composure Sam continued on his way. The notice meant little to him. He wasn't a man for theatre performances.

On reaching Seaton's office he was a little alarmed when his friend's manager informed him that Mr Campion had not been to the office that morning and that he had had no word from him. Sam immediately left and made for Seaton's house in Bagdale.

The maid showed him to Seaton's study. Seaton rose from behind his desk to greet him.

'I was worried when I found that you had not been to your office.'

Seaton gave a wan smile. 'I had a lot to think about.'

'Possibly something to do with the debt?'

'Yes. Only natural, surely, now that the wedding is not to take place?' Seaton was worried that Sam might suggest his third son for Alicia's future husband. He would not want to inflict on her someone who was going to be at sea for most of his life, and someone he did not rate in the same class as Martin or Ben.

'Then worry no longer, Seaton. I do not intend to call in the debt immediately. I don't want to see a friend of long standing in impoverished circumstances. I am sure something can be worked out and, no doubt, you can make your firm and its subsidiaries more profitable. Holding back on any repayment will give you a chance to do that.'

'That is most generous of you, Sam, and I am deeply grateful. A glass of Madeira to seal the new arrangement?'

'Why not?'

Seaton rose and crossed the room to a cabinet from which

he started to take a decanter. He stopped and said, 'Dorothea and Griselda are out but may I break the news to Grace and Alicia? I know they are as anxious as I.'

'Of course.'

Seaton rang the bell, and when the maid appeared asked her to tell Mrs Campion and his eldest daughter that he would like to see them in his study. He returned to the cabinet and by the time his wife and daughter appeared had glasses of Madeira waiting for all.

When they entered the room Sam rose to greet them. 'Grace,' he said, 'you can dismiss that worried frown. Seaton and I have come to an arrangement.'

His words confirmed what she had suspected when on entering the room she had noticed her husband with the decanter in his hand. He certainly wouldn't have charged the glasses if the news had not been good.

There was concern in Sam's voice when he greeted Alicia. 'I hope, my dear, that you have recovered from the shock of yesterday?'

She nodded. 'I have, though I must say I was shattered. But I have resolved that there is still a life for me.'

'Of course there is, and I am pleased to hear that you have a strong appetite for it.'

Alicia was bracing herself for the suggestion she thought might come, one she had been determined to refuse though she realised it would take a strong will to condemn herself and her family to hard times. Her thoughts were interrupted when she realised that her father was speaking.

'. . . and so everything is held in abeyance which will give me time to realise more profits from the firm in order to repay my debt.'

Alicia's heart raced, joy sang in her mind. She would not be faced with an awkward decision.

'That is most kind of you, Sam,' said Grace.

'We have a lifelong friendship, I would not want to mar that.' He raised his glass. 'The future.'

The Campions reiterated his toast with relief.

Sam, wanting to relax the atmosphere all the more, then came out with a suggestion that surprised even himself when he made it. 'I would like you, all the family, to be my guests at the theatre next Wednesday. I see that *She Stoops to Conquer* is being performed.'

'That would be delightful,' said Grace. 'Wouldn't it, Alicia?'

'It certainly would. I know Dorothea and Griselda will be excited when we tell them.'

'Good. I'll have Sarah and Dina with me. I don't think Eric will come.'

'Next Wednesday,' said Grace thoughtfully. 'Why don't you all come here for a meal beforehand?'

'We wouldn't want to put you to any bother.'

'It won't be any bother. It will be simple. We'll save more elaborate dining for another time.'

'Splendid,' said Sam. 'I look forward to it. I am sure it will take all our minds off recent unpleasant episodes.'

The following Wednesday, wondering what on earth he had been thinking about to suggest an evening at the theatre when it wasn't his usual sort of entertainment, Sam strolled into his drawing-room. He took a watch from his waistcoat pocket and, seeing that he had half an hour to spare, poured himself a whisky, cut and lit a cigar and settled himself comfortably in front of the fire. Maybe his suggestion was out of consideration for Alicia? She had suffered at the hands of his son. He hoped he could ease some of that hurt.

Ten minutes later the door opened and Sarah walked in, followed by Dina.

He sat up. 'My, I have two lovely daughters. Your dresses are exquisite.'

They kept their surprise to themselves. Their father was not generally one to notice such things, let alone make complimentary comments such as this.

Sarah had taken particular care in choosing a plain muslin

dress that showed much more of the natural figure now that tight-lacing and hoops had been cast off by the fashion of the times. It fell straight from the high waist with a flair at the back towards a short train. Its colour was a light shade of blue with no ornamentation. Her shoulders were bare, with the neckline of the dress level with its short puff-sleeves. She carried a small velvet bag and a cotton shawl, both in a darker shade of blue than the dress. Dina was similarly dressed but had chosen a pale yellow shade. The noticeable difference was in their hair styles. They had both piled their hair on top but whereas Dina had decided to hold hers in place with a latticework of thin red ribbons, Sarah relied on no such support. She had pinned hers so that at one side it swept from the top down towards her cheek.

'I suppose we had better be going,' said Sam, rising to his feet. He threw the remains of his cigar into the fire, drained the last of his whisky and made for the door which he held open for his daughters.

As they put on their outdoor coats Dina whispered to Sarah, raising her eyebrows as she did so, 'Father's on his best be-haviour?'

Sarah, with a little smile, nodded.

The meal with the Campions was relaxing and got everyone in a mood to enjoy the rest of the evening.

People were milling towards the theatre entrance around which extra oil lamps had been placed so the whole area across the street was illuminated for the safety and convenience of the theatregoers. Their party joined the throng with Sam and Alicia bringing up the rear. The jovial atmosphere that emanated from the crowd was getting to Sam who was finding himself drawn into the frivolity. His gaze ranged across the people beyond them. He bent towards Alicia and whispered a comment about a couple a short distance ahead of them. She followed his gaze and, catching his meaning, threw back her head in laughter. The amusement suddenly died from her lips and eyes. In its place came an expression of smouldering hatred. Astonished by the sudden change, Sam followed the direction of her eyes.

Ben and Ruth!

They were passing by, arm in arm, on the periphery of the crowd.

In that moment their eyes met.

Sam gripped Alicia's arm, an automatic reaction as if to give her support and caution her not to react.

Ben's step almost faltered but Ruth gripped his hand tighter and kept him moving. She too had seen the hatred in Alicia's eyes.

Alicia had stiffened as if frozen to the spot. Sam, who had noticed that no one else in their party had seen Ben and Ruth, bent close to her and whispered forcefully, 'Strength, my dear. Be strong. Don't let them see you weaken.' He pressed her elbow gently, inviting her to move forward. 'Forget that you ever saw them.'

Alicia shuddered with reaction to the shock. With her determination strengthened, she became aware of Sam holding her arm and, strangely, found comfort in that. 'Thank you, Sam.' Immediately they both became aware that she had not used the term 'Uncle' as was the custom between their families.

'I'm sorry you had to see that,' said Ben as he and Ruth made their way towards the bridge.

She shivered. 'It was the hatred in Alicia's eyes, Ben . . . It was horrible.'

'I know, love. Don't worry about it.'

'Ben, be careful.'

'There's nothing to worry about. Alicia cannot touch us.'

'You never know.'

They walked on in silence. Ruth knew Ben had been affected by the expression in Alicia's eyes, but she knew equally well that he would brush it aside so that tomorrow it would be as if it had never happened. She must try and do the same. There was no better time to start so when they reached the bridge she stopped to gaze along the quiet river on which silver moon-beams broke into a myriad sparkling jewels. The river was idle; no boats broke its surface. Ships lay quiet at the quays, their masts and rigging trellising the sky in black silhouette.

'It's beautiful, Ben. Don't let what happened spoil this.'

'It won't,' he replied, pleased that she seemed to have thrown off the pessimistic mood that the meeting with Alicia had caused in her.

Chapter Fourteen

Although Alicia was fully occupied with her everyday life, visiting friends, shopping with her sisters, helping her mother to entertain, pursuing her interests of needlework, painting and reading, her mind often drifted back to that visit to the theatre. Remembering Ben and Ruth together set animosity surging through her and a renewal of her determination that one day she would find revenge. Only Sam, of their party, had noticed the young couple, so the subject was never raised. She had been thankful for that, just as she was thankful for the extra attention he gave to her, as if trying to ease the hurt she had felt.

Ten days after the visit to the theatre she was in the drawing-room reading to her mother who was busy putting the finishing touches to a table cloth she was embroidering. They heard the door bell and the maid announced that Mr Sam Coulson was requesting to see them. Although Alicia expressed surprise, she had to admit to herself that she was not as astonished as she might have been.

'My dear ladies,' Sam greeted them affably as he strode into the room. 'I hope I am not disturbing you?'

'Not at all, Sam,' replied Grace. 'We are delighted to see you.'

He crossed the room and took her proffered hand, then turned to Alicia and smiled as he said, 'I hope you have got over the hilarity of the play, my dear?'

Alicia chuckled to recall that evening when she had laughed so much at the antics of the cast, but wondered at the same time if there was a hidden allusion to their sighting of Ben and Ruth behind his question. 'Indeed I have. I recall the evening with pleasure.'

'Good, good, I am so pleased.'

'We were grateful for your invitation, Sam,' said Grace, indicating for him to sit down.

'We've been friends a long time, Grace. As for that evening, you made it most enjoyable by providing a splendid meal beforehand.'

'Ah, that was nothing elaborate but I do intend to have you and the family here for a more formal meal soon. It is just a matter of my working out when it will be most suitable. In fact, at the moment I am thinking of making the invitation around Christmas.'

'That would be splendid, Grace. It will be nicely spaced and allow me to state my reason for being here. I came to invite you and all the family to an evening at the Angel next Tuesday. I have had a word with the landlord and that will be a suitable day for him – the private room is free.'

'That is most kind, Sam. Isn't it, Alicia?'

'Indeed it is. I am already looking forward to it.' An excited light had come to her eyes. She wondered if this was another move by Sam to make up for Ben's actions.

'Then there is nothing more to be said. We will all meet up at the Angel at six-thirty next Tuesday.'

During the afternoon of that day a little ceremony was taking place outside the workshop of Adam Gale. A newly completed coble was being manoeuvred to the water with the aid of a wheeled undercarriage. All the Holmes family and Ben were watching with eager anticipation as the boat neared the water's edge. Adam Gale eyed the boat with pride as he oversaw his assistants, not allowing them to make any mistake that might damage the coble. He reckoned it was the best he had ever constructed, but he felt that about every latest creation. They had reached the water but he called a halt before the boat touched it.

'Now, Captain Holmes, I think we ought to have a launching ceremony. Who's going to name her and set her off into the water?'

'Come on, Georgina, you do it.' Gideon gave his wife a smile.

She gave a little shake of her head. 'No, Gideon, let Ruth. She and Ben are starting out on a new life, so let her do it.'

Ruth began to shake her head in protest but Gideon would have none of it. 'Come on, lass. Just give her the name we agreed on and then help push her into the water.'

Ruth knew she could not avoid the performance as everyone encouraged her. She moved near the bow, took a deep breath and said, 'I name thee *True Love*, and God bless all who sail in thee.' She pushed at the bow, and when everyone saw this they all exerted pressure and ran the boat into the water, cheered on by a group of onlookers who had gathered around when they realised that a ceremony was taking place.

As the boat began to float, Gideon and Daniel stepped on board, steadied its movement and held it so that Ben could join them. He almost lost his balance but having maintained it, sat down on the centre thwart. Gideon took up position at the tiller and Daniel went to take the oars closest to the bow. The boat rocked gently on the water, and when he judged the time right Gideon called on his crew to dip their oars. Daniel did so with ease but Ben was a little clumsy. However, once settled, determined not to fail, he slipped into the rhythm and the boat glided forward.

Gideon was delighted with the feel of the coble. To inexpert eyes they were all the same, but they were not, each had its own individual stamp and Gideon immediately fell under the spell of this one. He praised the expert craftsmanship of Adam Gale, knowing they had a good vessel that would serve them well. Having assessed the boat, he turned his mind to Ben. Would he wilt under the pressure when conditions were not as gentle as here within the shelter of the stone piers? Maybe he should give him a little taste of less friendly waters, though today the sea was calm.

Daniel, facing his father and noting the direction he was guiding the boat, read his intention and smiled to himself. It was only when he saw the piers that Ben realised Gideon was taking them to sea. He was moving into unknown territory. True he had been on a whaling voyage, but he had never been employed in one of the boats; he had been on board the 323-ton vessel all the voyage. That had been enough for him. Now as they headed towards the open sea he began to chide himself for suggesting he should become a partner in this boat which looked as if it could very easily be swamped. He cursed himself for entertaining such thoughts, and with his fear came a renewed determination not to make a fool of himself.

With his back to the bow he could only estimate their progress by their position in relationship to the piers. He realised that once clear of them they would lose their protection and feel the swell of the sea. It came a few moments later when he felt the boat lift and then dip as it rode the undulations.

He had got the feel of the oars and now concentrated on his rowing in an endeavour to keep his mind off the queasy feeling that was beginning to grip his stomach. Row. Row. Row. He kept repeating the word to himself, hoping it would focus his mind on one thing. But suddenly he could hold out no longer. He shipped his oars in haste, flopped with his head over the side and retched and retched and retched. He felt awful. In a matter of a few moments life held no joy for him and he wished he could die. Nothing else mattered. He heard mocking laughter but could not respond. He heard a voice but could not distinguish what it was saying. He raised his head to try to bring himself some relief but it made matters worse. In that moment, through half-closed eyes, he had seen the piers and knew they were heading back for their protection and the tranquil river.

The rise and fall of the boat gradually lessened. The stones of the piers were a welcome sight, exuding stability and offering the solidity of firm ground. Ben sat upright, and despite a head that did not feel like part of him, started to struggle with the oars.

'Leave them, Ben.' Gideon's sympathetic voice exonerated him from any more effort and he was glad.

Gideon guided the coble to a convenient place beside a wooden ladder let into the stonework of one of the quays on the east side of the river. As he came forward to help, Daniel slapped Ben on the shoulder. 'Enjoy that?' he chuckled.

All Ben could do was grunt. He wanted the feel of solid earth beneath his feet. With the boat tied up, Gideon called out, 'Come on, Ben.'

He climbed unsteadily to his feet. His head still spun but he managed to clamber to the ladder. Daniel had already reached the top and stood waiting for him. Ben gave a sickly smile of thanks as Gideon steadied him in his attempt to start up the ladder. At the top he was grateful for Daniel's helping hand. He gave a great sigh of relief at the feel of the ground and slumped on to a bollard, holding his head in his hands in an attempt to stop it spinning. He was aware of voices but could not be bothered to distinguish what they were saying.

The gyrations slowed gradually. He looked up and saw Daniel grinning. Though Ben wanted to retaliate to the amusement in his eyes, he could not. Instead he was thankful for his support as Daniel said, 'Come on, we'll get you home to bed.'

Ben wanted to remonstrate but didn't. He would be too thankful to lie down. When they entered the house in Grape Lane, although she was amused by Ben's reaction to his first encounter with a coble, Ruth fussed him into bed where he gave a great sigh and was thankful when sleep overcame him.

'We'll have to set off without him.' There was a touch of annoyance in Sam's voice as he looked at his watch.

'Eric did say he might be delayed,' Sarah reminded him. 'He's rather keen to sail on the *Water Nymph* again next season, so didn't want to miss the interview with the new captain you appointed, Captain Ormson.'

'And he did say that he would join us at the Angel.' Dina added weight to her sister's words in defence of her brother.

'I know.' Sam nodded.

They stepped outside, wrapped well against the frosty air, and made their way to the inn.

There they were welcomed warmly by the landlord, who was always ready to oblige Sam Coulson. Stay on the right side of him and this influential merchant could push more custom his way. He realised that Sam and his daughters had arrived a shade early so that they could appraise his efforts to entertain their guests in the seclusion of a private room.

'Thanks, Jed,' said Sam as the landlord bade his staff take the Coulsons' outdoor clothes.

'Come this way, sir,' said Jed, fussing around them as he escorted them to the room he had set aside for their use. He stood to one side while Sam cast critical eye around him.

A long table, set for nine, was positioned down the centre of the room which was large enough to give a feeling of space but not so large that guests might experience a sensation of being out of touch with each other. The table had been carefully laid with the best cutlery and the glassware's sparkle was reflected in the highly polished tabletop. At the end of the room, beside the door that gave on to a passage leading to the kitchen, was a solid oak sideboard set with all the necessary accoutrements to serve the meal. On a small side-table was a bowl of steaming punch.

'I hope everything is to your liking, Mr Coulson?'

'It is indeed, Jed. And I am sure that the meal will match it.'

The landlord gave a little nod of acknowledgement at Sam's praise and assured him that what was to be served would not disappoint any palate. 'Would you like a glass of punch now, sir, or will you await the arrival of your guests?'

'We will wait, thank you, Jed.'

'Very good, sir. I will be on the lookout for their arrival.'

'Thank you.'

When the landlord had left the room both girls commented with enthusiasm on how delightful the room looked.

'Influence pays off,' replied Sam. He eyed his daughters. 'It will be most gratifying when I can include two young gentlemen of your choosing in our gatherings.'

Dina knew her father was implying a criticism of her relationship with Rowan, of which he did not approve, and hinting too that Sarah should be casting aside all thoughts of the love she had so tragically lost.

'I like Rowan, Father. So would you if only you would get to know him.'

Sam was about to make a remark in reply but was prevented from doing so as Dina continued quickly, 'I suppose you won't raise any objections to Sarah's latest beau?'

'What?' Sam looked questioningly at his eldest daughter.

'Dina, he's not my beau,' snapped Sarah with marked indignation.

'He must like you to make such an invitation.'

'What's this all about?' demanded their father.

'A little while ago, Ben and I attended an exhibition of paintings here in the Angel. We got into conversation with a young man, Ryan Bennett, nephew of Miss Bennett, who has come to join her at Mulgrave Hall.'

'I have heard of her,' replied Sam thoughtfully. 'A very rich lady, I believe. Family made their money in coal. And the invitation?'

'Is to a concert being held at Mulgrave,' Sarah explained.

'Then you must accept,' he told her.

'Well, I'm not sure . . .'

'Of course you must,' he insisted.

Before the conversation could proceed any further there was a knock at the door. It was opened by the landlord who announced, 'Your guests are here, Mr Coulson.'

'Thank you, Jed.' Sam greeted Grace and her daughters effusively and then shook Seaton warmly by the hand. Sarah and Dina welcomed the Campion girls with pleasure and they were soon exchanging gossip.

'Eric not with us?' Seaton enquired.

'He should arrive any time. He had an interview with

Captain Ormson and is coming here straight after. Let us have some punch to drive out the evening cold.' Sam gave a nod to a manservant who immediately started to serve the steaming wine.

The atmosphere became convivial and everyone relaxed, chattering in friendly fashion. They were interrupted when the door burst open and Eric rushed in.

He had a broad grin on his face as he greeted them. 'Hello, all. Sorry I'm a little late.' Hilarity overtook him then. 'I saw the most wonderful sight on the way to see Captain Ormson . . . our Ben, as green as a high cheese, staggering from a coble! He slumped on to a bollard and held his head in his hands, then had to be helped away.'

'What was wrong with him?' asked Sarah with concern.

'Well,' chuckled Eric, 'it seems he'd been out in the coble and was seasick. Imagine it? Seasick!'

'What was he doing in a coble?' Sam demanded.

'He didn't see me, I'd kept out of the way, but I discreetly enquired from some bystanders and learned that he has gone into a fishing partnership with Captain Holmes and his son Daniel. They'd just launched their new coble and went out beyond the piers for the first time, with the result that Ben was sick.'

So that was why he sold the ropery. Damn him for helping Holmes! thought Sam, but only said, 'Serve him right. Come, let us be seated.' He directed everyone to their places. He was at the head with Sarah, as hostess, at the bottom. He had arranged for Alicia to be at the top on his right hand and Grace on his left.

As they settled into their places he said quietly to Alicia, 'I hope that didn't upset you, hearing about Ben?'

She shook her head. 'No, it didn't. In fact it amused me. What a picture that would have been, Ben with his head over the gunwhale!'

Sam chuckled. 'Indeed it would.'

And that's not the only thing that will embarrass him, if I

have my way, she thought. Aloud she said, 'Do you think he'll ever make a fisherman?'

Sam laughed. 'I doubt it! He won't like being tossed about in a coble for one thing, and for another they're not going to make a fortune and that will bother Ben. He's going to have to adapt to a different style of life from that which he has been used to. I can't see it lasting. He'll want more from life. But after what he did to you, he needn't come begging for help from me.'

At the foot of the table Sarah did not have her mind fully on the conversation with Seaton on her left and Dorothea on her right, though they were not aware of it. Her mind kept drifting back to the news Eric had brought. She was concerned for Ben. He was doing something completely foreign to his nature. Knowing his determination, she realised that any misgivings he had about having to share the practical side of a fishing partnership would be kept hidden from Captain Holmes and his son. Ben would force himself on in spite of any discomfort; she only hoped that did not put him in increased danger. She knew fishing could be a dangerous trade and that whoever was engaged in it needed all their concentration, not only to be successful but to survive. One small lapse of attention at a critical time could spell disaster.

She badly wanted to see Ben and that desire grew stronger over the next three weeks during which Eric was only too eager to report the latest stories he had heard about his turncoat brother. Well, he, Eric, had the last laugh now. He was heir to Sam Coulson's fortune while brother Ben barely scratched a living fishing, if indeed he could cope with the physical aspects of the life.

During those three weeks, Ben suffered torments in the bobbing coble but sheer determination carried him through. Thankfully his bouts of seasickness did lessen until finally one day he was not sick, even though he still felt queasy.

'Have I conquered it, Daniel?' he asked anxiously as they

stepped ashore and walked along the quay, leaving Gideon securing the boat for the night.

'Aye, maybe. How do you feel?'

Ben pulled a face. 'Not good.' Then added with all the enthusiasm he could muster, 'But at least I wasn't sick.'

'Ben,' said Daniel, a serious note in his voice to match the thoughtful expression on his face, 'up to now we've been concentrating on getting you used to the sea and to handling the coble. I know Father wants to start fishing soon and intends to do so tomorrow, if the weather is right. The serious business begins then and throws more responsibility on each of us. None of us can afford be a weak link if we want to make good catches and survive any difficulties we may encounter. If you want out of the partnership now there would be no disgrace in it, and I think I could get someone to buy your share.'

Ben stopped, grabbed Daniel's arm and turned him towards him. 'Don't dare suggest such a thing,' he snapped angrily.

'I was only thinking of you.'

'I'll be all right. I won't let you down if that's what you were meaning.'

'I know, I know,' put in Daniel quickly, wanting to soothe him. 'I only wanted you to know that we would understand if you wanted out.'

'I don't!'

'Right. I'm pleased to hear it, and I do think you are handling things well and will continue to do so as long as you can keep your mind off the sickness. I've seen you fighting it and that can take your attention off what you are doing.'

'It won't!'

'Good, then it's a drop of ale in the Black Bull for us, a drink to tomorrow's success.'

'Right.'

Daniel slapped Ben on the shoulder and they fell into step.

A cacophony of conversation over which orders had to be shouted assailed them when they entered the Black Bull. They got to the counter and were awaiting their beer when they heard a shout.

'Ben Coulson, over here!'

He turned and saw Ralph North and Warren Laskill, gesticulating for him to join them. Ben raised his hand in acknowledgement. Undecided, he glanced at Daniel.

'Who are they?' his brother-in-law asked.

'I used to see quite a lot of them. Ralph North is the thin one, Warren Laskill more broad-shouldered.'

'Quite a contrast.'

'Aye, but they're both lively characters.'

'So I gather.' Daniel was aware of the two men still loudly cajoling Ben and himself to join them.

'I think we'd better,' suggested Ben.

'Aye, all right,' agreed Daniel. 'It might quieten them down a bit.'

'Don't be too sure!' Ben laughed, and, taking his drink, led the way to their table where there was one spare seat.

Warren, on seeing them coming, jumped to his feet and dragged another chair to the table. Daniel eyed him as he did so. His rugged features had a determined set but that was soft-ened by the light in his blue eyes which were alert to every-thing around him. There was power in his body and Daniel judged that he must be able to take care of himself or he would not be coming to an inn such as the Black Bull. His jacket cut to the waist had knee-length tails. Its large revers gave into a high rounded collar. His waistcoat was of a similar blue to his jacket. He wore trousers, the incoming style, and Daniel was in no doubt that this gentleman would be pleased by the change in fashion. Trousers suited his figure better whereas Ralph still wore tight-fitting breeches to calf-length. His jacket and waist-coat were of similar design but fawn in colour.

'Sit down, Ben, sit down and tell us what you've been doing. We've missed you. I say, we've missed you.' Ralph waved his arms at the vacant seats.

'Oh, shut up, Ralph,' said Warren. 'Ben's brought a guest,

let him introduce us.' Warren grinned at Ben and gave him a light tap on the shoulder.

He raised an eyebrow in amusement at Daniel. Warren and Ralph had obviously had what might prove to be a little too much to drink.

Ben made the introductions.

'Daniel Holmes,' slurred Ralph. 'Hah, that's a slap in the face for your father, Ben, you in the company of a Holmes!'

'Oh, shut up, Ralph,' said Warren again, flopping back in his chair. 'You remember – Ben married a Holmes.'

Ralph straightened in his seat. 'So he did! Whatever happened to the lovely Alicia? The way you two behaved at all those parties, we thought . . .'

'Shut up,' snapped Warren who saw that this could be embarrassing for Ben in front of Daniel. He went on quickly to divert the others, 'Ben, you never invited us to your wedding. I thought we were your friends?'

'You are, Warren, you are, but the wedding was a very quiet affair. We wanted it that way.'

Ralph swayed forward. 'Well, if that's the way you wanted it, you had every right to have it that way. Hadn't he, Daniel?'

'Aye, he had.'

Warren stood up and moved round Ben, looking him up and down. Then he looked at Ralph. 'Have you seen his clothes, Ralph? He's dressed very oddly.'

Ralph narrowed his eyes at Ben as if that would enable him to see him better. 'So he is. What you dressed like that for, Ben?'

He winked at Daniel. 'Because I'm learning to be a fisherman.'

'Fisherman!' Warren and Ralph gasped together. Their mouths fell open in amazement, then they started to laugh. It grew louder and longer, interspersed with cries of, 'Fisherman? You?'

'Aye,' put in Daniel with a wry smile. 'And he'll make a good one.'

That brought more laughter from the pair. 'We must see this! Tell us when you are going. We'll get a boat and come and watch the fun.'

Ben grinned. 'I don't think you could get up early enough.'

Warren looked at Ralph. 'Early? Now *that's* a sobering thought. Maybe we'll wait and get an account from Daniel here. You'll tell us, won't you?'

'Aye, I'll do that.' He was quick to agree lest these two changed their minds. He wouldn't put it past them to hire a boat and that could spell disaster for the fishing.

'You will?'

'Aye, I've said so.'

'Hurrah!' cried Ralph. 'We can stay in our beds. Now, Ben, we've missed your company. I can understand why you've not been on the town, you've a little lady now, but remember this, old friend – Warren and I still frequent our old haunts if ever you feel like speculating on the cards. And we still keep our ears alert so if you ever want to have a flutter, you can find us.'

'I'll remember, Ralph.'

'We've made a penny or two in our time.'

'Yes, we have,' agreed Ben. 'Maybe again, some day.' He drained his tankard. 'We'd better be going, Daniel.' He stood up slapped his two friends on the back.

They nodded and, bleary-eyed, shook hands with Daniel, saying. 'We're glad to have met you. We can see Ben will be in good hands when he's fishing. Look after him.'

'I will.' Daniel followed his brother-in-law from the Black Bull. 'They're a right pair of characters,' he said when they got outside.

Ben grinned. 'They are that. Harmless, though, and they're good sorts. Drink too much, but it never gets the better of them. They can sup all night and be little worse than you've already seen.'

'Where are they from?'

'Both their families have estates higher up the Esk Valley.

They've known each other since they were youngsters.'

'I'm surprised they chose the Black Bull.'

'They'll drink anywhere and with anyone.'

'Have you known them a long time?'

'Yes. They were always at the parties I used to attend in Whitby and the county.'

'With the lovely Alicia, as they put it?'

'We'd been friends from childhood.'

'So some of the stories about you are true?'

Ben grinned. 'Maybe, but all stories get exaggerated, especially when drink, gambling and girls come into them.'

Daniel nodded. 'Do you still crave a bit of excitement?'

'You're quizzing me, Daniel. Thinking of your sister? Ease your mind, I've other things to think of now.'

'I hope it stays that way.'

'It will.'

Chapter Fifteen

Dina could not settle. Knowing that her restlessness irritated her father, who was trying to concentrate on the newspaper he was reading, she had come to her room earlier than usual but had left her door slightly ajar so that she would hear Sarah's return from the concert in Mulgrave Hall.

The fire gave her bedroom a cosy warmth, the chair was comfortable and eventually she began to feel drowsy. It became a struggle to keep her eyes open but finally she succumbed only to wake with a start. Her eyes flashed to the clock on the mantelpiece. Twenty minutes since she had last looked at it. Had she missed Sarah's return?

She sat up. There were voices below. They must have woken her. Relief swept over her. She heard footsteps cross the hall and start up the stairs. She jumped to her feet and glided swiftly across the room, closing the door gently and remaining close to it, listening for Sarah to reach her room.

'Good night, Sarah. I'm glad you had an enjoyable time. He seems a pleasant young man.'

'Good night, Father.'

Dina strained to hear the two doors shut. The first one she heard was the nearest to her room, Sarah's. She waited, tense, willing her father not to be long. Then she heard his door close. She waited a few moments more before quietly slipping into the corridor and tripping light-footed to Sarah's room. Dina tapped gently on the door and stepped quickly into the room without waiting for an answer.

'Come on, tell me all about him. Did you have a wonderful evening? What's he like? What's his aunt like?' The words poured out of Dina as she sat down expectantly on the bed.

'There's nothing to tell,' replied Sarah, trying to sound casually disinterested as she hung her coat in a cupboard.

Dina, knowing it was only a put-on attitude, said, 'Don't tell me it was boring? I'll bet it was all so exciting!'

Laughing, Sarah sat down on the bed beside her. 'It was, Dina, it was. And he's very interesting and attentive.'

'Come on, tell all. Why did he send a coach for you and not come himself?'

'A business appointment came up at the last minute. It was important and took longer than he'd expected. Ryan was very apologetic.'

'Sincerely so?' Dina put the question with just a little suspicion.

'Oh, yes And his aunt supported him in his explanation.'

'What's she like?'

'Appears formidable when you first see her, but that comes from never having been married and always having to look after everything herself. She's thin, carries herself well, her face is longish, eyebrows arched so that her eyes appear bigger than they are, but they're shrewd too, never missing a thing. I learned in the course of the evening that she has a sharp brain and an alert mind.'

'Did you like her?'

'Yes. She's a person you wouldn't want to cross but would be a very supportive friend. She idolises her nephew, He's her only relation apparently.'

'Oh, well, he's worth cultivating then. Do you like him?'

Sarah pursed her lips thoughtfully. 'Well, I'll tell you that when I've seen some more of him.'

'So you *are* seeing him again?' Dina twisted on the bed so that she could prop herself on one elbow and see her sister's response to this question.

'Yes. He brought me home and asked Father if he could take me to dine at the Angel next Monday.'

'And Father said yes?'

'He did.'

'Lucky you! I wish he'd approve of Rowan.'

'Be patient, Dina. Maybe he will in time. Don't you think he's been rather more amiable lately, a little more appreciative and attentive to us?'

'You might well say so when he's given his approval to your seeing Mr Bennett.' Dina pouted.

'No, apart from that, don't you think so?'

'Well, yes, I suppose so.'

'It seems to have stemmed from the time we all went to the theatre. Do you think he's seeing someone?'

'You mean, a lady friend?'

'Yes. Why shouldn't he be?'

'No reason, I suppose. But if he is and she puts him in a better temper, long may it continue.'

Sarah sat up on the edge of the bed. 'I overheard something at the concert . . .'

Dina sat up beside her. 'What?' she said, eager to hear a bit of scandal.

Sarah laughed and shook her head. 'Nothing like that. It was about Ben.'

'Ben?'

'Two people sitting behind me were discussing us, the Coulsons. They didn't know who I was. Among other things they were commenting on Ben's marriage and how it had led to his going into a fishing partnership. They were saying how foreign that would be to him. But the point I am getting to is that they happened to mention that he would be going fishing for the first time the day after tomorrow. I feel guilty that I haven't been in touch with him as I said I would, but the opportunity has never arisen. I must make an effort. Tomorrow I shall find out what time they are likely to be sailing and will go to see him off.'

'And I'll come with you! Rowan hasn't gone on a second winter voyage. I know where he'll be tomorrow. I'll ask him to find out what time Ben will be leaving and where from.'

*

'Your first fishing expedition, how do you feel?' asked Daniel as he and Ben walked to the Fish Pier where their coble was tied up. Gideon, anxious to check once again that everything was ready, had left the house in Grape Lane half an hour before.

'I'm ready. I only hope I can remember everything you and your father have told me.'

'You did well on our last two practices. You'll be all right. You handle the oars well. You'll be in the bow, as you have been since you got used to the oars, so you can take your rhythm from me. Father will be at the tiller as usual. If we get under sail, he'll not fasten the sheet but hold it so that if he wants the boat to lose way he can let go. You've seen what happens – the sail will flap, but don't be alarmed by that. Your job, as we've told you, will be to bail if necessary, and that's more than likely, while I'll be busy with the blocks.'

Ben grinned. 'Thanks for reminding me. Let's hope we get a good catch.'

When they turned on to the Fish Pier, Daniel eyed the sky which had become bright with the morning light. 'Looks as if the weather will be set fair.' He glanced in the direction of the boat. 'Hello, it seems we have someone to see us off.'

The two figures already there caught Ben's eye. His pulse raced with excitement. 'My sisters! What are they doing here?'

'Come to see their brother off on his first fishing voyage, I expect.' There was a touch of hostility in Daniel's voice. After all, these were the daughters of the man who had wronged his father. Without acknowledging them, he turned away to join Gideon who had kept himself aloof since Sarah and Dina had arrived on the Fish Pier.

Hearing footsteps, the girls turned to see their brother. 'Hello, Ben.'

'What are you two doing here?' There was a touch of concern in Ben's tone as if he feared they were the bearers of some sort of bad news.

'We're here to see you off on your first fishing venture,' replied Sarah. 'I'm sorry I haven't been in touch before.'

'That's all right,' he replied. 'Thanks for coming. I'm sorry about their attitude.' He inclined his head in the direction of Gideon and Daniel.

'It is quite understandable in view of what Father did,' replied Sarah. 'How are you?'

'Very well, thank you.'

'Happy?'

'Immensely.'

'Then I'm happy for you.'

'What about the fishing, Ben?' asked Dina. 'It isn't your trade.'

'I've learned.'

'But it's the sea!'

Ben grinned. 'I'm getting used to it.' He added tentatively, 'How's Father?'

'He's well,' replied Sarah.

'We think he's more amiable than he was before,' put in Dina.

Ben raised a questioning eyebrow to express his doubt that this could be so.

'It's true,' insisted Dina. 'We think he must be seeing a lady and that she's influenced his outlook for the good.'

Ben laughed. 'You think that? Have you any proof that he is seeing someone?

'It's just a suspicion since he seems more mellow.'

'I'll believe that when I see it. Look, I'm sorry, I'll have to go.'

'One last quick bit of news,' said Dina in a manner that revealed she had been wanting to break this to him. 'Sarah has a new beau!'

'Dina!' she chided. 'He's not my beau.'

'You said you liked him, and he's taking you out again.'

'Well, come on, who is it?' pressed Ben.

'Ryan Bennett, nephew of Miss Bennett of Mulgrave Hall.'

'Oh, the young man we met at the art exhibition at the Angel. Good, I'm pleased for you Sarah. Now I must go. Thanks for coming. I hope we'll meet again.'

'We will,' promised Sarah.

'Good fishing,' said Dina.

Ben hurried to the coble, slipped her ropes and stepped on board. They pushed off, and once clear of the pier Daniel and Ben unshipped their oars and, in a rhythm that had come from long practice, propelled the craft towards the sea.

Sarah and Dina watched until it became a dot on the horizon. As they turned and walked slowly from the Fish Pier, Sarah wondered what the future held for them all.

'There is a gentleman asking to see you, miss. Mr Warren Laskill.' The maid had brought the message to Alicia's bedroom, situated at the front of the house and with a view across Whitby towards the ruined abbey high on the east cliff. She had turned this room into a cosy retreat, a place where she had dreamed of a life with Ben Coulson – a dream that had now turned sour and left her with a burning desire to revenge her humiliation at his hands.

'Show him into the second drawing-room. I'll be down in a minute.'

'Very well, miss.'

Alicia sat for a moment pondering this visit. Well, there was only one way to find out why he'd come. She rose from her chair, viewed herself in the mirror, smoothed her dress and patted her hair, then went to join him.

Warren was standing looking out of the window but swung round when he heard the door open.

'My dear Alicia, it is so good of you to see me.' He smiled as he came to greet her, taking her hand and raising it towards his lips.

She smiled to herself at such a display of proper etiquette from the man with whom she had shared much laughter and ribald humour at country house parties where she had also watched him triumph at cards, quickly learning to match him and being bettered only by Ben.

'Warren, thank you for calling. You have brightened my

day.' Alicia knew he liked a bit of flattery. 'Do sit down.'

He waited until she had taken her place in a chair to one side of the fireplace, then took the one opposite.

'We have not met for a while and under the circumstances that is understandable. May I commiserate with you? We all thought that you and Ben were meant to marry and that his appearance at the ball with someone else was only temporary aberration.' Warren felt remorseful when he saw that his words were causing Alicia some pain. He shrugged his shoulders. 'Well, what has happened has happened and life must go on. We cannot see the lovely Alicia hiding herself away. That is why I am here. I have been invited to a party at Danby Hall. The invitation includes a guest, and I would be honoured if you would accompany me?'

Alicia did not reply immediately. She did not want to seem like a recluse waiting for such an invitation.

Misreading her hesitation, Warren went on, 'I think the usual crowd will be there and probably some new faces. It will do you good to get out among them all again.'

'It's very thoughtful of you, Warren. I do appreciate your asking me.'

'Of course, I will formally ask permission of your parents.'

Alicia smiled to herself. He was certainly trying to appear proper. In the past such a situation hadn't arisen as it had always been understood by their friends that Ben would be escorting her. Had Warren some ulterior motive in mind now that he knew she was free from any commitment? Maybe he wouldn't be such a bad catch, but at the moment she was not prepared to pursue that possibility. But here was an opportunity for her to get back into the old life. Sam had seen that she did not hide herself away and had gone out of his way to be kind to her, but this was different and could give her opportunity to win her revenge.

'I am sure it will be perfectly all right, but if you wish you can see Mother now. She's in the other drawing-room.' Alicia rose from her chair and Warren followed her.

'Mother, Mr Warren Laskill would like a word,' said Alicia as she walked into the drawing room.

Her mother looked up from the embroidery she was doing. 'Ah, Mr Laskill.'

'Mrs Campion,' said Warren in the most pleasant tone he could muster. 'Indeed, it is a pleasure to see you.' He took the hand she held out to him and raised it to his lips as he bowed graciously. 'I trust you are in good health?'

'I can't complain.'

'I am pleased to hear that, just as I am to see Alicia looking so well. I hope that Mr Campion and your other daughters are the same?' He took the seat indicated by Mrs Campion as Alicia sat next to her mother.

Grace laid down her embroidery. 'Now, Mr Laskill, to what do we owe the honour of your visit? I'm sure it is not me you came to see.'

Warren, though a little taken back by her forthright manner, saw the amused twinkle in her eyes and threw up his arms in surrender. 'Meeting you has made this visit all the more pleasurable. But you are right – I came to see Alicia. I have asked her if she would like to accompany me to a party at Danby Hall two weeks from today. Now I seek your permission for her to do so.'

Grace shot her daughter a glance and what she saw was sufficient for her to know that Alicia wanted to go. 'That is most kind of you. As far as I am concerned, and I have no doubt Mr Campion will agree, you have my permission.'

'Thank you, Mrs Campion. The party will be all the more pleasant now that Alicia can accompany me.'

'It will do her good. She has not been socialising these last three months, as you will have noticed. It will be good for her to be among old friends again. Now, I am sure you two have a lot of news to exchange.' She turned to Alicia. 'Why don't you go and have a chat with Mr Laskill? I'll have some chocolate brought to you.'

'Thank you, Mother.' Alicia rose from her chair.

Warren sprang to his feet. 'Thank you so much for giving your permission, Mrs Campion, and for your hospitality.'

Grace acknowledged this with a little inclination of her head. He hurried after Alicia, opened the door for her and they returned to the second drawing-room.

She smiled as the door closed. 'Chocolate? I think you'd rather have something stronger?'

He smiled. 'Indeed, though I would not like to disparage your mother's kindness.' As they sat down he added, 'Everyone has missed you, Alicia.'

'I'm sorry I've not been around but it was due to force of circumstances.' She certainly wasn't going to tell him it was because she had expected to be married. That would only fuel to the speculation that she knew must be flying round, especially when Ben arrived back in Whitby married to Ruth. 'But now that's past and I'm able to resume the life I've missed. Thank you for asking me to this party.'

There was a knock on the door and a maid came in with a tray bearing the chocolate.

'Thank you, Eliza. Just leave it, I'll pour.' When the door closed Alicia said, 'Now tell me all the news?'

Warren settled back, accepted his chocolate and told her the latest gossip about all their friends. He was careful not to refer to Ben, though.

When he seemed to have exhausted his news, Alicia said, 'Come on, Warren, you've not mentioned what they all thought to Ben's marriage. I know you are avoiding the topic but if I am to meet our friends again, I would rather know something of their attitudes to that marriage.'

'Well, I must say, it came as a shock to us all. We had expected he would marry . . .' He hesitated to say it.

'Me?' she finished for him.

'Well, yes. We all thought it was a match made in heaven.'

Alicia gave a wan smile. 'So did I.' She shrugged her shoulders. 'But such is life.'

'I met Ben yesterday.' He put the statement tentatively.

'You did?' She couldn't help her curiosity, just as she couldn't help asking, 'How was he?'

'He looked well.' Warren hesitated again.

'Yes?' she prompted, wanting to know more.

'I was in the Black Bull with Ralph when he came in with Daniel Holmes. He's taken up fishing with Daniel and his father.'

'Has to earn a living somehow, I suppose.'

'But it's hardly him.'

'I know.'

'What a change for him! What on earth was he thinking of, marrying a Holmes, after what happened in the Arctic?'

'I was surprised the Holmeses didn't move away.'

'I suppose that would have looked as if Captain Holmes accepted that he was to blame for the tragedy,' reasoned Warren.

'Even if he was innocent, they can never prove it.'

'I suppose not.'

'Now, tell me more about this party at Danby Hall? I have never been there.'

'Nor have I but I am assured it is a splendid place. The host family are called Robson, and moved there about two months ago. They have four children all about our age, and this party is for them to get to know local people. They came from the East Riding apparently. Ralph knew them from the time he spent down there. It's through him that I received an invitation, as have more of our friends.'

'Sounds interesting, and it will be entertaining to meet some new people.'

'Good, I will call for you with my carriage.' He waved his arms flamboyantly and swept them across himself, bowing from the waist as he said, 'And you, Miss Campion, shall be carried away to dance all night.'

Alicia laughed at his antics. 'I can't wait.'

Ben felt greatly relieved when they rowed the last few yards to the Fish Pier. He shipped his oars and, as rehearsed, was the first ashore to tie up. People were already there, eager to buy fresh fish, and the crew of the *True Love* were pleased to be the first coble back in port, for it meant they could get a good price for their fish.

The day had been hard but by sheer determination Ben had kept pace with the two more experienced men. He had had all his work cut out to do that when Daniel started to haul in the lines, while Gideon, at the oars, kept the coble on a steady course and speed so that his job and Daniel's were coordinated. There had been no let-up for Ben as he gaffed the fish as they came to the surface and then unhooked them. Now came the job of gutting them and laying them out for customers to make their choice. Though they had given him some practice over previous days Ben still could not keep pace with Daniel and Gideon, the former being much the quicker. Half their catch had been sold before other cobles appeared and by the time all their catch was taken they were ready for home, a meal and their beds to recover for a repeat performance tomorrow, weather permitting.

With advice from her mother, Ruth saw to Ben's needs and sympathised with his desire to be left alone once he had tumbled into bed. As tired as he was, sleep did not come easily to him. He lay staring at the ceiling, wondering how he had come to such a life, and felt the stirrings of a new determination. He must relinquish it before too long but for now that was a secret he would keep to himself, not even sharing it with Ruth.

'Have you seen Ben again?'

Warren was surprised by Alicia's question as they drove to Danby Hall. He had thought that the subject would be taboo with her.

'I have, as a matter of fact. Saw him in the Black Bull again.'

'And?' She pressed him for more information, something that may enable her to make Ben pay for what he had done to her.

270

'He looked well but a bit drawn about the face, and there was a tiredness about his eyes. From what he said, or more the way he spoke, I gathered he was finding the life of a fisherman hard.'

'But still doing it?'

'Oh, yes. You know Ben. He won't want to be seen weakening, but I believe if he had the opportunity he'd be out of it. Mind you, that's only my impression, it comes from nothing he said.'

'Only the way he said it?'

'I suppose so, but I could have been reading more into it than there is.'

'You're probably right. Ben was never cut out for that sort of life. I'll bet he wishes he still had his ropery. It was a stupid thing to do, selling out in order to help the Holmes family by going into partnership with them.'

'When I saw him I suggested he should join the usual group for a game of cards at the Angel. He didn't commit himself but he turned up.'

'Did he?' Alicia's tone expressed surprise but also indicated that she would like to know more, without appearing to press Warren. He was drawn into the trap.

'Yes, and by the time the evening was half over he was beginning to relax and enjoy himself. He left earlier than in the old days, though. I told him we were pleased to see him back and that he'd be welcome any time, something that was reiterated by everyone else.'

'So his taste for his previous life is still there?'

'Oh, yes, I'm sure it is, but from something he said I gathered that money was a bit tight and likely to become more so. The greater part of the proceeds from the ropery will have gone on this fishing partnership – a new coble and all the equipment, that's not cheap.'

'Ah, well, it was of his own choosing.' Alicia adopted an unsympathetic attitude but she had stored the information away. It could prove useful. A word placed judiciously here or carefully dropped there sent all sorts of stories circulating. Some people were only too eager to gossip. Warren could be worth cultivating to get further news of Ben. She slid a little nearer to him and Warren was not one to deter her. He knew Alicia for a flirt, she always had been, but while he'd thought that she and Ben . . . Well, that hadn't happened. Maybe now there was a chance for him.

'Enough of Ben, we're going to enjoy ourselves.' The tempting promise in her voice was not lost on Warren.

'Ben, what is the matter?' Ruth was sitting at her dressing-table adjusting her hair to a new style that she hoped he would notice. She wanted to look her best for him this evening especially as it was his first Christmas Eve away from his own family. It would be a big change for him and, although she knew her mother was going out of her way to make this a special occasion in spite of times being a little harder for the family, she was sure she could make their first Christmas together memorable. But she wanted him to be in a better mood than he had been over the last few weeks.

'Nothing,' he replied, buttoning his shirt.

'I think there is. Please talk to me. You've become distant over these last few weeks. I know marrying me changed your life. Do you wish you hadn't?'

He came to her, his shirt sleeves hanging loose, the neck unbuttoned. He stood behind her and slid his hands over her shoulders until his fingers touched the curve of her breasts. He bent and kissed the top of her head and looked at her in the mirror. 'I love you, Ruth. Please never think that I regret marrying you.'

'Then what is it, Ben?' Eyes fixed on his pleaded to be told the truth. He hesitated so she continued, 'You miss your old lifestyle? I know you've been frequenting the Angel, meeting your old friends in the back room for cards.'

A startled look came to his eyes. 'How did you know?'

'Word gets around, sometimes on purpose. There are always

272

those ready to talk, people who thought you and Alicia should have married and will see that rumours come my way, hoping to upset our relationship. Oh, maybe they're not so malicious, but they do take pleasure in salacious talk.'

Ben sighed. 'I might have known it. I'm sorry, Ruth.' He kissed the top of her head again. Her hand came up to his in a gesture of forgiveness. 'Yes, I do miss the life I knew, but I would not return to it without you. It's just . . . I'm not cut out to be a fisherman. Oh, I'll not let your father and Daniel down, and I'll continue with them until something else turns up. It might help if we had a place of our own.'

'Aren't you happy here?'

'Yes, but—'

'I know, Ben. Sometimes I feel the same, but what can we do?'

'I have a couple of investments I did not realise, keeping them back in case of emergency. I could cash them in now and we could get a house of our own.

Ruth swivelled on her stool and stood up. She slid her arms round his neck and leaned back against his arms so that she could look into his eyes. 'Maybe this will help you to decide.' The twinkle in her eyes mesmerised him. 'I'm going to have a baby.'

Time stood still for a moment until he burst out, 'What?' It was a question that needed no answer. He hugged and kissed her passionately

'You're pleased?' she asked when their lips parted.

'Of course. I love you so very much.' He kissed her again.

She realised this was a further responsibility she had pushed upon him, but had no doubts that he would rise to it.

'And I love you, too.' He looked into her eyes and she felt a new bond between them.

'We'd better finish dressing,' he said, and started to turn away but she stopped him. 'Ben, we'll find a place of our own after New Year if you think you can afford it.'

'We will.'

'And I don't mind your going to the Angel and seeing your old friends occasionally.'

'Ruth, you are wonderful!'

When everyone was relaxing after a delicious meal Ruth made her announcement to the family. The momentary hush broke into pandemonium as congratulations reverberated from the walls and chairs were pushed back. Kisses and hugs were exchanged. Ben felt his arm would be pumped off and his back would be black and blue from being thumped in congratulation.

'This calls for a toast. Fetch the special bottle, Daniel,' said Gideon.

He soon had glasses filled and Abel handed them round, saying, 'I'm going to be an uncle, I'm going to be an uncle,' as if he needed to convince himself of his new role in life.

Gideon made the toast to his daughter, son-in-law and grandchild-to-be.

When the excitement had abated Ruth made her second announcement. 'After New Year, Ben and I are going to find a place of our own.'

For a moment there was shocked silence. Gideon broke it with, 'There's no need—'

'Yes, there is, Father. It would not be fair to any of you to bring a baby into the house. Apart from which we have put on you long enough.'

'We appreciate all you have done for us,' said Ben quickly to support his wife. 'You are all very dear to us, but we think it's time we had our own home.'

Gideon started to protest again but Georgina silenced him. 'Gideon, let the young ones have their way. I can understand them wanting to be on their own. I remember how I felt when we were first married and had to spend a month with your parents until our cottage was ready. It will be for the best, and they won't be far away.' She added then as if to halt any further objections, 'Do you know where you would like to live?'

'We haven't thought about it, Mother. We'll start looking.'

About that time on the other side of the river the Coulson family were approaching the Campions' house. They had all wrapped up well against the sharp bite in the air and were in a Christmas mood. Grace, who had suggested a meal for the two families near the period of festivities, had eventually decided on Christmas Eve. Sarah and Dina had witnessed a softening in their father's temperament as the day approached. Once again it had made them wonder who or what might be responsible for this easing of what had previously been an unbending character. Not that they minded; in fact, they welcomed it for it made for an easier life for them, though they were still careful about mentioning certain subjects, one of which was Ben. It was inevitable that his name should slip out sometimes, though, and on those occasions they saw their father's eyes darken and witnessed his newly genial temper become edged like a sword.

They had raised their eyebrows when he had suggested a shopping expedition to buy presents for the Campions. They wondered why he had insisted on similar silver necklaces for Mrs Campion and Alicia, but that Alicia should also have an exquisite jet pendant. Surely *she* couldn't be . . .? They dismissed the idea that had entered their minds when they talked about it after shopping. He must be making the extra present to Alicia because of Ben's treatment of her. There could be no other reason.

Laughter and jollity filled the atmosphere when they entered the Campions' residence, shook off their coats, exchanged greetings and added their presents to the pile in the drawing room to be opened later. A warming punch was served and accepted to combat the evening cold.

Staring at the flames, with the warm cup cradled in her hands, Sarah wished that Ben was with them and hoped that his first

275

Christmas away from the family would be a happy one.

'A penny for them,' Alicia offered as she and Dina came over to Sarah.

She started and gave a wan smile. 'Nothing really.'

'We don't believe it,' said Dina, and turned to Alicia. 'She's mooning over Ryan Bennett.'

Alicia's eyes lit up with curiosity. Here was some news. 'Who?'

'Ryan Bennett, nephew of Miss Bennett, the spinster who moved into Mulgrave Hall recently.'

'Now, Sarah, what have you been hiding from me?' said Alicia

'Dina makes more of this than there is.'

'There must be something in it. She was introduced to him at an art exhibition. He invited her to a concert at Mulgrave Hall and has since dined her at the Angel, and we are all invited to the Hall on Boxing Day.'

'Sarah, his interest must be serious,' said Alicia with a teasing twinkle in her eyes.

'We are friends,' she replied tersely, casting a dagger look at her sister for giving so much away, especially to Alicia whom she knew liked nothing better than to be in possession of news.

Alicia knew better than to pursue the subject now, but she would find out more about Ryan Bennett. Maybe Warren would be able to tell her. She turned to Dina. 'Well, what about you? Are you and Rowan still . . .'

'Of course she is,' replied Sarah quickly so that she could get her own back and not allow her sister to deny it. But Dina had no intention of doing so.

'I see him when I can. I'll sneak away tomorrow when Father doesn't know and visit him with a present I have for him.'

'Your father doesn't approve yet?'

'No, but I'm hoping he might be relaxing his ideas.'

'Has he said anything?'

'No, but he is a bit more amiable these days.'

Alicia shot Sarah a questioning look.

'I think he is too.'

'We think he might be seeing a lady,' Dina blurted out.

Once again Sarah shot her sister a hostile look for saying too much.

'That's an interesting speculation,' remarked Alicia, but before their conversation could continue the call to dine was made.

It was a most pleasant meal, taken leisurely with conversation flowing easily all around the table. Sam found himself seated opposite Alicia. From her position, Sarah noted the attention her father gave to her friend, and that he also kept observing her even when they were in conversation with others.

Alicia was not so naive as to be unaware of the attention Sam was paying her. Others may not notice it, or if they did would put it down to concern for the girl his son had hurt deeply. Later, when the presents were distributed and she found she had a special present from Sam, she began to wonder if there was more to his attention than an attempt to alleviate hurt. She began to feel flattered and to link other incidents together. And that made her think even further. A relationship with someone old enough to be her father? But he wasn't so old, and besides, she did get on well with older men. Well, most men. Maybe in this case it could develop into something more and directly benefit her family because she could use marriage to Sam to eliminate her father's debt once and for all. She covertly observed Sam.

He was still a handsome man, rich, well thought of in Whitby by most, respected by others, hated by some who dare not move against him. To live alongside such a man would give her status. Did the prospect horrify her? She found it did not. And there was the added incentive of making sure that Ben continued to be out of favour. She might very well inherit what he regarded as his. Alicia resolved to play the situation slowly and shrewdly, to her own best advantage.

It came as no surprise to her when, after they had retired to the drawing-room, Sam kept paying her particular attention. Now it was up to her.

When Ben woke on Boxing Day his wife was still asleep. He turned his head and watched her, counting his blessings in an outpouring of silent love.

When Ruth woke she opened her eyes to find him still looking at her. She smiled. He leaned over and kissed her. 'You're beautiful.'

'I'm glad you think so.' She reached out and strolled his cheek. 'Thank you for marrying me, Ben Coulson.'

He kissed her again then turned on to his back and held out one arm so that she could cuddle close with her head on his shoulder. They lay in the blissful silence that only true lovers share. They wanted time to stand still so that they could share eternity just as they were, lost in each other's love. But time does not stand still.

'Ruth, you know how close Sarah and I were and still are?'

She gave a little nod. 'You miss her?'

'Yes. I would like her to know about the baby. I'm going to visit New Buildings today. Come with me?'

'If that is what you want, but what if your father is there?'

'He won't answer the door. We'll ask the maid if he is at home. If he is, we'll ask her to give a message to Sarah asking her to meet us.'

Two hours later they were approaching New Buildings. As they walked towards them Ruth said wistfully, 'But for that accident, my family might have been living on this side of the river by now.'

'They will one day, love.'

The door of the Coulsons' house was opened by a maid whose eyes widened with surprise when she saw Ben.

'Hello, Jenny. Is my sister Sarah at home?'

She gave a little shake of her head. 'I'm sorry, sir. All the family have gone to Mulgrave Hall for luncheon.'

Ben was not only surprised but mystified. 'Then will you give her a message when she returns?'

'Yes, sir.'

'It's for Miss Sarah only, mind. No one else must know we have been here. You understand, Jenny?'

'Yes, sir.'

'Tell her we called wanting to see her, and ask her if she will meet us at the Angel tomorrow morning at eleven o'clock. You've got that Jenny?'

'Yes, sir. The Angel at eleven tomorrow. And no one else must know.'

Prompt at eleven o'clock the following morning Sarah arrived at the Angel to be shown to a small private room where Ruth and Ben were waiting. There was concern on her face when she came in.

'Sarah.' Her brother came quickly to meet her, hands held out to take hers in greeting. He kissed her on the cheek and said, 'Take that worried look off your face.'

She let go of his hands and came to Ruth who rose from her chair, embraced her sister-in-law and kissed her on both cheeks.

'I've hardly slept a wink all night, wondering why you wanted to see me. I imagined all sorts of things.'

'I'm sorry. I should have told Jenny that it was nothing to worry about.'

'Well, what is it?' asked Sarah, looking from one to the other.

'I ordered chocolate to be served when you arrived, let's wait for that.'

'Don't keep me in suspense any longer! What is it that was so pressing?'

Ben and Ruth exchanged glances and Ben's slight nod told her to proceed as arranged.

'You are going to be Aunt Sarah,' Ruth announced quietly.

For that split second Sarah looked as if she had not heard aright and then her face lit up with pleasure. 'Ruth, Ben . . . oh, I'm so happy for you.' A lump came to her throat and her eyes dampened. She hugged Ruth, and then with one arm still round her she held out her other to Ben. The three of them were united in a joyful embrace.

'Take your things off, Sarah, stay a little while,' Ben suggested.

He was pleased when his sister agreed and shrugged herself out of her outdoor coat. She removed her bonnet and patted her hair before sitting down in the chair held for her by Ben.

The maid arrived with a tray and set it on a low table that stood between them. Ruth poured the chocolate as Ben enquired about his family.

'Eric is Eric, still full of his own importance though he has no reason to be. He's very keen on whaling. Though that's genuine enough, I suspect it's also because he sees it pleases Father. Dina is in good health and as bright as ever. Nothing gets her down.'

'She still sees Rowan?'

'Oh, yes, whenever she can.'

'Father hasn't relented yet?'

'No.'

'When you visited me on the Fish Pier you said you thought he was more amiable, nowadays. Is that still so?'

'Yes.'

'Now, Sarah, what about you?' asked Ruth. 'When Ben returned from his first fishing he told me you had seen him off and that Dina had said you were seeing a young man who was living with his aunt at Mulgrave Hall. When we called on you yesterday the maid told us that all the family were at a luncheon there. So do we conclude that this relationship is serious?'

'I don't know. I like him and he seems to like me.'

'Does Father approve?' asked Ben.

'Well, you know Father. If there's money there he'll approve. Miss Bennett is reputed to be rich and Ryan is her only relation . . .'

'Don't let him bully you into anything you don't want,' advised Ben. 'Go where your heart is.'

'Like you did,' commented Sarah admiringly as she looked at the couple seated in front of her and saw their hands clasped together lovingly.

She was never able to say why but that gesture made up her mind for her about her feelings for Ryan.

Chapter Sixteen

During the third week in January Ruth and Ben found a small house towards the south end of Church Street. It was not what they would have liked but it was what they could afford and they were determined to be happy there. Their finances were unstable as so much depended on the fickle weather. With a serious loss of income in February, Ben was beginning to grow worried.

The problem was on his mind when, one evening, knowing that Ruth was at her mother's he made his way to the small room at the back of the Angel. When he walked in he was greeted as a long-lost friend.

'We thought you had deserted us again,' cried Warren.

'You always make the games more interesting,' called Ralph.

A murmur of agreement went up from other friends around the room.

'Where have you been?' asked Warren as they made a place for him at the table.

'Busy moving into our own house.'

The announcement startled them all but it was Warren who really wanted to know more.

'Where?' he asked.

'Small place towards the south end of Church Street.'

'Bit of a change from New Buildings,' commented Ralph.

'Maybe, but we're happy there. Ruth's at her mother's tonight so here I am. I have to call for her in two hours.'

'Watch out, Ben, if it's mother and daughter talk,' someone slurred.

'I think it will be baby talk.' The words were out before he could stop them.

His admission was taken up by all around the table and ribald comments followed, filling the air with hilarity until someone shouted, 'Are we here to play cards or do you want to continue talking about babies?'

'Play!' the dealer called as he picked up the cards.

Warren, eager to impart Ben's news to Alicia, extended an invitation for her to accompany him to a meal at the Angel a week later. He had hinted to Jed Crowther that he would like a discreetly placed table and, knowing Warren for a good customer, he had only been too ready to comply.

When they were shown to a table in an alcove that shielded them from the rest of the dining room, Alicia smiled to herself. She wondered if this was all building up to a proposal of marriage, or if he just enjoyed her company and revelled in being the bearer of gossip. Well, no matter, she was enjoying herself. Marriage to Warren would never seriously be considered, but she would play him like a fish to hear news of Ben.

So she enjoyed Warren's attention and, realising from his attitude that he had something he was eager to tell her but was holding back to tease her, pretended she was not all that interested.

Finally, as they waited for their tarts, jellies and syllabubs, he could hold out no longer. 'Would you like the latest news of Ben?'

'It appears you are dying to tell me.' Alicia smiled, meeting his questioning gaze with a flirtatious glance so that he would hold nothing back from her.

He leaned forward and lowered his voice.

'Ben's going to be a father.'

Though it was something she had expected in the natural way of events, Alicia felt a little jab of shock, only for it to be taken over by an intense jealousy of Ruth. It was she who should have been having Ben's child, not Ruth. She could feel tears prickling behind her eyes and tensed herself with a determination not to let them flow. 'Oh, well, I suppose that was bound to happen. Good luck to them.' She forced her voice to stay even.

'He and Ruth have moved into a house at the south end of Church Street,' went on Warren.

'Oh, I suppose that follows.' She laughed mockingly. 'Quite a comedown for Ben Coulson, though.'

'Exactly what we all said.'

'We? I suppose you mean the usual group that gathers in the back room at the Angel.'

Warren smiled. 'How did you guess?'

'That's where you get your information, isn't it? Ben must have visited your game again.'

Warren waited until the servant who had brought their food moved away.

'Yes. He told the news himself.'

'Was he pleased about it?'

'I suppose so, though he didn't say too much. I got the impression that he was concerned about the added expense what with the fishing not having been so good recently. In the past week he's been free to visit us three times.'

Alicia raised an eyebrow. 'Because he wants to escape or because he is he expecting to make money that way?'

'He seems to be pleased to be back among his old friends but I reckon he hopes to go away better off than when he arrived. Remember, he was always a clever card player. Knew exactly when to bluff or not to bluff. Just as he always seemed to have good luck with his investments.'

Alicia looked thoughtful for a moment then with a serious expression said, 'Maybe we could help him.'

Warren looked puzzled. 'How?'

'Well, Ben can't be completely short of money. If we hear of anything that sounds like a good investment, you could give him a hint. Oh, he may not have the same amount to invest as he used to, but every little will help him.'

Warren pursed his lips thoughtfully then said with bright-ness coming to his eyes, 'That's a good idea, Alicia. It means you and I will have to be in touch more frequently.'

She was amused at the way he thought he had turned the situation to his own advantage but kept her amusement to herself.

During the second week in February with all their catch sold quickly after tying up at the Fish Pier, Gideon, Daniel and Ben were considering themselves lucky that they had made any profit. The catch had been small as the worsening weather had driven them home early.

After looking around and seeing everything was left as he liked it, Gideon said, 'Let's away home. Ruth will be at our house. Georgina said she would have something for us all and she'd send word to Ruth to come round.'

Ben nodded, but made no comment. This was happening almost every time they put to sea. He wished he could just go to his own home and have a meal alone with his wife, but he did not want to offend anyone especially Gideon on whom his father's wrath had been unjustly poured. His thoughts were interrupted when he heard Daniel speak.

'Just a moment, Father, I'd like to say something.' Gideon stopped and turned to face his son in the middle of the Fish Pier. 'I want to say it before we get home. It concerns the three of us.'

Ben's curiosity arose.

'Well?' prompted his father.

Daniel licked his lips as if that would help him to start, but he was not one to skirt around a point. 'I want to sell my share in the *True Love*. I think you both understood that I would return to the whalers this year?'

The announcement shocked Ben but that was banished almost immediately when he realised that what his brother-in-law said was true. He hadn't given it a second thought but now he was faced with it, realised that losing Daniel would be a blow to him. A different partner, one whom Gideon would see was experienced, could mean that Ben's own deficiencies would be more obvious. A new man might not accept them as Daniel

285

had. His world was being turned into turmoil again.

'Yes, I knew that, son. I always said your place was with the whalers. I'm grateful to you for giving up your winter voyages to get my enterprise under way. Knowing this might happen, I have been giving thought to another partner. I won't have much difficulty in finding one. I think we have impressed everyone with our catches.'

'Gideon, please sell my share too.' The words were out almost before Ben realised it.

Gideon and Daniel stared at him in disbelief.

'You don't mean it?' gasped his father-in-law.

'Why?' Daniel's question came almost at the same moment.

'I do, replied Ben in a voice that showed his determination. 'It's not the life for me.'

'But you've done so well.'

'Thanks to your tolerance. With Daniel gone it would not be the same. A new partner would probably see me as a hindrance. You've covered for my shortcomings many a time. I'd be better ashore.'

'But you need to make a living. You've Ruth, and a baby on the way.' Gideon, for the sake of his daughter, had to remind Ben of his responsibilities.

'I know that. And I shall look after them.'

'But what will you do?'

'I don't know yet, but I'll find something.'

Gideon saw the light of determination in his eyes. Though he did not approve of the action his son-in-law was taking he could see it would be no use arguing with him. That way could only lead to a family rift. He did not want that to happen. He nodded. 'All right, Ben, I'll see what I can do. And I'll get a good price for you.'

'Thank you.'

Gideon looked at them with sadness in his eyes. 'I'll miss you both. Let's go home and break the news.'

Ruth cast a questioning glance at Georgina when the three men walked in. She knew her mother too had felt the tension between them. Their usual banter was missing as they took off their working clothes.

'Well, you three, what's wrong?' No one answered immediately. 'We don't eat until Ruth and I know.'

'I have to find two new partners before I sail again,' replied Gideon bluntly.

Mother and daughter stared at the men in disbelief. 'Why?' Georgina asked.

'Daniel wants to return to the whalers. That I expected, but Ben also wishes to leave.'

'Why?' demanded Ruth with a frown.

'It's not the life for me, love,' replied Ben quietly.

'But we . . .'

'I'll explain later.'

Georgina, sensing tension between the two young ones, stepped in quickly. 'The meal will be ready, let's go to the dining room.' She knew Ruth and Ben needed to discuss the situation privately without any interference from her or Gideon or anyone else.

The meal was not its usual carefree affair. Ben knew his news had hurt Ruth and was glad when they could escape from the house in Grape Lane.

They had reached Church Street before she broke the awkward silence between them. 'What do you intend to do?'

'I don't know,' replied Ben lamely.

'What? You give up something that was bringing in enough for us to live on and you don't know what you are going to do next?' Disgust was added to the hurt in Ruth's voice. 'You have a double responsibility now.'

'I know, I know,' replied Ben, irritated that he was being reminded again. 'Your father's already pointed that out.'

'And so he should!'

'It has nothing to do with him.'

'He's only thinking of me.'

'And what about *me*? I'm no fisherman. Hate it every time we put to sea.'

'Not man enough to take it?' she mocked.

'I've taken it, Ruth, but I'm not taking it any more.' He stopped, grabbed her arm and turned her to him. 'I want a better life for us.'

'Maybe you should have married Alicia then!' She pulled her arm away and walked on with a quick step.

Her scathing words stunned Ben. He stared after her for a few moments, tempted to turn round and find solace in the Angel, but wisdom prevailed. He could not let her walk home alone in the dark with mist rolling in from the river. He ran after her and fell into step beside her. 'That was uncalled for, Ruth.'

She did not reply, but, holding herself very straight, kept up her quick pace until they reached home. As he lit the oil lamp left ready on a small table beside the front door, he could tell she was still angry with him by the way she flung off her cloak and threw her bonnet on top of it.

She followed him into the front room where he lit another oil lamp. Ruth went to the window and pulled the heavy curtains together with all the force she could muster. 'Ben Coulson, if you don't want this sort of life then you'd better go and find another!'

He came and stood in front of her, locked eyes with her. 'It's the fishing I don't want. I want my life with you, and I want it to be better than it is now. I want it for you.'

'Noble words, Ben, but how do you propose to live without an income?'

'We'll have the money from my share of the boat.'

'We can't live on that forever!'

'I'll find something else.'

'Where? Will your Angel friends help?' The mockery in her voice made him smart.

'They might.'

She gave a laugh of derision. 'They're more likely to fleece you.'

'They're not like that.'

'And how much have they taken from you recently? Oh, I know you've been going there more frequently.'

'And whoever told you that, did they also tell you that never once have I come away the loser?'

'So that's it, Ben, is it? You think it's easier than fishing and that we'll be able to live off your winning from cards?'

'Aye, maybe we can. You wouldn't cry foul against my friends then, would you?

Dampness came to Ruth's eyes. She bit her lip, hoping it would hold back the tears and curb the rising anxiety that churned in her stomach. She took a step towards him. There was a plea in her voice as she said, 'Oh, Ben, Ben, why are we quarrelling? What is happening to us?'

He reached out, took hold of her waist and drew her gently to him. All the while his eyes were fixed on her and the love that was in them rekindled hers. 'I love you, my darling, more than anything in the world. Please trust me.'

She nodded. 'I do, Ben. I do.'

Their kiss lingered, wiping away all the harsh words that had come between them and reaffirming a love that would overcome all adversity.

The Monday of the second week in March dawned with every indication that the weather was set fair for the whale-ships to leave for the Arctic. Whitby folk were pleased for there was nothing more daunting than for their men folk to depart if the prospects looked foul. Fair weather put them in a good mood to face the hazards they knew were ahead even though the loss of Martin Coulson and his crew still lay on their minds.

Whitby turned out in force to see them sail. Among those flocking to the quays, staithes and piers were Warren and Alicia. He had promised to escort her and she had readily accepted, hoping to receive confirmation of a rumour brought home one day by Griselda. As soon as they left New Buildings she lost no time in seeking confirmation.

'Is it true that Ben has given up his fishing?'

'Oh, you've heard?' replied Warren, disappointed that he was not going to be the first to give her this news.

'Well, is it?' she asked sharply.

'Yes. He's been coming to the Angel, but didn't tell us immediately. We only got to know a few days ago. He was not very forthcoming but I got the impression that he was tiring of that life.'

'So what's he doing now?'

'He had something from the sale of his partnership but that can't last long. I think he's trying to supplement it from cards.'

'And is he?'

'A little, but I reckon he could be in trouble if he suffered a big loss. He's more cautious than he used to be, but I think he'd be tempted if a big stake came along.'

Alicia locked the information away in her mind. One day it might prove useful.

'Where would you like to go to see the ships leave?' Warren asked as they neared the bridge.

'The West Pier. We're much closer to them there.'

He guided her among the crowds until they reached a place from which they would get a good view of the ships.

'I saw your father the other day,' said Warren, 'I didn't think he looked his usual self. I hope he's well?'

'He's had a lot of business worry lately. It has been upsetting for him, though he tries to hide it.'

Warren was curious but he knew better than to try to elicit more information when it was not forthcoming.

'He also has the added worry of Griselda.'

'Oh?' He hoped his exclamation warranted an answer.

'You know her beau, Roger Cawthorne?'

'Yes, went out to the Bahamas last year.'

'That's right, to see his elder brother Richard who had been invited there two years previously by their uncle. He had been a loyalist in the War of Independence and left America for the Bahamas where he took up agriculture and cotton growing. Made a success of it, too. He had lost his family during the war and invited Richard to look at the situation with the idea of his taking over the developments his uncle had made. Griselda has had a letter from Roger. He's in London and coming to Whitby in ten days' time. Father fears that he may be tempted to return to the Bahamas and might want to take Griselda too. As his wife, of course.'

'And your father wouldn't want her to go?'

'He wouldn't relish it, but I don't think he would forbid it if that is what she wants and she is really in love with Roger.'

'And you think that is worrying your father and making him feel out-of-sorts?'

'Yes, that and the business.' She glanced upstream and saw a whale-ship moving slowly in their direction. 'Here's the first,' she cried excitedly, steering their conversation away from the Campion family.

As the four ships came down the river Whitby folk gave each one a rousing send-off. With never a thought for the dangers, Whitby men headed into the cold northern waters to hunt the whale and contribute to the prosperity of their home port. The people of Whitby gave them the departure they felt they truly deserved, one they would hold in their memories until they came in sight of their home port again in five or six months' time.

With the ships having successfully cleared the river and taken to the sea, the crowds began to break up and return to their daily lives. As Alicia turned to retrace her steps along the West Pier she saw Ben and Ruth joining the flow of people. Ben glanced round and for a brief moment their eyes met. He averted his gaze without any sign of recognition, but Alicia knew that he had seen her. Her lips tightened. 'Ignore me at your peril, Ben Coulson.' There was hatred in her words that no one else had heard.

A week later as Dorothea was on her way to bed, she turned into Griselda's room. 'Are you getting excited?' she asked as she sat down on the bed and eyed her sister through the dressing-table mirror.

Griselda smiled. 'Yes and no. Roger's been away for a year. I don't know if he will still feel the same way about me.'

'Surely he indicated that in his letter?'

'Well, he sounded a bit constrained.'

'That's your interpretation. Maybe you haven't understood his words correctly.'

Griselda gave a little shrug of her shoulders.

'How do you feel about him?' pressed Dorothea.

She swung round on her dressing-stool to face her sister. 'I still love the man I knew, the one who left for the Bahamas saying he would be back for me in a year.'

'So why the doubt?'

'What if he's changed?'

'Surely not.'

'He's seen new places, new people, a different way of life, and that may have changed him.'

'What if he hasn't changed? What if he wants to return to the Bahamas with you as his wife?'

'I would hate leaving you and Mother and Father and Alicia, probably never to see you again, but . . .' She left the rest of her feelings unspoken.

Dorothea, seeing that her sister was troubled, came and knelt in front of her and took her in her arms. 'I would hate you to go.' She gave a slight pause and then added in all sincerity, 'But follow your heart.'

Roger Cawthorne arrived at the Campions' house displaying all the zest for life he had shown when he had resided in Whitby. It had not been dulled by his sojourn abroad; in fact, if anything it had been enhanced. The tan he had acquired gave a startling new cast to his handsome features and Dorothea saw that her sister had fallen in love with him all over again.

The Campions welcomed him with warmth and affection. Seaton and Grace had liked the young man from the first moment he had sought their permission to approach their daughter Griselda. They had seen a romance develop between the young couple and were pleased, but that had been shattered when he had announced that he was going to the Bahamas for a year at the invitation of his uncle. It was good that he was back but how long would he stay in Whitby?

'Knowing that you would have no one in the town to go to, I have had the guest bedroom made up for you,' Grace informed him when the welcomes were over.

'That is most kind of you, Mrs Campion, but I could have stayed at the Angel. I must say, though, it will be much more pleasant here, and more useful, if you will allow me to use your home as a base? I have several people to see on behalf of my uncle in the Bahamas, some in London but in particular his brother in Northumberland.'

'That should present no difficulty, should it, Seaton?' Grace turned to her husband as they entered the drawing-room.

'None that I'm aware of.'

Dorothea glanced at Griselda and gave her a wink. She smiled back happily.

'Do sit down, everyone,' Grace called over her shoulder as she went to the bell pull which she tugged three times.

It was obviously a signal for in a matter of moments two maids appeared carrying tea and scones.

'I'm sure you are in need of some refreshment after your journey, Mr Cawthorne,' said Grace, reaching for the teapot.

'Indeed, ma'am. It will be most welcome. And please, not Mr Cawthorne, I'm Roger.'

'I trust you found your brother and uncle in good health?' queried Seaton, who had been eyeing the young man keenly in the few minutes since his arrival. He liked what he saw but feared that the light that had come to Griselda's eyes could mean but one thing.

'They were, Mr Campion. It is a very agreeable climate.' Roger went on to extol that aspect of the islands.

'And the prospects of—' Seaton's enquiry was cut short as the door burst open and Alicia hurried in.

'I'm so sorry I am late.' She kissed her mother on the cheek and turned to Roger who had risen from his chair. She held out her hand to him. 'Welcome back, Roger.'

'Thank you, Alicia.' He took her hand to his lips as he bowed, then waited for her to sit down before he resumed his seat.

Once tea was over he was shown to his room and informed that the evening meal would be served at six-thirty.

When they went upstairs to dress, Griselda grabbed Dorothea's hand and guided her to her room. 'What do you think?' she asked excitedly.

'I could see from the moment he stepped into the house and you saw him that you were head over heels in love again.'

'Yes . . . yes, I am. I must see him on his own to find out how he feels!'

'Then do it now.'

'Go to his room?'

'That's where he is.'

'But . . .'

'No one need know.' Dorothea went to the door and opened it a little so she could see along the corridor. There was no one there. She opened it a little wider to look the other way. Again the corridor was empty. She turned and signalled to her sister. Griselda slipped past her and tripped quickly and quietly to Roger's room. She tapped lightly on the door and looked round, hoping that no one would appear. The door opened. As soon as he saw who it was Roger stepped back and allowed her to enter. He closed the door gently, and as he turned round swept her into his arms and kissed her passionately.

'Oh, Roger, I just had to see you.'

His smile sent her heart racing. 'I love you, Griselda. You have been in my thoughts all the time I have been away.'

'I love you too, Roger. I've missed you so, but absence certainly makes the heart grow fonder.'

'Will you marry me, Griselda?'

'Oh,' she gasped. She had not expected this so soon after his arrival.

'Is it too sudden for you?' he asked with concern.

'No – no, it's not.'

'Then say you will?'

'Yes, I will.'

'I intended all the while to ask you as soon as possible. There isn't a lot of time. I must return to the Bahamas in three months.'

'You want me to go there as your wife?'

'Of course! Does that present a problem?'

'No . . .'

'There's something troubling you. That wasn't very convincing.'

'Well, Father has not been in the best of health lately and has had a lot of business worries. But I'm sure he'll not let that get in the way of giving his permission for us to marry.'

'Good, then I'll ask him at dinner this evening when all the family are there.' He kissed her again before she could reply and then said. 'Now, off with you, and let me get ready.'

Griselda hurried back to her room to find Dorothea still there. 'He's asked me to marry him,' she announced excitedly.

Dorothea gasped. 'So soon?'

'He has to return to the Bahamas in three months.'

'And you will be going too?'

'Yes.'

'Oh, I'll miss you, but I'm happy for you.' The sisters hugged each other.

'Say nothing to anyone,' warned Griselda. 'He's going to ask Father this evening during the meal when everyone is there.'

'That's unusual.'

'I think he wants all of you to know at the same time.'

'Or maybe it's linked with something else?'

'It can't be.'

The relaxed atmosphere that had been generated in the drawing-room prior to the evening meal was carried over into the dining-room. Seaton had quietly continued to assess the young man recently returned from the Bahamas. He saw from Roger's mannerisms and speech that his self-confidence, which had not been lacking before he left, had grown. He carried himself and spoke with more assurance now. This was certainly a young man Seaton would not mind his daughter marrying provided his prospects were good. Without asking details of Roger's personal affairs, he casually elicited information about life in the Bahamas. Conversation flowed as the Campions learned more about the islands and life there, and Roger caught up with Whitby news.

When they had returned to the drawing-room and everyone was seated comfortably, Roger cleared his throat. Looking at Seaton, he said, 'Sir, may I ask you for Griselda's hand in marriage?'

Seaton showed no surprise. He had sensed this coming though he had expected it to be done man to man. Except for Griselda, the others gave little gasps of surprise, not at the fact that he had made this request but that he should do so soon after arrival and with them all present.

Seaton did not reply immediately but rose to his feet and moved to stand with his back to the fire so that he could view them all. He knew no one would speak until he had done so. The glance he swept across them all noted the eager light of anticipation in Griselda's eyes.

'My first thought, young man, is that it is unusual to make such a request with the whole family present.'

'I know that, sir, but I have a good reason for doing that, though would rather explain it later.'

'In other words, your explanation depends on my decision?'

'Yes, sir.'

Griselda frowned. This was most unusual. What was Roger trying to do? She had thought it would be a simple request with a simple answer given between the two men. But here? What was Roger thinking of?

'Well, young man, I suppose if I give my assent it will mean that my daughter goes with you to the Bahamas?'

'I hope she would agree to that as I am proposing to make my home there.'

'You have told us a great deal about the Bahamas but little about your prospects and whether you would be able to provide a good quality of life for her in such a place.'

'Sir, the loyalists who left America after the War of Independence, among them my uncle, have created a lifestyle of which you would be proud. As regards my own prospects – well, as you know, my brother went there at the instigation of my uncle. It was an exploratory visit for both of them. They got on well and my brother saw that my uncle's cotton plantation could be expanded along with some agricultural developments. They realised that another partner would be a great advantage and that is why my brother encouraged me to go and have a look for myself. I liked what I saw. The prospects are good and I have the assurance of my uncle that, as he has no family, my brother and I will inherit all he has.'

'If you are not painting too rosy a picture then a prosperous settled future seems to lie ahead of you. I am sure that Mrs Campion has been impressed not only by the picture you paint but also by your person.' He caught the slight nod of approval from her. 'Therefore, young man, I am pleased to say that I offer Griselda's hand in marriage to you.'

Roger jumped to his feet. 'I thank you, sir, and assure both you and Mrs Campion that I will love and cherish Griselda for the rest of her life.'

Excitement charged the room and tears of joy flowed as hugs and kisses were exchanged. When a degree of calmness had returned, Roger and Griselda were standing side by side holding hands.

'Mr and Mrs Campion, I said I would give you an explanation of why I made my request in front of the whole family rather than just to you, sir. I now want to do so.' He gave a little pause, making sure that he had everyone's attention. He sensed Griselda's anxiety as she wondered what was coming and gave her hand a reassuring squeeze. 'Griselda gave me to understand, sir, that your health has not been too good lately. I could tell she was worried about you and anxious about leaving for the Bahamas. When she told me this I had an idea. I don't wish to be presumptuous about your health nor about your affairs when I make this suggestion – but why not come to the Bahamas with us? I mean, the whole family?'

An astonished silence descended on the room as each of them tried to grasp what this meant.

Dorothea was the first to appreciate the prospects that the proposal held, but she kept her enthusiasm to herself. The decision would have to come from her parents but for her part she would welcome the idea. She would still be with Griselda. She had nothing to hold her in Whitby.

Alicia's mind set against the idea but, like Dorothea, she said nothing. Her father must speak first. She did not want to leave Whitby. There were things she wanted to do here to purge her heart of the hurt it had borne, and the only way to do that was to stay and work towards her vengeance on Ben. To leave now would be to dash all the plans that had been forming in her mind.

Grace saw it as a way of casting aside the threat that hung over them. They could escape the debt without any upset or finger-pointing, and she would still have her family around her.

Similar thoughts were forming in Seaton's mind, but could he give up all that he had worked for and built up in Whitby? Could he face making a new life? And the big question was, what could he do in the Bahamas?

'My goodness,' he said, 'you have given us all a lot to think about.'

'Sir, there is no need to make a decision now. Obviously it needs a lot of thought.'

'Indeed it does, young man.'

'I have told you about the climate and have no doubt that it would suit you very well. I know that you will be wondering what you would do. With your experience as a merchant, I am sure you could set up a lucrative business trading from the Bahamas, particularly with America. I know my uncle is looking for new investments and think you and he would make good partners.'

'You have indeed surprised us, Roger.'

'I know that you need time. May I add at this point that I must return to the Bahamas in three months, not only because of my business arrangements but because I must sail before the hurricane season. I would like to be married here in Whitby before Griselda and I go.'

Seaton swallowed hard. 'You must give us a while to discuss this. It is a big step and there will be a lot to consider. You said you had some business to see to over here?'

'Yes. I leave the day after tomorrow for Newcastle and then for Edinburgh. I will be back a week today.'

'Very well. I will have an answer for you then.' Seaton glanced round his family. 'I suggest that you all give this careful thought and the day after tomorrow, when we sit down to our evening meal, you give me your opinions and we will discuss them.'

Chapter Seventeen

Every member the Campion family had much to occupy their mind when they sat down to their evening meal two days later. Only their mother and father had freely discussed the implications of leaving Whitby for a new life in the Bahamas. Griselda had no decision to make, but Dorothea and Alicia had kept their thoughts and conclusions to themselves. Now came the moment of truth for them all. They waited for Seaton to speak but he held his silence on the subject until the meal was finished. It was as if he was still wrestling with his decision.

When the maid had finally cleared the table and had left the dining-room, he leaned back in his chair and gazed at his daughters. 'Your mother and I have discussed thoroughly the proposal made by Roger and I think I should give you our conclusions. But first I should say that, in our opinion, if Griselda is going to marry Roger as we believe she is . . .'

'Of course I am,' Griselda interrupted quickly.

'. . . then she should go with him. You all know that I am in debt to Sam Coulson. If we went to the Bahamas I could free us from that debt because I am sure that Sam would take my business in repayment. As long as we are here I don't believe he will call it in because of our long friendship. If we go, the load of that debt, which has weighed heavily on me, will be lifted. The little money we have saved plus what we would receive from the sale of this house would no doubt pay our passage and give us something on which to build a new business over there. As Roger pointed out there is every chance of my forming a partnership with his uncle in a trading venture.

So as far as your Mother and I are concerned, we think it could be a move for the best.'

'I agree with your father,' said Grace wanting to present a united front to her daughters.

'I was hoping that your decision would be to go,' put in Dorothea quickly. 'It will mean I will still be able to share much with Griselda.'

All eyes turned on Alicia. Expectancy charged the air. The tension was palpable.

'I don't want to go and I will not!' Her voice was low but filled with resolute determination as she deliberately emphasised every word.

The intensity of her delivery brought a stunned silence to the room. If her parents had expected any opposition they had not thought it would be as forceful as this. They immediately gained the impression that there would be no compromise, but they had to try.

'We can't stay just for you!' cried Dorothea. 'You must come.'

'There is no must about it,' snapped Alicia.

Tears welled in Dorothea's eyes. She bit her lip to hold them back.

'Alicia, we cannot leave you,' said Grace.

'You'll have to if you want to go.'

'Going will solve my problem,' said Seaton. 'I'll be free from debt.'

'Won't it be exciting to build a new life?' put in Grace.

Alicia drew a deep breath and drew herself up. 'I have thought a lot about this since Roger made his proposition. I can see how you view it, Father, you too, Mother, and it is natural for Dorothea to want to go. Your decisions are as I expected them to be. With them in mind, I considered my own desire to stay in Whitby. I knew it would bring problems for you but will not change my mind about leaving here. So, Father, I considered your business. Because you have no son you have involved me in it to a certain extent. I propose that between now and your departure you train me to take it over.'

'But you couldn't, not in a man's world!' Grace raised her arms in a gesture of shock horror.

'Poppycock!' snapped Alicia. 'The barriers they put up to preserve their precious male enclave want breaking down. A challenge from a female trader will do them good. I know most of them and I'm sure I'll receive respect from most. Those who don't accept me will soon know, in no small measure, that I am here to stay and someone to be reckoned with. Besides, if I needed help or advice, I'm sure Sam . . . Uncle Sam would be willing.'

'That would mean I would have to leave with my debt hanging over us, or else try and pay it off from the venture I set up in the Bahamas.'

'I would not want you to do that. I know if I came you would hand the business over to Uncle Sam in repayment, but it would hurt you to do so. I believe you would rather keep it because it means so much to you. If I stay here the firm will still be yours. I'll work hard so that you can receive some income from it and will direct the rest of the profits into a fund to repay Uncle Sam.'

'You think it will be that easy?'

'No, Father, I don't, but because I don't want to leave Whitby, let me try. If I fail then we can still let the business go to repay your debt and I'll come and join you later. Please let me try?'

'But, Alicia, if you stay we will not be able to sell this house and your father will have no money to finance his business in the Bahamas,' Grace pointed out.

'You can sell the house. I have plenty of friends with whom I could stay.'

'But you couldn't put on them for long.'

'That would be the least of my worries. Something will turn up.'

Grace, wanting Seaton to come down firmly on the idea and say no, looked pleadingly at her husband.

He caught the meaning in her eyes. He did not want to hurt her but he had read deep determination in his daughter and knew she surprisingly competent. Whether she could hold her own among Whitby's merchants was another matter. He admired her determination to try and make them accept her. He would love to see her using her charms to that end, but he couldn't have everything. With everyone else wanting to leave and he himself tempted by new prospects in the Bahamas, especially the climate, the only course was to agree with Alicia. If he did not make the decision now he knew Grace would use all her charm and wiles to make him insist that their eldest daughter accompany them.

'Very well, Alicia, you can stay.'

'Seaton, she can't be left on her own!' cried his wife.

'I have considered this carefully as we have been talking. Everyone else wants to go so I say we should.'

'I know that, but Alicia must come with us.'

'And be miserable? Spoil it for the rest of us? No, Grace, that is not the solution. It is not a step I am prepared to take even though the majority of people in this town would disagree with me. Alicia is very capable. She must demonstrate that by applying herself wholeheartedly to the business between now and our departure.'

'I will, Father. I will.'

'I'm rather glad it is not going out of the family. But, Alicia you must promise me that if things do not go well, you will give it up and present it to your Uncle Sam?'

'I promise that, Father.' She jumped from her seat and rounded the table to hug him. 'Thank you so much.'

Grace knew it was no good trying to alter the decision that had been taken. She must forget her objections and remember that her daughter was twenty-three. She would see that everything went smoothly and that Alicia was firmly settled before they left. She stood up and held out her arms to her daughter who came to return her embrace.

Dorothea and Griselda flung their arms round each other, joyful in the knowledge that they would still be together.

'I will see Sam tomorrow and appraise him of the situation.

I'm sure he will help you all he can, Alicia.'

As she went to her room Alicia hugged herself. She had got what she wanted and, with the germ of a plan already in her mind, would make sure that Sam would be of more use to her than her father imagined.

'Good morning, Seaton.' Sam Coulson rose from behind his desk when his friend came into his office. He held out his hand in greeting and Seaton took it as Sam added, 'What brings you here so early?' He indicated a seat and the two friends sat opposite each other.

'I've a surprise for you, Sam. I'm emigrating.'

Completely shocked by this unexpected announcement, Sam was unable to speak for a moment. Then 'What?' burst from his lips.

Seaton grinned. 'I thought that would surprise you.'

'Surprised? I'm shocked. You can't be serious?'

'Oh, yes, I am.'

'But . . . what's this all about?'

He explained about Roger Cawthorne's arrival, his proposal to Griselda, and the suggestion that they should all go to the Bahamas. 'The prospect was attractive because he painted a picture of a perfect climate. I have not been too well lately and thought it might be advantageous for me. It depended on the opinions of the rest of the family, however.'

'Obviously they agreed, so I suppose you are here about your debt?'

'Partly. I had expected to ask you to take over all my trading assets in settlement, but I am not doing that. Instead I am asking you to let things stand as they are, at least for the foreseeable future.'

'You mean, until you leave?'

'No. Beyond that.'

'But you won't be here to run your business?'

'That's right. But, you see, not everyone wanted to go to the Bahamas. Alicia wishes to stay.'

Sam attention was fixed on him keenly.

'So what are you saying?'

'You know I've involved her in my business?'

'Because you have no son,' put in Sam.

'Yes. Fortunately she's always showed interest. Well, now she wants to take charge. She is determined to repay my debt to you and keep the business going.'

'Brave girl.'

'You know Alicia, Sam. She's a resourceful and committed young woman when she has her mind set and, I don't mind telling you, she's that way now. I'm going to give her intensive training between now and our departure. But, Sam, can I ask you to keep your eye on her? I've told her to come to you for advice. I hope you will help if necessary?'

'Of course. Tell her, any time.'

'Thank you. That eases my mind.'

Sam gave a chuckle. 'I'll be helping to get my own money back after all! But seriously,' he added, 'will she continue to live where you are now?'

'I need to sell the house in order to release some capital for the Bahamas. Alicia says she has plenty of friends with whom she could stay until she gets settled.'

Sam nodded thoughtfully for a moment. 'Why don't I buy the house? Then she could stay there.'

'Well, I . . .' Seaton hesitated.

'I don't need it for living purposes. Alicia needn't move. It will give her one less worry and enable her to concentrate more fully on the business. I'll be getting a good piece of property, so it's an investment for me, and it's going to save you the bother of selling it on the open market.'

'That is most thoughtful and generous of you,' replied Seaton.

'It's a deal then?' Sam stood up, leaned across the desk and held out his hand. The sale was settled there and then. 'All I ask,' he said, 'is that I receive an invitation to the wedding.'

'That goes without saying,' replied Seaton.

'And the other thing I ask is that our two families should

dine together at the Angel the night before you leave Whitby.'

When Seaton reached home the whole family was pleased by the outcome of his visit to Sam, and none more so than Alicia. She would not have to move from Whitby and this sharpened her anticipation of revenge.

After Seaton had left, Sam sat for a long time with his thoughts. If Alicia had gone with the family the Campion business could so easily have been his, but as she had chosen to stay it was still as far away as it had been. He could foreclose but would then be seen as an ogre taking advantage of a woman on her own. But that woman could be vulnerable in other ways, one of which he had already subtly started to manoeuvre.

When Roger returned to Whitby he was delighted to learn that the Campions had chosen to come to the Bahamas. He knew how strongly attached Griselda was to her family and that life would be much easier with them nearby.

Wedding arrangements were put in motion immediately and a month later Griselda and Roger were married in the parish church on the East Cliff. An invitation had been sent to Ben as an old family friend, but knowing that it would mean seeing his father and possibly souring the day, he refused while wishing the bride and groom every happiness.

Ryan Bennett had been included on Sarah's invitation and she was delighted with the immediate rapport there was between him, her family and friends. She was only sorry that Ben was not there and explained the reasons for his absence to Ryan.

'I'm sorry too,' he said, 'but I understand.'

'We will remedy that the day after tomorrow. Now that he and Ruth are living on their own, I will take you to meet them.'

'I look forward to that. I can tell you think a great deal of him.'

During the reception Sam engineered a few moments alone with Alicia. 'You are taking on a tremendous responsibility running your father's company, and I admire you for what you are doing.'

'I intend to succeed,' she replied firmly.

'That's the right spirit, but you will find it can be a hostile world, so if ever you need advice or help, call on me.'

'That is kind of you, Sam. I will remember.' Her hand had strayed near his as she was speaking and on the last three words she squeezed it gently.

It was a gesture he noted with satisfaction. 'And if ever you need company, remember, the girls and I are not far away.'

Sarah felt joyful as she and Ryan headed towards Ben's house in Church Street. She was about to introduce the two young men of whom she thought so highly. She was sure they would like each other. Nevertheless her heart beat a little faster when Ryan rapped on the door.

A girl who could be no more than thirteen opened it a few moments later. She looked harassed and unsure of herself.

Sarah gave her a reassuring smile and enquired gently, 'Are Mr and Mrs Coulson in?'

The girl looked startled by the question and nervously tried to push a stray wisp of hair back under her mob-cap. 'Er . . . yes, ma'am.' She did not move.

'May we see them, please?' asked Sarah softly.

'Oh.' The girl appeared to be trying to remember something. Then, realising what it was, said quickly as if she must get the words out before she forgot them, 'I'll see if they are available, ma'am.' She started to turn away, then stopped and looked back. 'Oh, please step inside. Who shall I say is calling?'

'Miss Sarah Coulson and Mr Ryan Bennett.'

'Yes, ma'am.' She was mouthing the names silently as she left them.

Sarah smiled at Ryan who she hoped was not put off by this unexpected reception. He gave an amused twitch of his lips and a knowing smile.

'Should we step inside?' he whispered, giving her a little bow as she did so. He closed the door behind them.

They were in a passage leading past the stairs. At the end

307

was a door which was closed. There were two other doors to the right, the further one of which stood slightly ajar. It opened quickly and Ben strode out in great haste followed by the maid who still looked flustered. She paused a moment to stare at them and then fled through the kitchen door.

'Sarah, what a great pleasure this is,' said Ben, taking his sister in his arms and kissing her on the cheek. 'This must be Ryan.' He held out his hand and Ryan took it.

'I'm glad to know you, Ben. I've heard so much about you.'

'All good, I hope?'

'I don't think your sister would ever say a wrong word about you. In fact, I'm jealous.'

'I can sense what she feels for you so you have no need to feel jealous. Come in, come in.' Ben ushered them forward, calling out, 'Ruth.' But she was already coming from the other room.

'Sarah!' Her delight on seeing her sister-in-law was immediately evident.

'I've brought Ryan to meet you,' said Sarah. 'Ryan, this is my sister-in-law Ruth.'

He bowed and raised her hand to his lips. 'This is indeed a great pleasure for me. Sarah's descriptions do not do you justice. I can see Ben is a very lucky man.'

Ruth blushed. 'I think your eyes are deceiving you, but I thank you for your compliment.'

When they entered the room Sarah saw that it was modestly furnished but there was a comfortable atmosphere about it. This was a home in which lived two people who were very much in love.

'I'm sorry, if your reception was a little unusual,' said Ruth as they settled down. 'We've just acquired Betsy. This is her first job and we are having to train her.'

'She was very refreshing,' said Ryan with a smile.

'I hope she will do better with the chocolate I've told her to bring.'

When the pleasantries were over, Ruth asked, 'Was the wedding enjoyable?'

'Splendid. I'm sorry you weren't there but I understand that it could have been embarrassing. You do know that the Campions are emigrating to the Bahamas?'

'No!' gasped Ben with Ruth equally surprised.

Sarah explained how this had come about.

There was a knock on the door and Betsy appeared with a tray of chocolate. She placed it carefully on a table in front of Ruth who cast a quick glance over it. Nothing had been forgotten. She looked up and smiled encouragingly at the girl. 'You have done very well. Thank you, Betsy.'

Delighted at the praise, she smiled and left the room with a confident step.

'You say Alicia is staying in Whitby?' Ben sounded puzzled.

'Yes. She told me at the wedding. She did not want to go and persuaded her parents to let her stay. You know she always took an interest in her father's business. Now she wants to run it.'

Ben gave a little grunt. 'And she will, but I'll bet there are some among the Whitby merchants who'll not want a woman entering their world.'

'Apparently Uncle Seaton agreed only if she promised that, if there were any difficulties, she would consult our father.'

'You told me he was being more amiable than he used to be. Is that still the case?'

'Yes.'

'Well, I hope for Alicia's sake he continues to be.' Ben turned to Ryan. 'I'm so sorry to be engrossed in our affairs.'

'No need to apologise. It is one way of getting to know the people Sarah values.'

As Ruth and Sarah began to exchange news, Ben turned to him. 'And you, Ryan. You are staying with your aunt at Mulgrave Hall, I believe?'

'That's right. She is my only relative.'

'How long are you going to be there?'

'I originally came for a few weeks, but I think that my aunt has the idea that I might move in with her permanently and made this invitation to see if I liked this area.'

'And do you?'

'Oh, yes.' The enthusiasm in his voice coupled with a swift automatic glance in Sarah's direction was not lost on Ben. 'I have made up my mind to sell my interest in two firms in London and move up here.'

'And what will you do?'

'I'll be comfortably off and, living with my aunt, there really will be no need for me to do anything, but that's not my nature. I'll find something that interests me. I might need some advice though, Ben. You know the area and the people I might deal with here.'

He gave a grimace. 'At the moment things are a little difficult for me.' He went on to explain his situation. Ryan listened with interest though he knew some of it already from Sarah.

'A pity you sold the ropery. It might have been something we could have expanded together.'

Ben shrugged his shoulders. 'It seemed the right thing to do at the time and it did help Ruth's father out of his immediate difficulty.'

'But now you are left in a precarious situation?'

'Well, we are managing.'

'I have to return to London to see to my affairs. It will take maybe six months, but I'll be back and forth in the meantime. Will you look out for opportunities for me and keep your eyes open for something that we can go into as partners?'

'But I could not match your capital input,' he pointed out. 'Besides you do not know me.'

'Ben, the faith and love for you that I have seen in your sister is all I need to know. She has told me that apart from being very shrewd you like a bit of a gamble, particularly at cards, but that you have the sense to know never to overstep the mark in that respect. I like that in someone. It shows a sensible sharp mind. I think you and I could get on well. Will you keep your eyes and ears open?'

'Gladly.' Ben was overjoyed at the prospect opening up for

him. Six months . . . Things might be difficult meanwhile but they would manage.

'Good. Then it's a deal.' They shook hands.

The action caught the attention of Ruth and Sarah. 'What's going on?' they asked.

Ben quickly, and with great enthusiasm, told them of Ryan's proposal.

'This is wonderful,' enthused Sarah.

Ruth looked overjoyed. 'Ryan, you do not know what this means to us, and particularly Ben. I feared he might become depressed when things were going against us. This has given us new hope.'

'I'm sure things will turn out well. We'll make them. We may as well form this partnership right away so that I can put money at Ben's disposal. It will be a recompense for the work he will be doing in connection with seeking for new opportunities for the partnership Bennett and Coulson.'

'But I couldn't—'

'Of course you can. You'll be working for us while I'm busy tidying up my own affairs.'

'This is most generous of you.'

'Not at all. It is a business arrangement and I am sure that I won't lose by it. I know my aunt will be delighted that I have found something, apart from someone, that will bring me permanently to Whitby.'

There were tears in Ruth's eyes as she thanked him.

'Not at all.' He dismissed her thanks with a wave of his hand. 'It is I who am fortunate in finding a partner so readily. Now I have two suggestions to make. The first concerns this partnership. I think it would be best if it were not mentioned to anyone else for a while. It will be better that no one hears of it until we are ready to release the news.' A murmur of agreement came from everyone. 'The second suggestion is that Ruth and Ben should come to dine one evening at Mulgrave Hall and meet my aunt. When I tell her what has transpired here this morning she will be anxious to meet you. I will let you know a convenient date. And of course you will come too, Sarah.'

When they left Ruth and Ben, Sarah immediately thanked Ryan again. 'It will certainly ease the strain on them, knowing that there is some tangible prospect in the future. I know Ben will not let you down.'

'You have no need to assure me of that,' Ryan replied. 'From what you have told me of him and what I saw this morning, I knew I had found an ideal partner. I quickly saw that he has a strong mind, is willing to take calculated risks, knows much of Whitby's trading, and as a Coulson no doubt has connections. Though in view of his alienation from your father, I realise not all those connections will be readily available to him.'

'That would only be true if it was Ben himself seeking a new venture. If his part in this were kept secret, at least for the time being, and you made the approaches, no one need know.'

'Very true,' Ryan replied brightly. 'I see I am going to acquire a very astute lady for my wife.'

Sarah stopped in her tracks and gaped at him. 'Was that a proposal?'

He laughed. 'I suppose it was.'

'You didn't know you'd said it?'

'It slipped out, but it must have been on my mind for it to do so. Sarah, I have thought about it ever since I met you. It was love at first sight for me. Oh, dear, this is not how I imagined it to be – on a crowded street with people going about their daily tasks giving all manner of looks because we are in their path. But I have said it and I mean it. Will you?'

'Oh, yes, Ryan, yes!'

If any passer-by had taken the trouble to study the two people who appeared to be deep in earnest conversation they would have seen a young couple who were immensely happy. They both glanced along the street, then, as their eyes met, burst out laughing.

'I don't think this is quite the place to seal our commitment with a kiss, do you?' said Ryan.

Sarah responded, 'I don't think it is, but it's a proposal I shall always remember and treasure in my heart even if, when we are quietly by ourselves, you go down on your knee and propose again. When will you see Father?'

'Right away, if you wish it?'

Sarah pondered a moment. 'Maybe it will be better if you wait for a while. He's sure to want to know what you propose to do when you settle in Whitby and I think it would be best not mention any partnership with Ben for the time being.'

'I will leave it until business matters are settled. Maybe in the future we could use it to reconcile your father with him?'

'I doubt that will ever happen. Ben's married to a Holmes.'

'Is there nothing that can be done?'

Sarah gave a shake of her head to match the doubt on her face. 'The only way would be to exonerate Captain Holmes from the death of Martin but I can see no way of doing that.' There was regret in her voice.

'Some day maybe your father will realise it is no good continuing with this attitude.' Ryan tried to sound reassuring as they walked on.

After four days honeymoon in Scarborough, Roger had to leave his new bride to complete his uncle's business. When he returned he found the Campion household in a state of upheaval as they prepared to leave for the Bahamas. Grace found her task made easier by the fact that Alicia was staying behind. Selling the house to Sam made the transaction simple so Seaton was able to devote more time to making Alicia more familiar with his business. He admired her ability to assimilate quickly and build on what she already knew of his way of operating. He was pleased that her relationship with his manager, Simon Yardley, was strengthened by her charm when he was told that the Campions were emigrating but that she was staying behind to take charge of the business.

A week before they were due to leave Ryan returned from

London, and as soon as he was in Whitby called at the Coulson house.

When told by the maid that Mr Bennett was here to see her, Sarah hurried into the hall to meet him. 'Ryan!' She held out her hands to him.

'Sarah, you are as beautiful as ever.' He took her hands and kissed her. 'I've missed you so.'

'And I you.' She led him by the hand towards the drawing-room. 'Come, tell me all about your visit to London.'

He dropped his coat and hat on a chair and followed her into the room. 'All went well. I settled most of my affairs there. I may have to return but not for a while yet. I received good prices for the shares I had in two companies so that will give us a sound basis for whatever it is that Ben and I develop.'

'I am so pleased. It is going to be an exciting time, I just know it.'

'I'm so happy that you are happy.' He took her in his arms and their kiss lingered in the expression of the love they felt for each other.

'I've visited Ruth and Ben on a couple of occasions while you have been away. Ben has a few ideas to discuss with you.'

'Good. I look forward to hearing them. Now, we must arrange for them to meet my aunt. They'll be thinking I have forgotten. And I think it's time I saw your father about us. I know we said we would wait a while but I think we should do so now. I can tell him something of my prospects without mentioning Ben.'

'Ryan, may I say something about that?' She saw alarm come in his face at her serious expression. 'Can we leave it a little while longer, at least until after Ruth has had the baby?'

'Of course, my love,' he replied readily, relieved that his momentary fear was not to be realised. 'But why?'

'I think that she has the idea the baby might bring about a reconciliation with father. It was just a hint she let drop. I also think my father might use my proposed marriage to you to humiliate Ben by comparing the two matches in the way *he* wishes to view them. I don't want that to happen before Ruth has had a chance to try to bring about a reconciliation through the child.' Sarah grimaced at her own words. 'Oh, Ryan, I'm sorry you've stepped into such a hornet's nest.'

'You have nothing to be sorry for, my love. I love you for your loyalty to Ben, and admire you for treading the thin line between him and your father with such care. Now I must away and let my aunt know that I am back.'

'One more thing before you go – Father is giving a farewell dinner for the Campions at the Angel next Wednesday, the evening before they leave. He said if you were back from London, I was to tell you that you are invited.'

'Tell him it will be my pleasure to accept. I don't suppose Ben will be there?'

Sarah gave a wan smile and shook her head. 'No. Father won't have invited him.'

Three days later, an invitation having been sent to Ruth and Ben to dine at Mulgrave Hall, a carriage drew up outside the small house in Church Street. They settled into it in a state of nervous excitement, one that increased as they drew nearer and nearer to the Hall. They passed between two stone piers supporting high iron gates and drove up a long gravel drive that curved in front of an imposing mansion. Four stone steps led on to a terrace that ran the full width of the six-bayed house. The graceful sash windows were tall and matched by six more on the first storey.

As the carriage drew to a halt, a manservant appeared from the front door. He bustled down the steps to the carriage, the door of which had been opened by the coachman. Ben was quickly to the ground, turning to help Ruth from the carriage.

'Welcome to Mulgrave Hall, ma'am, sir,' said the manservant. 'Please follow me.' He led the way into the house, and Ruth and Ben found themselves in a hall that was furnished with choice pieces of furniture and paintings. They were quick to judge that they were in the home of someone with impeccable taste, a judgement that was confirmed when, after discarding their outdoor clothes, they were shown into a drawing-room.

'Ah, Ruth, Ben.' Ryan and Sarah, who had been at the Hall since the middle of the afternoon, greeted them. 'Welcome to my aunt's house,' Ryan continued. 'She will be with us in a minute or two. She was resting in her room. One of the maids will have informed her of your arrival.'

'She is not unwell, I hope?' said Ruth with concern.

'Oh, no.' Ryan smiled. 'She always takes a short rest prior to the arrival of guests. Says it prepares her for the evening by making her more agreeable and attentive.'

'Maybe we'll all be following her example in years to come,' said Ben.

They all turned when the door opened. A tall thin lady walked imperiously into the room that was immediately filled with her presence. She held herself very erect and though she carried a black ebony walking stick it was difficult to judge if it was there from necessity or for effect. Her features were sharp but her perfect complexion took away any note of severity. Her hair had been given careful attention, being plaited and pinned up at the back, the rest being brushed smoothly forward where it waved across her forehead. Her black dress was of the finest cotton, perfectly plain, the only ornamentation being the delicate lace that trimmed the high neckline. The dress flared only slightly from the high waist, adding to the elegance of her slim figure. Light reflected from the only piece of jewellery – a marcasite lizard – which she wore just above her left breast. Ruth could not but admire the elegance of this lady who she knew must be seventy-five. She was even more surprised when she spoke for her voice was as soft as suede and, even from the first few words, Ruth knew she could listen to it all night.

'Good evening to you all. I am honoured that you are here to dine with me tonight.' She looked to her nephew to make the introductions.

'Aunt Cecilia, I would like you to meet Ruth Coulson.'

'Good evening, ma'am.'

'Welcome, my dear.' Then with a query in her eyes with which she had cast a sharp glance towards Ruth's stomach, she asked, 'When is the baby due?'

'Six weeks, ma'am.'

'Then you take care. I know there are people who would advise you to stay at home instead of going on a visit.'

'I don't like mollycoddling, ma'am, and felt sure that this visit and seeing you would do me good.'

'Flattery, my girl, flattery, but I like it. It does an old lady good.' She turned to Ben. 'And you must be Ben Coulson, of whom I have heard much from my nephew?' She gave him a little poke in the chest with her stick as she said, 'You take good care of her, you hear? She's a precious young lady.'

'I know, ma'am, and I will.'

'Good. Now let's all sit down. Some Madeira for everyone, Ryan.'

'Only a little for me, please,' said Ruth, and saw Miss Bennett give a nod of approval.

'Young man,' she said, looking at Ben, 'my nephew tells me that you and he are going to form some sort of partnership. Now tell me something about yourself?'

Ben did not really know what to say but realised this lady would appreciate openness so told her what he thought was relevant, including some facts he would not normally have told a stranger at first meeting. She listened intently without interrupting and he knew she was not only assessing what he told her but also making up her mind about him.

Cecilia Bennett was good at creating a relaxed atmosphere, a skill she'd developed at an early age, knowing it would enable her to learn more about the people with whom she was dealing. This atmosphere continued throughout a splendid meal during which she led Ben, Ruth and Sarah to talk of life in Whitby, its standing as a port and trading possibilities. She learned something of their personal histories without seeming to probe and the young people found themselves talking freely about their lives so that by the time the meal was finished she knew about the Arctic disaster and the rift it had caused between the Coulson and Holmes families. She commented on the bravery of Ben and Ruth, marrying in the face of opposition, and saw it as an indication of their deep love. This settled her mind about Sarah's relationship with her nephew for she thought, Like sister, like brother. Once they were back in the drawing-room she manoeuvred the females into a group without its being too obvious so that Ryan and Ben were left to continue their discussion about the prospects for a partnership, a discussion she had guided them into as they left the dining-room.

Seated comfortably with coffee served – 'I get this sent from London' – she chatted about the latest fashions and then drew Ryan and Ben back into the general conversation, turning it to the King's failing health, and the renewal of the war with Napoleon after the short uneasy peace.

'Unless that little upstart succeeds in invading England, something I expect to falter before the guns of our Navy so ably commanded by Nelson, I see no reason for your partnership to fail,' she pronounced. 'I am not going to make funds for it available, you must use your own resources, Ryan. But remember, you may call on my help if necessary. I shall always be here with advice if you need any. These are my conclusions after a most pleasant evening.

'I admire you, Ben. I like your frankness. I know you would not be so with everyone and that gives me reason to believe you are a good judge of people and situations which, together with your local knowledge, will be a major asset to Ryan. You have a sensible, knowledgeable girl for your wife who I can see is devoted to you and will be a tower of strength. Treasure her, Ben.

'Now, if you will excuse an old lady, I will go to my bed and leave you young people to chat for a while.' She rose to her feet as she was speaking. The others, out of respect and admiration for an elegant lady who had won their hearts, rose too.

'Ryan, you will escort our guests home when they are ready. The coach and driver are standing by.'

'Thank you, Aunt.'

Ruth and Sarah expressed their thanks profusely.

'Sarah, I am glad my nephew found you. I had formed that opinion before tonight but now it has been confirmed. Ruth, take care of that baby. It will influence your future.' She turned last to Ben. 'I like you, young man, not the least that cautious gambling streak of yours. You have been frank with me about much of your private life. From what you told me, I'd advise you to beware of Alicia Campion, she could be trouble.'

Chapter Eighteen

Alicia stood on the quay ostensibly alone. There were people milling around: friends of passengers watching the *Esmerelda* head for the sea, labourers tidying up after she had slipped quietly from the quay, people passing by oblivious to the fact that another ship was departing Whitby. To Alicia the shouts and hubhub around her meant nothing. She felt forlorn. The tears that she had held back when the goodbyes were being said now flowed. The tightness of regret contracted her chest. Doubt beset her. Should she have gone too? She fought against the lost feeling. She had chosen her path. If she had given way and deviated from it she would never have lived with herself. The only way she could cauterise the deep humili-ation Ben had inflicted on her was through revenge and she could not have done that from abroad. She stiffened her resolve.

Last evening's dinner given by Sam had been a success though overshadowed by the prospect of departure and the severing of a long friendship. Everyone there had put on a brave face against the impending departure and had kept the evening free from regrets, replacing them with talk of the adventure ahead and hopes for success in a far-off land. Seaton had requested that no one but Alicia come to the quay in the morning and everyone understood this desire for a private parting.

Alicia could still see her family near the stern. They raised their hands in a final farewell. She raised her arms in reply.

The *Esmerelda* passed between the piers and took to the sea bound for London where, three days later, the Campions, Roger and Griselda would embark on the *Star of the Sea* bound for the Bahamas in comfortable cabins booked by Roger during one of his visits to London.

Alicia turned and walked slowly along the quay. Her future seemed so empty. She tried to comfort herself with the knowledge that she had plenty of friends around her still and a staff, both at home and at work, she knew would be loyal and give her their support. All would be well. She would see that it was so and that the purpose of her staying here was fulfilled.

She turned to avoid a stack of wooden crates waiting to be loaded on to a nearby ship when someone stepped into her path as if he were avoiding them from the opposite direction, but she knew otherwise. He must have been watching and waiting until the ship sailed.

'Oh, Sam, you startled me.' She feigned shock.

'Alicia! I'm sorry if I alarmed you. You've just been seeing your family off?'

She knew he had no need to put that question. He knew the answer very well. But she replied, putting a sob in her voice, 'Yes. I'm going to miss them.'

'You will, but remember what I said – I am here if you need me.'

'Thank you, Sam, I won't forget.'

'Are you on your way to the office?'

'Yes. I thought if I got straight into some work it would occupy my mind.'

'Then let me escort you there.'

'That is kind.'

'You have a very competent manager in Simon Yardley,' commented Sam.

'Yes, I'm very fortunate. I have been working closely with him ever since my parents decided to emigrate. I know Father briefed him about supporting me. I should come to no harm, having you and Simon to consult.'

'I know you are a very astute young woman and not afraid of making decisions, but there will be people who will resent your coming into a man's world so there might be times when a show of support from me could be beneficial. Don't be afraid to ask for it.'

'I won't. And let me tell you, Sam, that I am determined to make this a success, for my father's sake. You can be sure you will be repaid the money he owes you.'

'You have some deals in mind already?'

Alicia smiled. 'Ah, Sam that would be telling.'

'But you can trust me. I could judge if they were sound.'

'We are not partners, Sam, merely friendly rivals.'

He laughed. 'That puts me in my place!'

They had reached Campion's office so Sam had no excuse to linger.

They stopped by the door. He was about to open it for Alicia when he stopped. 'I don't think you should be on your own this evening, the first without your family. Come to us for dinner. I'm sure Ruth and Dina would be most pleased to see you.'

'Thank you, Sam, that is most thoughtful of you.'

'Half-past six.'

Alicia smiled to herself. She could not have worked things better if she had tried. Spider and the fly . . . and she wasn't the fly.

Sam's step was brisk as he walked away. His manoeuvring had borne fruit earlier than expected. He too felt like the spider and the fly, and he too reckoned he wasn't the fly.

That evening Ben made his way to the Angel. He was going with Ruth's approval for she knew it was there that he was most likely to pick up information he could pass on to Ryan. He, for his part, promised that no matter how tempting it might be to slip into his old gambling ways, he would stick to a limited outlay.

The game was under way when Warren remarked, 'Well, the Campions have gone.'

'Aye,' remarked Ralph, 'and leaving Alicia behind. The way's clear for you now, Warren.'

Ben stiffened at the implication behind the remark but kept his lips tight.

'I reckon that'll be the end of Campion's, leaving her in charge,' someone remarked. 'I ask you, a woman trying to do something only a man is capable of!'

'Maybe,' muttered Warren as if he half-disagreed with the last remark.

Ben seized on this to say, 'You'd better not pass any tips on to her, Warren, better to let me have them. I could do with making money from somewhere other than taking it off you lot.'

'Getting cocky with his cards again is our Ben,' commented one of the players. 'Come on, let's stop him winning this time.'

'It is good of you to have me this evening,' said Alicia when Sarah greeted her on her arrival at the Coulsons' house.

'It is a pleasure and the least we can do, especially this first evening alone.' She escorted Alicia to the drawing-room.

Sam dropped the paper he was reading and jumped to his feet. 'My dear girl.' He came to her and took both her hands in greeting, kissing her on the cheek. 'Come, do sit down. A glass of Madeira?'

'That would be pleasant, thank you,' she replied.

Sam glanced at Sarah who took it as an indication that he wanted her to pour the wine. She went to the sideboard on which there were glasses and a decanter.

'How did you get on at the office after I left you?' he asked.

Sam had told his daughters that he had met Alicia and invited her for a meal but had not indicated that he had been at her office. It was a little fact that somehow lodged in Sarah's mind, though she did not realise it at the time.

'Very well. There were several items that Father had left for me to attend to but they were all straightforward and Simon was very helpful. A bit over-fussy, but I suppose that was to be expected.'

'He's a good man. Your father set a lot of store on his know-ledge.'

323

'I know, but there was one thing I asked him about today on which he was a little vague. He could tell me few of the details about the operations of the firm you and Father set up to trade in wine. And Father never told me much about it either, saying that as you were involved you would keep it right and there was little need to clutter my mind with it at the moment.'

'Quite right. You have plenty more to think about. Some time I'll tell you all about it.'

'I look forward to that. I really would like to know.'

The door opened then. Dina came in and greeted Alicia pleasantly.

'I'm so glad you are here, Dina,' said Sarah. 'Help me to keep these two from talking business all night.'

Alicia raised a hand in mock surrender. 'Sorry, Sarah. It's all new to me. All right, no more business talk.' She called to Dina who had gone to pour herself a glass of Madeira, 'Did Rowan sail with the whale-ships?'

Typical of Alicia to ask that knowing her father opposed her relationship with Rowan, but what did it matter? 'Yes,' she called over her shoulder.

Realising she was to hear no more on that subject Alicia turned to Sarah. 'And how is Mr Bennett?'

'He's very well, thank you.' Sarah blushed.

'He's a handsome man and I'm told wealthy in his own right, though goodness knows what he will inherit from his aunt. Have you met her?'

'Yes.'

Sarah offered no more but Alicia was not going to leave it at that. 'So what was she like?'

'Formidable.'

'A battle-axe?'

'No, far from it. She is most pleasant, a good conversational-ist and very shrewd.'

'And dotes on her nephew?'

'She is very fond of him, yes.'

'So, charm the aunt and you win the nephew? Have you done that, Sarah?'

Seeing his daughter a little embarrassed, Sam put in, 'Ah, but he would have to meet with my approval first.'

'Naturally, Sam.' She was about to add, 'Unlike Ruth and Rowan,' but held the comment back. Retreat from the subject was better at this stage. The conversation turned to other topics and continued pleasantly throughout the meal and into the late-evening until Alicia said it was time she should be going other-wise she would be late into the office the next morning, and that was not a good example to set her staff.

'A good maxim,' Sam approved. 'It keeps them alert. I will escort you home, my dear.'

When they stepped outside the last remnants of cloud were being driven from the moon, leaving Whitby washed in a silvery light that made their walk easier. Nevertheless, Alicia slipped her arm through Sam's, ostensibly for support but it carried more meaning than that. She was pleased to note Sam's response.

When they reached the house in Bagdale, they paused on the steps before she let herself in.

'Sam, I really would like to know about that wine deal.'

'You shall.'

'Soon, please. Come to dinner the night after next. By your-self. We can talk then without boring other people.'

There was a husky note of enticement in her voice that he could not resist.

'All right. That sounds like a good idea. I can see you are someone after my own heart as far as business is concerned.'

'And maybe more,' she added, kissing him quickly on the cheek. 'Good night, Sam.'

'Good night, Alicia.'

As he walked down the path he raised a finger to his cheek where her lips had touched him. Over the years he had sought solace with a number of women, but this was different. An attractive young lady – young enough to be his daughter, in fact. That was quite a challenge, and there was more – the prospect of a future trading empire, with its headquarters in Whitby, beckoned.

The following day Alicia was in her office when one of her clerks announced that Mr Warren Laskill was asking to see her.

'Show him in, please,' she replied.

A few moments later Warren breezed into her office.

'My dear Alicia, it is good to see you looking so well. I had thought that being left behind might have had an adverse effect on you. I am glad to see it has not.'

'It was my choice so I won't let it affect me adversely, though I must say that it is strange with only the servants sharing the house. Now, Warren, what has brought you here? I don't believe it is merely concern for me.'

'My dear Alicia, that was indeed the prime purpose, but there is another.'

'I thought so.'

'You remember you thought we might help Ben without his knowing it?'

'Yes.'

'Well, I saw him last night and believe he is getting a little desperate regarding money. He dropped a hint that he wouldn't mind a decent tip or two that would help him.'

'Well, I think it would be most kind of us to help an old friend.' Alicia fought to keep the sarcasm out of her voice. 'So we'll keep our ears open. And he must never know where the information comes from.'

'Still have a soft spot for him?'

Alicia shrugged her shoulders. 'I've got over any feelings I once had.'

'I thought hatred would burn in you heart forever after what he did to you.'

'Oh, Warren,' she said smoothly, 'we can't be vindictive all our lives. Besides, there are other fish in the sea.'

He felt some satisfaction. Maybe he was one of those other fish . . . maybe the only one.

'A glass of wine before we eat, Sam? After all, that is what we are going to talk about,' Alicia commented once he had entered the drawing-room.

'That will be most acceptable.' He had noted the bottle on the sideboard and established from the label that it was one of the best he and Seaton were importing.

'Do sit down, Sam,' Alicia said as she turned from the sideboard with two glasses of wine in her hands.

He took one, and when she sat down noted that she had left the wing-chair for him. He raised his glass. 'To you and the future.'

'Wait.' She stopped him before the glass touched his lips. 'That should be, "To us and the future".'

'Very well.' He smiled. 'To us and the future.'

As she drank she met his gaze with smouldering eyes. 'Now, the story of this wine agreement between you and my father?'

'On a trip to London I overheard two young men expressing a desire to import special wines from Spain. They had the contacts to do this but had no knowledge of shipment and storage. I told them to look no further, I had a friend who could do that for them – your father. I had no knowledge of the wine trade myself, had never gone into it because of an unwritten agreement between us that we would not rival each other in individual aspects of our trading.'

'So you passed this deal entirely over to him?'

'Not exactly. We formed a special partnership.'

'And what did you put into it?'

'My contact with the two young men.'

'It seems strange that my father would accept that as your only input?'

'There was no need for capital. Your father already had shipping facilities and storage in place.'

'But wasn't this cutting across the wine trade he already conducted?'

'Expanding it, my dear.'

Further discussion was interrupted when it was announced that dinner was ready, but it gave Alicia time to consider what she had learned.

Once the soup was served and they were alone, she took up the topic again. 'I think there is a little more to it than what you have told me, Sam. If you had never competed before why did Father allow this . . .' She stopped as realisation dawned on her. 'Father told us about his indiscretion and that you had come to his rescue.' Her eyes narrowed as she added, 'You used that in order to get him to make you a partner in this lucrative trade. You pressured him into it, threatening to call in your debt if he didn't do so.'

Sam spread his hands in mock surrender. 'I needed some return on the money I had laid out.'

There was a charged silence and then Alicia gave a little smile. 'You are a devious man, Sam Coulson. And was the object of my proposed marriage to Ben to get an increased influence on my father's firm? After all, he had no sons. I can see from your expression that it was.' She started to laugh. 'And Ben really upset that, didn't he? I was devastated that night he walked in with Ruth and announced he was married, but what must you have felt? My father's firm was so close . . . and then it was dashed away. Life has certainly dealt us some disappointments, Sam. We've just drunk to us and the future, what does that hold for us now?'

'You are a very perceptive young woman, Alicia. With your sharp mind I can see you succeeding in a man's world. And I wouldn't be surprised either if you would not be averse to using, shall we say, underhand methods.'

'How right you are, Sam.'

'I see that I have a formidable opponent.'

'How can I be that? I'm hardly experienced.'

'No, but you are very astute; have a sharp mind, will make quick decisions and follow them with immediate action.' He gave a small knowing smile while keeping her under tight observation. 'Oh, yes, I've been keeping my eyes and ears open since you decided to stay in Whitby.'

She smiled and raised her glass to him. Was he merely interested in seeing Campion's prosper so that, in the long run, he would benefit too? Or did he have an ulterior motive? Knowing Sam Coulson's hard-headed, uncompromising methods she thought the later more likely. She must beware of being drawn into a web from which there could be no escape – unless she could turn that situation to her own advantage.

'Should I be flattered by that? Or has it been for your own ends?'

'Read it as you will.' His slight pause emphasised his next query. 'Should I trust a woman?'

'Who knows? You've never met one who was your rival in the commercial world before.'

He smiled. 'Then maybe it's time that I did. It could become very interesting.'

During the following weeks Alicia was aware that Sam's suggested investments were not always as good as he made them out to be. Some paid dividends, others did not, and she realised that the latter had been deliberately put her way so that she would seek his advice all the more. This she did not mind, for the more she was in Sam's company the more she could weave the charms she hoped would lure him into her web.

They both enjoyed the cut and thrust of dealing with and against each other. Sam's admiration for Alicia grew and he found that it was going beyond their commercial relationship. She was aware of his mounting interest and that pleased her; she could wind him in when she pleased as the angler reels in his catch.

They were discreet about their personal liaisons and, on Alicia's suggestion, dined more and more often at her home, invitations that Sam was only too willing to accept.

*

329

One evening when they were settled in the drawing-room after their meal, he asked, 'Did you follow my latest suggestion about timber?'

'Yes, Sam, I did. It was certainly a good idea of yours to buy into that trade.'

'You purchased the stand of oaks near Helmsley that I recommended?'

'No.'

Sam was immediately alert. What did this mean? Had his plan for her to make a bad investment under the guise of a good one gone awry? 'I thought you said it was a good idea?'

'The idea to go into the timber trade was, but not with that stand of oaks.'

'What was wrong with it?'

'I think you know very well, Sam. On most occasions I have followed your recommendations implicitly, but not this time. Something told me not to buy that timber, especially for the shipbuilding trade, without seeing it. Now, I'm no expert on timber so I took Mr Fairburn with me. He told me that particular stand was no good for building ships so I didn't buy it. But I did buy another he recommended and I'll make a handsome profit from it. No thanks to you.' Her voice had become cold. 'I believe you suggested that particular stand knowing that it was not worth buying.'

'Why would I do that?' he protested.

'You wanted to see me lose heavily so that you could come forward with a rescue act and put me under a further obligation to you. Maybe even force a foreclosure on my father's business, knowing you could then make a reduced offer that would not cover his debt and force me to find the rest of the money elsewhere. From my more successful investments.'

'Would I do that to a friend, someone who has my growing admiration?'

'Knowing you, Sam, and seeing how you operate, yes, you would, if it was for your benefit.'

'Alicia, what can I say?' He spread his hands in acceptance

of defeat, but his mind was intent on how to turn this situation back to his advantage.

'Say nothing, Sam. Don't even start to apologise. You and I are of the same calibre when it comes to manoeuvre and counter-manoeuvre, so with that understanding we will continue our friendly rivalry, but on a closer basis.' She had let her voice imply more than was on the surface of those last three words. She could tell by his attitude and the look he gave her that she had him hooked.

Their eyes met and held, a world of meaning passing between them.

Sam leaned forward, eyes still intent on her. 'You and I shouldn't be rivals, not even friendly ones. Marry me, Alicia, and we'll work as one.'

She allowed the silence that filled the room to become charged.

Sam broke it. 'I know I am old enough to be your father but . . .'

'And I am young enough to be your daughter but . . .'

Silence descended between them again.

This time Alicia broke it. 'Don't think that by marrying me you will get to run my father's firm. That may have been your intention by forcing me to marry Martin and then Ben. You knew I would not see my family impoverished. Well, that no longer applies thanks to their new life in the Bahamas. I stayed behind for two reasons. One you don't have to know about, the other was to clear my father's debt to you. I'll marry you if you call off that debt and I can send him the documents to prove it.'

Sam's mind raced. He was close to achieving the aim he had had when he first put his proposal to Martin. Alicia may think he wasn't getting his hands on her father's firm but he was close to it. Once he had married her he would bide his time to close that gap, maybe it would take little more than nine months . . .

Before he could say anything she went on, 'Don't answer

me at once because there are other conditions. I know you have liaisons with certain women from time to time. That must stop or you will suffer the consequences.'

Sam had no need to ask what these would be. This was a determined young woman speaking to him.

'The other condition, to put it more politely than a blunt invitation, is that there will be no need for you to go home tonight. You may change your mind after that. I have given you my answer and conditions. I will expect yours, with no conditions, in the morning.'

Alicia stretched as she watched Sam dress. The thin sheet did not hide the sensuality of the gesture and she knew he was aware of it.

'Well, Sam?' she asked huskily, and he knew from her intonation that the night they had shared would be one she would remember, and that she was inviting him to reciprocate.

He came to the bed, stood for a moment letting his eyes bore into hers, then he sank down and pulled her to him. 'For more nights like that, I would tear up a hundred debts.'

'Then I am yours.'

Their lips met and fused into a passion that sealed their future.

'I'd better be going,' Sam said eventually as he reluctantly rose from the bed.

'I think it would be wise to keep our proposed marriage a secret from everyone for the time being,' said Alicia.

'But I thought we could wed soon?'

'Just give me a little time. There are a few things I would like to see to first.' She had slid out of bed as she was speaking. 'Please Sam, do it my way. You'll not regret it.' Her arms slid up his shoulders and she looked at him with pleading eyes in which there was also promise.

'Very well.' He kissed her and took her arms from around his neck. 'Now I must go. And I don't think you should be late to the office either.'

'I won't be.'

'Tonight?' he queried.

She gave a little shake of her head and was amused to see the disappointment that clouded his face. 'Sorry, Sam. I have an appointment this evening.'

He cocked a querying eyebrow at her but saw from her expression that he would learn no more.

Alicia smiled to herself as the door closed. She had hooked Sam Coulson and liked the stab of jealousy she had just witnessed. She could use it to her own advantage.

Sam's step was brisk as he walked to New Buildings. He was in the dining-room when his daughters came downstairs. They were surprised to find him in talkative mood. He generally had little to say at breakfast. He led the conversation to Ryan Bennett. 'Do you know what he intends to do in Whitby?'

Sarah gave a shake of her head. 'He hasn't decided yet, but I believe he is looking into some business proposals.'

'If there is anything I can do, tell him to contact me.'

'Thank you, Father. I rather think he is someone who likes to stand on his own.'

'A little advice might help.'

'I'll tell him.'

'Are you seeing him today?'

'No. Tomorrow he is taking me to a party at Hawsker.'

'You'll be getting a few invitations,' put in Dina, 'now that Ryan is here permanently. People will be curious about him and his aunt.'

'You're missing out, Dina,' said Sam, 'you should have found yourself a young man such as Ryan.'

'I'm happy with Rowan.'

He gave a thoughtful nod. 'You've always been quite sure about your feelings for him. Maybe I should find him a job ashore and see if he has the ability to cope with my type of work.' The hint behind that was not lost on the sisters. 'It could eliminate any chance of similar heartaches to those we suffered over the loss of Martin.' He shook himself. 'Now, we mustn't let ourselves get morbid. You'll need a new dress for that party, Sarah. Can you find one ready-made?'

'I can try.'

'Well, if you can't, put one on order for the next event. You get one too, Dina. Now I must be off.' He rose from his chair.

The girls were profuse in their thanks as their father left the room. When the door closed behind him they looked at each other in amazement, and a silence charged with curiosity lay between them.

'What's got into him?'

'Talkative, pleasant, generous . . .'

'And considerate – look at his remarks about Rowan.'

'Once he would never have mentioned him, or certainly not in friendly tones.'

'Must be a woman.'

'I don't think he came home last night. I was awake a long time, thinking of the Campions and wondering how they were getting on.'

'I've known him stay out all night before but he's never been in this sort of mood after it.'

'Do you think he's found someone of whom he is fond and who is fond of him?' Sarah put the question seriously.

Dina shrugged her shoulders. 'Who knows? But if it puts him in this mood, let it be so.'

'Who can it be?'

'We could speculate all we like and still not come up with the answer. Maybe one day we'll know. In the meantime let's make the most of his good mood. Come on, there are dresses to be bought!'

Alicia was engrossed in some paperwork that morning, after which she spoke to Simon Yardley.

'I have been studying some figures relating to our purchase of local produce for onward shipment to London. I think we could increase that trade by as much as thirty percent, and if that goes well increase it again later. Will you look into the possibility of our suppliers being able to meet that demand, or perhaps approach new sources?'

'Certainly, miss,' replied Simon. He was pleased with the way Alicia had kept the emphasis on expansion since she had taken over responsibility for the firm. He liked a challenge and hoped her enthusiasm did not wane. The possibility of testing that resolve came unexpectedly an hour later.

'Miss, there is a gentleman, a Mr Thomas Bowman, asking if he may see you?'

'Do you know anything about him?'

'I have never heard of him. He says that he has opened a new stone quarry at Aislaby.'

'I wonder how he thinks that can interest us? Show him in, we'll soon find out.'

'Yes, miss.' He left the room to return a few minutes later and announce the stranger.

'Mr Bowman.' Alicia rose from her chair and offered the caller her hand. As he took it she eyed him critically. She judged him to be in his forties, well-dressed, well-groomed, a man who took pride in his appearance. He was just beginning to show signs of putting on weight and his florid complexion was maybe a sign that he was not averse to taking a drink, but she judged that if he did so the drink would be of the choicest.

'Miss Campion, thank you for seeing me. I deem it an honour.' His voice was soft with a slight trace of a southern accent.

'Do sit down, Mr Bowman.' She indicated a chair on the opposite side of the desk. 'You don't mind if my manager sits in on whatever it is you want to talk about? You may know that I am fairly new to running this firm and Simon served my father for many years.'

'I quite understand. When making enquiries about who might handle some business for me, I heard that your father had emigrated to the Bahamas and that you were now in charge.'

Alicia smiled. 'And you thought you might be able to take advantage of a young lady's inexperience?'

Thomas Bowman raised his hands as if dismissing her comment, and quickly interposed, 'I will admit I was curious to see what it was like dealing with a lady in what is almost entirely a man's world.'

'You know of others?' Alicia was curious to hear his answer.

'Not personally. I know of two other ladies who have ventured into the world of commerce, and people who have dealt with them.'

'And what was their experience?'

'One disastrous, the other satisfactory.'

'And now you want to see for yourself. So what can we do for you?'

'As I told your manager when I introduced myself, I have an interest in a stone quarry at Aislaby. You probably know that the area is a very good source of deltaic sandstone. It is highly workable and has the virtue of hardening as it weathers, so it is prime stone for building. I'm sure that you know it is shipped out of Whitby to various places. I also have interests in a number of building projects in London and the south coast. I decided that, instead of buying the stone from an existing supplier, it would be advantageous to have my own quarry but came across a stumbling block when it came to the matter of transportation. It seems that the stone-moving vessels are already working to capacity so I must look for alternative arrangements.'

'And that is why you are here. You think we could organise it for you?'

'I sincerely hope you can, otherwise I may have to give up the idea altogether.'

'So you do not own your quarry as yet?'

'No, but I am at the point of doing so if I can organise transportation of the stone.'

'You would want us to organise transportation from the quarry to London?'

'Yes, or to whatever other destination I specify.'

Alicia turned to her manager. 'What will this entail, Simon?'

'We would have to engage wagons pulled by oxen to transport the stone from Aislaby to Whitby.' He glanced at Bowman. 'I presume your quarrymen would load the wagons?'

'Yes, if that is the way you want it.'

'We would expect that,' Simon went on. 'We would be responsible for lading on to the ships we would have hired. The unloading to be your responsibility, Mr Bowman?'

'Yes.'

'That seems a fair distribution of work, miss,' said Simon, giving the deal his approval.

She eyed Bowman. 'Very well, sir. In broad outline that seems satisfactory, so provided we can reach a financial agreement. I believe we can work together. We will work out the details. Can you return the day after tomorrow, at, say, ten o'clock in the morning, and we will confirm that we have a deal?'

'I most certainly can, Miss Campion,' Bowman replied enthusiastically and rose to his feet. 'It has been most pleasant dealing with you and I am sure it will continue to be so. I look forward to seeing you in two days' time. Good day to you.'

After Simon had seen Mr Bowman to the door he returned to Alicia's office.

'What do you think, Simon?' she said, indicating for him to sit down.

'I think this looks to be a good prospect. It will need some organising and will be of a nature we have never undertaken before. We must work on the figures first.'

'Then let us start straight away.' Alicia paused and added wistfully, 'I wonder what father would have thought.'

'I think he would have been proud of the way you handled it, miss.'

'I wonder if he would have turned it down?'

'Maybe, miss. I think your father was content with his lot and had little desire to expand further, but I don't think he would have disapproved of the ambition you show and, if I may say so, miss, I am pleased to see it.'

'Thank you, Simon, that is reassuring. I suggest we both think further about this proposal and then this afternoon we will discuss our ideas.'

'Very well, miss.' He started for the door.

'One moment, Simon'

He turned back. 'Miss?'

'Let us keep this to ourselves for the time being. Say nothing to anyone. If word gets out someone might try to undercut us.'

When Simon returned to Alicia's office at two o'clock he found her sitting at her desk looking very thoughtful. She glanced up and without a word indicated the seat opposite to her. He sat down and remained silent so that he did not interrupt her train of thought, waiting patiently for her to speak. At the end of another three minutes she nodded as if confirming to herself that she had made the right decision.

She looked seriously at him and said, 'You will no doubt have given the practical side of Mr Bowman's problem some thought?'

'I have, miss. We'll have to hire ships which should present no difficulty. We will have to organise men to load the ships here and make sure we have a convenient quay when we know that stone will becoming from the quarry. We will have to hire wagons, oxen and teamsters. We'll have to look into that part of the operation very carefully as it is new to us.'

She gave a nod and assumed a look of satisfaction. 'We should be able to handle all these things ourselves, but I too have given the situation serious thought. What I propose is something radical, a departure from our usual methods. I suggest we engage someone else to run the whole operation for us. He will oversee everything, even directing the bills to be issued by, and paid directly to, the firms he engages to do the particular work. We will know the individual amounts, and the firms he has engaged will pay us, through him, a percentage of their receipts for our work in setting this up.'

Simon waited for her to go on. He admired her initiative and hoped that her idea would prove a success.

'Do you think it will work?' she asked.

'I see no reason why it shouldn't. It will depend a lot on the honesty and organisational ability of the person you engage.'

'Rightly said. I have someone in mind – Mr Warren Laskill.'

A look of doubt crossed Simon's face.

'I see you have reservations about my choice?'

'Well, I can't deny that.'

'You probably only know him from his reputation as a frequenter of Whitby's inns and as no mean card player. People say he is doing this off his father's money. I know differently, Simon. His appearance hides a sharp brain, and his organising ability is evident from the way he has run his father's estate in the Esk Valley. I also know him to be entirely trustworthy and that there is no one better at keeping a secret. Though he is a gossip, he knows what can be told and what cannot.'

'I bow to your judgement, miss.'

Alicia gave a little smile. 'I can see you are wondering why I am suggesting this method?'

'I can't deny that either, miss.'

'I want the whole operation to be kept secret so that it appears that we have nothing to do with it. I have my special reasons for that. I will require absolute secrecy from Mr Bowman, Mr Laskill and yourself.'

'You have my assurance, miss.'

'Good. Then I will contact Mr Laskill, and when Mr Bowman calls we will get everything settled and papers signed.'

'Are you confident enough for me to start on the necessary documents now? They will have to be carefully worded so there is no ambiguity and I will have to do it personally if our part in the business is to remain a secret. We cannot allow clerks to write them out.'

'I am certain this will work. Yes, start right away drawing up the documents.'

When Simon had left her office Alicia sat for a few moments considering her scheme. With a plan of action clear in her mind, she picked up a pen and wrote a note. She folded the sheet of paper, wrote a name on it and sealed it with wax. She sat for a few moments tapping the paper thoughtfully then rose quickly and left the office. She paused on the step, looking to right and left. Seeing two boys idly watching a ship being loaded, she went up to them.

'Want to earn a coin?' she said as she neared them.

They spun round to see who put the question. 'Yes, ma'am, but it depends what thee wants?'

'Take this to the Angel and ask the landlord to give it to the person to whom it is addressed.'

'Yes, ma'am.' One of them reached out for the paper.

Alicia held it back. 'Don't throw it away. I'll know if you do and have your hide.'

'Trust us, ma'am. It will be there in a few minutes.'

'Evening, Mr Laskill,' Jed Crowther greeted Warren when he arrived at the Angel that evening. 'There's a note here for you.' He picked it up from the counter behind the bar and handed it to Warren.

'Thanks.' Wondering who would be sending him a note to the Angel, he took it to a chair and sat down. He broke the seal, scanned the writing, stood up and stuffed the note into his pocket. 'Jed, tell the others I won't be playing tonight, I'm called away.'

'Yes, sir.'

Warren left the Angel and walked with a brisk step in the direction of Bagdale. What did Alicia want that warranted sending him a note? No matter. Whatever it was there might be other advantages to be gained from a young lady who lived alone.

The maid took his coat and hat and showed him into the drawing-room. Alicia rose to meet him when he was announced.

'Warren, thank you for coming, I'm sorry if it has interrupted a night of cards.'

'My dear Alicia, seeing you is far better than all the kings and queens I might have been looking at.'

She gave a little laugh, appreciating his flirtation. 'A glass of Madeira?' She indicated a chair to him as she put the question.

'That would be appreciated.'

'I have arranged a light supper to be brought to us a little later.'

He made no comment but wondered where all this was leading. He accepted the wine and she sat down on the sofa opposite to him. Pleasantries were exchanged for twenty minutes during which time a second glass of Madeira was poured. Then Alicia rose from her chair and went to the bell-pull. Three tugs was a signal for two maids to appear carrying trays. These were placed on a sideboard and a low table placed in front of the sofa.

'This is indeed an unexpected pleasure,' commented Warren, eyeing the selection of cold meats, bread, pickles and salad.

'Please do help yourself,' said Alicia. 'It might be easier for you if you sat on the sofa with me.'

Warren needed no second invitation to change his place. At that moment the maids reappeared with dishes of fruit pie and creams. He eyed them with appreciative anticipation. 'You know my weakness,' he commented.

'Are there others?'

'Well, there are other ways to a man's heart than his stomach.'

She made no comment in response but did wonder what his reaction would be if he knew with whom she had shared her bed last night.

When she saw that Warren was enjoying the food Alicia came to the point of her invitation. 'You remember I said we might help Ben in his financial difficulties?'

'Yes, and was surprised that you wished to do so.'

'Well, I do, and I think I have found a way. I do not want him to know anything about what I am thinking of putting into place, though, so it will mean strict secrecy.'

'This sounds intriguing.'

'If Ben got a whiff that I am behind this, I think he would refuse and I don't want that.'

'Very well, tell me what you have in mind.'

'I was approached yesterday to organise the transportation of stone from a new quarry at Aislaby to London.' She went on to explain what this entailed. When she paused, Warren, who had been wondering why she was telling him all this, asked, 'What has this to do with me?'

'I would like you to organise the whole operation.'

'Me?' He gave an amused smile.

'Don't play yourself down, Warren. I know you can do it. If you are a little bit reluctant, just tell yourself you are doing it for me.'

'I thought we were doing it for Ben?'

'Yes, we are, but I want everything to go through with nothing to show Campion's firm connected with it.'

'But . . .'

Alicia cut short the objections he was going to raise about her ability to do that. 'Hear my ideas through before you see snags.' She went on to explain what she had in mind and then added, 'The only way Ben can benefit from this is by supplying the wagons and teamsters to convey the stone from Aislaby to Whitby. I suggest you tell him you have had this contract from Mr Bowman and propose that he should benefit by organising the wagons.'

'You've certainly thought this through, Alicia.'

'I have, because it is important to me.'

Warren wondered at that admission. Why was it important to her to help Ben, going to such lengths as well?

'Well, what do you say Warren? Will you help me with this?' Undecided whether his hesitation was feigned to extract the best deal for himself, she plunged on, 'It will be worth your while. If you want a contract in writing you shall have it, but I am sure you would not want any extra benefits that might be involved also putting in writing.' A hint of what she meant was conveyed in the suggestive look she gave him.

'Put like that, Alicia, how can I refuse?'

As she got ready for bed that night Alicia wondered what she had got herself into with such a promise, but she needed Warren, he was her only contact with Ben, and through him lay the road to revenge.

Chapter Nineteen

'Good day, Mr Bowman.' Alicia rose from her chair and came round her desk meet him. They shook hands and he accepted the chair she indicated to him. 'I would like to get down to business straight away. My proposal may seem a little unusual to you but I assure you I have made careful consideration of what I am going to put to you and am certain it will work very well to the benefit of all parties.'

'This sounds interesting,' he said a little cautiously.

'Your request brings us into a trade we have never handled before but I believe we can set things up to your satisfaction. I have someone coming here shortly whom I want to take charge of the whole operation.' She went on to explain the organisation she had in mind. She saw that she had his full attention and surmised he was intrigued by the way she was proposing the deal to be set up.

'There is one thing I must insist on.'

'That is?' he queried as she paused to let her request sink in.

'There must be absolute secrecy. No one must know that my firm is involved in this. That is why I have set the operation up this way.' She saw suspicion cross his face. 'I hasten to assure you there is nothing underhand involved. As you have heard all my proposals are quite straightforward, the method of payment is just a little unusual. The reason for this secrecy is purely personal and will not affect you or the operation in any way.'

Mr Bowman nodded thoughtfully. 'I agree it is a little unusual to require secrecy on something that could win you future orders if it was known Campion's was organising stone shipments. But if that is the way you desire it and I am impressed by the man you are engaging, then we have a contract if your terms are acceptable.'

Alicia picked up a bell from her desk and gave it a sharp ring. A few moments later the door opened and Simon came in carrying four sheets of paper.

'Thank you,' said Alicia. 'The figures, Mr Bowman,' she added as her manager handed the papers to him.

He studied them with intense concentration.

'If you have any questions, Simon will no doubt have the answers.'

Mr Bowman made no response but continued studying the papers. He pursed his lips thoughtfully when he eventually looked up. 'You have obtained these figures from the firms who will be involved?'

'No, sir,' replied Simon. 'Because of the secrecy I have made estimates which, though I say myself, I have been able to calculate from my long-standing knowledge of what goes on in the port of Whitby. I think they will be very near any figures you could obtain elsewhere.'

Mr Bowman nodded. 'I worked on some estimates myself before I left London and I must say yours seem very satisfactory.'

'Then all that remains is for you to meet Mr Laskill.'

'He is already here, miss,' said Simon. 'He arrived just as I was bringing the figures to you.'

'Good, ask him to come in.'

Introductions were soon over and in the next half-hour details were discussed. Mr Bowman was impressed by the sharpness of Warren's mind, his ability to grasp detail, and the fact that he had obviously given the operation much thought.

With all parties satisfied, the contracts were signed and would come into force the moment that Mr Bowman acquired his quarry, negotiations for which were at a very advanced stage.

'I think that we will be taking out the first stone in two

weeks. Can you have everything in place for then, Mr Laskill?'

'All will be ready, sir.'

'Come in,' called Alicia in answer to a knock on her office door.

'Mr Sam Coulson to see you, miss,' announced one of the clerks.

'Send him in, please.'

She came from behind her desk to wait for him. Sam smiled at her admiringly. He held out his hands, which she took, and they kissed.

'Why this visit, Sam?' she asked coyly.

'Two days are too long without seeing you, my dear.'

She gave a little laugh as she swung away from him to return to her chair. 'More frequently could set people talking and I don't want that. Well, not yet anyway.'

'Does that mean you are going to refuse an invitation to have lunch with me tomorrow at the Angel? I thought it might lessen any opposition to your becoming part of Whitby's commercial world if certain merchants saw you in my company. Many of them meet in the Angel for luncheon. It's a place where news is exchanged and deals are struck. You should not be on the outside of that. If you are seen in my company it will be a mark of my approval and that carries a lot of weight.'

'It's very thoughtful of you, Sam, and I accept.'

'Then I will call for you at half-past eleven.'

'You are looking very smart, my dear.' Sam eyed Alicia with approval the next day. 'If you can't win over Whitby's traders then there is something wrong with them. They'll be buzzing round you like the bees to a honey pot, and I've no doubt that when the wives get to know they'll tighten the reins on their husbands. Beware of jealous wives!'

Alicia laughed. 'This sounds as though my life will soon become particularly interesting.'

'Then let us go and see.' He smiled, gave a small bow and held out his arm.

She took it for a moment, until they reached the door.

'Good day, miss. Good day, sir,' Jed Crowther greeted them when they walked into the Angel.

'You have my table ready?'

'The exact one you picked, sir.'

'Good.'

Their outdoor clothes discarded and taken by one of the servants, Jed escorted them into the dining-room where Alicia was quick to notice that the table which Sam had chosen was in a prominent position. No one entering the dining-room could fail to notice them. They had already attracted the attention of two men who were dining at a table across the room. Their heads had drawn closer together and Alicia was amused to see the glances that kept coming in her direction.

'You are attracting attention already, my dear,' whispered Sam when Jed moved away.

So it continued during the two hours they spent over the meal. Merchants, ship-owners, ship builders, sail makers, ropery owners, in fact every trade that made up this thriving port was represented by the men who came to the Angel that day. Alicia knew many of them by sight or by name. Some she had met at social occasions attended by her family but never had she been near them in her new capacity as head of a mercantile company. Many came over to have a word, others to say hello to Sam but really wanting an introduction to the attractive young lady who sat at his table. A few ignored them both, making a point of showing their disapproval of Alicia's daring to enter a man's world, and indicating they did not condone Sam's support of her.

Alicia revelled in the attention, was quick with her replies and comments, and shared with Sam intimate observations, both serious and amusing, about various diners.

She dabbed her lips with a napkin at the end of the meal.

As she laid it on the table she said, 'That was most enjoyable, Sam. Thank you.'

'It was my pleasure, my dear. Now, most of the people you have seen here will gather in the other room for a drink or two and to exchange information. They may even make some deals, or keep each other up to date on what is happening in other ports and the likely direction new trade will take. Do you feel like venturing into the lion's den?'

Alicia's eyes twinkled as she said, 'Sounds like an experience, but it will be fun, I'm sure.'

He smiled his approval. 'Let's go.'

The room he took her to was half-panelled in dark oak. Above the panelling the walls were white and on each one there were two small seascapes in oils. A continuous wall bench encircled the room and four tables were placed so that they did not obstruct free movement.

When Sam walked in with Alicia an immediate hush fell, tinged with hostility, but out of respect for a lady the men had risen to their feet.

Sam grasped the situation. 'Gentlemen, some of you will know Miss Alicia Campion through her family, others may never have met her, but may I introduce her as someone now following the same calling as ourselves? Miss Campion runs the firm her father founded, Seaton having emigrated to the Bahamas with the rest of his family. Gentlemen, I give you, Miss Alicia Campion.'

There was a moment's quiet as if the men were trying to come to terms with the fact that a woman had penetrated their inner sanctum. Then someone clapped. It was taken up and the room soon resounded with the noise and the buzz of welcoming comments.

Alicia smiled and gave an inclination of her head. She then held up her hands and quietness descended on the room. 'Gentlemen, thank you for your welcome. I hope that I will be an asset to the commercial fraternity of our wonderful port and look forward to meeting you all in one capacity or another. Please do sit down.'

The buzz of conversation broke out again as they resumed their seats but not before several had jockeyed to make room for Alicia to sit beside them. It was not lost on her that amid all the fuss three gentlemen showed their disapproval by leaving.

Alicia realised this was not an opportunity to be missed and throughout the next two hours listened carefully to what was being said, made discreet queries, heard opinions about trading prospects and their future potential. She witnessed three deals being struck, and noted some that could not be agreed.

'That was quite an education, Sam,' she commented as he walked her to her house in Bagdale.

'You made a stir, but that was only to be expected. And you definitely made an impression with the knowledge you showed.'

'I had a good teacher in my father.'

'You certainly had.'

'And now I have another to whom I can turn.'

'Flatterer.'

'No. It's true. If you hadn't been there, Sam, I don't think I could have coped.' She wasn't going to tell him that the need for revenge on his son would have motivated her in his absence.

They reached the door of the house.

'Tonight?' he asked.

'Not tonight.'

'Are you having second thoughts?' His frown held a touch of suspicion.

'No, Sam, I'm not. Just let me adjust to my new life.' The pleading light in her eyes touched him as she'd intended it should.

'All right, my dear. I do understand.' He kissed her on the cheek and waited until she had gone inside.

Sam walked back to his own office thinking of the pleasures to come once she had adjusted, and with them his own control of the Campion business.

Alicia leaned back against the door when she closed it and stood for a few moments gathering her thoughts. She had Sam hooked, and when she cast him loose she would be left in sole charge of the biggest trading firm in Whitby.

The following morning Alicia made a quick visit to her office and, after signing some papers, left it to recross the river to Skinner Street.

'I would be obliged if I could see Mr Nettleship,' she said to one of the clerks who greeted her when she entered the premises of Nettleship & Son.

'Yes, ma'am.' The young man could hardly get his words out, his breath taken away by the appearance of this attractive young woman. 'Who shall I say wants to see him?'

'Miss Alicia Campion.'

The clerk blushed at the assumption he had made. 'Yes, ma'am . . . miss.' He scurried away down the passage but was quickly back with the request, 'Please follow me.' He led the way to a door halfway down the passage, knocked and opened it. 'Miss Campion, sir,' he announced. He stood to one side to allow Alicia to enter the room and then closed the door.

'Mr Nettleship, it is so good of you to see me without an appointment,' she said brightly, extending her hand.

He took it and bowed. 'It is my pleasure, Miss Campion. Please do sit down.' He indicated a chair and then, to make the occasion seem less formal, did not return behind his desk but sat down in another chair that he drew at an angle to hers.

'You will remember me from yesterday, Mr Nettleship?'

'Who could forget you?' He smiled and ran his right forefinger across his moustache which, like his hair, was beginning to grey. It gave him a distinguished look which was enhanced by his slim figure and straight bearing. He gave a little chuckle. 'You certainly stirred up our gathering. I know there were those who objected, but let me tell you, your presence was a breath of fresh air. And if it changes the face of trading in this town, Whitby will be the better for it.'

'You flatter me, Mr Nettleship. All I want is to hold my own and succeed, and so fulfil my father's trust in me.'

'I am sure you will do that. Now there is obviously something behind this visit. I'm sure it is not just a social call.'

'You are right. It is in relation to something I overheard you tell another gentleman yesterday.' She raised her hand in an apologetic gesture. 'I assure you I was not eavesdropping but I was near enough to overhear you say that you have a consignment of wine in Hull you do not want. I would be interested in purchasing it from you.'

'What you heard is perfectly true, but what you may not have heard is that it is poor wine.'

'I heard that too,' said Alicia, smiling to herself at the mystified expression that came over his face.

'Miss Campion, I couldn't let you buy the wine, it would not be right . . .'

'It will fit in perfectly with something I have in mind.'

'I am reluctant to say yes. It was a trade I had never been in. I saw your father running a successful wine interest and when this offer came along, thought it too good an opportunity to miss. I was careless. I failed to look into it sufficiently, something I've never done before. On closer examination I found that I had been duped. A few bottles of good wine had been placed where I could see them and the labels on the other bottles which contained an inferior wine had been replaced.' He gave a shake of his head. 'It is not a good vintage.'

'Mr Nettleship, I would like to make the purchase no matter what the wine is like. I can make good use of it.' He looked at her with a mixture of curiosity and doubt. 'I am serious,' Alicia went on. 'Don't ask me why I want it.'

'Well, if you really have your mind set.' His voice trailed away. 'No, Miss Campion, I can't sell you an inferior product.'

'Mr Nettleship, you don't need to trouble your conscience. You will be selling me something I want.'

He spread his hands in a gesture of resignation. 'Well, if you really want it, who am I to say no to getting rid of something that is an embarrassment to me? All right, I'll let you have it for half what I paid for it.'

'There is no need for such a generous offer.'

'It will help me to rest easily.'

'Very well.'

'Maybe it will lead to our doing further business in the future.'

'I will certainly bear that in mind. There is one more thing about this deal, Mr Nettleship – it must be kept secret. No one must know that you have sold this wine to me. Just tell me where it is and it will be removed at some time in the future. It is imperative that this transaction should remain secret between you and me.'

'I won't breathe a word about it. I have a warehouse in Hull, it is stored there.'

'Will you instruct whoever is in charge that when my representative comes for it, they should let it go?'

'I will. Should I have a name to pass on?'

'No names, Mr Nettleship. Besides I am not sure who I will ask to do it, but it may be a little while before I can have the wine removed.'

'Whenever it is convenient. I shan't need the space it is taking up. In fact, I am thinking of giving up that particular warehouse.'

'Then let me buy it from you and the wine can sit there until I am ready to move it.'

'Are you sure you want to go that far?'

'I can see a warehouse in Hull might be advantageous for distribution purposes.' She gave a sharp little nod. 'Yes, Mr Nettleship, I will take the warehouse. I want you to promise secrecy on that too. Will you have the necessary documents drawn up, but that must be attended to in Hull so that no one in Whitby is aware of this transaction.'

'Very well, Miss Campion, I will see to all that for you. Call on me a week today.'

'Thank you, Mr Nettleship.' She stood up. 'It has been a pleasure dealing with you.'

'And for me.' He escorted her to the door where they shook

hands, sealing their negotiations and the pact of secrecy.

As she walked back to her office Alicia felt a strong feeling of satisfaction. She had put things in place to ruin Ben Coulson.

That same evening Warren made his way to the Angel, not only anticipating an enjoyable evening of cards but hoping that Ben, who had been missing from their game for nearly a week, would be there. He knew Alicia would be growing anxious in her desire to help his friend, though why she was bent on doing so he could not understand. Still, his not to question why, but to help Alicia all he could.

'No Ben again?' he said as he settled down at the table.

'Ruth must have tightened the shackles,' someone replied.

'Never marry, you can always be satisfied elsewhere and still have your freedom. Heed that, Warren, and get your eyes off Alicia Campion.'

'Now, she'd be something to be tied to,' someone muttered.

The insinuation that came with the comment peeved Warren. 'Shut up and let's play,' he snapped.

The cards were being dealt when the door opened and Ben came in. Greetings flew in his direction.

'Thought you'd gone for good without giving us the chance to win our money back,' someone said.

'Now would I do that?' returned Ben.

'Are you getting short of money again?'

The remark nettled Ben but he made no comment. He could easily slip up and reveal his association with Ryan Bennett.

They started to play and for the next hour concentration was directed at the cards. When they took a break to replenish their drinks, Warren managed to have a quiet word with Ben. 'If you are looking for a good prospect then get yourself to Aislaby. Contact a Mr Bowman who is opening a new quarry there. Tell him you'll transport the stone to the ship in Whitby that will be conveying it to London.'

'But I haven't the means of doing that.'

'Get it,' hissed Warren. 'This is a prime opportunity, but

you'll have to provide the oxen and carts. You can do that, you'll be speculating on a certainty.'

Ben looked doubtful.

'I'm trying to help you, Ben. Don't say a word to anyone else or they might step in and snatch this chance from you. One other thing – if you do contact this Mr Bowman under no circumstance mention me. Just say you've heard that he's looking for someone to do this job.'

'How do you know about it?' queried Ben.

'I keep my ears open.'

The others started to take their places at the table again.

'Come on, you two,' someone called.

'This is an opportunity, Ben, take it,' said Warren quietly and slapped him on the arm.

'Ruth, I'm going to have to go and see Ryan this morning. Will you be all right?' He was concerned for her during breakfast. Ruth had been off colour the past week and was only toying with her food this morning.

'Of course I will. I was all right when you were out last night. And I have Betsy if I need anyone.'

'This is important. I had no luck at cards last night but Warren passed on some news that could be profitable to us.' He told her quickly what his friend had said.

'There's no reason for you to suspect it's not genuine?'

'None.'

'Well then, you must go and see Ryan. We are dependent on him to a very great extent. Stand by his judgement.'

Within half an hour Ben had hired a horse from the stables at the White Horse and was riding out of Whitby in the direction of Mulgrave Hall. He was shown into the study where Ryan was writing some letters.

Ben quickly acquainted him with the information Warren had given him.

'This sounds just the thing we need to start us off. I'll go to Aislaby right away. Come with me. You can tell me where I

354

might hire or obtain carts and oxen. You can wait for me outside Aislaby then no one need know of our connection.'

By the time they reached the village Ben's local knowledge had proved invaluable and Ryan became well acquainted with all the possible sources for the carts, oxen and men they could hire.

Ben waited impatiently for his return. He considered himself lucky to have fallen in with Ryan, for a promising partnership could develop if everything went well. He was thankful that by being herself Sarah had attracted this young man and so had brought about a valuable association. He only wished he could regain his father's friendship and approval, and could but hope that at some time in the future that would come about. But at the present it was a distant hope. The chief concern that occupied his mind was Ruth's health. She told him he fussed too much but he could not help it. Nothing must go wrong.

He was shaken out of his reverie by the sound of a horse approaching. He could sense from Ryan's attitude that all had gone well. Relief swept over him especially when his friend confirmed that he had sealed terms for providing the transport of the stone from Aislaby to Whitby. Ben appreciated his financial help but he did not like being dependent on him. Once haulage payments started to be paid by Mr Bowman, he would be free from any such obligation.

'Mr Bowman reckoned that four wagons would suffice to begin with. I said that would not be a difficulty. I hope I was right?'

'We'll manage that. We'll hire them from the timber merchant in the Esk Valley. I'll take you there tomorrow.'

'And the teamsters?'

'Will come with the wagons and the oxen. We can do it all through the timber merchant.'

Two days later, Warren called on Bowman to tell him that a ship would be at his disposal in two weeks' time and that the necessary labourers to load the ship had been hired to start that day.

'Excellent.' Bowman showed his delight. 'We'll have the first stone out of the quarry by then.'

'What about the transport of the stone to Whitby?'

'All organised. I had a visit from a young man who seemed very efficient – Ryan Bennett. He just awaits a date to move the first lot of stone. Now, I can give him that when he visits me again.'

Warren hid his surprise but his mind was filled with annoyance. He had failed Alicia and knew she would not like the news he would bring her. How had Ryan Bennett got to know of this business?

When he reached Whitby he went straight to Alicia's office only to find that she was not there. Ah, well, it might be more advantageous to visit her in her own home this evening.

As he crossed the bridge he saw Ben coming from the west side. They exchanged greetings and then Warren added, 'Did you follow that tip I gave you?'

Ben grimaced. 'No, I couldn't.'

'Why not?'

'I haven't the sort of money I would need for such an enterprise.'

'Surely you could borrow?'

'I'm not prepared to do that, not at the present time with an increase in the family not far off. I'm sorry I couldn't take it up but I am grateful for the information. Thanks for thinking of me.' He wanted to tell his friend that he had benefited from the information but this was not the time to reveal his association with Ryan Bennett.

When Warren was shown into the drawing-room in Bagdale he sensed that Alicia was a little agitated and wondered if his unexpected visit had not pleased her.

'Well?' she asked sharply.

'I thought you would like to know that Ben did not take advantage of the information I fed him.'

'What?' Alicia tightened her lips in exasperation. The first part of her scheme, the one intended to lure Ben in, had come unstuck.

'I met him earlier today and asked if he had followed my information. He said he couldn't afford to and was not prepared to borrow at the moment.'

Alicia cursed silently. 'So now we'll have to find someone who will organise the transportation of the stone?'

'No. I rode out to Aislaby this morning. Bowman thanked me for sending him such an efficient young man with whom he'd struck a deal to transport the stone.'

'What?' Alicia was mystified. 'Did he say who it was?'

'Ryan Bennett.'

'How on earth had *he* got to know about it?'

Warren shrugged his shoulders.

'Well, I suppose it can't be helped. My good intentions to help Ben have come to nought, but something else will turn up.' She glanced at the clock on the mantelpiece. 'Warren, I'm sorry, but I must ask you to leave. I'm expecting someone in a few minutes.'

'But, I thought we might—'

'No, Warren, I'm sorry. I made this arrangement a while ago. It is important.' She was already moving him towards the door. He could do nothing but oblige her.

As he walked down the path from the house he wondered who she was expecting? Who was causing her to get rid of him quickly? The visit must be imminent. Curiosity got the better of him. When he reached the gate there was no one in sight. He quickly found a place from which he could observe the house without being seen.

He had not long to wait before he heard footsteps. Warren waited until he heard their rhythm change and knew that whoever it was had reached the gate. He peered cautiously from out of his cover. His eyes widened with shocked surprise and his pulse started racing. Sam Coulson! Not wanting to betray his presence Warren waited patiently until he judged Sam to be in the house. All the while questions filled his mind. They continued to do as he walked to his Whitby house. No cards for him tonight. Was it just a case of a family friend looking after Alicia's welfare? Was it a business meeting, maybe conducted over a meal or a glass of wine? But she had been agitated and had wanted him out of the house, as if she did not want him to see who her visitor was. Did that indicate that there was more to this visit that might be supposed? Surely not? Sam was old enough to be her father. But what did age matter? She was an attractive young woman and he had to admit that Sam Coulson presented the appearance of a much younger man.

If there were a relationship between them, what would Ben have to say? With that thought Warren resolved not to tell him what he had just witnessed, or at least not until the appropriate time.

As much as he would have liked to waken Alicia, Sam left the house early the next morning. They had arranged it that way so that he was clear of it before the servants were about. So it was no surprise to Alicia when she awoke that she was alone. In fact, this morning she was rather pleased for she wanted time to consider the news Warren had brought yesterday evening. There had been no time for that once Sam had arrived.

She stretched in the luxury of the soft bed and gave some fleeting thought to the night she had shared with Sam, but quickly dismissed this from her mind. Similar nights would come again but for now she must consider what to do about Ben.

He had not been tempted by Warren's suggestion. Why? It had seemed a golden opportunity and if it had been successful he would have trusted any other information she fed him that way. And how had Ryan Bennett got to know anyway? She pondered the question then realisation of what could have happened hit her like a thunderclap. Ben's sister Sarah was close to Ryan Bennett. Had Ben seen his sister and told her of the offer, and when he had said he could not take it up, had Sarah passed the information on to her sweetheart who was looking for some local interest in which to invest? That was the only explanation Alicia could think of but a few minutes later, as she was dressing, another came to her. Could Ben and Ryan Bennett be working together: Ben, knowing Whitby's commerical world, supplying information and advice, with Ryan acting upon it? If that was the case her chance of ruining Ben had vanished, because if she assumed correctly that Ryan was the true investor he could always veto any risky proposition that Ben put before him. But supposing they were true partners? She could see why Ben might want to keep that a secret for the time being. The question began to intrigue her. Supposing Ryan Bennett had the final decision, what would happen if some enticing expensive deal, one that needed an immediate decision, cropped up when Bennett was out of Whitby? Would Ben be tempted to act alone? Alicia smiled to herself. Maybe all was not lost and that warehouse of wine would still prove useful. She must try to ascertain when Ryan Bennett was next away.

It was three weeks before the opportunity arose and it only occurred through a chance meeting. At the time Alicia wondered if fate had played into her hands.

The rain of the previous evening had cleared away, leaving a sky of broken clouds that were gradually dispersing. From her window, Alicia watched their shadows skim across the roofs of Whitby until the sun glinted off the tiles a clear sea of red.

Too good a day to spend in the office, she told herself. I'll treat myself to some shopping.

She was strolling along Baxtergate when a shop door opened and a young woman hurried out. Her head was down as she adjusted a packet that had started to slip off her basket. She crashed into Alicia, sending her staggering and the offending packet toppling to the ground.

'My goodness . . .' The admonishment that sprang to Alicia's lips froze. 'Sarah!' she gasped.

'Oh, dear.' Sarah's heart had started to race. 'Alicia! Oh, I'm so sorry. I hope you are all right?'

'Perfectly. It was just the sudden shock.'

'It was so careless of me. I should have looked where I was going. It was that awkward packet.' She stooped to retrieve it.

Alicia was straightening her bonnet and smoothing her dress. 'It's surprising what little things can do.'

'Let me take you to Mrs Sumerbee's coffee house.'

'That is very kind. Thank goodness it was never turned into a tavern.'

'Indeed. Let us go. We both could do with a drink to settle us down, and it will give us a chance to catch up on any news.'

In a few minutes they were comfortably seated in an alcove in the coffee house. A teenage girl, neatly dressed to Mrs Sumerbee's strict standards, took their order and once she had gone they started to exchange news.

'How are you coping on your own?' asked Sarah.

'Very well, thank you.'

'I must say, you appear to be blooming.'

Alicia smiled. 'I think it must be the independence.'

'Doesn't running a business worry you?'

'Not really, though I must admit that the responsibility does weigh a bit heavy at times. Your father has been helpful on the few occasions I have needed advice.'

'I'm so glad he has been of assistance.'

Alicia wondered how glad Sarah would be if she knew of the true relationship that existed between her father and her friend.

Good coffee with a pungent aroma was served to them with a small slice of parkin.

'I'm surprised Dina isn't with you today,' said Alicia as she stirred her coffee.

'She's gone to see Rowan's mother.'

'She's still sweet on him then?'

'Oh, yes.'

'Doesn't she worry when he's away with the whale-ship?'

'I think so, but she makes light of it.'

'I thought your father was opposed to the relationship?'

'He is or was – I'm not sure which.'

'Was?' Alicia's curiosity had been aroused by Sarah's statement.

'Well, Father's mood seems to have mellowed a little recently, and he has indicated that when Rowan returns he might find him a job ashore within the firm.' Sarah gave a little chuckle and leaned forward as if implying that what she was about to say was in confidence. 'Dina and I wonder if he has a lady friend somewhere – it might account for this softening of his attitude.'

'Does he have the same opinion of Ryan Bennett?'

Sarah laughed. 'Oh, no. He took to Ryan immediately, but you know Father's attitude – anyone with position or money is automatically all right. If they have both then they are more than all right.'

Alicia smiled at the inference. 'Then you are lucky. How is Ryan, by the way?'

'He's well and busy. Wants to build up a trading firm locally and has got a start transporting stone from Aislaby to Whitby for shipment to London.'

'Has he a partner, someone local who would be able to advise of local possibilities? It would seem the sensible thing to do.'

'Not that I know of. He has never said anything and I'm sure he would have told me if he had.'

'You are that close then?'

Sarah coloured a little.

'No need to answer that,' put in Alicia quickly with a smile.' I can see you are. I'm so pleased for you, Sarah. Do you see a lot of each other?'

'Whenever we can but I'm going to miss him for three weeks. He's going to London the day after tomorrow to tidy up some of his aunt's affairs that were left pending when she moved to Whitby.'

Alicia felt a strong sense of satisfaction. She had gained the information that she wanted quite by accident. Fate had indeed delivered Ben Coulson into her hands.

Chapter Twenty

When they parted outside the coffee house Alicia did not go straight home as she had intended but in the direction of her office. As she walked along the quay, opposite the building from which the business of Campion's was conducted, she kept a sharp lookout for the two boys she had employed before.

Spotting them, she called out as they started to play chase around a large stack of crates waiting to be loaded on a nearby ship for the London market. They pulled up sharp on hearing their names called by a lady instead of the curses often flung their way by sailors and labourers working the ships. They looked around and, seeing Alicia, shot each other a querying glance. Then, as one, they raced to her.

'You called, miss?'

'Yes. Do you want to earn another coin?'

'Same job, miss?'

'Yes.'

'Aye, we'll do that.'

'Come with me then.'

She set off and they followed in her wake. When she reached her office she ushered them inside and told them to wait with her clerks until she had written a note.

Within ten minutes they were racing to the Angel, one of them clutching a sealed paper, the other making sure he did not drop the two coins that had been presented to them.

'A note for you, Mr Laskill,' Jed called as Warren entered the Angel.

He guessed what it was before he opened it. He scanned

Alicia's writing and left the inn immediately. The maid who admitted him to the house in Bagdale had, from the haste with which she conducted him to the drawing-room, obviously been told that he was expected.

'Well, Alicia, what errand do you expect of me this time?' he asked coldly as the door was close behind him.

'Oh, come, Warren, don't be like that.'

'I hear nothing from you for nearly two weeks and then you expect me to come running like a little lap dog? And all without reward.'

'Have I said there will be no reward?' Alicia said coyly. She knew very well what he was hinting at, and though she did not want to go that far with him, she realised she may have to if she was to achieve her revenge on Ben.

'No, but I . . .' He was almost about to tell what he had seen but drew back. 'The last time I was here you were in some haste to be rid of me. Is there someone else?'

She stared at him for a moment and then broke into laughter. 'You think I had a beau to entertain? It was a business appointment, Warren. I didn't want you to know who was coming because then you might have guessed what we were going to discuss and it has to remain a secret for a while yet.'

Warren bit his lip. An element of doubt nagged at him, yet she sounded so plausible. Maybe he was over-reacting to what he had seen and had put two and two together and made five.

'Come here and sit beside me,' she cajoled.

He did as he was bidden and sat beside her on the sofa. She slid her hand into his. 'Don't be so suspicious, Warren. Suspicion is generally unfounded and can play havoc with good judgement. I think a lot of you, Warren. We have been friends for a long time and I know we both have Ben's welfare at heart.'

'I'm sorry, Alicia,' he said. 'Forget that I ever doubted you.'

'You are forgiven.' She rubbed his fingers. 'This could be a long night,' she said, and saw that Warren had not missed the note of enticement she had put into her voice. She met the anticipation in his eyes and, leaning forward, brushed his lips with hers. She rose from the sofa slowly, letting her gaze make the suggestion.

He followed her to the door.

'Was that reward satisfactory?' she asked as they lay side by side in her bed.

'I will do any task you want if that is to be the pay.'

'There *is* something I want you to do . . .'

'I thought there must be when I got your note.'

'We failed to help Ben last time. I know of something else that might bring him more profit than transporting stone.'

'And what is that?'

'This must remain a secret between us. You merely have to see that he gets the information by whatever means you choose.'

'Very well, what is it?'

'There is a warehouse in Hull in which there is a big consignment of wine. If Ben purchases it and sells it on, he will make a handsome profit.'

Warren sat up and turned to lean on one elbow so that he could look at her. 'How do you know about this?'

'That needn't concern you. All you need to know is that it is there. I will tell you the location of the warehouse and how payment for it should be made. We'll need to use an account that cannot be traced to me, and that will be that. But you must tell Ben that if he is to take advantage of this he will have to act quickly, certainly within the next four days. I know other people who would like the wine.'

'If it belongs to you, why aren't you selling it?'

'That would cut across the trade arrangement that Campion's and Coulson's have and I don't want anything to upset it. That is another reason for this secrecy.'

'Then why did you buy it in the first place?'

'Because I saw it would help Ben.'

'And is that all?'

'You are getting suspicious, Warren. You know what I told you.' Alicia reached out and pulled him to her. 'Forget it now. There are other things to occupy us.'

The following day Warren called on Ben and was thankful when he found him at home. Betsy had remembered the instructions Ruth had given her and had enquired if Mr Coulson was at home to receive Mr Laskill. Informed that he was, she had shown Warren into the drawing-room.

'It must be urgent to bring you here, and so early,' said Ben on greeting his friend. 'Where were you last night? We expected you at the Angel.'

'I had some business that prevented me from coming. Did you have a good night?'

'Yes. I bluffed and did well out of them. It's not the same when I haven't you pitted against me, though.'

'Thanks for the compliment.'

Ben had expected a smile but Warren's expression remained serious. 'Why so solemn?' he asked.

'I'm concerned for you, Ben. You can't go on hoping to make a living from cards. You missed out on moving that stone. I hear Ryan Bennett got it and is doing rather well. That could have been you, Ben.'

'This sounds as though you have another scheme in which you think I could be interested?'

'I have, but it will need prompt action.'

'I'm listening.'

'I heard a rumour about a large consignment of wine for sale in a warehouse in Hull. Thinking of you, I decided to find out more.'

'And you did?'

'Of course. This is a very good vintage and a quick sale is wanted so it's going at a low price.'

'Who is selling?'

'That is something I failed to learn but the sale is to be conducted through an agent in Hull and the money placed in a bank account in the town. That way the seller remains anonymous.'

When Warren revealed the grower, the number of bottles and the price, Ben gasped. 'Are you sure you've got that right?'

'Pretty sure. But you can always go to Hull and check.'

'If that wine is genuine it is a very good price indeed, but even so I haven't the money to buy that quantity.'

'Ben, with the Coulson name you'd be able to borrow and I'm sure it wouldn't be for long. You'll sell that wine in no time, probably wouldn't even have to move it from Hull.'

He looked thoughtful. This was a good opportunity. If only Ryan had been here he could have put him on to it, but he wasn't. He hadn't the authority to complete a deal such as this. It needed Ryan's stamp of authority. But what if he made the purchase on his own account? If Warren was right, it was a chance not to be missed and Ben had no doubt he could borrow to finance the deal.

'I was told that if I was interested I would have to be quick. The sale has to be completed within the next four days so you can't dawdle over your decision.'

'It is very tempting,' pondered Ben.

'You can't take it on my say so. Why don't you go and see it?'

He looked thoughtful. 'Will you come with me?'

'If you think I'll be of any use. I like a glass of wine but I'm no connoisseur.'

'You'd be company on the ride, and your advice would be useful.'

'All right, I'll come.'

'If I decide to go, I'll hire horses from the White Horse and meet you there at half-past eight in the morning. If I'm not going, I'll leave word for you at the Angel. Will you be there tonight?'

'Yes. I take it you won't be?'

'No. Not tonight.'

The door opened and Ruth came in. 'Hello, Warren.'

'Hello, Ruth.' He jumped to his feet. 'It is good to see you. I trust you are well?'

'Very well, thank you. If I am not interrupting anything, may I offer you a cup of chocolate?'

'That is very kind of you, Ruth, but I must be away. We have finished. No doubt Ben will tell you my reason for being here. Encourage him to think seriously about what I have told him.'

She gave him a puzzled look but did not hold him back with further questions. When Ben returned to the drawing-room after seeing Warren out of the house, he found his wife sitting down.

'Well?' she asked as he sat down on the sofa beside her.

He explained what Warren had told him.

'You can't act without Ryan,' Ruth pointed out.

'That's true but this chance will have gone by the time he returns.'

'Can you act on your own or does your agreement with him preclude that?'

'We have no written agreement. We trust each other not to act alone if the other is available to discuss whatever chance comes along, but Ryan isn't here so I see no reason why I cannot act on my own account. I would not hold it against him if he did so when I wasn't here.'

'Well, then, act on Warren's information.'

'I'll have to borrow to do it.'

'From what you tell me it sounds a good proposition, but you'll have to go to Hull. Why not go to see Mr Chapman now, and then when you see this wine you will have the finance in place and can complete the transaction. If you decide against buying it, you will have lost nothing and can cancel the loan when you return. I don't see that you have anything to lose, and you have a lot to gain.'

'You are very wise.' He leaned close and kissed her. 'And lovely, and I love you very much.'

The following morning Ben was waiting at the White Horse with two horses already saddled when Warren arrived.

'Not late, am I?' he gasped.

'No, it's me who's early. Thinking about your proposition gave me a disturbed night so I was up with the sun.'

'So you're keen on this?'

'Yes. Everything is in place if I decide to buy when I see the wine.'

'Good. Let's away.'

The two friends swung into the saddles and once out of Whitby put their horses into a steady pace that covered the miles without being too tiring.

They were thankful that the weather, though not particularly sunny, was fine. They kept to the east of the great expanse of moorland but swung around the west side of Scarborough beyond which they found the track leading south across the vast, undulating tract of farmland that made up the Yorkshire Wolds. Cattle grazed, birds sang, rustling sounds came from hedgerows. All seemed well with the world. The tranquillity that lay across the landscape seeped into them and they relaxed in the saddle, allowing their conversation to drift around many topics without once mentioning the mission they were on. Each kept their thoughts about that to themself, each wanting it to succeed for different reasons yet each intent on Ben's welfare.

They broke their ride after a couple of hours to take refreshments at a wayside inn, but did not linger long. When they emerged from the inn they were pleased to find that their horses had been well taken care of and, like themselves, seemed eager to be on their way.

Reaching Hull, their enquiries soon led them to the area in which they were likely to find the warehouse. They swung from their saddles and secured the horses. The street was quiet and a sombre atmosphere emanated from the brick buildings. Three men were rolling barrels from a warehouse further along the street and loading them on to a flat cart.

Warren glanced around. 'Over here,' he said, indicating a green-painted door on the opposite side of the street.

They found the door unlocked and, stepping through it,

emerged into a large square yard. Spotting an open door at the far side, they hurried across the cobblestones. Warren rapped on the door and a few moments later a man emerged. He was tall and broad with it. He was in his shirtsleeves which, rolled up, revealed muscular arms. His hair, though cut to a reasonable length, was ill-kempt. He was heavy-jowled and glared at them from suspicious dark eyes.

'What y'want?' he growled. Though they were travel-stained these two young men, confronting him were too well-dressed for his liking. What right had they to be in this part of Hull?

'I was told I could collect a key here to the warehouse on the opposite side of the road,' said Warren.

'Where y'from?' His eyes flitted from one to the other.

'Whitby,' returned Warren.

The man grunted and without further explanation walked back into the building. Warren shrugged his shoulders in response to Ben's querying glance. A few moments later the man reappeared with a large key in his enormous hand. He was clearly not inclined to hand it to them but growled, 'Follow me.'

The two friends padded along in his wake without attempting to engage him in conversation. Warren knew he must be under instructions and did not want to question the man for he knew that Alicia must have had a hand in them. Ben wondered from whom Warren had received his instructions, and who it was who had told this man to expect a visit from someone interested in the wine. He was clearly not prepared to speak of it.

The lock to the warehouse turned smoothly. Though gloomy and dank inside, there was sufficient light from the windows high in the walls to enable them to pick their way to an area stacked with cases.

'This is what y've come to see.' Even now the watchman's tone did not exude any desire to be friendly.

Ben nodded and walked around the stack doing a quick mental estimate of how many crates there were. With twelve bottles to a case there was a considerable amount of wine here.

'Some barrels of the same over there,' growled the man.

Ben saw there were twenty barrels stored against a wall.

'This case is open,' pointed out Warren.

'I'm tasting before buying,' said Ben, coming to join him.

Warren carefully extracted a bottle and examined the label, being particular not to disturb the wine. He handed the bottle to Ben who read the label carefully.

'This should be a good wine,' he commented.

''ere.'

They turned to see the man thrusting two glasses at them. They weren't the ideal shape or quality in which to assess a wine of this calibre, but they would make it possible to have a taste.

Ben took the glasses and Warren very carefully uncorked a bottle. He poured them a taste. They both savoured it respectfully.

Ben gave a nod of satisfaction and then, as if to confirm his assessment, took another sip. 'Yes,' he said, and looked at Warren.

He took another taste and nodded his agreement, eyes widening with excitement as he anticipated what Ben was about to say.

'It's too good a chance to miss.'

'It is at the price quoted,' approved Warren.

Ben looked at the man. 'I'm going to buy this wine. I understand you can tell me who I must see about that?'

'Aye. Mr Pease in Charlotte Street.'

'Where might that be?'

He gave them quick directions. 'Y'can walk there. Leave y'horses, I'll see them right.'

Ben eyed him curiously. 'For whom do you work?'

The man glared at him as if astounded that he should be asked such a question. 'Anyone. I ask no questions about them so I can tell nay lies. Y'd be advised to do the same.' He walked away. Back in the street he merely said, 'That way,' and pointed to the left.

As they walked to Charlotte Street, Ben said, 'What do you make of that?'

Warren shrugged his shoulders. Then he gave a little laugh. 'I wouldn't bother about it, I reckon you've got a bargain. You'll make a nice profit when you sell that wine.'

'I'll have to return to do that. Though there is no hurry, I may as well sell it as soon as possible and have the proceeds in my pocket, or rather my bank.'

The transfer of the money was soon arranged with Mr Pease and they sought his advice on where to stay for the night.

'I recommend the Cross Keys in the Market Place,' he said. 'It is one of our leading coaching inns and has stabling for over forty horses. You'll be well looked after there.'

So it proved. They had comfortable rooms, ate well and slept soundly, though Ben lay awake for a while considering his purchase and what it would mean when he had sold it on. His financial situation would be eased and he would not then need Ryan's generous support, which he felt would make for an easier relationship between them.

They left Hull early the next morning, and, with Ben concerned about Ruth, made good progress. They rode straight to the White Horse in Church Street and, after settling the hire of the horses, left the inn. When they reached the corner of Grape Lane they stopped.

'Warren, I am indeed grateful for your help. Thank you for your concern about my welfare. You are a true friend. I'll not forget what you have done.' Ben held out his hand. There was the warmth of long friendship in the grip they exchanged.

Within a few minutes Ben was in the house in Grape Lane, and after Ruth's mother had discreetly left them he was enquiring with concern about his wife's health.

Ruth laughed at the worry on his face and smoothed away the furrows on his brow with a soft touch of her fingertips. 'I'm in good health. The baby is not troubling me yet. I hope you weren't worrying all the time you were away? Now tell me all about it. Was it worthwhile?'

He took her hands and led her to the sofa. They sat down and he related with enthusiasm his trip to Hull and its results.

'Oh, I'm so pleased for you,' cried Ruth. 'When will you make the sale?'

'As soon as possible! I'd like to make it next week if it is all right to leave you again?'

'Of course it is. I'll come here, Mother will be pleased to have me. Take as long as you need. Get the best deal you can.'

A week later Ben set out for Hull again. He had checked with Mr Chapman that the money had been taken care of and hoped that when he returned to Whitby he would have repaid the loan and be left with a handsome profit.

Reaching the town, he rode straight to the Cross Keys where he was recognised by the landlord as one of the two young men who had stayed there the previous week and had spent well. He welcomed Ben with bonhomie and allocated him one of the best rooms. The landlord's friendly disposition encouraged Ben to make enquiries about the wine merchants in the town.

The next day, armed with the names of three of them and directions that would lead him to their offices, he left the Cross Keys.

The first name he chose was Carberry & Son in Nelson Street. When he was shown into the office of Mr Harland Carberry he found himself facing a tall, well-built and imposing man in his early-fifties who stood in front of his desk with a hostile glare.

He spoke first, not giving Ben time to say a word. 'My clerk tells me you are Ben Coulson from Whitby. Are you related to Sam Coulson?' His voice was charged with rancour.

Taken aback, Ben almost reeled and could only nod.

'Then get out. Out! And damn your father for what he did to me.' He saw the amazement on Ben's face and knew that this young man did not know to what he was referring. 'Went back on his word, he did. Lost me a lot of money and the

372

goodwill of several traders. And all for his own ends. Now, out!'

Ben knew it was no use pursuing the reason for his being there. He left the office and the building without so much as a word. Bemused, he thought about Mr Carberry's attitude which naturally turned his mind to his father. He knew of Sam's ruthless streak in business but had not known it had spread as far as Hull and that it was of such proportions that it had resulted in this vitriolic outburst.

He took the note from his pocket and scanned it for the next address. He hoped he would receive a better reception here than the one he had just experienced. He found the offices of Girdling & Nephew in Whitefriargate. A little apprehensive, he was shown into Mr William Girdling's office and faced a small, quiet-spoken man, who welcomed him with a smile and made no queries about his origins.

'I am pleased to meet you, Mr Coulson.' His handshake was friendly. 'This is my nephew Peter.'

Ben judged him to be of about his own age. His firm handshake matched that of his uncle. Though Ben felt himself under scrutiny, there was friendliness in the light blue eyes. Ben relaxed.

'Do sit down, Mr Coulson, and tell us why you are here?'

He took a chair on the opposite side of the desk from the uncle and nephew, quickly explaining that he had recently bought a quantity of wine that was at present sitting in a warehouse in Hull, and was looking to sell it.

'And what wine might this be, Mr Coulson?'

'Spanish, from the House of Juan Calatrava.'

A slight expression of surprise crossed Peter's face. 'I think we could be interested in that, don't you, Uncle?'

'Indeed I think we might. But, Mr Coulson, we should want to see it first.'

'Of course,' he agreed. 'It can be viewed whenever you like.'

Uncle and nephew exchanged glances and a slight nod of Peter's head led to his uncle saying, 'There is no time like the present.' He rose from his chair and the two younger men followed suit.

Within twenty minutes they were being admitted to the warehouse. Glasses were produced, a bottle uncorked, and after sampling it both the Girdlings agreed that it was in prime condition.

'Then you are interested in taking it?' said Ben, pleased that he was on the verge of a sale.

Mr Girdling raised his hands in a gesture to prevent their negotiations going further for now. 'We want to examine the consignment first.' He turned to the man who had admitted them to the warehouse. 'Will you move that row of cases?'

The man glowered at the unexpected work that was being thrust upon him. Reluctantly he started to move the cases that had been indicated.

William Girdling continued to direct the removal of more cases. Ben wondered why he was doing this but kept his question to himself.

'All right, that will do,' said William, having received a signal from his nephew.

Peter opened one of the cases and drew out a bottle which he examined carefully. He passed it to his uncle who also examined it with care. As he was doing so his nephew opened a second case and withdrew another bottle. Uncle and nephew went through the same procedure with five more cases picked at random from those that had been moved. They had set the bottles they had removed aside and now proceeded to open each one in turn and sample them. They kept their expression neutral and when they had finished the elder Girdling handed Ben a glass. 'Will you please sample each of those bottles?'

Mystified, Ben took the glass and poured and tasted a sample from each in turn. The first matched the original bottle they had opened, but the second made him look up sharply and he saw that both men were watching him intently. Shocked at the taste, Ben passed quickly to the other open bottles and was

374

horrified when he tasted their contents. His face was a mask of incredulity when he examined the label on the last bottle and saw that it was exactly the same as that on the bottle of their first tasting. He stared at the Girdlings in disbelief.

'I don't understand.' His eyes ran over the stack of cases. How many more of them contained bottles of poor-quality wine under false labels?

'I am afraid, Mr Coulson, that we will not be interested in that wine, and frankly I don't know who will be.'

'Mr Girdling, I assure you I did not know. I only bought this wine recently on the recommendation of a friend.'

'And so you did not examine it as we did?'

'No. I tried a bottle out of that case.' He indicated the one that had been open when they had arrived.

'No doubt you were directed to that one when you arrived to buy?'

'Yes.'

'I've seen this trick played before, but whoever set this up went to a lot of pains to have all the bottles labelled the same. Mr Coulson, you have been the victim of gross deception. If I were you, I would see the friend who directed you here. If he is answerable then he is no friend, but maybe he did not know. You will have to be the judge of that.'

'With your experience, tell me, is there no place I can get rid of this wine?'

Peter Girdling gave a sad shake of his head. 'I'm afraid not. Most of the wine is only worth tipping down the drains. That is normally what would have happened to it at the place of origin. Someone has gone to a great deal of trouble to set this up. I don't cast any aspersion on your friend, but if you have enemies, look there. I am sorry to tell you this, for no doubt you will have lost a great deal of money. The wine we first sampled was not cheap.'

Ben's lips were tight. He felt numb. His world was shattering around him. Then anger welled in him. He swung round on the warehouse man who had stood by saying nothing, for he deemed it his place only to answer questions. 'Who hired you?' Ben snapped.

'I comes with the warehouse and only do as I'm told,' the man growled back.

'Who hired you to see to this wine?'

'I dunno. Wine comes and I get a message to let anyone see it who wants to see it. And that's what I do.'

'Who gave you those orders?'

'A note came with the wine.'

'Let me see it.'

'I ain't got it, threw it away.'

Ben turned from him in exasperation. 'Mr Girdling, I'm sorry that you and your nephew have been troubled.'

'My advice to you, Mr Coulson, is to come away with us now. There will only be more heartache and trouble for you here. Tell this man to pour all that wine away. If you wish, I will instruct him what to do.'

'Please do, Mr Girdling. I feel so shattered I can't face doing so.'

'As I thought.' He gave Ben a sympathetic pat on the arm and turned to the warehouse man instructing him in firm terms as to what he had to do, and leaving no doubt in the man's mind that if he did not do exactly what he had been told he would be in serious trouble. Mr Girdling did not want any of this wine coming on to the market, not even illicitly, for it would damage the reputation of those engaged in Hull's wine trade. He pointed out to the warehouse man that he would hear if any of this wine were being sold. In payment the man was told he could keep three bottles of the best wine and that seemed to satisfy him.

'Come, Mr Coulson, try and forget what is going to happen here and then seek out the reason it has happened.'

It was late-afternoon when Ben reached Whitby the following day but he had no hesitation in riding straight to Warren's house on Cliff Street.

The coming confrontation with his friend had been on his mind ever since he had left the Girdlings; it had kept him awake for a considerable time but in spite of the lost hours of sleep he was up early, anxious to be on his way. Thoughts of Warren troubled him. Had his friend known of the deceit? If so why had he lured Ben into this calamity? For calamity it was. He could not repay the bank loan and had little prospect of being able to do so now. Had he been lured into this debt on purpose? He could think of no one who would do it yet it had been done and Warren was implicated. Where had his friend received his information? That was the vital question.

He swung from the saddle and in a few moments was hammering the brass knocker. The door opened to reveal a maid, startled by the impatient pounding.

'Is Mr Laskill in?' snarled Ben.

The girl was taken aback not only by the noise but also by the dust-covered person who stood before her. For a moment she did not recognise Ben then, realising who he was, spluttered, 'Er, yes, sir.'

With that Ben strode past her. He glanced at her, query in his eyes.

'There, sir.' She indicated the door to the right.

He flung it open without ceremony and strode in.

Startled by the sudden intrusion, Warren, who was reading a book, sprang to his feet. 'Ben!' he gasped, surprised to see his friend's dishevelled appearance. 'You look as if you've ridden hard.'

'I have,' he snapped. 'What do you know of that wine I bought?'

Warren looked mystified. 'What do you mean?'

'I've just ridden from Hull. I was there yesterday trying to sell it.' He glared at his friend. 'Do you know where it is now? Down the drains!'

Warren knitted his forehead in puzzlement. 'What do you mean? Was there an accident?'

'Accident be damned!'

'Well, what happened?'

'The wine was rubbish.'

'Rubbish? That wasn't rubbish we tasted.'

'No, it wasn't, but most of the rest was and I want to hear what you knew about it.'

'Ben, calm yourself. I don't understand what you are getting at. Sit down and tell me everything?'

Ben glared at Warren and reluctantly sat down. His friend appeared to be puzzled, or was he merely good at playacting? Ben related his story. Warren listened carefully without interruption. As the story unfolded a chill struck at his heart. Had Alicia purposely given him wrong information? If she had, it looked as if she had deliberately set up this deception. She had sworn she wanted to help Ben, but she had also said that he should never know that she was behind it. She had said that it was time to forget the past. But had she? Or had she used him to get at Ben?

He finished his story and said, 'Warren, I want to know where you got that information about the wine?'

His mind raced. He could not tell Ben about Alicia. He did not know where she had got her information about the wine, she would not tell him. She might be just as innocent as he was, though Ben would not think so.

'I overheard two strangers talking when I was in Scarborough,' he lied. 'One of them showed particular interest and that is why I thought you should move quickly rather than miss what sounded like a good opportunity.'

'Instead I've damned well made things worse. I now owe the bank for an outlay that has just gone down Hull's drains. Could you identify these men you heard talking?'

Warren made a gesture of hopelessness with his hands. 'I'm afraid not. They could have been from anywhere.'

'You weren't involved any more than that?' Ben looked at him closely.

'Would I deliberately put you in this position? We've been friends all our lives. I thought I was helping you. Believe me,

378

if I had known . . .' Warren punched his fist into the palm of his hand and cursed through tight lips. 'Why didn't I think to examine the other cases?'

Ben saw that his friend's attitude was genuine. 'I should have thought of it too, so don't blame yourself.' He rose to his feet. 'I'd better break the news to Ruth.'

'Can't you hold that back, at least for a while?'

Ben gave a shake of his head. 'She'll want to know all about it and will obviously wish to know what profit I have made. I can't hold anything back from her.'

Ben was in a thoughtful mood as rode his horse across the bridge into Church Street where he turned into the yard of the White Horse. With a stableman taking over the horse, he settled the hiring fee and hurried the short distance to Grape Lane.

Ruth and his in-laws were pleased to see him back. Not wanting Gideon and Georgina to know the true outcome of his visit to Hull, he said that his trip had been successful. He declined their invitation to stay, saying that he would rather get home and remove the stains of travel before he relaxed over a meal.

'Well?' said Ruth when they left the house. 'Now you can tell me how it really went.'

'Was it so obvious that all was not well?' he asked with concern.

'Only to me, love. I know you better than Mother and Father.'

'It was a disaster, Ruth.'

'What happened?' She slipped her hand into his, sensing that he was going to need comfort and support.

'Wait until we get home, it will be easier to talk there. It's not far.'

She respected his silence, realising that he was trying to sort out in his mind the best way of telling her what had happened.

Reaching their home, she did not press him immediately for an explanation but led him to their room where she poured water from the ewer into a bowl for him to wash in. As he was doing so she laid out fresh clothes for him and then went to instruct Betsy to prepare something for them. After that she returned to their room where he was finishing dressing.

'Now you can tell me,' she said, sitting down on the edge of the bed.

Ben made an emotional explanation of what had happened in Hull. Cold fingers seemed to close round Ruth's heart. This was a disaster they did not need. Their position now was untenable. They faced poverty. They could go back to her mother and father, but that would not answer their financial problem. She knew her father would offer some money to help, but that, even with the little they could realise on the sale of this house, would not be enough to repay the bank, and no doubt when Mr Chapman heard of the outcome in Hull he would call in the debt.

'Oh, Ben, what are we going to do?'

Chapter Twenty-one

Warren waited a few minutes after Ben had gone; he did not want his friend to see him leaving the house. They were minutes that brought Warren's anger to near boiling point. The question that had whirled in his brain while Ben had been telling him of events in Hull reasserted itself. Could Alicia really have set this up? There was only one way to find out.

Fury dogged his every step between Cliff Street and Bagdale; rage resounded in every rap he made with the doorknocker.

Wondering who could be seeking admittance in such a manner, the maid was wide-eyed when she opened the door. Warren strode in without ceremony.

'Where is your mistress?' he demanded brusquely.

The maid could only splutter 'In there' as she indicated the drawing-room door.

Warren swung round and was at it in six strides. He flung it open with such force that it sprang shut behind him of its own accord.

'What the devil are you up to?' he demanded.

Alicia, having heard the unusual hammering on the knocker, was already on her feet. At the sight of Warren's fury she drew herself up in defiance. She ignored his question and let her gaze sweep over him in cold contempt. 'What do you mean by bursting in here like this?'

'You played me for a fool,' he hissed.

'What are you talking about?' she asked imperiously. She swung round and sat down, still holding herself erect.

'Ben!'

'Ben? What has he to do with this?'

'You know full well.'

In the slight pause that followed the tension in the room reached an unbearable level.

'Well?' she demanded, wanting him to disclose what had happened and how much of it he attributed to her.

'You plied me with information to pass to Ben, knowing that if he followed it he would face ruin.'

Alicia gave a little smile of satisfaction. 'So he did, did he? Then more fool him.'

A cold heavy lump under his heart, Warren stared at her. In the back of his mind he had hoped that he was wrong about Alicia, but here she was admitting it. His temper snapped. He stepped closer and glowered down at her. 'You bitch! You've ruined a good man and used me to do it. I see now that your attempt to get him to invest in hauling that stone was only to get him to trust anything I told him.'

'And blinded by the personal favours I granted you, you'd fall for anything I told you and do anything I asked.'

Warren's lips set in a grim line at her taunt. He raised one hand as if to strike her.

She met his angry gaze without flinching. 'Hit me then,' she said with a cold challenge that carried the threat of untold consequences should he do so. He let his arm drop. 'Weakling,' she sneered. 'And you'll do nothing about what you know.'

'I'll tell Ben,' he said quietly, not really knowing if that was the best thing to do.

'You tell him and I'll reveal a lot about you to your friends. Ralph North will revel in it. You'll be the butt of their jokes whenever you show yourself in the Angel. You wouldn't want them to know the things I could tell them.'

'Made-up lies,' he countered.

She gave a little shrug of her shoulders. 'And who are they most likely believe? Me? You? They'll readily latch on to a bit of scandal and believe there is no smoke without fire. And those sorts of rumours grow until there'll be no telling what you've been up to.'

'And what if I tell Ben about you and his father? Don't deny it, I saw Sam Coulson visit you the night you wanted me out of the house so quickly. I wondered why and waited to see.' Even as he made the threat he sensed it would be hopeless. The only satisfaction he received was a momentary flash of doubt in her eyes, but it was gone so quickly he could have been mistaken.

Alicia laughed in his face. 'Go ahead if you want those stories about you to go even further *and* you want to be ruined by Sam. You've seen what he did to Gideon Holmes, and what he has done to other people who have crossed him. He could do it to you.'

Warren knew he was defeated. He looked away.

Alicia gave another sneer of contempt. 'Don't come here with any of your threats again. In fact, don't come here at all Now get out!'

'Bitch! Bitch!' He swung on his heel and left the room, slamming the door behind him, more angry at himself now for being duped so easily.

Alicia sat back in her chair smiling to herself, euphoria at having succeeded spreading through her. She needed some more information now to be absolutely sure of the path she wanted to follow.

The next day she sought an interview with Mr Chapman at his bank. She put on her most charming and beguiling manner when she sat down opposite him.

'I am thinking about investing in a consignment of wine that I have learned is being sold in Hull, but it will require a considerable loan for me to do so.'

'I should be pleased to do business with you, Miss Campion, though I will need more details before I commit myself.'

'Of course, Mr Chapman. I will get them and visit you again if the terms of the sale and the wine are to my liking. This was just an exploratory visit to make sure I could come to you if necessary.'

'I will look forward to a further visit, and might I say that any time you want to do business, I shall only be too glad to listen.'

'That's very kind of you.'

'It's strange that you should come enquiring about a loan to buy wine in Hull. I had a similar request only recently.'

'Oh, my goodness. I wonder if it is the same wine?'

'I wouldn't know, Miss Campion. I made the loan available but I don't know if the wine has been purchased. I have not had any demand note for the transfer of the money yet. If it is the same wine and it is still available, you may have to move quickly if you still want it. But I will warn you, if it is, you will need a considerable loan.'

'Thank you for that advice, Mr Chapman.' Feeling exulted by what she had learned, and allowing him to feel flattered by her charm, Alicia let the conversation drift awhile before taking her leave.

On her way home she called at the Coulsons' residence and was pleased to find Sarah and Dina at home. At one point she subtly steered the course of the conversation to Ben.

'I saw Ruth yesterday,' replied Sarah. 'He seems to be well from what she told me. She said he was away in Hull on business, she didn't say what but was hoping everything would go well as they've had a hard time since he gave up fishing with Captain Holmes.'

'I hope he succeeds then. When is the baby due?'

'About another six weeks. Ruth is hoping it is a son who will bring about a reconciliation between Ben and his father.'

Alicia felt a tremor run through her at that though she contained her alarm in an outward expression of acceptance of this possibility. It was something she hadn't envisaged. If this happened it would bring Ben back into his father's favour and plans of hers that were nearing fruition would be for naught. Something would have to be done about it and there was only one thing to do. She curbed her impatience to leave, only doing so when she deemed etiquette would be satisfied.

Alicia had intended going straight home from Bagdale but instead she made for the bridge, crossed the river and went straight to Coulson's offices. On making her request, she was shown to Sam's office.

He rose straight to his feet when she walked in and came from behind his desk to greet her. He took her hands in his and kissed her on the cheek. 'Is this business or pleasure, my dear?'

'A visit that I hope will lead to pleasure,' she replied with a suggestive lowering of in her eyelids. 'Come tonight.'

'I need no second invitation.'

'Sam, you remember you asked me to marry you previously, and I said later. Well, the waiting time is over. We can marry as soon as possible.'

They were lying on their backs, side by side, each reliving in their own mind what had just taken place between them.

At her words, Sam sprang up and twisted over so that he could look down at her. 'You mean that?' he asked. Every night he could share a bed with this irresistible young woman?

Her arms slid round his neck and she looked into his eyes. 'Yes.' She pulled him slowly to her, her body inviting. Their lips met and held.

It was some time later that he said, 'You have made me a very happy man.'

Their hunger sated, Alicia took up talk of their wedding and soon had Sam twisted round her little finger and agreeing to a quiet ceremony as soon as possible.

'I have no relations here, and there really are no guests I want to invite,' she pointed out.

'Well then, I shall keep my guests to family; that means Sarah and Dina. Eric is away with the whale-ships.' Sam gave a little chuckle. 'He'll get a surprise when he returns but he won't be bothered. All he can think about is sailing to the Arctic again.'

'What about Ben?' she asked tentatively.

'No! I kicked him out after what he did to you and he stays

out. He's no longer one of my family.' Sam laughed. 'Just as well he jilted you otherwise I wouldn't have got you.' He grabbed her and they rolled together, their laughter sealing a joyous future. Finally Sam flopped on to his back, one arm still around her as she snuggled close.

'What's so funny?' she asked.

He chuckled, 'Well, I had designs on your father's firm and all that went with it. I thought that if Martin married you, I would get my hands on it.'

'Because Father had no sons? And he agreed to the marriage because you paid his debt.'

Detecting no resentment in her voice he went on, 'Correct, but Martin was lost.'

'And you replaced him with Ben who forestalled you.'

'And hurt you.'

'So you saw the only way left was to offer to marry me and hope that I would accept?'

'As you have.'

'I could change my mind.' A teasing smile appeared on her lips.

'But you won't because I agreed to the conditions you laid down.'

She started to chuckle.

'What's amusing you?'

'You set out to get the Campion enterprises . . . well, I'll admit that my original intention was to get Coulson's by agreeing to marry you. But now I have fallen in love with you and . . . !' She left him to draw his own conclusion.

He turned to face her. 'You are of more importance to me than Campion's.'

Alicia gave him a beguiling smile. 'Then, if we are of the same mind, we should amalgamate both firms and that way we will both have achieved our objective.'

'Brilliant!' Sam kissed her but while she accepted his gesture she pulled away quickly. He looked surprised.

'But, Sam Coulson, if I agree to this we must be equal

partners, and I must have an equal say in running the business. We must share the decision-making, one not acting without the other. And I want proper partnership documents drawing up.'

'Of course, my love. It is the only sensible way. We both get what we want. I'll see to it . . .'

'No, Sam, 'she interrupted quickly '*We* will see to it.'

He gave a wry smile. 'All right, we'll start on it as soon as we are married.'

They kissed but this time it lingered as a seal was set on their whole future.

Eyebrows were raised, heads came together and tongues clacked when it became known that Sam Coulson and Alicia Campion were to marry.

'Old enough to be her father.'

'Could have the pick of anyone her age.'

'What can she see in him?'

'She'll not have a life worth talking about with him.'

'Amalgamation? If this marriage brings that then we're up against a formidable trading organisation.'

'Sam Coulson will rule trade in Whitby.'

'She'll be virtually handing over all her father built up. What on earth would he think?'

When their father told Sarah and Dina, their immediate reaction was shock. They found it hard to curb their protests, but if Alicia was the reason behind Sam's more amiable ways of late, then let him marry her. Besides he had pointed out that it did not mean they would have to leave their home for he would be moving in with Alicia.

Ben returned from a meeting with Ryan regarding the income from the transporting of stone from Aislaby to Whitby to find Ruth in a state of some excitement.

'You look as if you have some news?', he said after her welcoming kiss.

'I've heard that your father is going to be married.'

'What?' Ben was dumbfounded.

'It appears to be true.'

'To whom?'

'Alicia.'

Ben was so stunned that for a moment he could not speak. 'Alicia?' He gave a little shake of his head. 'That can't be true.'

'It is.' From the way she pronounced those two words he knew the veracity of her information.

'Good grief!' He sank on to a chair as if the news had drained all strength from him.

Seeing that he was grappling with this news, Ruth waited a few moments before she spoke. 'Does it bother you, Ben?' she asked tentatively.

He started. Not sure what lay behind her question, he took her hand and said, 'If you mean does it bother me that Alicia is getting married, then no, love, it doesn't. My own position? Well, I suppose at the back of my mind I'd always hoped there would be a reconciliation, but I really think I was resigned to the fact that there never would be and therefore I stood to gain nothing from my father. What concerns me is whether Sarah and Dina be provided for.'

'They've been friendly with Alicia since childhood, surely she would not do anything to harm them?'

Ben gave a little shrug of his shoulders. 'Who knows? She's been running Campion's. Maybe she sees this as a way of getting a grip on Coulson's assets too?'

Any more speculation was interrupted when their maid announced that the Misses Coulson were here.

'Have you heard?' Sarah asked as they came into the room.

'Ruth's just told me,' replied Ben.

'I heard it when I was out,' explained Ruth. 'I couldn't believe it at first but then I met Warren Laskill and he confirmed it.'

'What do you make of it?' asked Ben.

'If it keeps Father in the better mood we've seen lately then I'm all for him getting married,' enthused Dina.

'But what is your position regarding the house?'

'We are staying there. Father is moving in with Alicia. He is signing the house over to us and increasing our allowance,' explained Sarah. 'So we will be all right.'

'Make sure that will still be the case if anything happens to him,' said Ben. 'And get him to safeguard your interests in Coulson's otherwise it could all go to Alicia.'

The wedding took place quietly in the parish church on the cliff top. Ruth and Dina were bridesmaids and Sam asked Ryan Bennett to be the best man, hoping that it would help to draw him into the Coulson fold. When the trading fraternity of Whitby learned that the wedding was going to be a very small affair they lost interest and let speculation and talk die.

But there was one uninvited guest who slipped into the back of the church after everyone involved was in their place and left before the small bridal procession made its way down the aisle and out of the church. No one would ever know that Ben Coulson had witnessed his father's marriage to the girl everyone had once thought would be Mrs Ben Coulson.

When she left the church, her arm linked with Sam's, Alicia felt as bright as the day. She had directed life her way. Ben faced ruin when his debt was called in as inevitably it would be; Sam was hers and together they would form the biggest and most powerful trading company in Whitby and set it upon a course that would embrace wider horizons.

Sam smiled to himself, satisfied that he and Alicia would dominate trading out of Whitby. Expansion into many new commodities would be possible and the finances for that would be in place after his *Water Nymph* returned from the whaling grounds in the Arctic.

They took a honeymoon only a few miles away in Scarborough, but with both their minds on the businesses in Whitby they returned there after five days.

Content after a delicious meal, they were sharing the sofa in the drawing-room on the evening after their return when Sam said, 'I think tomorrow you and I should start examining the assets of both firms and set about consolidating.'

Alicia and Sam were so preoccupied with these arrangements over the next month that they had little thought for any social occasion or for anyone else. Then one day in late-July Alicia was coming down Skinner Street when someone hurried out of Well Close and almost knocked her down. Indignant, she swung round ready to give the person concerned a telling off. The words remained unuttered when she saw Ralph North who she knew was one of the card players at the Angel.

He was already raising his hat in apology. 'I'm so sorry, ma'am . . . Alicia! I apologise, my mind was elsewhere.'

'Ralph.' She adjusted her bonnet which had slid out of place under the impact.

'Are you all right?' he asked with concern.

'Yes, thank you. You must have been well and truly preoccupied not to have seen me.'

'I'm afraid I was, but that is no excuse.'

'You are forgiven,' she said smoothly. In some way the impact and seeing an old friend made her realise that she had been out of touch with everyone and had not been aware of what was happening in Whitby apart from its commercial world. 'If you are going my way, walk with me.'

'It will be my pleasure,' Ralph replied.

She gave him a sweet smile and took his arm. 'Now, Ralph, tell me all that has been happening in Whitby? I'm afraid Sam and I have been too preoccupied with business to know what is happening in the town.'

Ralph stopped and looked at her. 'You've not heard then?'

She had turned to him and from her expression he realised she had not. 'Heard what?' she asked, sensing she was about to be told something of importance.

'Ben and Ruth had a son yesterday.'

Alicia felt a thumping in her chest, leaving her feeling numb. She had forgotten that she had envied Ruth when she first heard she was pregnant. Now, this news drove sharply home what she had felt then. This child should have been hers! She steeled herself. This was no way to be thinking. Time and the world had moved on and her love for Sam had strengthened since then. She composed herself and said calmly, 'I had not heard. Are they both well?'

'I believe so.'

They started to walk again.

'Good. Now what other news have you for me?'

Ralph brought her up to date with Whitby gossip and Alicia felt she was back in a place that had once been her whole life, until she had concentrated on Sam and the business. Now that satisfactory arrangements had been made for the merger, she realised she would be free to participate in society again.

They reached the house in Bagdale and stopped at the gate.

'Thank you, Ralph, for seeing me home and for all the news that you have given me. Tell me one more thing: how did Ben react when he heard that I had married his father?'

'He showed no particular reaction except surprise, but that was momentary. He wished you well and smiled when he realised that you were now his mother-in-law.'

Alicia laughed. 'I never thought of that angle! But I am and he's my son-in-law and this child is my grandson. Who would ever have thought things would turn out this way? Goodbye, Ralph. Next time you see Ben, remind him who I am.'

Ralph stood for a few moments listening to her chuckle as she walked to the door.

Sitting having a cup of tea a little later, Alicia turned over all the news she had learned from Ralph and became curious. He had not mentioned Ben's circumstances. These should be in a precarious state after he had fallen into the trap she had set for him yet Ralph had not uttered one word about that. Was there something he hadn't told her or had he purposely avoided the subject? Or perhaps Mr Chapman hadn't called in the debt yet?

If she had been able to listen in to a certain conversation at that moment she would have had her answer.

*

'Is something wrong?' Ben asked when he walked into the Angel in response to a message from Ryan to meet him there.

He held up his hand in a gesture that warned him to wait a moment. Ryan went to the bar and a few minutes later returned to the alcove in which he had been waiting for Ben. He placed two glasses of whisky on the table. 'One way or another you might need that,' he said as he slid into the seat opposite his friend.

Ben looked at him askance. He had been pondering Ryan's serious expression while he had been buying the spirits.

'I've just come from seeing Mr Chapman,' his partner explained.

Ben's heart skipped a beat, and a cold hand seemed to settle on him. What did Ryan know?

'I went to ask him if there was any alternative way to finance future deals you and I may conduct. We are, as we agreed, putting profits from the present enterprise into a special account but they may not be sufficient if we want to widen our activities considerably. As you know I'm reasonably well-off but it would be better if I did not use my personal account, and although my aunt is rich I do not want to use her money though I know she would be willing. So I asked Mr Chapman if we might overdraw on our present account if the necessity arose. He questioned me more closely and when your name was mentioned his enthusiasm waned and he withdrew somewhat into himself. When I pressed him by asking if there was some obstacle, he suggested that, as he was not at liberty to discuss his customer's contacts with the bank, I should ask you.'

Ben diverted his eyes from Ryan's gaze and looked at his glass. He dampened his lips and took a swig of his whisky.

'Well?' Ryan prompted. He kept any hostility out of his voice. He liked Ben and believed there would be a good explanation, but naturally he wanted to make sure.

Ben explained what had happened while Ryan had been in London. 'I know we had agreed to consult each other on every deal before we went into it, but you were away and this seemed too good an opportunity to miss. I acted independently, borrowing from the bank in my name only so that I would be and am solely responsible for what happened. I thought nothing could go wrong. If it hadn't we both would have benefited but as it is I cannot draw you into this mess.'

'I appreciate your reasons for dealing with matters this way.' Ryan paused, frowned and said, 'It looks to me as though you could have been tricked.'

'But who would want to do that?'

He gave a shrug of his shoulders. 'Warren would have no cause to do so, would he?'

Ben shook his head. 'He gave me the nod about the stone and so far that is proving profitable. Naturally I took the information about the wine as being an equally good tip.'

'Where did he get it?'

'Something he had overheard apparently. He looked into it and thought it genuine.'

Ryan nodded thoughtfully then said, 'Ah well, what's happened has happened. There is nothing we can do about it – no, that's not right, there *is* something we can do about it.'

'I don't see what,' said Ben miserably. 'If Mr Chapman calls in my debt then I am ruined, and he's more than likely to do that now that you have spoken with him about what you have in mind. And I've ruined that too. You'll be better off without me. Take everything over as it stands. I'll just have to face Chapman with the truth and hope he is lenient with me otherwise it could mean a debtor's prison.'

'Does Ruth know of this?'

'Yes.'

'Go home and tell her that the debt has been transferred to someone who will not press for repayment but will accept it when it is possible. That should not cause her any worry.'

'But how can I tell her that when I don't . . .' His voice trailed away. 'You mean, you'll pay it?'

Ryan nodded. 'Yes, then everything will be taken care of. You can repay me as and when you see fit, with no interest.

Without that hanging over us we can concentrate on expanding our joint enterprises.'

Ben stared at him with astonishment charged with gratitude. 'I don't deserve this, Ryan, but I will be ever grateful to you. And from now on I'll not venture into anything without consulting you, even if you are away.'

'Good man.' Ryan stood up. He winked at his partner and went to the bar, returning with two more glasses. After he had sat down he raised his and said, 'Here's to our future.'

Ben acknowledged it with relief in his heart and mind.

'Oh, there is one thing about that repayment I must insist on.' Ryan's gaze was steady on Ben as he took another drink.

In that moment his mind filled with doubts.

'As interest on the loan, you can put in a good word for me with Sarah.'

Relief surged through Ben. 'I don't think there is any need for that. I think my sister's smitten.'

Eager to tell Ruth the good news, Ben hurried home.

'But we will still have that money to pay back,' she pointed out, her brow creased by a worried frown.

'Yes, we will, my love, but it can be done in our own time. It is not as if Ryan is going to call the loan in as Mr Chapman would have done. That would have been an entirely different situation with appalling consequences.'

Ruth relaxed. 'Thank goodness Ryan Bennett came into our lives and that he thinks so highly of Sarah. Do you think they will . . .?'

'I'm sure of it,' broke in Ben, anticipating the rest of her question.

'Then good luck to them.' Ruth pondered a moment and then said, 'Do you think Warren had anything to do with what happened?'

Ben shook his head. 'He had no reason to wish me ill.'

'Did anyone?'

'I can't think of anyone.'

Chapter Twenty-two

'Whale-ship! Whale-ship!' Word spread through Whitby, carried from mouth to mouth, shouted along every street, stirring excitement through the town. The hope and joy of everyone soared. Their men were back after braving the icy Arctic and battling with monsters. They would bring much-needed money to their families to see them through a winter that could be harsh on this north-facing section of the Yorkshire coast.

People left what they were doing, even those who had no direct interest in the men coming home or in the immediate wealth that would be generated from the catch, for everyone in Whitby in some way or other would be touched by the success of the voyages to the Arctic whaling grounds.

Eyes scanned the distance, seeking to identify the ships.

'The *Sunset*!' The name came from one mouth but immediately flowed like rushing water through the crowd on the East Cliff. It joined the same cry that had gone up across the river from the watchers on the West Cliff. The two sounds united below the cliffs and continued its way along the staithes and quays lining the river.

'The *Hunter*!' The second ship had been identified. Then the third, the *Wanderer*.

Expectancy gripped the crowds as they watched and waited for the ships to come closer and eventually sail into the river and be taken to the quays on the east bank upstream from the bridge. In that pause there was also the hope that the *Water Nymph* would be sighted. But no other ship broke the horizon.

The crowds cheered the three vessels to their berths.

Questions were asked. 'Did you see the *Water Nymph*?'

'Where was she?' 'Was she all right?'

And answers came. 'She was in good fettle, under sail, heading north in Davis Strait. Signalled she wasn't full.'

Those answers had to satisfy those who still waited. All seemed to be well. Anxious minds were eased a little especially when they realised that the three ships that had arrived were a little earlier than usual. There was still plenty of time for the *Water Nymph* to come home.

'There she blows! There she blows!'

The cry from the masthead brought a surge of relief through the crew of the *Water Nymph*.

'Whither away?'

'Port bow. One mile.'

Men rushed to the rail to catch sight of the rising blows. Eager excitement gripped them. There were plenty of whales ahead to add to the barrels of blubber stowed below decks, fill the ship and then head for home out of this God-forsaken sea. Captain Ormson's insistence that he would find more whales and return to Whitby with a full ship so as to avoid Sam Coulson's wrath had carried them northwards along the west coast of Greenland in Davis Strait. The further north they sailed so late in the season, the more the crew had started to grumble and mutter against their captain, but they knew better than to voice their worries and incur Captain Ormson's iron-handed authority.

The Captain had left his position beside the helmsman and had climbed the ratlines where he could get a better view of the whales. He allowed the ship to hold its present course, gaze sweeping the sky. Thankful that it was clear and there was no sign of deterioration he took little notice of the gentle breeze that came from the north-west. He eyed the distance between the *Water Nymph* and the whales and, when he judged the moment right, ordered the crew to heave-to. Sails were shortened and trimmed and the helmsman's cry of 'Helm's a-lee' completed the manoeuvre that brought no headway.

'Away all boats!'

In anticipation of the order men had already run to their allotted boats. They were lowered speedily and once in the water pushed away from the ship. Oars were quickly positioned in the rowlocks and with hands gripping the loom of the oar the men rowed as one, propelling the boats with increasing speed towards the whales. In each boat the boat-steerer, his eyes fixed firmly on the quarry, guided his boat towards the whales.

Judging the distance carefully, each boat-steerer called for the rowing to stop. The man rowing bow oar, who was also the harpooner, shipped his oar, stood up, balanced himself ready for the throw.

Nearer and nearer. The sense of expectation in the boats was palpable. So much depended on the harpooner making a good strike; then a full ship and homeward bound.

The whales, unaware of their presence, continued to idle in the water. Harpooners adjusted their grip. Close enough? Backs arched and then swung forward, arm coming up with the same motion. Harpoons flew through the air, each trajectory different depending on the judgement of the harpooner. Harpoons hit home and gripped. Pandemonium broke out. Whales were shocked into frenzied action. Water churned into a maelstrom around the boats.

Within the hour all boats were heading back to the *Water Nymph*. All but one had made a successful kill but even that crew was buoyed by the overall result and helped one of the other boats to tow its catch to the ship. The men were happy and rowed with a will. They could not leave the Arctic soon enough. They had already seen other ships leave for home; they seemed so alone in these empty wastes even though they could see land on the distant eastern horizon.

Captain Ormson had viewed the attack on the whales from the deck of the *Water Nymph* with a great deal of satisfaction. His decision to stay longer and head north in Davis Strait had paid off. He would be able to report a full hold to Sam Coulson and it would mean extra money not only in his pocket but that of every member of the crew. Winter would be easier for them all. When he saw the boats heading for the ship he supervised preparations for the flensing to begin once the first whale was brought alongside.

Men with spikes strapped to the bottom of their boots so that they could get a better grip when standing on the whale went about their business. Their long-handled spades with sharp blades were wielded with a dexterity born of long experience. Blubber was peeled from the dead whales and hauled on board where it was cut up, treated and stowed in barrels below deck. The whales were lined up and positioned so that they could be dealt with in turn. The ship was absorbed in this activity, each man concentrating on his particular job, working at speed, never letting up on the strenuous effort for one moment. The Captain and his mate were everywhere, supervising every procedure.

No one noticed that clouds were gathering in the northwest and with the freshening breeze being driven in their direction. It was only when one of the flensers nearly lost his footing that they became aware of the sea's increased motion.

The shout of, 'Rising swell!' caught the Captain's attention, but he had already felt the movement of the ship. He urged the men on the whale to finish their flensing quickly, and reluctantly called for the final carcass to be cast adrift. It floated away to the mercy of the sea and rising wind.

With the last piece of blubber on board the flensers scrambled on deck. The Captain's orders rang out and men were only too willing to obey and get the ship under way.

'Jenkins, get aloft!' There was urgency behind the Captain's command.

'Aye, aye, sir.' Jenkins was on the ratlines by then and climbing swiftly to the topgallant masthead, knowing exactly what was expected of him. He had been a lookout for ice many times before because of his exceptional eyesight. Reaching his precarious position, he seated himself as safely as possible on a plank of wood that served as a seat behind a canvas screen and immediately scanned the ocean for signs of danger other than the thin ice that had been forming along the coast during the past week.

'Ice!' The dreaded word resounded through the rigging, bounced off the sails to the deck below. Before the query came from the Captain, Jenkins was already answering it: 'Starboard quarter.'

Captain Ormson knew they would have to run. He called for more sail. The men needed no cajoling. Each one knew the danger that threatened them, but if conditions grew no worse they should be all right. Then came another foreboding shout from the masthead: 'Rising sea!'

All eyes turned to starboard but, apart from Jenkins in his lofty position, Captain Ormson was the first to see it. He had climbed the ratlines to get a more distant view than from the deck. What he saw sent a chill to his heart and confirmed the vagaries of the Arctic weather that could change from tranquil to treacherous in a matter of moments.

The distant waves were heightening, spray from their crests indicating the rising strength of the wind. Ice was being driven in their direction and its line could be seen stretching far to the south. If that continued it could lead to disaster.

Ormson weighed up the possibility of outrunning the moving ice but decided it was too much of a risk. To be caught by it even in the present sea conditions, which were in any case likely to worsen, could cause them to be crushed. Only shelter would enable their survival. He turned his gaze to the Greenland coast, but from this distance it was difficult to see if it offered any haven. He scanned the coastal ice and discerned there were leads through it. Maybe if he could reach one of those and pass through it he may find some sort of shelter, be able to ride out the storm and threatening ice. It was the only chance for them.

His orders rang out clearly so that there was no mistaking what he wanted. The ship came round to run before the wind. He cupped his hands around his mouth and looked upwards. 'Jenkins, whither the best lead?'

'Starboard ten degrees!'

Automatically the helmsman made the adjustment without the Captain's order.

Captain Ormson made no comment. He had implicit faith in these two men working together.

The ship ran on. The coast that had been but a mere hazy mass began to take on distinguishable features. The crew knew the Captain's intention but their hearts sank for at first sight there appeared to be only towering cliffs ahead. Captain Ormson knew there was nothing he could do but to let the ship continue on its course. They reached the coastal ice, which was thankfully still thin and with the leads still clear.

His orders rang out crisply. Sails were furled, leaving only sufficient for the ship to keep under way.

'Clear water!' The cry from the masthead brought some sense of relief to the crew.

Captain Ormston climbed the rigging to get a better view of the coast. Huge cliffs ran from the south, seemingly unbroken, but ahead there were three clefts. His gaze ran on and with it came hope. The cliffs lowered to the north before climbing again as they swung westward for about three miles before turning north once more. Captain Ormson blessed his luck. The lie of the coast at this point had formed a small bay with its shelf rising from the sea into small rock-strewn beach, beyond which the hinterland rose gently through a wide cleft in the towering wall of cliffs.

He quickly brought all his experience of the Arctic to bear to decide on the best point at which to anchor the ship. He chose a position that would shelter them from the rising wind and storm-lashed sea as well as one where the likelihood of their being crushed by ice would be minimal.

The men, knowing the ferocity of the storm that would hit them, found hidden reserves of strength to prepare the ship to weather it. When all was ready they knew there was nothing they could do but wait and hope that the foul weather was only short-lasting.

*

After five days during which the elements had never relented in their merciless attack on the ship there came a slight easing in the ferocity. Captain Ormson took the opportunity to go on deck and assess the situation. What he saw sent his heart plunging towards despair but he knew he must not show it and that his report to the crew must give hope.

The wind still howled and drove clouds that were heavy with snow towards their little bay. The sea ice from which they had run had thickened and had met the coastal ice. They had piled up into a mass and together formed an impenetrable barrier across the mouth of the bay. The temperature had plummeted and with the freezing grip of the ice there was no way the *Water Nymph* could force her way out of the trap even if the wind changed direction. They were caught and he realised they would be here for the winter.

Ormson was thankful that he had chosen this point at which to anchor, for here they were spared from the worst savagery of the ice by a small spit of land. He stared over a white land and sea and knew that he had long months ahead in which to keep up the morale of his crew and organise their time so that they did not turn in upon themselves or on each other. Food would have to be rationed and keeping warm would present a problem as the days drew on and the temperature dropped even further.

Captain Ormson stood for a moment longer, offering up a prayer for their survival.

As the month of September lengthened the pall of anxiety strengthened and hung heavy over Whitby. It could be seen in people's faces, in their slow step and their muted reactions to each other. People wanted to offer sympathy to those who had relations and friends on board the *Water Nymph* but refrained, for that would confirm they had given up hope of her return.

The likelihood of seeing the ship and her crew again occupied much of Sam's thoughts. To lose a ship and her entire crew was almost the worst thing that could happen, and it was magnified by the fact that his son was on board. To lose one son to the Arctic was bad enough, but to lose two was tragic. The fact that Eric would have died doing what he loved best was no consolation for a parent. And there would be Dina to comfort too; Rowan was serving on the *Water Nymph*.

Alicia, seeing her husband's depressed state when they were sitting at the table, left her lunch and came to him. She stood behind his chair, slid her arms down over his shoulders and bent to kiss his cheek. 'Try not to worry, love,' she whispered close to his ear. 'They may be safe.'

He put his hands on hers and looked up over his shoulder at her. 'You are a comfort, but each passing day makes their chances slimmer. The ice can be bad from now on.'

'They could have found shelter.'

'Even if they have, they'll be lucky to survive the winter.'

'Don't give up hope.'

He gave a wan smile and a slight nod of his head, but she knew his hope was faint.

She was returning to her seat when there was a knock on the door. A maid came in. 'I'm sorry to interrupt your meal, sir, but there is a lady here to see you. I've shown her into the drawing-room.'

'Who is it?' he asked sharply.

'Mrs Coulson, sir.' She saw his face darken. 'I thought it would be all right to let your daughter-in-law in.'

Sam's lips tightened, his face reddened as if he would explode into rage, but he held his anger in check and waved the maid away with a curt gesture that sent her scurrying from the room.

'I wonder what she wants?' he snapped.

'There's only one way to find out,' said Alicia.

Sam stood up and pushed his chair violently out of the way. 'I'll soon send her packing.'

'I'm coming too,' replied Alicia in a voice that would brook no opposition. Sam knew it was no use gainsaying her when she was in this resolved mood. He started for the door and she followed.

'What do you want, sullying my house with your presence?' he demanded of Ruth as he entered the drawing room.

She stood in front of the fire holding her baby in her arms. 'I thought it was time you met Alan Coulson, your grandson.' She eased the babe in her arms so that his grandfather could see him better, glanced at his wife and murmured, 'Alicia.'

She returned 'Ruth', coldly.

'He's a fine babe, don't you think?' asked Ruth, her eyes fixed on Sam.

He spluttered, trying to keep his gaze away from the boy, 'Yes, I suppose so.'

Ruth looked at her son and said, 'This is your grandfather, Alan, give him a smile.' Hidden by the baby's shawls she tickled him and Alan gave a little gurgle as his lips broke into a broad smile and his wide blue eyes sparkled with captivating beauty.

Sam automatically stepped forward. Seeing the movement, Alan stretched out his chubby hand. Hardly knowing he was doing it, Sam held out his own and felt the warmth in that innocent touch as the child's fingers closed around his thumb.

'He's a fine boy,' said Sam, not really knowing what to say. He did not want a Holmes in his house yet this tiny soul was guiltless of all that had happened. Had he been brought into life at this moment to replace Eric, lost in the Arctic? He looked into the blue eyes still staring up at him innocently.

'Mr Coulson,' said Ruth quietly, 'I came here because I thought it was time for you to meet your grandson, but also because of the joy he can bring you if you will let him. I hoped that through him, you and Ben might be reconciled.'

Tension had been heightening in Alicia as she had observed Sam warming towards the child. She could endure this no longer. 'Ben's heard about the *Water Nymph* and thinks that as the only son left he can step into Eric's place.' Her words were delivered with penetrating coldness to make Sam think. She got her reward when she saw him stiffen.

'Did Ben send you here?' he demanded of Ruth.

'No, he didn't, Mr Coulson. He does not know I am here.'

'I'll bet he does,' sneered Alicia, then more words poured out. 'I can see it all. He hopes for reconciliation through his son so that his father will take him back into the firm and pay off his debt to the bank. Don't listen to her, Sam. It's all a ploy. She thinks that if Ben and you are reconciled, this child will inherit everything.' Alicia gave her a look of contempt. 'Well, your schemes mean nothing. Sam's own child will inherit, not yours.'

A stunned silence filled the room for the second before Ruth spoke. 'That was not my intention in coming here. I came because . . .' She let her words fade away because she saw they were falling on deaf ears.

Sam's complete attention was focused on his wife. 'You mean . . .?'

'Yes, I'm going to have a baby.' Alicia's smile confirmed that she truly meant this. 'Now, get her out of here so that I can have you to myself.'

Ruth said nothing. She knew it was time for her to go. The reconciliation that she longed for, because she knew Ben wanted nothing more than to be within the family fold again, was as far away as ever. If Alan couldn't bring it about, who or what could? She was aware of Alicia's look of triumph as she walked from the room.

The anger that seethed in Ruth was all directed at her. She had sensed hostility from Alicia as soon as they came in. Sam had appeared to be softening towards his grandson, but Alicia had never given him a chance and had used her pregnancy to her own advantage. Ruth saw little hope now of Sam's ever granting Alan the recognition he deserved. His mind and attention would be all on his own new child.

She was also angry with herself for failing even though she knew Alicia had deliberately undermined her efforts.

'The bitch,' she muttered to herself, 'trying to make out that Ben was attempting to worm his way back into his father's favour in order to clear his debt. Well, she . . .' Then Ruth stopped. What had Alicia said: '. . . will take him back into the firm and pay off his debt to the bank'. Was that it? Ruth ran her mind back over the confrontation. Yes, she felt sure it was. Her lips tightened. How did Alicia know that Ben had borrowed money from the bank? She could only do so if she had had a hand in the wine deal. In fact, only if she was the recipient of the money. Had she known that most of the wine was poor and deliberately lured Ben into buying it? Warren Laskill had told him about the wine; Alicia was friendly with Warren. Could she have used him to convey false information to Ben? It was certainly possible and everything fitted neatly. Ruth quickened her step with one purpose – to see Ben as soon as possible. She crossed the bridge and turned into Church Street then remembered that he had gone to see Ryan. She would have to curb her impatience.

Two hours later when she heard the front door open she rushed into the hall to meet her husband. He saw the agitation in her but was thankful that it had an air of excitement about it and not one of worried despondency.

'I must talk to you right away, Ben.'

She turned back to the drawing-room and he followed her, shedding his coat and hat on to a chair as he did so.

As the door closed behind him Ruth told him: 'I took Alan to see your father today.'

'You did what?' Ben's face clouded with disbelief.

'I thought it was time he met his grandfather.'

Ben's disbelief turned to anger. 'Why? You know that after his treatment of you I want nothing more to do with him.'

'Ben, please don't be angry. I thought Alan might bridge the gap between you and your father. I thought if he saw his grandson : . .'

'And what happened?' snapped Ben.

Ruth explained everything.

'You might have known Alicia would put her penn'orth in. She certainly did that with her announcement.'

'I was hoping she wouldn't be there, but now I'm glad she was.' A new excitement had come into Ruth's voice.

405

'Why?' Ben frowned. 'Is there something you haven't told me?'

'Yes. Alicia was furious to see me there with Alan. Her mood was such that I believe she said something she normally wouldn't have divulged. She said that you had sent me to affect a reconciliation so that your father would take you back into his firm and *pay off your debt to the bank*.' She emphasised the last words so that there was no mistaking them or the meaning behind them.

Ben stared at her, trying to get his mind round the implication this information carried. 'She said what?'

'She implied that you were trying to get back in favour with your father so that he would pay off your debt to Chapman's.'

'You're sure that's what she said?'

'If I never speak again.'

Ben's lips tightened. 'How could Alicia know that?'

'No one else knew but us, Ryan and Mr Chapman.'

'And he wouldn't divulge clients' dealings.'

'Exactly.'

'Which means Alicia could only have known about it if she had been party to it.' Ben's tone was thoughtful. 'Well, there is one sure way to find out.' He started for the door.

Ruth knew there would be no stopping him. Besides she didn't want to; she too wanted to know the truth, no matter what the consequences were.

Ben's strides were long and quick as he made his way to the bridge and then to the house in Bagdale. The ramifications of this were enormous: Alicia had deliberately set out to ruin him. How far would a woman's scorn carry her? Was her marriage to his father also part of her desire for revenge? What else would she do to fulfil that desire? Ben hoped his father would still be at home; he needed him to witness Alicia's reaction when he made his accusation.

'I would like to see Mr and Mrs Coulson,' he demanded of the maid who answered the door. Recognising young Mr Coulson she had no hesitation in allowing him into the house.

'I'll tell them you are here,' she said as she closed the front door. She crossed the hall to the drawing-room leaving Ben waiting impatiently. She reappeared a few moments later and signalled that he was to come into the room. He nodded his thanks as he passed her.

His father had left his chair and was standing with his back to the fireplace, facing the door. Alicia was sitting in a chair to his father's left. He saw coldness and defiance in her eyes as if she knew why he was here. His father's gaze was hostile and held that piercing element that Ben remembered from his boyhood.

'What do you want?' growled Sam.

'My business is more to do with your wife, though you should hear it too,' he returned coolly, and turned to Alicia. 'Don't you ever try to ruin me again, or the consequences for you will be disastrous.' His eyes were narrow with disdain.

Sam stepped towards him, anger flaring. 'Don't you dare threaten Alicia!'

'What are you talking about?' She feigned innocent surprise.

'You know full well,' replied Ben. 'You duped Warren into passing on information that was false so that I would borrow heavily from the bank in my eagerness to invest.'

Alicia gave a little laugh. 'Oh, Ben, what an idea. You certainly have a vivid imagination.'

He looked at his father. 'Ruth visited you a short while ago and Alicia accused her then of coming in order to get me back in favour with you so that you would repay my debt to the bank.' He swung round on Alicia. 'You slipped up and gave yourself away in the shock of Ruth's visit.'

She glared at him but said nothing. She knew there was no use denying it for Sam had been there and must have heard. At the time he would not have known the significance of what she had let slip, but now he did. She could see it in his face.

'How did you know about my debt if you hadn't set up that wine deal to lure me into it and ruin me?' snapped Ben. 'You are despicable.'

'Don't you speak to my wife in that tone.' Sam grabbed him by the arm and swung him round.

'Wife?' he mocked, glaring at his father. 'Do you think she married you, a man old enough to be her father, for love? More likely it's just a scheme to get her hands on the Coulson assets.'

Alicia jumped to her feet and confronted Ben. 'I'll not deny that that was in my mind at first so that nothing would come to you or yours, and your father will tell you he had the same idea about getting his hands on Campion's, but when we really did fall in love our schemes meant nothing, for now we are as one.' Her eyes narrowed. 'And I can tell you that you'll still get nothing, nor will that brat your wife brought here. Everything will come to my son! Yes, my son by your father! Now get out and wallow in your ruin and loss. I'm glad I brought it about.'

Ben ignored her tirade. He had noticed that his father moved beside Alicia as she was speaking as if making a gesture of support. But at least all the facts were in the open now for Sam to query and make of what he would.

Ben stood there a moment longer. His eyes were cold but there was a touch of triumph in them. 'If you think you have ruined me then you have another think coming. It might interest you to know that I am in partnership with Ryan Bennett and that there is enough money available for us to cope with any setbacks, so don't think you can win by any more underhand methods. We are rivals but our dealings in opposition to you will be fair. Remember that, because if I suspect anything else is amiss, you'll feel my wrath.' His eyes fixed on his father for a moment. 'I hope you know what you have taken on, marrying this one with her poisoned mind?'

There was no love in Sam's eyes as he met his son's. 'Get out,' he hissed. 'Never come here or talk about my wife like that again.'

Ben swung round and started for the door.

'That's right, get back to that whore of a wife of yours,' Alicia shouted after him.

He stopped and swung round, glared threateningly at her. 'Say that again and . . .'

'Whore of a wife! We don't know what she got up to in France!'

Ben, his head set, his whole body threatening, strode towards her.

Sam stepped in front of Alicia. 'Don't, Ben!'

He stopped and glared for a moment at his father in an attitude that threatened violence to him as well.

'Then see she curbs her tongue about my wife and doesn't let her imagination run riot.' He hurried from the room, slamming the door behind him.

Sam stood staring at it for a few moments, his thoughts in confusion. When he turned around Alicia was sitting down.

'I remember what you said when Ruth was here,' he said quietly as he sat down opposite her. 'I take it that as Ben has seen fit to come here there is truth in what he says?'

Alicia smiled. 'I'll not deny it, Sam. I was burning with the desire for revenge after Ben turned me down and thought I had found a way to do it.'

He nodded and gave a dismissive wave of his hand as if he was not bothered by what she had done in that respect. 'Was marrying me part of that revenge, as Ben seems to think?'

Alicia came from her chair and slid on to the floor in front of him, her hands on his knees as she looked up into his eyes with all the sincerity she could muster. 'Oh, Sam, don't ever think that. We both admitted our original intention in marrying each other. We have laughed about it since because we found a real love we had not suspected was there. I love you, Sam Coulson.'

He leaned forward and swept her into his arms. 'I love you too.'

A few moments later they moved to the sofa to sit together.

'I'm sorry Ben has joined up with Ryan Bennett,' commented Alicia.

'Probably because of Sarah. I had hoped that because of their relationship I might entice him to invest some capital with us,' Sam said.

'That seems unlikely now, unless you can get Sarah to persuade him.'

'I doubt I can do that. If she's a mind to have him, I'll not spoil her happiness. Sarah's special to me. Besides, she and Ben were always close.'

'Is Sam Coulson going soft?'

He laughed. 'Not as far as business is concerned. We'll keep our eyes on those two and our ears open. You and I together will be too formidable for them ever to outdo us.'

'There's nothing more certain,' she agreed.

'But no more underhand methods, Alicia. Sharp dealing is a different matter.'

'And there is no one sharper than Sam Coulson as all Whitby knows.'

Chapter Twenty-three

Captain Ormson reached for his log and opened it at the next blank page. He stared thoughtfully at the paper for a few minutes then picked up his pen.

October 14th, 1804
Sunny. Sky clear. Bitterly cold.
We are still beset in our tiny bay. Though we have had a week of this weather there is no heat in the sun to melt the ice and enable us to break clear. If winter continues to tighten its grip we have no chance of escape and must set our minds to try to survive here.

'Sarah, they are not coming back.' Dina's voice was charged with resignation.

Sarah turned from the wardrobe and came to sit beside her sister on the bed. She put a comforting arm round Dina's shoulder. 'We must not give up hope,' she said quietly, though with no news of the *Water Nymph* and the year moving into November she felt in her heart of hearts that the ship's chances of survival were practically nil, but she must try and put on a hopeful front for the sake of her sister.

Dina turned to look at her. 'Oh, Sarah, after what Father said he would do, this would have been Rowan's last voyage!' The thought brought tears spilling down her cheeks. 'I've lost him, Sarah, I've lost him.' With sobs racking her body she fell against her sister who held her tight.

'And there's Eric,' Sarah whispered, as if reminding herself. 'We will have lost another brother, and Father another son.'

She bit her lip, holding back the tears and sadness. She must be strong for Dina; for them all.

Christmas Day, 1804,
More snow.
I conducted a small service this morning. I hope my
words were comforting to men whose hopes of survival
plunge daily.
I issued a small extra ration today. I doubt if our
meagre supplies will last the winter.
Despondency and boredom are our two worst enemies
at the moment though I believe it won't be long before
illnesses start to break out.
God help us.

It was a muted Christmas in Whitby. Everyone was aware that hope for the *Water Nymph* was practically non-existent. Those who had no one on board the whaler kept their Christmas celebrations to a minimum out of respect for families who had.

The old church on the East Cliff was packed for the Christmas service in spite of the inclement weather. Instinct told people that the Rector would mention the lost crew and felt the need to be part of that remembrance.

From the back of the church Ben saw his father and Alicia in the Coulson pew. His mind tumbled back over the years to the times when he had sat there with his father and mother and his brothers and sisters. What changes his life had brought him since. He had lost two brothers. His father had lost two sons. Now Sam sat there with only his young bride for company. Ben had a sudden yearning to lay a comforting hand on his father's shoulder, but after what had passed between them he knew that would be unwise. The gap between them had widened and Alicia would see that it was never breached. He wished his sisters were there. Had his father ostracised them because of their beau? Two minutes passed with more worshippers coming into the church. Then he saw Sarah and Dina. He caught

Sarah's eye and they made a slight gesture of pleasure at seeing each other. Dina gave him a wan smile and concern surged through him at the sight of her drawn pale face. He could see she was taking the loss of Rowan hard. They moved on to the Coulson pew.

The service was solemn. Whitby mourned its loss. All hope had gone.

January 20th, 1805
The snow of the last three days has stopped.
Jim Braithwaite became the fifth victim today.
Food is low.
Desperate measures must be taken.

Captain Ormson stood up, sighed and left his cabin. He went on deck and viewed the white landscape and formidable cliffs that almost surrounded them. They seemed to mock his thoughts, saying, Try it if you dare. He set his face defiantly. He would dare. He made his way with slow steps, each of which sapped a little more energy from him, towards the bow. Laboriously he climbed down to the fo'c'sle.

The ominous silence of despair hung heavy on the men lying on their bunks or hunched on the floor. Some glanced up to see who chose to enter what was rapidly becoming a place to die, others in their emaciated state had not the energy to do even that.

Captain Ormson stood for a moment. He could not ask any more of these men He started to turn away but stopped. If he did that he would be saying the Arctic had won. Their only hope lay in one last desperate measure.

'I need two volunteers.' His voice croaked from a dry throat.
No one moved.

'Two,' he repeated. 'You remember when we first came to this bay we explored the shore and saw signs that there had been human habitation here at some time. We hoped they might visit again. I want two of you to see if you can find any other

413

evidence. It may be a useless effort and you may never return but . . .'

'Sir, I'll go.'

The Captain started as if he didn't believe he had heard right.

'Dying doing something will be better than just sitting here waiting for the Reaper to tap me on the shoulder.'

'Thank you, Rowan.'

With an effort Rowan swung himself from his bunk.

'I'll go with him.'

The Captain turned to see who had spoken and almost refused the offer. If by some miracle he and whoever was still alive saw Whitby again, he might have to face the wrath of Sam Coulson for sending his son on a mission in which he had little chance of survival.

'Rowan's sweet on my sister, sir. I'll need to tell her what he did when we get back.'

'Well spoken, Eric. You two come to my cabin after you've put on another layer of clothes.'

Eight minutes later the two young men were standing in front of the Captain.

'We don't know when those signs of habitation were left here but it is known that there are people somewhere in this godforsaken land, though how they survive God only knows. I want you two to try and find some. We have little food left. I'll give you the rations you would have received for the next two days and some extra. It will be very little and you are weak already but I rely on you to do your best. Come on deck.'

They followed him outside and joined him by the rail which was thick with ice.

'I think your best bet will be to go through that ridge in the mountain range.'

'It's the only way anyone could reach here,' agreed Rowan.

'Right, lad. Make for it. I've studied the weather patterns and signs since we got here and I think it might remain fair for four days, maybe five. Work within that time frame and return

414

to the ship if you think the task is hopeless.'

'Aye, aye, sir.'

They started to swing over the side.

'I'll keep a look out for your return.'

Captain Ormson watched them go with only a tiny measure of hope in his heart.

'Have we a chance of finding anyone?' asked Rowan as they approached the long slope that led to the gap between the towering mountains.

'I don't know,' replied Eric. 'Why did you volunteer?'

'Why did you?'

In those two questions each man read the other's thoughts; it was better to die trying to do something than to lie in a bunk waiting for death.

They lapsed into silence, conserving their energy, depleted as it was, for the climb ahead.

They drew a little hope from the fact that the surface was not as formidable as they had imagined. The rugged contours of the ice gave them footholds that helped their progress, though that was slow enough due to their diminished strength.

The ridge drew nearer and nearer, beckoning them on to make one final effort. Drawn by this enticement they pushed harder and, finally, gasping for breath, fell face down on the ice. They sucked air into their aching lungs, ignoring the cold that seemed to carve into their insides.

Rowan slowly raised his head, hoping that what he would see would give them hope rather than dash it completely. He stared for a moment, narrowing his eyes against the glare of the sun which threw its brightness back off the ice. He reached out and placed his hand on his companion's arm. 'Eric,' he muttered. There was no response. 'Eric, look.' He forced encouragement into his voice.

Eric raised his head. His eyes swept the landscape ahead. He saw a long, snow-covered valley running between two mountain chains that widened gradually as it ran inland. The terrain looked more inviting yet held an atmosphere of isolation that could not be denied.

'What now?' he croaked.

Rowan looked back. The ship was a tiny dot between towering cliffs. It lay there, their only contact with the outside world. One step further and it would be gone from sight, to dwell only in their minds.

'We eat a little and then go on,' replied Rowan, firmly and hopefully.

Eric said nothing.

Though what they ate was only a small portion of their rations it eased the empty feeling in their stomachs.

They pushed themselves to their feet, looked back at the ship and stepped forward into the unknown.

Whitby started to resume its normal life. It had met tragedy before. Though there were heavy hearts for a time, the townspeople picked up and went on.

January 23rd 1805
The weather still holds fair.
I have kept watch for North and Coulson but have seen
no signs of them.
Merryweather and Ferguson died this morning.
Despondency grows stronger in the men. It is an effort
to keep them believing in our salvation. They grow
more resentful of my orders to go over the side and
walk in the sheltered pathway we cut in the snow
beside the ship. I have to remonstrate with them and
threaten them with being accused of mutiny if they do
not obey my orders to walk, something that is essential
to cultivate their circulation.

'Shouldn't we turn back, we've been longer than the Captain intended,' suggested Rowan anxiously.

They had progressed more easily than expected but time was

running out if they were to make it back to the ship before they succumbed to the intense cold through lack of food.

Eric hesitated. His gaze was distant. 'A bit further,' he whispered. He started towards an opening in the rock face on the right-hand side of the valley.

Rowan stared after him for a few moments. The faraway expression he had seen in his companion alarmed him. Was the vastness of this lonely wilderness affecting his shipmate? They should be turning back, not going on. Every onward step would diminish their chances of survival. Though death out here in the open might be better than in the confines of their ship, it was not an alluring prospect. His natural instinct was to be with the *Water Nymph*. Rowan drove his legs a little faster, stumbling with the effort.

'Eric!' His call came out as a croak, unheard by his companion who moved on persistently towards the opening in the rock face.

Rowan managed to be only a step behind when they reached it to find it was wider than expected and they could easily pass between two sheer walls of rock. A hundred yards on they came into a small amphitheatre-like valley.

Rowan's face was a mask of disbelief. He turned his head to look at Eric who stared at cave-like dwellings in the rock face outside which stood six human beings scraping at what looked like animal skins.

'Esquimaux,' whispered Eric.

'How did you know they were here?' asked Rowan.

The question startled Eric. The faraway look had vanished. He turned to Rowan. 'I didn't but I seemed to be drawn here.'

'We passed other openings and they didn't interest you. Why this one?'

Eric shook his head. 'I don't know, it was as if someone was telling me this was where we would find what we were looking for.' He grasped Rowan's arm. 'We're saved! We must get help back to the ship.' He started forward with as brisk a step as he could muster.

417

The movement caught the eye of one of the people. They all dropped their tools in surprise. One ducked into one of the dwellings while the others stood staring at the two men. In a moment five more people emerged. They hesitated a moment and then, having taken in the scene, ran to meet the strangers. Recognising their weak state they offered their arms for support. Eric and Rowan took them gladly. Questions flew from the Esquimaux' lips. Rowan urged them to help. Neither side understood the other, but the whalers did realise that the Esquimaux wanted to assist them.

In the next two hours Rowan and Eric were fed and though they did not know on what, it tasted good after the monotony of their short rations. Their footgear, which had become lacerated on the sharp ice, was exchanged for skin boots that the Esquimaux indicated would be better for them.

By signs and drawing in the snow Eric and Rowan were able to inform their saviours that they were from a ship. The Esquimaux knew exactly where that ship would be for there was only one place on the nearby coast that it could have beached. They also understood from signs that help and food were needed there urgently. Immediately the Esquimaux prepared to leave with food and clothing. They signed that two of them would go immediately and that Eric and Rowan, escorted by two other men, would follow at an easier pace.

It was with lighter hearts that they watched the two men, burdened with food and clothing, leave their tiny valley.

'They are talking about us,' commented Eric, eyeing their escort who had been joined by a third man, who kept looking in their direction.

A few moments later he came to Eric and Rowan and indicated that he wanted them to go with him.

The whalers scrambled to their feet and followed him. After about half a mile he stopped. Eric and Rowan glanced around but saw nothing that indicated why the man had stopped here. They looked askance at him. He pointed to the ground a few feet in front of them. When they frowned he bent down and started brushing away snow from what they thought was a jumble of ice, but after a few minutes it became obvious that it was not ice but a heap of stones in the shape of a grave. When the man turned to his left and started doing the same thing Eric and Rowan fell on their knees and helped him. Eyeing the mounds and wondering why they had been brought here they stood up.

The man pointed at them in turn and then at each of the graves. Rowan felt a moment of panic. Were they not to be taken back to the ship? Were they to end up here under a heap of stones? But then he saw the man's friendly smile and another gesture at the ground between the two graves. The Esquimaux bent down, pushed some snow aside and fumbled with something. When he straightened he had a lump of wood in his hand. He held it out and pointed at its surface.

A tremor of shock ran through the two whalers. Though it was faded the lettering could still be read: *Water Nymph*. They glanced at each other in disbelief.

'So that was it,' whispered Eric half to himself. 'This could only be from Martin's boat. He drew me here.'

'But there are only two graves,' said Rowan.

'You remember there was a storm? The others could have perished in that but somehow two of them made it to land and that could only have been in the bay where we are trapped.' He quickly drew an outline of the bay and then pointed at the board and the outline in the snow. The Esquimaux marked a place and the two whalers saw that it was on the opposite side of the bay to the present position of the *Water Nymph*.

'We don't know who lies beneath these stones,' said Rowan with regret.

'We'll say a prayer and leave them in peace.'

Each man made his own act of remembrance, and then Eric laid the piece of wood between the mounds. 'If anyone comes this way again they'll know two shipmates lie here.'

They nodded, their eyes registering their thanks to the Esquimaux who stood quietly beside them. No word was spoken as they walked back.

One of the women was standing close to a dwelling when they reached the encampment, holding something in her hands. The man nodded to her and she stepped forward, holding out the package wrapped in sealskin. Eric took it, wondering why they should be given a gift. He smiled his thanks and voiced some words he knew she would not understand but hoped his tone conveyed his appreciation. He guessed it had when she smiled back.

He unwrapped the object carefully and when it lay in the palm of his hand he gasped, 'Good God!' His eyes were wide with disbelief.

'What is it?' asked Rowan in a hushed voice.

Still staring at the object Eric said, 'It's Martin's diary.'

'What?' Rowan's gasp broke the spell.

'You know he always kept a diary of each voyage. He must have had this one in his pocket when he went after the whales.' He turned to Rowan, his eyes ablaze with excitement and wonder. 'One of those graves must be Martin's. He must have guided us here.'

Rowan had never had any time for premonitions and such like but how else could Eric have picked out this particular place in all this wasteland unless it had been with the help of someone from beyond the grave? He pulled himself up short from voicing his next thought. Had Martin guided the *Water Nymph* to the bay so that his last resting place would be found, maybe even the diary? Surely not, for that would have meant the death of some fellow whalers.

As he stood in this vast wilderness Eric felt a sensation of peace envelop him and offered his brother a silent prayer of thanks. He felt sure Martin had saved them; he sensed a communication between them and with it came the tranquillity of knowing where his brother lay in peace.

Rowan's disturbing thoughts were interrupted and banished when the two Esquimaux who were to escort them back to the ship indicated they were ready.

*

420

Captain Ormson sighed and laid down his pen. He had written what he had hoped he would never have to write.

January 28ᵗʰ 1805
Any hope of seeing North and Coulson again has gone.
I can only salute two brave volunteers who set out into
the unknown in the hope of finding help.

He pushed himself to his feet, picked up his spyglass and went on deck. He would keep watch one more time. He went to the rail and scanned the ridge where he had last seen his two crew members. Nothing but desolation.

He paced the deck for two hours to keep warm. With each passing minute his hopes of survival sank lower and lower. He had done all he could for his crew. There was no hope of escape for at least another six weeks and even then it would only be if the weather turned milder and the ice conditions changed. In that time the dread scurvy could reap its harvest.

His vigil was useless. He chided himself for clinging to a tenuous hope. May as well accept the situation. He raised his spyglass one more time. Nothing but a vast uncompromising land that seemed to mock the very existence of man.

He began to lower his arms but stopped. He must have been mistaken. He raised the spyglass again. Swept his gaze from the right, halted the movement, backtracked a little. Could it be . . .? Excitement gripped him. He started to tremble. Two figures. He sighed with relief. At least Coulson and North were safe. They had not perished alone in icy wastes so far from home. They could die among their companions. He looked again. Disbelief ran through him. These two figures couldn't be members of his crew. They were too bulky, moved too quickly for men who had suffered like North and Coulson. Bulky? They had something strapped to their backs and they moved with clear purpose in the direction of his ship. Was rescue in sight?

He raised his voice as best he could and those of the crew

who could manage it came stumbling on to the deck to see what had brought excited cries from their captain. Incredulous at what they saw, they lined the rail and let speculation run rife. In spite of the cold no one left the deck. The excitement of what they were seeing kept the blood coursing through their veins.

Even though they recognised the strangers as Esquimaux they called out words of welcome. The two men waved in reply and kept doing so until they reached the ship. Eager hands helped them on board. As the seamen crowded around, Captain Ormson had to call a halt to their eagerness to greet the men whom they saw as their salvation.

The Esquimaux managed to indicate by signs that they had seen two men from the ship and that they were being brought back. They opened the bundles and Captain Ormson saw what could only be seal-meat, and fish, but it was a more than welcome sight. Now there was every chance that the sick would recover and those who were still well would gain more strength and be ready to take the vessel home if and when the conditions became favourable.

Captain Ormson took the men and their goods below deck where he organised the storing of food. The cook chopped some of the ship's timbers for fuel and prepared a meal. From the signs they made Captain Ormson understood that the Esquimaux wanted to stay on board until their compatriots arrived with the two whalers. He was only too willing to comply.

Two days later four figures were seen crossing the ridge. By the time they reached the ship everyone, even those who were still in a serious condition, formed a joyful welcoming party. Eric and Rowan were overwhelmed by all the praise and it was some time before the Captain could intervene to say a few words of thanks on behalf of every man on board. He made gestures of thanks to the Esquimaux too and extended an invitation for the two newcomers to stay as long as they wanted.

The four Esquimaux held a short conference and indicated to the Captain that they were willing to stay and help in whatever way they could. They explained that they knew of a small area of sea that was only ever covered in a thin layer of ice and that from it they could keep the ship supplied with fish. Captain Ormson was only too glad to accept.

When things had settled down he called Eric and Rowan to his cabin to make their report. He was astounded by the story of how they had located the Esquimaux and amazed that they had come across the graves of two previous members of the *Water Nymph's* crew, one of whom they were certain was Eric's brother. When they explained the reason for their assumption, Eric handed Martin's diary to the Captain.

'Would you like me to send a party to recover his body and that of the other poor fellow, whoever he might be, and take them back for burial in Whitby?'

'No, thank you, sir. I considered that as we returned to the ship. I would like my brother to remain at peace where he is in the Arctic that he loved.'

'Then it shall be so.'

Two days later Ormson sent for Eric.

'Strictly speaking, Coulson, this diary should remain in my possession to be handed over to the authorities in Whitby. It sheds light on what happened, but it is a personal document that I think your father should see first. What action he takes next is up to him; whether he hands it over to the authorities or not is his decision. I will tell you now, and I will tell him, that I shall not speak of the diary's contents.' He passed it back to Eric.

'Thank you, sir.'

February 25th 1805
There is no sign of the ice loosening its grip. We must hope that it does so before long. The cold continues to be intense. We are nearing the point where we dare not take any more of the ship's timbers for the fire.
Thankfully illness has been held at bay since the arrival of the Esquimaux. They continue to supply us with

food. Though maybe not all to our taste, it is life-saving. The men gain in strength, but it will be some time before some of them can take on their duties again.

March 1st 1805
We have had three days of severe gales and driving snow. It curtailed the visits of the Esquimaux. The wind came from the north-west and pushed ice against ice towards the shore but in doing so broke it up. Today the wind is blowing from the north. It is bitter but it is starting to move ice southwards.

March 3rd 1805
Today hopes rise for our escape. The wind has veered to the north-east. Surely it must ease the ice away from the coast. We must be ready.

After that entry in his log Captain Ormson assessed the capabilities of his crew. Those whom he realised could not stand the strain of work he excused duties even though they were willing. The rest he organised into the best possible team to get them home.

Two days later he was amazed to see more figures cross the ridge. They had been used to visits from the four Esquimaux they had met in the days surrounding Eric and Rowan's return. Today there were eight of them and six women. Their leader indicated that the change in the wind would take some of the ice away from the shore and possibly leave open water. His party would cut and break the ice around the ship to enable it to make the open sea.

Captain Ormson took his cue from the Esquimaux whose judgement he trusted implicitly. At his signal his party started working at the ice around the bow of the ship. The Captain sent all the able-bodied men he could spare over the side. Armed with ice-axes and ice-spades they attacked the ice along the sides of the ship. When he judged it to be the right moment he sent men aloft to unfurl those sails that had not been shredded in the storm when they ran for shelter. There was sufficient to catch the wind and as they billowed the crew felt a judder run through the ship. The crew members who had struggled aloft now descended with caution on the icy ratlines.

A shout rang out from beyond the bow that drew the crew to see a crack in the ice opening in front of the ship. The Esquimaux and those members of the crew on the ice ran forward and endeavoured to widen the crack. Their efforts, together with the force of the moving ship, slow though it was, paid off. Ice cracked with what to the trapped men was a joyous and heart-lifting sound. Gradually the open water along the coast came nearer and nearer. Judging the distance, Captain Ormson called his men on board. No one had ever boarded a ship more willingly than they. Men came to the rail and with gestures and shouts made their thanks and farewells to the Esquimaux.

There were more cheers when the *Water Nymph* took to the sea and the men felt the ship ride the first waves. Cheer they might but each man knew there was still ice to face before they reached completely open water.

March 8th 1805
We are clear of the Ice. These have been rough days
when at one time we all thought we were to be crushed
by the force of ice streaming south but another fortu-
itous change of wind prevented that.
Now we head for home.
We must look a sorry sight.

Whitby gave her whaling ships the usual send off. People remembered the *Water Nymph*. She was lost and her crew with her but another whaling season had come round and Whitby must send more ships to the north with her blessing.

425

Chapter Twenty-four

For twelve days the tiny ship rode the Atlantic swell, pitching and tossing in a manner that threatened finally to end the days of this battered craft. But survive she did and the distant line on the horizon kindled new hope in the hearts of her crew.

At the mercy of the sea and the wind, Captain Ormson suspected his calculations regarding their position might be far from accurate. Weakness and mental strain could easily become masters of the mind. But he didn't care. There was land visible. He hoped he was taking his ship into Lerwick, but where didn't really matter.

The coast drew nearer and nearer. No one was certain where it was but spying a tiny inlet and some houses, Captain Ormson took the *Water Nymph* towards it. He eased her into land and was met by a small group of people who had emerged from the five houses there. They stared in amazement at the ship, her sails tattered, her boats cut up for firewood, and crew like scarecrows who stared helplessly at them from the rail, as if begging for help. The men ashore were galvanished into action and were soon on board helping to make the ship secure. Captain Ormson and his crew were relieved to learn that they were at Ronas Voe in the north of Shetland. They were safe!

Though they were eager to be on a homeward course the Captain deemed it wisest to remain where they were for three days to enable his men to regain some strength for the voyage. The crew realised that it was a wise decision, for with the food that the kind people of Ronas Voe were able to supply every man began to feel some measure of his strength returning.

They took on supplies but, tempting though it was to put into Lerwick, Captain Ormson knew his men wanted no further delay. He assessed the condition of those who had suffered most, concluding that the knowledge they were homeward bound without delay would serve them best. Then he set course for Whitby.

'Whale-ship! Whale-ship!' The unexpected shout startled Whitby folk who had settled into the routine that would take them through until the return of the whalers with their store of blubber. This sighting was all wrong unless one of the ships they had recently despatched had been forced to return. The call, which had been started by two youngsters playing on the East Cliff, spread quickly through the town.

Whitby's streets became choked with people hurrying to vantage points for a sight of the ship. Sarah and Dina, who had been shopping in Church Street, hurried to the Church Stairs and climbed the steps rapidly to reach the top, breathless. This did not stop them from hurrying to the cliff edge where other people were already gathering.

Sarah scanned the sea quickly and fixed her gaze on the distant outline. She watched it for a few moments, then her words came out in a long incredulous gasp: 'It can't be . . . ?'

'What? What is it?' asked Dina, knowing her sister's recognition skills were better than hers.

'It's the *Water Nymph*.' There was still disbelief in her voice.

'How can it be?' cried Dina who for one brief moment had had her hopes raised that Rowan was coming home.

Someone nearby who had overheard Sarah snapped, 'Rubbish! She was lost.'

She swung to face her detractor. 'Did we ever receive proof of that? That ship is the *Water Nymph!*'

'No vessel could survive a winter in the Arctic,' retorted the doubter.

'She has!' The certainty in her tone silenced any argument. Before long everyone knew she was right and the identification spread quickly among the people on the east side of the river.

'She's in a sorry state,' commented Sarah quietly.

Dina saw what her sister meant. The *Water Nymph's* bows were battered; planking on her sides was torn, sails in tatters, cordage flapped loose, her boats were non-existent, the fore-mast broken.

Boats filled with men eager to help others they knew would be suffering had put out from Whitby's quays. Reaching the ship, they were soon on board and taking over the ship's duties to see the battered vessel safely into harbour.

As she passed between the piers cheering rose from the cliffs, piers, staithes and quays. It died away to a solemn silence as the ship proceeded upstream and people saw her exhausted and dejected crew.

'They're not all there!' cried Dina, and turned to run.

Sarah was only a pace behind her. She knew her sister wanted to be at the quay. The steps flew beneath their feet. They raced through deserted Church Street until they came to that section that bordered the quays along the river. There they joined the flow of people making for the quay where they knew the *Water Nymph* would dock. Some seemed dazed by the return of the ship from the dead, others had anxiety etched on their faces as doubt and hope clashed in their minds. Was their loved one alive? The undercurrent of conversation carried with it hope and despair, joy and despondency.

Everyone watched anxiously as the ship was carefully manoeuvred through the swing bridge, and as it drew nearer and nearer they scanned the crew, seeking those dear to them. They were shocked by the emaciated appearance of the men who crowded the rail eager to make it known to their loved ones that they had survived. Joyous shouts cut through the air and arms were raised in greeting as identifications were made, but there were those on shore who felt their throats constrict when they did not see the person dear to them. They bit their lips, trying to hold back the tears while clinging to the hope that he might be too ill to come on deck.

'He's there!' shouted Dina as excitement and relief surged through her. 'Rowan! Rowan!' He heard her, saw her and waved.

'And Eric's with him. Thank God!' All the pent-up anxiety was expressed in Sarah's words.

'Indeed it is thank God.'

The sisters turned to see who spoke behind them. 'Father!' they both gasped together. This was unusual; their father had broken his own rule of never being there when the whale-ships left, nor when they returned.

He must have read their minds. 'When I heard the cry at this time I knew it must be something unusual.'

Ben had come to the edge of the crowd. He was relieved to identify his brother on deck. Seeing his father talking with Sarah and Dina, he instinctively started towards them, but then caught sight of Alicia squeezing through the mass of people. He turned and walked away.

The *Water Nymph* tied up and soon after the gangplank was run out there were joyful reunions but also shattered hopes. Tears of joy and of sorrow were shed; hearts soared and were broken, but everyone accepted the return of the ship as a miracle.

Dina held out her arms to Rowan. Not a word passed between them while they held each other as if they would never let go.

Eric clasped the outstretched hand that expressed Sam's relief at seeing his son. He looked at his father through eyes that were damp with emotion and appreciation to find him here but was too choked to say anything. He turned into Sarah's arms and hugged her tight, something he had never done before. Sarah, who had noted all this, wondered why it needed tragedy to unite a family more closely. She only wished Ben were standing with them.

Alicia slid her arm through Sam's, and nodded and smiled at Eric.

'I must see Captain Ormson,' said Sam. 'Only briefly and then we'll all go home. You too, Rowan.'

'Thank you, sir.'

Dina was elated at this sign that her beau had been accepted.

'Before I go on board, Eric, there is something I must tell you.'

He turned from Sarah but she kept hold of his hand.

'Alicia and I are married.'

Speechless, Eric stared from one to the other. He felt Sarah squeeze his hand, a signal to be careful how he replied. 'Er, congratulations, sir.'

'We'll talk shortly, son. Take them all home, Alicia. I won't be long.' Sam strode to the gangplank.

'Eric, you look bemused,' said Alicia gently. 'Your father and I fell in love.'

Still trying to get his mind round the news, he nodded and asked with a slight twinkle in his eyes, 'Do I call you Mother?'

His question broke the tension and brought chuckles from everyone present.

'I think I'll always be Alicia to you all. Come, let's do as your father said and go home.'

'But Captain Ormson hasn't dismissed his crew,' Rowan pointed out.

'I think Father will fix that with him,' said Eric.

'Captain, it is a great relief to see you safe,' said Sam, shaking Captain Ormson's hand. 'This is no time for you to be troubled with making a report. I'll hear something about it from my son and get your official report tomorrow afternoon, three o'clock at my office. Dismiss your crew now.'

'Yes, sir.'

'How many did you lose?'

'Six, sir.'

'Let me have their names, I must visit their relatives.'

'I have them here, sir.' Ormson withdrew a piece of paper from his pocket.

'Thank you.' Sam took the note and started to turn away.

Captain Ormson held back the query that sprang to his lips. It was obvious that Eric had said nothing to his father about the diary otherwise Mr Coulson would surely have asked him about it. What the reason was for Eric's not mentioning it as soon as he saw his father it was no concern of the Captain's. Better let Eric tell the story in his own time than report it now.

'Tell the men I'll see them all on board this ship a week today, if they have recovered enough. They're to be here ten o'clock in the morning.' Sam had already made up his mind that they should be compensated for the time they had been marooned in the Arctic and unable to contribute to the welfare of their families.

When he reached the house in Bagdale he found that Alicia had organised chocolate and scones for everyone and had ordered Cook to prepare a celebratory dinner for them all that evening.

When they were settled in the drawing-room, Eric took a sip of his chocolate and let out a moan of appreciation. 'There was a time when I thought I'd never taste this again.'

'You've had a harrowing experience, son,' said Sam. 'There's no need for you to talk about it now. I'll get a full report from Captain Ormson tomorrow afternoon.'

With that remark Eric realised that the Captain had said nothing about the diary, and was glad. 'Very well, I won't tell you it all, but there is something that Rowan and I must tell you now.'

He paused and in that moment Sam recalled what Eric had reported after the last voyage of the *Water Nymph* when Captain Holmes was in charge. Had there been similar incompetence on this voyage?

Eric started the story at the point where he and Rowan had volunteered to try to find help. Between them they related how they had come to the Esquimaux encampment.

'From your description of the country it was sheer good fortune that you chose that particular point,' commented Sam.

'Not good fortune, sir,' said Rowan.

Puzzled, he asked, 'What do you mean? What else could it be?'

'Eric felt drawn there,' replied Rowan. Sam frowned but before he could say anything, Rowan added, 'Let us continue the story, sir, and I think you will realise why Eric sensed that was where we had to go.'

'It's true, Father.' Eric took up the explanation again. 'At that time I didn't know why I went to that opening in the rock face, but I did. I just felt something was taking me there.' He licked his lips as he tried to find the right thing to say. The room was heavy with expectant silence and he saw he had the rapt attention of everyone. 'We found ourselves in a valley and there were the Esquimaux – our salvation.'

Rowan told them of the treatment they'd received and how they had managed to communicate by signs. 'Then, when we were nearly ready to leave, one of the Esquimaux signed that he wanted us to go with him. He took us further along the valley and showed us two graves. Lying between them was a piece of wood salvaged from a whale-boat.'

Everyone was hanging on his words but he allowed Eric to take up the story. 'We could make out the name *Water Nymph* on it.'

The silence that descended on the room became even more charged.

'But how could that be?' asked Sarah.

Comprehension was flooding Sam's mind. 'A whale-boat went missing on the previous voyage.'

'Martin's!' gasped Dina.

Eric nodded.

'We realised that it was the only place the wood could have come from,' said Rowan, 'and then we received further proof.'

'Only two graves?' said Sam quietly.

'Yes, sir.'

'Then you don't know who is buried there or what happened to the rest of the crew?'

'We could only presume that they perished in the storm.'

432

Sam nodded and glanced at Rowan. 'You said you had some other proof?'

'Yes, sir.' He glanced at Eric. This was the point where his friend should really complete the story.

'One of the Esquimaux gave me this package when we were leaving.' Eric fished it from his pocket and held it out to his father.

Sam took it with curiosity on his face. He unwrapped it slowly so that everyone could see. As the diary was revealed he gasped, 'Martin's!'

Everyone else turned their disbelieving eyes on Eric.

'It's true,' he said, 'and proves that he lies in one of those graves. If he had been lost in the storm the diary could not have got there.'

Treasuring the item in his hand, Sam looked up slowly. 'Did you not think of bringing him home?'

'Captain Ormson could have made the decision but instead he left it to me as a member of the family. I decided that Martin would rather lie in the Arctic that he loved.'

Sam hesitated and then nodded. 'You were right.'

'It is a pity we do not know who lies beside him,' said Alicia.

'Oh, but we do,' said Eric. 'I have read his diary which he kept until the very end. That was two days after the Esquimaux found their wreckage, so he mentions who was with him. It was Meredith.' He allowed their murmurs of pity to diminish before he said, 'But there is more in that diary that is revealing.' The tinge of regret that had come into his voice caught everyone's attention. 'It proves I shouldn't have made the accusations against Captain Holmes that I did.'

He stood up and went to his father. 'May I have the diary a moment?' Sam gave it to him; Eric sat down, opened it and carefully turned the pages so as not to damage them until he found the entry he wanted. 'I think this must have been written after the Esquimaux had found them because they are mentioned on the previous page.' He read aloud: '"This diary may never be found but I must write this in case by some miracle it is. I am to blame for the loss of the whale-boat. I was in command. I knew Captain Holmes's orders in case of a storm. Our whale had run. The ship had long been out of sight. I saw the storm coming. I should have cut the rope and returned to the ship but I was so obsessed with killing the whale that I ignored the warnings that were there for me to see. We were caught in the scvcrc storm. We lost all the crew but Meredith and myself. What good fortune brought us to land to be discovered by these friendly Esquimaux I will never know, but alas it was too late. I write my last words now: I disobeyed orders and endangered my crew. Captain Holmes is in no way to blame."'

Eric looked up. 'The writing gets worse, showing how weak Martin must have been, but I read these last pages many times and though some words are difficult to make out I believe that what I have read out is what Martin wrote. Rowan agrees with me.'

He nodded. 'Yes, I do.'

Eric handed the diary back to his father.

Sam sat staring at it then stood up and walked slowly from the room. No one moved or said a word, not even when a few moments later they heard the front door close.

Alicia looked thoughtful and left the room. She gathered her coat and hat and hurried after her husband.

'I think I know where you are going,' she said when she'd caught him up and slipped an arm through his.

He glanced at her. 'Do you?'

'To see Captain Holmes.'

Her gave a wry smile. 'You are a very perceptive young lady.'

'Do you want me to come with you?'

'I would like you first of all to go to Ben's.' He felt her stiffen and patted her hand reassuringly. 'Do this for me. Ask him and Ruth and the child to go with you to her parents' at once.'

'But I couldn't face them.'

'Please, for me.'

434

'What if they won't see me or refuse to come?'

'I believe you have great powers of persuasion.'

'Well, I'm not sure it is a good idea sending me. I'll go back and ask Sarah to do it.'

'No. Now you have offered to come with me, I would like you to do it. Off you go and get them. I will wait at the end of Grape Lane until I see you go into the Holmeses' house.'

Alicia said no more. She sensed Sam's determination. She had guessed he was going to see Captain Holmes but had not reckoned on his hoping that Ben and Ruth would be there too. Her joining him had given him a way to make it possible and he had seized on the chance.

She hurried off. Sam watched her go. His eyes never left her until she passed from his sight. In those moments he knew how much he loved her and saw their happy future together, working to establish a successful trading business to leave to their child. Ben's disclosures about her could be swept under the carpet, and maybe there was something else he could do for his son if things turned out as he hoped.

He took up a vantage point from which he could keep the Holmeses' house in view. A few minutes later he saw Alicia, Ruth and Ben, who was carrying the child, hurrying from the opposite end of Grape Lane. Alicia was talking and gesticulating, and from the dark cloud over Ben's face, and the look of irritation in Ruth's, Sam judged that his wife had not had an easy task. But his faith in her ability even under the most trying of circumstances had proved to be right. He waited until he saw the door close behind them and then went to the Holmes' house.

Recognising him, and knowing she had just admitted his wife and son, the maid had no hesitation in complying with Sam's request to see Captain Holmes.

Everyone seemed to be talking at once when Sam reached the drawing-room. He paused a moment by the door which stood slightly ajar.

'What is *she* doing here?' Gideon was demanding of his son-in-law.

'She told us we were wanted here.'

'Why should she do that?'

Ben shrugged his shoulders.

'What's going on, Ruth?' her mother asked as she took the child on to her knee.

'Ask her,' snapped Ruth, glaring at Alicia.

Sam pushed the door open. 'No, ask me!' His commanding tone silenced everyone.

'What the devil are you doing here?' Gideon's demand was full of hostility. Anger surged in him. 'How dare you come uninvited into my house? Get out, and take your wife with you.'

Sam adopted a defiant attitude and stood his ground. Alicia moved to stand beside him. 'Hear me out, Gideon Holmes.' Sam deliberately left out the title Captain, and Gideon noticed it. 'I have some important things to say which I want your daughter and my son to hear as well. That is why I sent my wife to fetch them.'

'What you have to say doesn't interest me but I guess it's no use refusing to listen, so say what you have to say and then get out.'

'Gideon Holmes, I have learned but a short while ago that I have wronged you and for that I humbly apologise. I hope that when you have heard the rest of my story you will find it in your heart to forgive me.'

Ben stared at his father in amazement. Sam Coulson apologising? He glanced at Alicia and saw that she had slipped her hand in to his father's as if she was giving him support. If this was the effect she had on him then long may their marriage last. His thoughts were interrupted when he heard his father speak again.

'As you will be aware the *Water Nymph* has survived a winter in the Arctic. She is in a sorry condition and some of her crew will never return.' He went on to tell them Eric's story and about the discovery of the two graves and the piece of wood.

'So somebody survived?' said an astonished Gideon.

'Aye, for a while. And we know who.'

'What? How?'

'From this.' Sam held up the diary.

Everyone looked mystified.

'There are some notes in here. I want to read you one of the entries.' His voice broke.

Alicia realised the thought of reading his son's last words was too much for him. 'Sam,' she said gently, 'let me read it.'

He bit his lip and passed her the diary. She found the piece that Eric had read out to them. Though as he had indicated the writing in places was not easily deciphered, she managed. Everyone was struck silent by this testimony from the dead.

As Alicia closed the book, Sam said, 'So you see, Gideon, I was wrong to blame you for the loss of my son. It was his fault for not following your orders. I am so very sorry for the distress I have caused you. I am having a new whale-ship built, she will be ready for next season. I would like Captain Holmes to take command of her.' His emphasis on the word Captain this time was not lost on Gideon.

'Thank you. It will be my pleasure.'

Sam held out his hand, which Gideon had no hesitation in taking. Then Sam turned to Ruth. 'I welcome my daughter-in-law into the family and hope that any wrong done to her can be forgotten. I hope that you and my wife will become good friends, Ruth.'

Alicia smiled condescendingly but in her mind said, 'Never!'

Ruth made a silent resolve to try for Ben's sake but knew from the look Alicia had given her that there would always be rivalry, between them.

Sam looked at his son. 'The last time we spoke there was hostility between us. I hope it can be laid aside and that you, Ruth and my grandson will come home whenever it pleases you. You indicated that your debt to the bank had been taken care of and that you are in partnership with Ryan Bennett, so I assume he satisfied the bank on your behalf? No doubt you still have him to repay?'

Ben nodded. 'His kind gesture relieved me of any time limit.'

'I will repay Ryan for you. That will be your inheritance from me. I have taken care of your sisters' future even though I suspect there will be two weddings in the family before long. Eric will have money put aside for him, and the rest of whatever there is when I die will go to Alicia and our child. No one must challenge that.'

Alicia smiled to herself. She had the love of a powerful man and her future and that of her child were assured.

Sam set his gaze on Gideon. 'Forget fishing. I will pay you as if you were on a whaling voyage now. Be at my office at ten o'clock in the morning to sign the necessary papers.' He turned to his wife. 'Come, Alicia.'

As they left Grape Lane she slipped her hand into his. 'That was a wonderful gesture, Sam.'

He smiled. 'Marrying you has changed me for the better. I will always be grateful for your influence and your love.'

She squeezed his hand. 'I love you too. More than anyone I have ever loved.'

'Even Ben?'

'Even Ben.'

Also by Jessica Blair,
available from Piatkus Books:

DANGEROUS SHORES

When Abigail Mitchell is a little girl her father, John, inherits a large estate in Cornwall from his uncle. He chooses to move his family from their comfortable living in Whitby to the rugged Cornish coast, in the hope of securing a more prosperous future in the South. John soon incurs the opposition and wrath of their neighbours, the Gainsfords, a powerful old Cornish family. However, as Abigail blossoms into a young lady, she finds herself mixing socially with the younger Gainsfords and attracted to the eldest son Luke Gainsford. She agress to marry him in spite of his rakish reputation and her father's objections to the match. Abigail soon learns she should have heeded her father's warning when she uncovers Luke's secret life . . .

978-0-7499-0928-4

REACH FOR TOMORROW

The year is 1891. Marie Newton is the daughter of a famous painter, Arthur Newton, and she has inherited much of her father's skill. Luckily her father is happy to encourage his daughter's talent, agreeing that she may attend a prestigious art school in Paris. Accompanying her on her journey is her best friend, Lucy, a young widow. The girls find themselves entranced by Paris and each finds a sweetheart though this does not bring happiness for Lucy. In order to help Lucy recover, Arthur proposes that the girls join him and his wife on a visit to America to visit relatives. But Arthur's past is about to catch up with him . . .

978-0-7499-3743-0